UP
NEXT

UP
NEXT

A
May
Morrison
Mystery

Nancy Star

POCKET BOOKS
New York   London   Toronto   Sydney   Tokyo   Singapore

POCKET BOOKS, a division of Simon & Schuster Inc.
1230 Avenue of the Americas, New York, NY 10020

Library of Congress Cataloging-in-Publication Data

Star, Nancy.
   Up next : a May Morrison mystery / Nancy Star.
      p.   cm.
   ISBN: 0-671-00893-5
   I. Title.
   PS3569.T33555U56   1998
   813'.54—dc21   97-32544
                                                        CIP

First Pocket Books hardcover printing July 1998

10 9 8 7 6 5 4 3 2 1

For Elisabeth and Isabelle,
and for Larry

UP
NEXT

1

HE STARED INTO THE CLEAR RIPPLE OF newly flushed water and wondered if this was where he was going to see the white light, the long tunnel, his life flash before his eyes. By now he'd produced enough shows on near-death experiences and reincarnation—including the ratings-winning one with Shirley MacLaine—to fully believe in the signs that presaged imminent death. Is this where they would come? In his toilet bowl? Or was it possible, after all this pain, he was actually going to live?

He stumbled back to bed thinking he ought to say something, to apologize at least. Then the cramps came again and his jaw clamped shut and his knees lurched to his chest as if he were a marionette whose strings had just been yanked. Only there wasn't anyone pulling his strings. There was just the still figure standing beside him watching him writhe. And now that he thought of it, when had the look of concern gone away? When had the blank stare arrived? When had that stare begun to look like contentment?

He closed his eyes, felt something cool on his forehead, reached a hand to feel the damp washcloth that had been placed there. The timing was perfect, he had to admit, since now his head felt as though a family of gorillas were smashing it with baseball bats.

"Fresh air," he heard, but he was so muddled he couldn't tell if he was the one who had said it. He stumbled to his feet, reached to straighten the billowed lumps of his crumpled quilt, but instead found himself being led by the hand out of the room, like a child.

Fresh air. That might revive him. He tried to think of what he'd eaten that could have made him this wretchedly sick, but the thought of food made his stomach heave again. Again he held in the bile and tore down the narrow hallway to the bathroom so as not to soil his white carpet.

When he was done, his mouth tasted as if he'd gargled with sewage. With effort he straightened and pulled the toothpaste out of the medicine cabinet, knocking down bottles of pills and syrups along with it. He fumbled to right them, then gave up, struggling instead with the toothpaste top. And he wondered, could it be soldered shut? Or could he be too weak to open it?

"I've never felt like this before," he managed to mumble as he wiped his mouth on the proffered washcloth. He watched it drop to the floor as if in slow motion. He wanted to scoop it up, to throw it away, out of sight, but all he could do was push it aside with his foot because now he was being gently guided again, by the elbow as if he were a blind man, to the French doors leading out to his landscaped balcony. He wanted to stop, to lie down on the soft white carpet, but it was plain a decision had been made. They were going outside, and he was too weak to protest it.

He drank in the biting cold air, let it sting his nostrils, slap his cheeks. For a second it felt great, like sticking his head in an ice bucket, but then the pounding began again and the balcony started to spin. As he was led to the edge, he suddenly realized a story was being told to him, an explanation. He struggled to focus, but between the throbbing and the spinning and his own steady movement forward and up—he stopped to wonder why he felt as though he was going up, then looked down to see that he'd been escorted atop his leather kitchen stool.

Then he was dreaming, half-asleep, dreaming that he was falling. He tried to stop himself, the way he did when he was lying in his bed and suddenly felt the world slip out from under him. But he wasn't in his bed, couldn't simply brace his legs against his hard mattress to ground himself. Only the sidewalk would stop the falling sensation this time.

When he thought of all the news crews that would rush to his body, he made one feeble attempt to button his jacket, then gave up and gave in to the free fall, thirty-nine stories, to the ground.

2

TO PRESERVE THE QUIET OF HER light-sleeping household May Morrison dressed for work watching the early morning news with the sound turned so low she was unintentionally learning to read lips. Staring at the woman reporting from the site of a burning factory, she made out the word *spectacular*, then turned her attention back to her opaque black tights, which were now stuck at her knees. Determined to prove she hadn't grown from size A to size B, she fought them, defeated only when the last yank caused a run the size of a Slinky to race down her leg. She hobbled to her stocking drawer, inches from the television speaker, and, as she ransacked for a fresh pair of tights, heard the newscaster whisper in her ear, "the death of James Barnett, executive producer of the popular morning talk show *Simon Says.*"

Her legs held together by black lycra one size too small, she hopped back to the front of the TV in time to see Barnett's smiling face displayed in a box in the upper corner of the screen. She slipped off the ripped tights, upped the volume, and heard, "shock upon hearing he'd jumped to his death."

She sat down hard on the bed, blinking, dazed. In the moment it took her to focus back on the set, the newscaster had moved on to the possibility of another inch of snow and a half-hour tie-up at the Lincoln Tunnel. Already her phone was ringing. She shut off the TV.

"Channel Seven. Turn it on. Barnett is dead." It was Margery Riegle, one of May's fellow producers on the talk show *Paula Live.* Margery lowered her already husky, sugarcoated southern voice. "Proving once and for all, there is a God. And don't go gasping," she snapped before May had a chance to take a breath. "You feel exactly the same way."

"I just wouldn't say it out loud."

"Which is why you get blotches on your face instead. Now, sugar, listen up. Since you're the only one of us who's got any friends at *Simon Says,* you're the one who's got to call over there and get the scoop on the dirt."

"If I have time," May offered.

"Damn. You're not going to call."

May smiled as she hung up the phone. Margery knew

her well, knew she was as likely to have extra time as she was to have a winning lottery ticket. May had recently done the math—in order for her life to run smoothly she needed at least eight additional hours a day. Since manufacturing time was not one of her many talents, and since sleeping six hours a night was one of her many needs, she made due with shaving minutes where she could. She dressed in monochromatic black to save several seconds of decision-making time in the morning. She'd recently convinced both her four-year-old daughter, Susie, and Delia, aged seven, to grow out their bangs so that they could make do with fewer haircuts. She found dry cleaners who picked up, milkmen who delivered, and even a doctor who could occasionally be cajoled into making a house call. She kept her checkbook and a folder of bills close at hand so that whenever someone put her on hold on the phone, she could pay the next one due. She installed a small TV in the bathroom so that she could watch the local news while washing up. She completely eliminated her social life.

Still there wasn't enough time. If she wasn't lugging home a mule's load of paperwork and overnight reading, she was carting a crying Delia to school, with some last-minute project precariously perched on her knees, pieces leaning from puddles of still-wet glue.

Now Barnett's untimely death would add hours of gossip, speculation, and anxiety, further shortening the productive hours of her workday. May caught herself, aware that she'd just reduced a man's life to so many minutes of inconvenience. The thought gave her pause, but not for long. There wasn't time.

She ran her fingers through her shoulder-length wavy brown hair, arranging it. While she spent a lot getting it cut by a man who called himself a hair director, it was a style that required no maintenance and could last up to four months if she avoided looking in the mirror for the last bit of it. She'd given up on highlights and color, though. That required too much of an outlay of money and time.

She began and concluded her makeup regime with a quick swipe of subtle lipstick, and then, thanking her genes for the clear, smooth skin and large hazel eyes that meant—for now at least—she required no further cosmetics, she raced downstairs.

Ovaa-Iita, the latest in the lineup of child-care providers she'd hired since Todd's surprise departure, had been up for hours, stuck, as if in protest, on Finnish time. Homesick and depressed, she found solace only while in the kitchen, kneading dough with her large, farmer's hands. The children remained aloof, suspicious, impatient with her limited grasp of English, but Ovaa-Iita held on to her conviction that it was all a matter of baking them the right dessert. This morning she struggled with a dense mixture of pears, granola, raisins, cinnamon, whole wheat flour, and butter. May saw it as Susie would, a mountain of putty-colored clay speckled with bugs.

"By any chance, do you know how to bake anything chocolate?" May asked as she slipped into her long navy wool coat.

"Wha?"

Carol, the au-pair coordinator, had assured her the language barrier would disappear within days, but it had stuck hard, as much a part of Ovaa-Iita as her daisy yellow hair and her glacial-lake-blue eyes. May tried again, speaking slowly. "Chocolate. Can you bake anything chocolate?"

"Do you need me chalk? How much is?"

May forced a smile. Ovaa-Iita just needed a few more

days to acclimate. "Forget the chalk. Just make sure the girls are up by seven-thirty."

The sitter blinked back a fresh crop of tears, then smiled bravely. "Happy tears. Nothing to worry me." She retreated to the kitchen, her sniffles drowned out by the sounds of cabinet doors opening and closing. Then there was silence. "You can go now," she called out to May in unexpectedly perfect syntax.

But May couldn't go. She was stuck as surely as if her feet were glued to her mud-stained jute hall door-mat. The knot she felt in her stomach every morning was becoming so familiar she considered giving it a pet name. Was she kidding herself about this baby-sitter? Was she leaving her children in the care of someone who needed a sitter herself? Or was she just worrying too much? After all, Ovaa-Iita's long list of references had been glowing, reverential. Maybe too reverential, now that she thought of it. How did she really know those employers weren't all part of one big, blonde ex-tended family?

Ovaa-Iita interrupted May's thoughts, striding into the hall with a box of Nestlé's Quik held in the air like a trophy. "I found chalk!" she boasted, her face, for the first time in America, lit up with joy.

"Great," May countered and, riding the wave of Ovaa-Iita's newfound happy competence, left, quickly walking up the steep hill to the train, her head down against the biting wind.

As she turned the corner, she forced her new au pair out of her head. She had to focus on the three shows she was juggling in preproduction for next week. She couldn't afford distraction. The way her house was sucking up money lately, she couldn't afford much of anything, least of all losing her job.

Her mind took a quick detour to a grisly image of

Barnett lying splayed out on the sidewalk and to the day, one week ago, when her executive producer, Gil Lee, had wished him dead.

The *Paula Live* production staff had straggled in to an early morning meeting in the conference room, where a large chart had been carefully perched on an easel as if it were an exhibit in a murder trial. Columns of numbers, huge and irrefutable, were lined up beneath the headings of three competing daytime talk shows: Her own, *Paula Live*, their newest competitor, *Tell Tonya*, and the current ratings king, *Simon Says*.

"I want to obliterate Tonya so fast people will forget what the hell she looks like," Gil had snapped. "I want Simon to want to kill us for our numbers.

"The choice is simple, people," he went on. "We can wait for Mr. 'Hot-Shot-Producer' James Barnett to step off the curb in front of a truck, so that he is no longer supplying Simon with every hot guest known to man and beating us to one why-didn't-I-think-of-that idea after another. Or we can hustle, people. Hustle."

The room had fallen silent. Now James Barnett was dead. May shook off a chill.

3

DETECTIVE PAUL O'DONNELL'S EX-partner liked jumpers because he knew once he'd stepped over the body on his way into the building, he didn't have to worry about getting his shoes sticky or the elbows of his jacket streaked with blood. Jumpers were neat.

O'Donnell hated them, hated how they gnawed at him, how they kept him up at night and edgy in the day, hated that even when they left a note saying "I can't go on," there was no guarantee the corpse didn't have a helpful friend giving him a little push. And if jumpers were neat, their helpful friends were even neater. They didn't leave behind a lot of clues.

Not that he enjoyed walking into a room splattered with the guts of a gunshot victim, where the plate-load of spaghetti and meatballs spread out on the floor turned out to be someone's brains. But it was part of the job, like long hours, nights sleeping on the couch, and a paycheck that took care of rent, food, and schoolbooks for the boys, but never quite stretched all the way to vacations or let him keep up with the number of in-line skates and soccer cleats that his growing boys' growing feet demanded. The boys were why he always wore his vest. But his gut, his goddamn noisy gut, was why he hated jumpers. It was unfinished business. You never knew for sure.

So here he was again, going through the apartment one more time. This guy left no note, at least not one they'd found, though the way his new partner had eye-balled the furnishings, O'Donnell could have taped the note to his own ass and Paradiso wouldn't have noticed it. Too young to be wearing a detective's shield, if you asked O'Donnell, the kid didn't have a degree in art history, couldn't tell a Picasso from a painting on black velvet, but he appreciated what he saw on the walls, his mouth hanging open like a thirsty mutt as he took in the deceased's own artwork. Oil paintings and water colors hung in every room, all of nude figures, all of women, all with the dead man's name scrawled on the bottom right corner. Maybe they reminded Paradiso of the brightly colored photographs on the calendar he'd hung inside his locker door—Miss January in her goose-bump coat. "Imagine," Paradiso had said, "having all this and jumping."

Just like that, he'd decided the guy had jumped. He'd been looking, gaga, at the high-class furnishings, the stainless-steel kitchen, the leather couches, the granite coffee table, the Arctic white rugs, and the paintings, the reclining torsos, the upturned, downturned, and low-slung breasts. His reaction just confirmed what O'Donnell's gut had already told him—Paradiso had spent too long in Narcotics, too long hanging around crack houses and handball courts at three in the morning waiting to make a buy. Narcotics might think Paradiso was a star, but now, on top of everything else, O'Donnell was going to have to retrain the kid and do it so he didn't even notice.

Maybe the first thing he'd tell him was to start using his nose, to sniff his way into a crime scene the way O'Donnell did, the way a dog would. Paradiso could learn a lot by shutting his mouth, closing his eyes, and sniffing. He might smell anything—gunfire, old age, old dogs, cheap perfume, fine wine, piss. And then there was the smell of death.

Different people handled the stink different ways, some better than others. Maybe it was because his nose was so damn good that O'Donnell had a tougher time of it than most. He'd long ago given up trying to tough it out and hide that, though. Now, if he knew ahead of time he was meeting a body that had been hanging around for a while, he just made sure to hold a hand-kerchief over his nose before he inhaled its putrid odor.

Probably Paradiso's nose didn't even work anymore, thanks to his success in Narcotics. That was the only way to explain why the same guy who had commented on the top-end stereo equipment and wide-screen TV hadn't found it worth mentioning that an overwhelming stench had come up like a wind from a sewer the closer they got to the bedroom and again at the balcony, where the guy jumped. *"Ooh,* yeah, right," was all he said when O'Donnell finally mentioned it.

By now the apartment was packed with the regular crew, scurrying to get the job done so they could move on to the next. Photographers were shooting pictures of the bed, the balcony, the pristine, never-used kitchen. Technicians were dusting the French doors, the door-knobs, the dresser tops, the toilet flusher. No one was being particularly careful. They all figured they were just there for the record. The mood was light, a kind of office-Christmas-party goofiness, different from the depressed silence that sat on them when, say, a young kid got shot by a stray bullet.

But when O'Donnell had first toured the place with the Uniform, he had been struck by how still it was, how quiet and perfectly clean. The guy had been a neat freak who had a hell of a housekeeper, and the housekeeper figured to be the only woman visiting the premises on a full-time regular basis. This place was all man—gray, steel, cold. He'd seen it before. Some hotshot decorator brought in enough high-tech equipment to stock a small store, enough uncomfortable furniture to start a trend, then bailed out. The look ended up more walked-through than lived-in. The only personal touches were the victim's art-class nudes on the wall staring down from every angle and the bedroom-dresser-top display of candles, about two dozen in assorted heights and widths, with drips attesting to their having been regularly used to set the mood. O'Donnell had sidled up to them, touched a few, found the thin ones were still pliable from recent use.

The bed had been the only other place he'd found a sign of life. He'd spotted it right away, the depression, shaped like a question mark, in the overstuffed down quilt. He pictured the scene as clearly as if he'd been there, the guy lying curled up in a ball on his big fat bed. Combine that with the smell of puke that had permeated the place and what he'd gotten was that the victim went through some bad news pain-in-the-gut suffering before he went overboard. Pills, drugs, a bad oyster?—that was for the medical examiner to reconstruct. Now, as he paced through the rooms again, O'Donnell tried to reconstruct the more immediate question nagging him: What the hell had happened here?

He imagined the guy on the bed, saw him racing to the can, getting sick all over his nice clean tiles. It must have been one hell of a stomachache if, as Paradiso's current theory went, it made him climb up and over his balcony just to end the pain. Like a wrong-sized shoe, no matter how hard O'Donnell tried, no way that story fit.

He opened the French doors leading out to the balcony and took in the view. Up here was the only place the city really seemed like the New York he knew from the movies. Sounds drifted up, music, laughter, shouts, but you couldn't actually hear the scumbag language. Cars looked like toys, people were dolls, and you couldn't tell that half the dolls were the dregs of the earth.

The snow was starting to fall sideways now, hitting him in the face. He couldn't hear the horns blaring, but he knew that they were. Between the weather and the crime scene, the street below had turned into a giant parking lot.

For the second time he looked at the stool pulled close to the iron rail. Why, he asked himself as he checked his notebook for the name—Barnett—why did Barnett step up on the stool before jumping when without it he could have easily climbed up over the railing?

He eyed the balcony, covered now with several inches of hardening snow. When he'd first come on the scene, the snow had been fine, and soft as dust. The pen, peeking out of a newborn drift, had stood straight up like a tiny flag just waiting for him to see it. He'd pulled a plastic coin envelope out of his pocket, scooped up the find, glanced at it through the plastic bag, read its insignia, and pocketed it. Too bad snow worked hell on fingerprints.

He came back in, leaving damp footprints on the white carpet. He didn't hear Paradiso at first. He was busy, turned inward, letting the facts seep deep into his brain, where if he was lucky, they'd put themselves together in the right order, making everything suddenly clear. When he finally noticed Paradiso standing a nose away from him with the look of an overeager puppy waiting to be pet he said, "What?" but it wasn't much of an invitation to talk.

"That sucker got mighty sick in there," Paradiso reported, motioning to the bathroom, as if this was some kind of news.

"So get yourself a spoon and scoop yourself a taste," O'Donnell told him just to bust his balls. He knew if Barnett had left any smelly gifts behind, the crime team would already have sampled them and sent them to the lab. If Paradiso didn't know that, he deserved the job of doing it again, for nothing.

"It's been cleaned already," Paradiso explained, then lifted up a plastic bag, heavy with something. "But I found a washcloth stuffed behind the toilet."

When O'Donnell nodded, a kind of benediction, Paradiso galumphed off to see what other prizes there were to be won. O'Donnell knew he was doing it only to impress him, that he didn't really see the point. After all, Paradiso thought any moron could tell the guy jumped.

O'Donnell stood silent and still, a picture of calm, except for his gut, which was going into spasms. Paradiso was wrong. The crime-scene team was wrong. But because he couldn't explain exactly why yet, he said nothing.

The thing was, this morning his sons had complained that the holidays had made him grumpier than usual. The little one had warned him not to go out and arrest any good guys by accident. The big one looked him dead in the eye and told him, whatever he did, he better not get shot. But what got him was the middle one, who wouldn't even look at him at all.

What O'Donnell needed was to coast for a while, till his kids, till his life, got a chance to settle down. What he didn't need was to stare at this guy's name, Barnett, on the homicide board for the next month while foamingat-the-mouth reporters followed him home, got the cameras rolling every time he swallowed. The guy was a big shot somewhere, that was for sure. So O'Donnell would let Paradiso tell the story of how the big shot jumped. He'd let the vultures report it that way, knowing they'd drop it fast, as if it were something catching. Meanwhile he'd sniff around in the shadows until he found something to prove his noisy gut was right again. And the press, the goddamn horny press, would leave him alone while he got the job done.

Two hours later he and Paradiso walked in on the scene of a domestic squabble that had worked out poorly for the now dead man sporting a tiger tattoo on both his upper and lower right cheek. His sobbing girlfriend clutched a cleaver, the dark red streaks oozing off the wooden handle and dripping down over the silver lightning bolts painted on the tips of her fingernails.

By the time they got back to the station house, the tiger man's name was listed, last one in, on the board. The case was tight. Tiger man would be erased, case closed, before the week was out. As for Barnett, Paradiso had written his name in real light, as if he were already a ghost, not worth another thought.

4

THE ELEVATOR STOPPED ON NEARLY every floor, giving May ample time to finish wondering about how many tickles it had taken for Ovaa-Iita to cajole Delia out from under her covers this morning, how many pieces of bread had gotten tossed before the au pair figured out the particular shade of brown Susie had in mind when she asked for toast. May made a mental note to call as soon as she got to her desk, then quickly moved on to worrying about the effect of Barnett's suicide on Paula's psyche.

Without question there would be repercussions. Despite her on-air demeanor of confidence and power, off-screen Paula was a petri dish of phobias. The cough of a stranger standing next to her could completely convince her that she'd come in contact with tuberculosis. A casual conversation with someone who blinked a lot was reason enough for her to urgently dispatch her secretary, Patty, to the drugstore for a shopping spree-selection of eyedrops, just in case Paula developed a tic, too. And no one who knew her well would dare yawn in her presence. That was one of her most well developed fears—that one day, in the middle of a show, she'd let out a yawn so big and long that the entire home audience would yawn back and then sleepily reach over to turn off their sets in the middle of her sentence.

Sometimes her quirks had more serious consequences—like the week before, when she'd fired Joan, her senior producer, after taping a show on bad skin. Joan's crime had been to allow her dermatologist guest to bring along three patients—two befores and an after—who were even more unpleasant to look at than the oversized color photographs the doc displayed of an acute skin condition featuring large purple boils.

As soon as the show was over, Paula fled to her bathroom. It was the perfect hiding place, its ancient castle motif—limestone bricks running up the walls, faded tapestry towels, slightly uneven terra cotta floor—providing a fitting backdrop to her terrified damsel mood. The castle theme didn't extend to the fixtures, though. She flicked on the high intensity make-up lights and using a specially constructed magnifying mirror, began examining each pore on her face. Only after Gil, armed with faxes of statistics he'd frantically gathered from five top dermatologists, barged in and swore on his job that her smooth-as-glass skin would not suddenly go cystic, that the skin conditions of the guests were certified not to be contagious, did she tentatively emerge.

The aftermath was even uglier than the boils. This show, like all failed shows, was followed by a painful meeting, a postmortem at which Paula stood before the entire production staff and attempted to piece together and elaborate endlessly on all the reasons why the show had died. At the postmortem on the dermatologist debacle, their senior producer, Joan Budney, insisted—as the producers always did—that both Paula and Gil had approved and signed off on the entire show from concept to completion. Paula, however, swore that the show she signed off on was about what to eat to get great skin.

It should have been over quickly. Joan Budney knew as well as any of them, the job of a producer in their postmortem meeting was to sit perfectly still and let

Paula rail until her fury ran its course. Any prolonged defense of a show only meant prolonged suffering. But for reasons no one else was privy to, Joan Budney came to this postmortem armed with her own copy of the "Folder."

Every show had a Folder, and the one Joan threw on the table was no different from any other, an inch thick. In it was the detailed bio of her guest and his patients, a copy of the jacket from the book he wrote, and half a dozen articles about him. There was the usual concept page, several fact sheets, as well as copies of the index cards that contained "bullet points"—information Paula could use to draw out the doctor and his patients if any of them got stuck. The bullet points included questions the guests had been prepped to answer and key words to prompt anecdotes they'd rehearsed and demonstrated they could retell well, as if for the first time.

The night before any show was taped, the producer of that show would give Paula the Folder to take home. It was never known for sure how carefully she would study it. Never before had anyone kept a copy to thrust in her face, a tangible "I told you so."

"It's all here," Joan had said. "A copy of every single piece of paper that was in your Folder. I have witnesses who saw me hand it to you last night." She made her case quickly with evidence it was difficult for Paula to refute. She was promptly fired.

If a bad boil could result in a firing, May hated to imagine what kind of fireworks would be prompted by Barnett's demise. All she could hope was that Paula had decided to spend the day at home in bed, consulting with coveys of psychics and palm readers who, for a steep fee or the promise of a plug on the show, would calmly assure her that her long lifeline hadn't splintered in half overnight.

As the elevator doors opened on the twenty-second floor, Linda, the receptionist, waved May over, directing her to hustle to the meeting already in progress in the conference room. She slipped in and sat down next to Margery, who shot her a look of warning.

"Is that too much to want to know?" Paula boomed. They taped two shows a day Tuesday through Friday, but today was Monday, so Paula was dressed in her off-air clothes. Frighteningly expensive French jeans, gold-toned—her new defining color scheme—Missoni sweater, thick honey-colored hair hastily tied back in a knot of itself, and pure undisguised fear. "Is he dead because of work, or was it something else?"

Whatever little color there was in Gil's normally cadaverous face drained away, leaving him with the perfect complexion for a stick of chalk. The burden of keeping Paula's blood pressure low sat squarely on his narrow shoulders. As he stood before her now, May thought she could see him swaying from the strain of balancing on such a narrow sliver of power base. The production company honchos who promoted him after firing the previous executive producer—the one who, with Paula, had created the show—had given Gil a clear mission: keep the ratings high; keep Paula's panic low. To that Gil added one of his own weaknesses, Emmy envy. It made for a volatile mix.

"How could it be work?" Gil chewed on the blue plug at the top of his Bic pen. Other executive producers May had worked for on other shows coveted fancy pens, Montblancs and Watermans, but Gil eschewed fine writing instruments, was addicted instead to chewing on the tops of Bics when he was nervous, which was several seconds short of all the time. To make sure his preference for Bics was not misinterpreted as a sign that theirs was a low-budget show, he special-ordered the pens by the gross from a calligrapher in New Hampshire who inscribed them with gold-flecked ink.

"Barnett was golden," he reminded her. "Simon loved him so much he made him his partner. His partner, Paula." He was gentle. This wasn't the time to press that point. "It was something in his private life. He had a past."

"As opposed to you," growled Bunny, their most seasoned producer, "who hatched this morning?"

"I'm talking about a past with a capital *P*." Gil walked over to Paula, stood behind her, began gently massaging her shoulders. "I promise you have nothing to worry about."

She pushed his hands away. "Because if this job is going to end up making me want to jump, I'd rather stop off on my way to the roof and offer my services to QVC. If Cher could do infomercials, I can do infomercials. They run for an hour, don't they?"

May hadn't noticed the question had been directed to her. Her attention had wandered to thoughts of Barnett's final descent. She pictured him standing on his balcony, arms overhead, fingertips touching, as if he were readying to dive into a pool. Then, moments before he jumped, the face in her mind morphed into Todd's. The corners of her mouth turned up in a smile as she pictured her ex-husband's splat. It fell off her face just as fast when her mind jumped to the thought that she needed to call home, to make sure the girls were okay.

"What were you grinning about?" Paula snapped.

"Let's keep this in perspective," Bunny interjected to save her friend. Bunny didn't like much, but she did like May; she liked her unaffected, straightforward manner, and she liked her brains. "I don't think suicide has made it to the top-ten list of communicable diseases just yet."

"Y'all know how much I hate to agree with Bunny," Margery said. "But, honestly, I don't think any of us believe his job made Barnett jump. People jump because they did something illegal or immoral or because they think they're going to get caught. You haven't done anything illegal, and you're no more immoral than the rest of us."

For a second there was silence. Then Paula unknotted her hair and shook it out. She knew how to use it, to let it surround her like a halo. "Maybe you're right. Anyway I hate heights. And the impact." She shivered at the thought of her carefully sculpted body hitting concrete. Before anyone could blink, she switched gears.

"Okay. Since I'm not jumping off any rooftops, let's talk about professional suicide instead." Her eyes scanned the room.

5

IT WAS LIKE WATCHING SOMEONE FLICK the spinner to a giant board game. Everyone waited, fists, jaws, or stomachs clenched, to see if the arrow would stop on them. Who would get beaten up today? Whose area of expertise was going to be strip-searched?

Like newspaper reporters, each producer on the show covered a carefully guarded beat. Bunny specialized in perennials, shows that never went out of style: mothers who were sluts; grandmothers who gave birth; fathers who were women. The perennials could be aired anytime and were perfect when the show went on hiatus, the months when production shut down and the staff dwindled to a skeleton crew. That's when the hot shows, the ones with big stars promoting big movies or brand-name authors touting mega-books, turned, like old milk, into garbage. Once the movie opened and then closed, once the book hit the stores and then moved to the bargain table in the back, the appeal of watching Paula schmooze about them vanished, too. Bunny's shows, on the other hand, were long-lasting.

The downside was they were constantly getting bumped for something hotter. Bunny no longer protested or even bothered to keep track of all the shows on adopted children reunited with their birth mothers that were put on hold because of a news-breaking cataclysmic kidnapping or a high-profile avalanche survivor. She'd simply absorb the news with a snarl and move on. Moving on was the key to her longevity, she'd explained when May first joined the show. Since Bunny was known throughout the industry as one of the first women to break into television production, May listened carefully to her advice. It proved to be the glue to their unlikely friendship.

May's own specialty was heartwarming, tear-jerking human interest. While the shows Bunny produced were introduced by the chirpy *Paula Live* theme song, May's shows, more often than not, started out with a somber, slower version of the same tune, one that tipped off the viewers at home that they only had a few more seconds left to go get that box of Kleenex.

Any avalanche survivor celebrating with Paula was there because May or her production assistant, Henry, had vigorously pursued them until they were convinced that *Paula Live* was the best place to bare their soul. May could make them believe—without doubt—that of all the talk-show hosts around (providing Oprah hadn't called them) Paula Wind was the most honest, forth-right, and caring, the one who would most quickly make them feel at home on TV, the one who really felt and could ease their pain. May was so convincing because she believed it herself. She saw how Paula drew out her guests, how some guests healed on camera, before her eyes.

Her cohort Margery Riegle's guests didn't heal quite as fast. Margery's guests vacillated between the bizarre and the lurid, with a smattering of heartbreak thrown in. Her beat was true crime, the weirder the better. She adored crime, adored hanging out with cops and be-friending assistant district attorneys, and lots of cops and assistant district attorneys adored hanging out with her. But what made her great at what she did was the ease with which she could charm victims and perps alike into coming on the very same show.

"Talk to Paula, sugar," she'd tell the victims or their survivors. "Never mind if that ugly old killer is going to be on a remote from his jail cell. Paula wants so bad for everyone to hear your side."

The celebrity beat belonged to Colleen, who was also the self-appointed queen of the kingdom of self-help. Colleen had uncanny radar capable of zeroing in on exactly which book on "getting a man and keeping him" was going to hit the best-seller list, on which actor poised to leap to stardom would actually make a safe landing. She was also a one-woman work-in-progress laboratory. She'd had tucks, peels, implants, and ex-plants, tried every diet from no-fat to no-protein, every purge from grapefruit to garlic juice. She'd done the green-tea thing, the tai-chi thing, and now the Frenchlifestyle thing. She believed in each with the devotion and conviction of a monk. A perfect one week ahead of every trend, she was one reason Paula was so fiercely current.

Together the production staff raked the planet for information. Their goal, and they were good at reaching it, was to make sure that every day of every week Paula Wind had the opportunity to harvest a show on any subject around and to sound as though she knew it better than anyone else. Their nightmare was to find out that one of their competitors had aired a show on a topic they had never considered. Considered and rejected, they could live with it. If no one had thought of it, there was hell to pay.

Mostly that didn't happen. Despite frequent fighting, territorial-boundary wars, petty jealousy, and enough competitive spirit to fuel the Olympic teams of several small countries, when it came down to it, the producers knew their enemies were not each other but Paula's panic and Gil's ire. To keep those two at bay, even Margery and Bunny would occasionally collaborate. Now they were all struggling to keep calm in the wake of the storm of Paula's hyperkinetic and highly contagious worrying.

The moment of truth arrived. The spinner stopped. Paula's eyes rested on May.

"I'm getting nervous about Valentine's Day."

May's color rose. She knew producing the Valentine's Day show gave her temporary combat status. Paula, a self-described romantic, viewed the holiday as one created especially for her, like a second birthday. Worse, the show aired directly in the middle of the February sweeps, when ratings immediately translated into dollars. May knew this, and still she'd volunteered.

But if Valentine's Day for Paula was like a second

birthday, for May and Todd it had been like a recurring nightmare. How, she'd ask Todd year after year, could he pretend the holiday had surprised him again? Was she really expected to believe he was oblivious to all the cupids pasted on their neighbors' front doors, to the school-packs of Dalmation-puppy tear-apart valentines the girls left strewn about the house for weeks like love notes?

It had been an impulsive decision to mark this year's holiday by volunteering to produce the show and one she now regretted. Not that she didn't remain convinced it would be an award winner. But now she wondered if maybe she'd had another motive for taking it on. Was it possible she harbored the ridiculous hope that Todd—sitting in the million-dollar Malibu beach hut belonging to his new, beautiful, young companion and toilet-tissue heiress, Chloe—would turn on the show and think, *Wow, what a woman; I must have been a jerk to leave her?* Wouldn't it have been wiser to let Colleen round up and deliver to Paula the usual Hollywood lovebirds? Then May could have concentrated on baking the four-dozen heart-shaped sugar cookies she'd volunteered—in a weak moment of mother guilt—to bake for both Susie's and Delia's class parties.

She snapped back to hear Paula insist, "I have to know. How ugly are they? I've had it with ugly guests."

May stayed calm. "They're not ugly at all." Even though she'd known from the moment she'd tracked down the couple they would be a tough sell, she'd developed the show anyway. Their story—they met in a shelter, lost everything until they found each other, would marry on air—was a modern fairy tale. It would strike a chord.

Gil jumped in next. "What about methadone?"

"They're not drug addicts."

"Thorazine?" he tried.

"You can take a look at the Folder now if you like," she offered carefully as the producers, thinking of Joan Budney, shifted uncomfortably, in their seats. "What it will tell you is that Lianna is in the shelter because she lost her house and her mother in a fire. Miguel got laid off from his custodial position because of a chronic back problem."

"She wants me to talk love to a janitor," Paula moaned.

"At least she doesn't want you to make love to a janitor," Margery pointed out.

"That I've done."

May pushed on. "It's because you're willing to take a chance and do a show like this that you rise miles above those sleazoid trash-pickers who shouldn't be allowed to call themselves hosts." She was going for broke, going for one of Paula's soft spots. Paula loathed being confused with that other kind of talk-show host, the kind whose dreams of perfection rose no higher than fistfights and hair-pulling spectacles. "It's shows like this that keep *Paula Live* one of the few class acts in town."

Paula sighed, resigning herself. "Look at her." She pointed to May's face. "She's heating up. Now her hair is starting to frizz. She's not going to let go of this quietly."

May hated that people could read her like a thermometer, but it was beyond her control.

"The photos will decide it," Gil called out, making an entry on his notebook computer. "It sounds heartwarming, maybe award winning, but Paula's got to sleep at night. Get me two nice full-front head shots of your headless couple so I can show Paula how pretty they are."

"Homeless," May reminded him. "Not 'headless.' "

Either way it was a headache for him. Gil released a mouthful of anxious air.

"I'm sure it will be fine," Paula said. It was safe for her to be supportive now. Gil wouldn't let this show happen until she approved the photos, and if the pictures weren't totally convincing, he'd send out a video crew. "I mean if May says they're beautiful, they must be beautiful. What she promises she delivers."

May knew this bouquet came only because last week her show on real-life heroes—the one where Paula and most of the studio audience struggled to choke back their tears—had ratings so beautiful Gil, upon news of them, cried freely and without shame. May enjoyed the glow of her success, but she knew as well as anyone that Paula never let her producers glow for too long.

"Speaking of that," Gil broke in. "Paula and I wanted to take this opportunity to announce we're finally ready to fill that senior producer spot."

Both Gil and Paula were staring at May, but because she absolutely didn't want a promotion, couldn't bear any more responsibility, more work, more hours away from the girls, she convinced herself someone else must have entered the room behind her. She swiveled to find no one was there. When she turned back, her colleagues were standing, applauding her. Gil motioned for everyone to sit. Paula beamed like a proud mother waiting to hear what May had to say.

May considered the politics of turning the promotion down. Though her ex-husband, Todd, PowerBook on his lap, lay on the beach doing a perfect rendition of a suddenly hot screenwriter, their divorce decree had conveniently predated his income-earning success. Each week she fully intended to squirrel away a portion of her paycheck to build up an emergency fund in case she ever lost her job and to begin college funds for the girls. But her house, as if sensing available funds, invariably sprang another leak or came down with a case of termites or toilet failure.

May found herself thinking of the ashen look on Joan Budney's face when Gil's assistant, Wendy, had led her by the elbow out of the conference room to her office so she could pack up her things. Joan, who instead of kids had a trust fund and a high-paid stock-exchange-trader husband, had looked as though she was going to throw up, and that was just from crushed ego and shock. May didn't worry about ego damage. She worried about the snow boots and down jacket that Delia had outgrown overnight with the winter not yet over, about signing up for spring session ballet lessons and karate, about the deteriorating oil tank under her front lawn and the antiquated burner in the basement, about constant pleas to go to Disney World or anywhere.

She couldn't afford to lose her job. She couldn't afford to turn down the promotion.

"Thank you," was all she could get out. And then, "I'll get you those pictures. You'll see. Lianna is a natural beauty, and Miguel will be Holly-wooed by the time you go to first break."

"All right. If it will make you feel better, take the pictures." Paula reknotted her hair, then stood up. "Meeting over?"

Gil swallowed his Bic nib, took another pen out of his inside jacket pocket. "One more thing. About Barnett. Anyone know if he was chasing a hot story?"

Paula sat down. "You think someone killed him? I didn't want to say it out loud, but that's what I think, too."

Big mistake, May thought, planting that little notion in Paula's hyperactive imagination.

Belatedly Gil realized it, too. "He killed himself,

Paula. He jumped. Off a building. What I meant was, what if before he killed himself he didn't have time to tie up all his loose ends? What if he left a couple of hot stories, half-done, sitting on his desk? There might be a potential guest out there ripe for the plucking. Who has a friend at *Simon Says?*"

All eyes went to May. For someone who had no time to socialize, who hadn't sat down over coffee with a friend in twenty years, she did a great job of having superficial relationships with half of New York. But no way would she call up her friend Judy to steal Barnett's remains. "I'll call when I have a free minute," she offered easily, knowing that would be never.

"Terrific," Gil enthused.

"That's my senior producer," Paula said, before rushing out of the room.

"Wait up," Bunny called after her. "I've got the Folder on your second show tomorrow." She stood and started toward the door, but Gil intercepted her, motioning for her to sit back down.

"Before you go, can we all agree to go easy on the uglies for a while? I'm not saying every guest has to be gorgeous," Gil explained. "But, people, can you make our lives easier and, for at least a while, give a rest to grotesque?"

"Honey pie, you're not being very politically correct," Margery observed.

"Don't give me that shit," Gil countered. "This is a talk show, not Congress. Paula's talent. She's allowed to be difficult. You're not. Think fluff," Gil counseled the group.

Margery laughed. "What's the latest in fluffy crime? Snow White stealing from the seven dwarfs?"

"All right, children, let's pretend it's a fairy tale. Think of Paula as the queen. Anyone who brings her an ugly dwarf will get their heart cut out by the hunter, who is me."

"Don't go getting yourself another ulcer, sugar. From now on any crime is fine with me, so long as the perp is cute. May I be excused? I have a meeting with an adorable pedophile."

"I have to go, too," Colleen announced, as she buffed her bronze bangles with the edge of her sleeve. "I have to go find another job. One where star power, the value of what I do, is understood and rewarded." She couldn't hide her suffering. From the moment Joan Budney had walked out the door, she'd wanted, expected, assumed she'd get the senior producer spot. Sure, May was the nicest one in the bunch, but since when did that count for anything? Could any of May's shows ever match the ratings of, say, Colleen's show with Lisa Marie? Could any of them even come close?

"I understand your power," Gil said. "I adore your power."

Colleen fingered her Rolodex, the biggest model available, the size of its wheel approaching that of a small tire. She took to heart the notion that the size of a Rolodex determined the size of a producer's paycheck, and because she was too paranoid that someone younger and more cunning might steal it, she lugged it with her wherever she went. Jammed with cards, it was so difficult to flip through her cuticles had been rubbed into permanently raw patches that even her manicurist couldn't repair. More than once May had suggested she use the address book software in her computer instead, but Colleen laughed her off. "I like to hold the cards in my hands," she admitted, adding in a whisper, "and if they've ever screwed me over, I like to burn them when they die."

"Let's go have lunch," Gil suggested. "Let's find a way to make you feel better."

"There is a brand-new place I've been dying to try," Colleen admitted. "If you can get a table."

"Where's that?" He loved places where it was hard to get a table.

"Gil," May interrupted. "Can we get back to work?"

"All right. All right. But I'm worried, people." He chewed harder, faster. "You're making me worried."

"Don't worry," May said, easily taking on the role of facilitator. She might not have wanted the promotion, but Gil and Paula had chosen wisely. Her conciliatory nature made her perfect for the job.

"We'll put all our hard-edged shows on hold," she told him, "and just give Paula pretty shows about pretty people getting prettier. We haven't done a makeover show yet this month. How about haircuts for everyone?"

"You're canning your homeless couple?" Gil smiled, blissfully relieved that she'd finally come round to seeing his point of view even before he'd had a chance to fully express it.

"No. I'll get them new haircuts, too. They're beautiful, Gil. You'll see from the pictures. They'll be uplifting. Inspirational."

"We are not on the Christian Cable Network," Gil grumbled.

"And this show is not an Emmy. It's an easy Emmy."

It worked every time. Gil wanted a collection of those statues on his mantel at home so badly it was rumored he'd called up one of last year's winners with a hard-to-refuse offer to buy theirs.

He shut down his computer. The meeting was over. Wendy, his assistant, hovered in the doorway, waving her hand to get his attention. Gil ignored her, staring into space, his jaw crushing his plastic nib with brutal determination. When she started waving both hands, everyone but Gil looked her way. May noticed that Wendy's usual cold shield of efficiency was broken by dark brown eyes that looked tentative, vulnerable, scared.

"Gil," Bunny mumbled, "I think Wendy's about to have a seizure."

Wendy dropped her arms and stiffened.

Gil looked up. "Yes?"

Not wanting to address the whole crowd, she mumbled quickly, "Someone to see you."

"Someone to see me? This is how you deliver a message?"

"Mr. O'Donnell is here to see you," she said quietly.

"Who the hell is Mr. O'Donnell?"

The visitor, uninterested in lengthy introductions, brushed past her. "Gil Lee?" He extended his hand. "Detective Paul O'Donnell, New York City Police Department. This is Detective Paradiso." His partner, standing behind him, made no move to come forward and take part in the niceties. O'Donnell spoke quietly, but everyone heard. "We'd like to speak to you. In private, please."

The producers quickly left the room, then stopped, clogging the hallway outside as they lingered, struggling to listen in. Wendy, pushing her way through their ranks, carefully closed the conference room door. Then, arms folded, legs astride, stare impenetrable, she stood in front of it until one by one first May and then her colleagues slunk away.

6

"OVAA-IITA FROM FINLAND." THE AU pair announced herself after answering on the tenth ring.

"Hi. It's May."

"Okay. I can check." The thump of racing footsteps receded, followed by silence. Moments later the feet stomped back. "She can be at work still. You can try later."

May held the dead phone in her hand for a second, then jammed the speed-dial button. As soon as the au pair picked up, May blurted out, "Ovaa-Iita, don't hang up. It's me. May."

"Oh. Someone just called to you."

"I called. To see if the girls got off to school okay."

"It was awful. Susie's whole bagel came out."

"Is she sick?"

"Not yet. What means 'melted'?"

"Is Susie home? Did you pick her up early?"

"It's okay with me. I can see you then." Once again the phone went dead.

As May slammed down the receiver, her thoughts turned to Todd. She pictured him, like Barnett, about to jump. But this time his descent was into the part of the Pacific Ocean he now considered his own, and the fate she drew for him ended with a large school of hungry man-of-war jellyfish he hadn't noticed congregating below. She considered, with not a little satisfaction, it was probably a painful way to die.

Now that Todd was gone, she realized neither of them had ever appreciated how lucky they'd been that he was there for the kids every day after school. When May had thought of it at all, it had been with jealousy. She thought it was a perk that came with working at home and didn't know until it was too late that Todd viewed it as an unemployed screenwriter's booby prize.

Her thoughts were cut off by a sharp knock. Her door opened quickly.

"We've got to talk." Gil sat down across from her, his arms folded, his jaw chomping hard.

"Do I get to pick the topic?"

"Don't argue with me. You don't have time to argue with me. You have a show to put together. You're taping the day after tomorrow."

"What happened?" While "sweep" shows were planned months in advance, the rest of the time they worked a week ahead. That meant one week to come up with the idea, locate and screen the guests, research the subject, and fine-tune the spin. Only catastrophes— earthquakes, celebrity murders, presidential scandals— happened faster. Those were the real ulcer-growers. There was never enough time, all their competitors were chasing the same guests, and since the stories involved real life, things could change in a blink. Wars could be settled; irate mistresses bought off and silenced; hot guests snatched. It had never happened on *Paula Live,* but less than a month ago Iris Ehrlick, *Tell Tonya*'s senior producer, had wooed away one of Simon's guests half an hour before taping, from a stall in the second-floor powder room of the St. Regis Hotel.

But May's radio had been on, like white noise, in the background. And Henry checked the wire services through his computer at least every hour. If a disaster had struck, she'd have heard about it.

"What is it?" she asked again. Gil was struggling, which made her think it was bad.

"Tipping," he got out. "We'll tape Wednesday."

She laughed. "You're going to think I'm crazy." She laughed again. "I thought you said 'tipping.' " She got serious. "What did you really say?"

When Gil defended it with "It's information everyone wants," she knew it wasn't a joke.

"I can't do it. I'm still pulling Valentine's Day together. I'm working on my prodigies. I've got the pit bull who saved the little girl's life. You need tipping, give it to Bunny. She's probably done it ten times already."

"Paula thinks she undertipped her doorman at Christmas time. She had Joan working on it. She's still waiting for it. Now it's yours." He got up and dropped his squashed nib into her wastebasket.

May opened her well-stocked top desk drawer, handed him another one—feeding time at the zoo—and said, "I can't do it. Henry just got back from escorting Lianna over to my dentist. She's getting half a mouth of new teeth as we speak, compliments of you."

"Are her new teeth going to go bad? She'll flash them to the camera a few days later, that's all."

It was the unnaturally high pitch of his voice she noticed first, his shirt collar next, made dark by sweat.

"Your collar," May said, "it's wet. Are you sick?"

He sat down, leaned close to her, and whispered, "No sicker than you'd be if you spent an hour with two New York City police detectives."

"What did they want to know?" May whispered back.

He leaned closer. "They found a pen in Barnett's apartment. One of these." He picked a *Paula Live* Bic off her desk, then threw it back down with such force the plastic cartridge split. Blue ink began to seep through the pile of mail that hid May's blotter but she didn't care. Her mind was busy ticking off the implications, filling in the missing pieces as if she were putting together a show. Barnett was a suicide. But the cops were questioning Gil as though he was a suspect. Only there were no suspects in a suicide. It didn't make sense, unless Paula was right and Barnett had been murdered.

When the intercom buzzed, they both jumped. Henry's disembodied voice shot out of the speaker box. "Paula's looking for Gil."

He popped up. "You'll get all the support you need to keep your love story alive," he told her, dropping the subject of death faster than it had taken Barnett to hit the sidewalk. "You'll lose two days, tops. And"—he paused for effect—"I'll lend you Wendy."

It was pointless to explain to him that getting assistance from Wendy was like asking the girls to clean up their rooms. They'd stonewall, play deaf, play dead until she arrived at the right level of threat. Likewise, though Wendy was a miracle worker for Gil, everyone but Gil knew that when mere mortals sought her help, she became as useful as a dead battery.

"You're not going to let me down now, are you?" he asked. It was a rhetorical question. May was constitutionally unable to let anyone down.

As soon as Gil hustled off to Paula's office, May called home again.

"Good morning to you. Ovaa-Iita from Finland," her au pair sang out.

"It's May again. I need to be clear." She enunciated carefully, speaking as slowly as she could. "Did everything go all right with the girls this morning?"

"Is too much to worry with in America," Ovaa-Iita

observed. "Everything here is right. How are you? Awful?"

"Yes, thanks," May said, and clicked to the next button to call her friend Judy at *Simon Says*.

It wasn't her favorite part of the job, playing the part of a vulture, picking through the remains of people's lives. But of all people, Judy would understand. Judy, like May, suffered from an overdeveloped and difficult to satiate curiosity. It came with the job, an occupational hazard. It's what drove them to scour dozens of newspapers and magazines every day, tracking down story ideas. It's what emboldened them to call grieving widows, offering them a chance to tell their story on TV. It's what made them producers.

"Was Barnett murdered?" she asked when Judy got on the line.

"Don't tell me you're putting together a show on him."

"I'm not."

"Good. The official word is suicide, but considering all the cops crawling around here, speculation is otherwise. Fess up. What are you working on?"

"The truth? Tipping."

"My condolences."

May saw Henry's shadow stretching across her office floor. Of course, he'd never confess to listening in. He'd claim he was just waiting to see her. She hung up the phone quietly, let him strain to hear her as she crept stealthily across her small office, then popped her head into the hall, surprising him.

"I was just waiting to see you," he said, defending himself, as if she'd accused him of something worse. He quickly changed the subject, handing her a set of photographs of Lianna and Miguel. "Dr. Foust said only another dentist could tell which of Lianna's teeth are her own. You want to know which ones he did?" He pointed to a spot on Lianna's tiny Polaroid smile.

"Hold on," May said. "We have a crisis."

He quieted instantly.

"We got bumped today, with forty-eight hours to groove up a show on tipping."

Henry was at a rare loss for words. May went on. "I want you to look at this as an opportunity. Show me you're ready to be an associate producer." Due to budget constraints she'd had to make do without one for six months. That left Henry handling the administrative duties he loathed—and did poorly—at the same time as he struggled to learn how to put together a show. So far he'd demonstrated the bloodhound instincts of a producer, but still lacked the polish. "If we get this show done and keep our Valentines on track, I'll try my best to make my promotion mean a promotion for you as well."

The creases in Henry's forehead multiplied into an intricate web. He was panicked—so close to getting his first big break that he could finally smell the foul odor of failure.

"Okay. Okay. I'll check articles and pamphlets."

"And books. Look for books," May advised.

"On tipping?" He was nearing hysterics.

"You can do this," May reassured him as she escorted him back to his computer. She continued on down the hall to make her pilgrimage to Wendy, hoping Gil had remembered to direct her to be helpful.

"Good morning," Wendy murmured when she saw her, offering no more than that, civility.

"Where's Gil?" May asked, trying small talk for starters.

"He just left for the afternoon viewing. Barnett's," she

said when she noticed May's blank look. "I sent a memo around," she added defensively. "Didn't you read it?"

"I haven't had time to read anything this morning," she lied. Henry's secretarial skills, simple ones like passing along memos and messages, had been fading fast, as if he knew he wouldn't need them much longer. She'd have to deal with that later. "What do you make of it all?" she asked, trying small talk to ease the way before asking for help. "Do you think Barnett killed himself?"

Wendy looked up slowly, deciding whether or not it was her place to say. As footsteps headed down the hall outside her small cubicle, she quickly shook her head, a silent jerky motion May took to mean no. The footsteps faded, but it was clear Wendy was finished speculating. She put her pen in her desk drawer, her hands on her impossibly clean blotter, and raised an eyebrow, waiting.

May was a firm believer in having administrative allies. Paula's secretary, Patty, had been an easy get—a few lunches was all it took to make her friendly. But Wendy's friendship had so far remained out of reach. She'd let down her armor exactly once, the day last year when May arrived at work red-eyed and undone with news of Todd's surprise departure. The rest of her colleagues had offered little solace, since none of them liked Todd at all. Their consensus was that his leaving should be cause for celebration, not despair. Wendy was the exception. Surprising May, she suggested lunch, where at a corner table in the Plaza's Oak Room, she confided their new commonality. Her husband had run out on her, too.

Until then all May—all anyone—knew was that Wendy lived alone, without the son whose fleshy face smiled crookedly in photographs displayed from one edge of her window ledge to the other. But over that lunch Wendy shared more: she told of the day Charlie was born, underweight and unresponsive, immediately diagnosed with a multitude of syndromes. She told how her husband first denied the boy was his and then, when that didn't work, how he walked out. Only years later did he begin sending money, hefty guilt-driven checks that enabled her to send the boy to the fine Connecticut facility where he lived with round-the-clock care.

Her life, she told May, was completely devoted to the boy. She visited him every weekend and spent nearly every lunch hour at the post office sending packages of comic books and candy for him to share with his caregivers. Her point, she explained, was that if she could survive her abandonment and accept that she'd foolishly married a snake, no doubt May, who carried far fewer burdens, would soon be able to do the same.

The women returned from that lunch with swollen eyes and raw noses. Wendy was so depressed she went home early. For the first time in six years she called in sick the next day, causing Gil to drop by May's office and advise that if, in the future, she needed to spill out her guts, she should try psychotherapy like everyone else. He must have laid down the law to Wendy, too, because for a time after that she avoided May completely before eventually resuming her normal stance of cool distance. As for currying favors from her, May had no illusions that it would be easy.

"Did Gil talk to you? About helping me out on the tipping show?" She didn't wait for Wendy to volunteer. "I need an audience the day after tomorrow. Two-thirds waiters, chambermaids, hair stylists; the other third people who have complaints about the service industry."

Wendy stared back at her, revealing nothing.

"Gil told me to ask you."

Wendy shifted her gaze to her computer, opened a file, jotted down a name on a small, yellow Post-It, and stuck it in May's hand. "Try her. She's a travel agent who can help with rounding up the complainers. Tell Henry he can use my name when he calls."

"It will take Henry two weeks to put together this audience. I have two days. Gil said you'd do it. Do you want to tell him you won't or shall I?"

Eye contact was terminated. Wendy hit the buttons on her computer again, muttering a barely audible, "What do you need?" She would do the job. The tipping audience would be dense with waiters, beauticians, and gripers. But Gil and Paula would be sure to know who had made it happen. And May would suffer for the help with innumerable difficult-to-document slights.

When she got back to her office, Henry was sitting in one of her guest chairs, waiting. "Number one, Lianna wants a makeover at Elizabeth Arden," he told her. "Number two, she must have really enjoyed the nitrous at Dr. Foust's because now Miguel says his teeth are bothering him, too."

The phone rang. Reluctantly May picked it up to find it was Pete Jackson, the Howard Stern–loving contractor currently camped out in the kitchen of what she laughingly called her new house. She and the girls had moved less than a month after Todd left for Malibu, but there was no honeymoon period, no romantic courtship for May and this 1910 post-Victorian cash sucker. Like the rest of her life, it seemed to constantly become unglued. Pete, rebuilding it around her, phoned nearly every day now.

"How much?" she asked as soon as she heard his voice. "In hundreds."

"I can't be sure till my roofer gets here, but my guess is today you should start thinking in thousands. And before you hang up, your baby-sitter wants to know if you're feeling any better, and two girls are standing next to me waiting to say hello."

"Me first," she heard Susie scream.

By the time she got off the phone, took another four calls, read half a dozen faxes, and had a meeting with a publicist it was five o'clock. Five o'clock and her favorite show was in jeopardy, her house had sucked out more money that Miguel and Lianna dreamt of making in a year, and her mind was being pulled back again and again to Barnett's lifeless body.

Gil burst into her office. "You know why Iris Ehrlick was not at James Barnett's wake today?" He didn't wait for an answer. "She was out building Tonya a Valentine's Day show about the best-kept secret romance in Hollywood."

"I give up," May said. "Who are they?"

"How the hell am I supposed to know? That's what I pay my staff to know." He stomped down the hall screaming. "Iris got Tonya a Hollywood scoop for Valentine's Day, and we're giving Paula a man who scoops poop for a living. What's wrong with this picture?"

When May came out of her office to keep the peace, she ran right into Stephanie Lee, Gil's wife.

If nothing else, he had married well; his father-in-law was a powerhouse who ran a major television network, sat on the boards of several museums, and remained a frequent White House guest through four administrations. As for Stephanie, she was born to all the breeding and connections Gil could only ache for, and her gene pool had seen to it that she was as smart as she was beautiful, smart enough to stand behind her man and work the controls from the rear.

"He's shaken up," she confided to May as if they were best girlfriends, her cool soft hand resting lightly on

May's wrist. She tilted her head, and her lightly sprayed hair moved just enough to look natural but not messy. "The wake was very sobering. He's quite upset. Don't pay too much attention to anything he says. Not now," she added quickly, as an afterthought.

"Where the hell is my hat?" Gil called from the hall. "Hey, Colleen. Why don't you take Iris Ehrlick out to lunch tomorrow. Pick her brain. Raid her Rolodex. If she won't share her contacts, try taking her up to Barnett's balcony to admire the view."

"Maybe if he got to know that headless couple better, he'd be more comfortable with them," Stephanie suggested. "I could make a dinner."

"They're not headless," May told her. "They're homeless."

"Oh." She shifted slightly in her perfectly serious gray Chanel suit. "I see you've lost your sense of humor, too. Look, May, we all need to unwind a notch. How about you come up to the house tonight for a late dinner?"

"Why is it that Tonya's going to have Beauty and we're giving Paula the Beast?" Gil droned on like a drunken man. "And where the hell is my scarf?"

"Try your hat rack, where it always is," May called.

"You're so good with him," Stephanie told her.

"It's not there. Why is nothing where it's supposed to be? Why can't we get anyone decent to come on this show? Why is nothing ever done right the first time around here?"

"On second thought, tonight is not a good idea," Stephanie said. She disappeared inside Gil's office, where she linked arms with him and guided him to the elevator, whispering calming words along the way.

Even though May was ready to leave, too, she stalled so she wouldn't have to ride down in the elevator with them. She still had plenty of time to make her regular train. But ten minutes later, when she got to the lobby, she decided to give in to the nagging voice of her curiosity and take a detour past Barnett's apartment instead.

Any idea she had of casually wandering over and interviewing his doorman was put aside when she saw the crowd hanging around in front of the dead man's home. From her post across the street, half-hidden behind a lamppost, she watched them, half a dozen men—cops or reporters, she couldn't tell which—wearing dark raincoats, their off-kilter belts hanging down to the sidewalk, shifting like tails as they nervously paced.

"Twenty-five, twenty-six, twenty-seven." A woman next to May was counting quietly, her head bent back as she looked up the balconied front of the tall, narrow building.

"What are you doing?" May asked, keeping her voice friendly.

"Same thing as you," the woman barked, annoyed that now she'd lost her place. "They said on the news he jumped off thirty-nine." She moved several feet away from May and started counting all over again, tipping her head way back to get a better look at the upper floors.

The woman looked familiar. May thought she might be one of the faithful. All the shows had them, people, women mostly, who showed up for every taping, whose presence served as assurance that the host had a loyal group of fans, whose absence was often taken as an omen that the segment they were taping would go badly.

May opened her purse to find one of her business cards. It came to her in a flash, that it might make a fun show, one on talk-show junkies. But as she rifled through her wallet, she suddenly felt a rush of embarrassment. She owed Barnett more respect than this. She snapped her purse shut and checked her watch. She'd missed the wake. She'd missed her train. At least she could spare several minutes for a few moments of silence to pay her respects. Almost immediately the woman interrupted.

"He worked for *Oprah*. A real ladies' man, it said in the paper. Did you ever go to *Oprah?* I'm going to see *Montel* next week. I just love *Montel*. But the one I'm dying to get into is *Rosie*. Have you gone to *Rosie,* yet?"

May smiled politely, drew her collar closed, and decided to pay her respects with a long, silent walk downtown to the train.

TONYA HAD BEEN ON A RAMPAGE FOR hours, ever since reading in Page Six of the *Post* that *Tell Tonya* would be a memory by Memorial Day. To fix this one Iris Ehrlick did so much ego massaging she developed carpal tunnel syndrome. Miraculously she got the Page Six people to agree to a troika lunch at Nobu the following Tuesday. Then Tonya, deciding it would be a better idea to play hard to get, canceled it. This was the part of being a producer Iris loathed. She delighted in the hunt for a hot story, the cunning that went into plotting the pursuit, the joy of stealing a guest from a competitor right before show time. But time spent hand-holding her host was nothing less than torture.

The topper was now she had to go to this surprise engagement dinner that had been cloaked in enough nauseating mystery to qualify as a high school senior's idea of a good time. They were meeting under the blue whale in the Museum of Natural History. At least this was across the street from her apartment, so if it was really a fiasco, she could go home and check her mail and it wouldn't be a total waste. Then they were to migrate to cocktails and dinner at some as yet undisclosed eatery. The invitation, typed on plain paper like a chain letter, had said three times that it was imperative the party be kept a secret lest the media at large get wind of the event. The bride's engagement had occurred in the kind of total news blackout only the very best publicist could deliver. The guests were directed not to RSVP, an unnecessary instruction considering Iris had no idea who was hosting the party. Even finding out who else was invited had proved to be a nightmare. She called a couple of people she assumed would be on the list, but after hinting around no one fessed up, so she gave up, figuring they, like her, were too afraid of blowing it to risk allowing a confidence.

The gift was to be something for the boudoir. *How affected can you get?* Iris wondered as she ducked into Bergdorf's and bought the most expensive pair of mules they had, satin ones, with pom-poms of dyed blood-red ostrich feathers.

"Latecomers risk ruining the surprise," the invitation threatened so Iris got there early, only to find herself alone with the giant whale. The school tours were over, the tourists back in their hotels, the remaining museum regulars crowding onto the fourth floor to see the reconfigured fossils as if the exhibit itself were threatening to become extinct. It was just Iris and the animals, a stuffed polar bear devouring a fish, a walrus basking on a rock.

For a moment she wondered if it was possible that everyone else had been too busy to come, or too irritated by the mannered melodrama of the invite. But that was unthinkable. This was a bride no one in their right mind would snub. That Iris had been invited at all meant she was finally a player.

She was considering the possibility she'd gotten the time wrong when she was joined by a second guest, who, she realized, had been sitting all along at a nearby café table, hidden by the dark, nursing a drink. It was champagne, the guest explained, one of two bottles smuggled in to toast the bride. Iris didn't refuse the proffered glass of Cristal. It wasn't a secret among those who knew her; she enjoyed her daily drinks, all the more if it was something good.

She shared with her new companion her smoldering annoyance, but her anger was suddenly sideswiped by the onset of a cannonball headache that arrived with a throbbing so explosive it made blinking painful. She felt as if she was going to be sick, stood up, sat back down, overcome by dizziness. She didn't want to get sick in the Museum of Natural History even if the only one watching her was the giant whale.

Her friend asked if she'd seen today's *New York Times* story about a debilitating stomach virus pummeling the city's population. Although she'd missed it—strange since she'd skimmed every article and thought that one would have caught her eye—it was some comfort to hear about, since at the moment she felt as though she was about to keel over and die, that in fact dying might be preferable to living with the throbbing pain behind her eyes and the rolling waves of nausea that were coming faster with each shallow breath.

When her fellow guest offered to accompany her across the street to her apartment, she could barely nod her assent. Like a baby she limply offered her arms, let herself be bundled up in her coat, let a scarf be tucked inside and a hat—was it even hers?—gently placed on her head. She hobbled out through the Planetarium exit.

The temperature was in the single digits, flirting with zero. The cold revived her. If she could just make it across the street, Bill, her doorman, could call an ambulance. But her new friend spent so much time fussing with the scarf and the hat that by the time they crossed the street, Bill was halfway down the block, helping old Mr. Butler into a cab.

Her legs wobbled like Jell-O. She didn't trust that she could stand up long enough to wait for Bill to come back and call the paramedics. When her friend suggested bed rest might do the trick, she nodded her assent. Anyway she was too weak to argue. They rode up in the elevator alone. She made it to her bed and instantly collapsed onto it.

Her friend tended to her, helping her off with her coat, then her boots, laying the neatly folded outerwear on the armchair next to the bed, lining the footwear up beside it. A cup of tea was offered and a dish towel soaked in ice water for her blazing headache. She couldn't remember mentioning her headache, but she was so dizzy now she couldn't be sure. When she leaned over to vomit, her small bathroom wastebasket was there to catch the spray. It was as if all her needs had been anticipated.

When she finally tried to get up again, she found it too hard, so she lay still, giving in to the sharp sting of the cold compress that had been placed on her forehead in exactly the right spot. As the compress warmed, the throbbing started up again. The damp cloth began to smell. Her forehead itched. She was going to be sick. Just in time the cloth was lifted off her head. She moved her hand to scratch the spot where it had been, but a sudden pressure around her throat took her breath away. The compress, itchy, warm, smelling like wet wool, was tied around her neck, too tight. She lifted her heavy lids, tried to say the pressure didn't feel good, but found she couldn't speak. She felt her stomach heave, and when she tried to get up, she was pushed, firmly, down. The pressure around her neck continued. With a surge of energy she tried to force the strong arms away, but then the throbbing worsened, the room began to spin, and she let her body go limp.

She was vaguely aware of someone fussing with her, arranging her, then walking around her apartment tidying up. She had no idea how much time had passed when she noticed the room was still. The best she could do was roll off the bed and hope her neighbors below were home to hear the thump of her crash landing.

She didn't wait to find out if they had. Cursing herself for moving the phone to her desk at the far end of the room, she half-crawled, half-rolled, inching toward it, the wet wool still knotted around her neck, making it difficult to swallow and to breathe. Finally she reached her desk chair and heaved herself up.

She struggled to get her fingers to move, pushed 611 by mistake, got telephone repair, depressed the receiver again. Finally she heard the sharp voice of the operator.

"Nine-one-one. What is your emergency?"

As Iris opened her mouth to speak, something tightened around her throat. The phone was pulled from her hand. She grasped for the receiver, got instead the huge calendar she kept on her desk. She died, clutching a page of it, the wrong month, while the voice of the 911 operator called out in vain, "This is nine-one-one. Can you tell me your emergency?" followed by the garbled sound of patrol cars being summoned.

8

EVERY EVENING WHEN HER TRAIN rolled out of the station, May's eyelids rolled shut. Before the last car disappeared into the first tunnel, she was gone, to a sleep that flirted with dreams. True, it sometimes seemed to last no longer than a sigh, as if her time-pressed brain had figured out the fewest possible seconds necessary to constitute a cat nap, but without it she'd be useless at home. Susie would have to tuck herself into bed. Delia would have to close up the house.

Tonight her head tipped slightly, righted itself, then tipped again, to an awkward angle that gave her the look of a corpse. Her arm jerked reflexively when the newspapers in her lap were gently tugged away. For a second she thought, *Why isn't Todd answering the phone?* Then her eyes snapped open, and she was staring at the boyish grin of her next-door neighbor, Carter Cooper.

"To what do I owe the pleasure of finding you on my train?" he asked her. "Working late on something special?"

May looked at the newspaper Carter held in his hand,

the one that had been resting on her lap. He followed her gaze.

"Oh. Sorry. Do you mind? I noticed you had the Tampa/St. Pete paper, and I happened to see, when I checked CNN on-line, that a high school student in Tampa was stabbed today after squirting someone with a water gun. That's a show, right?"

"Sally Jesse's already got it in the works."

"Damn. I have to log on earlier in the day."

Carter was only kind of kidding. A successful lawyer, a member of the Kiwanis, the Rotary, and several other clubs that May didn't and wasn't supposed to understand, her neighbor stood an even six feet tall, had matchstick straight sandy hair, a square chin, and a palpable aura of confidence. But clean, strong looks and an easy smile weren't enough for Carter. He was on a constant campaign to prove he was the best at whatever he did. It was Carter who had recommended Mr. Jackson, "the best contractor in New Jersey." Carter also claimed to employ the best landscaper, the best plumber, and the best French-drain man in Essex County.

When May moved onto the block, she nearly ruined his life. Up until then Carter had the best job, too. His company car was a red Mercedes. He had use of an oceanfront beach house in Cape May Point and a villa in Jamaica where he took his wife, Emily, and the five boys every January for at least a week. But none of this was showbiz. The day his boys heard their new neighbor worked in television, Carter watched his self-esteem, as reflected back through their eyes, slip ever-so-slightly away.

Carter, however, was successful in no small part because he knew how to turn just such problems into opportunities. So he quickly restructured his thinking.

Now he boasted that he had the best neighbor in television, May Morrison—and the _Paula Live_ show was the best morning talk show on the air.

"I've got everyone in the office taping your show. If you see a blip in your ratings, it's thanks to me."

She'd quickly learned with Carter even a smile could be too much encouragement—especially now that he'd decided he wanted to get into television, too. In a life composed of ever-new challenges, his current goal was to come up with an idea for a show that May would produce. Then he could tell people his best neighbor, who worked on the best program, took his advice in producing what turned out to be the best hour in talk-show history.

"Emily and I were discussing this last night," he said, leaning in close enough for her to smell the Tic Tac on his breath. "How about a show on dentists? Em and I have a friend who's done some damn famous teeth. Think about it for a minute." He waited, allowing her more than enough time. Then he asked, "Does Sharon Stone have cavities? Are Tom Cruise's teeth really his own? You're curious, right?"

"It's a great idea, Carter, but we already have a dentist show in the works."

"Damn." The train pulled in to their stop. He scooped up the papers that fell off her lap and stuffed them back in her bag.

May smiled, noncommittal, then stepped down off the train. As it did every night when she got close to home, her desire to see, to hug, her children rose to a nearly desperate urge. She walked fast, almost running. Carter's long legs matched her quick steps easily. As she turned up her front path, he tried one last pitch.

"What about lawyers?" he called from the sidewalk. "You ever do a show on lawyers?"

"Only convicted ones. Good night." Her door was wide open. She disappeared inside.

"Mommy's home," the girls yelled as they came running toward her from the kitchen, each grabbing one leg.

"Mommy, I have to make a diorama of a Native American family and Ovaa-Iita doesn't know what a diorama is. She keeps telling me to eat bananas. She thinks I have diarrhea," Delia reported.

May laughed.

"It's not funny. It's due tomorrow."

"A diorama," May began, slipping off her coat, "is a little scene, like a slice of life. You make it in a shoe box."

"Mommy, Mommy, Mommy," Susie interrupted. "Look."

"A what?" Delia yelled, to be heard.

May looked over at Susie. "You're finally wearing your new panties," she cheered. "That's terrific."

Pete poked his head out of the kitchen doorway. "Hey, Mrs. Morrison. I got those numbers for you on the roof, the ceiling, and the door." He said the last with a smirk.

"What door?" Suddenly she noticed how cold the house was and that her children were walking around wearing their down jackets zipped up to their necks. She swung around and looked at the walk-through opening where her front door used to be.

"But I don't have a shoe box," Delia worried. She worried about everything. "And I don't know what 'a slice of life' is."

"The good news is I found an old door in the back of the garage that's the right size, if I cut a couple of inches off the top," Pete explained. "I'll put it in for the meantime. I can jimmy up a lock that will hold for the night." He leaned closer to confide, "It was your old lock that got her." He gestured upstairs, where Ovaa-Iita could be heard lumbering around. "She must have got the key stuck in the door and then she went a little berserk trying to get it out."

"Mommy." Susie tugged on May's sleeve.

"Ovaa-Iita," May called. The au pair came running down the stairs, burst into tears, then ran right back up. The phone rang. Pete wouldn't meet her eyes but couldn't hide his smile.

"Mommy." Susie tugged again, then began to cry. "I'm wet." She was standing in a puddle. She looked at her sister for help. "Delia, I'm wet."

"Mommy, Susie's wet," Delia said, taking a step aside to avoid getting herself wet, too.

"May Morrison," May said into the phone, forgetting she was home.

"Honey pie, you won't believe this," came Margery's silky voice. "I just got a hot-tip news flash. The Wicked Witch of the Upper East Side, Miss Iris Ehrlick, is dead."

"Is this a joke? I don't have time for jokes right now."

"This isn't a joke, sugar. This is a trend. One, I hasten to add, that I hope not to follow. I've been holed up with Gil in the conference room checking the facts, and it's true. He's on the phone now with the local news yokels trying to get the full story. He wants to be able to fill us in tomorrow before Paula tapes her first show. She's having a severe case of panic, I might add, interviewing bodyguards as we speak."

May dropped her voice. "Was Iris murdered?"

"I imagine if she'd suffered a heart attack, our Miss Wind would be interviewing Oprah's chef instead."

Her sobs ignored, Susie upped the volume. Delia, seeing no advantage in waiting quietly, began to cry, too.

"Don't go out dancing tonight, sugar. Don't stay home alone. And definitely double lock your doors."

"I haven't gone dancing in a decade," May replied. "I couldn't be alone if I wanted to be, and for reasons you're not interested in, I don't even have a door to lock. Do you hear what's going on here?" The girl's cries were now joined by the guttural sound of Ovaa-Iita's sobbing. May stared at Pete's back as he walked by her carrying an old mint green painted door.

"I suppose I can't convince you to make a few calls," Margery purred, then lowered her voice. "Bunny and I aren't exactly on speaking terms at the moment."

"Mommy, I said I spilled," Susie screamed, pointing to her wet pants.

"Never mind, sugar. I'll call her myself," Margery signed off.

"I spilled," Susie shrieked.

May hung up the phone and scooped Susie up. "You didn't spill," she explained, struggling to find the midline between reassurance and indulgence as she carried her upstairs. "You had an accident," she yelled to be heard over the sound of Pete banging the new door in. "Everyone has accidents."

Regaining control instantly, Susie yelled, "Ovaa-Iita had an accident today, too. She spilled the front door."

"What am I?" Delia called out, pushing past them up the stairs. "A ghost? Fine. I won't bring in a diorama. Fine." She slammed herself inside her bedroom.

"Not that one," Susie screamed when May tried to put on her green pajamas.

May opened Susie's drawer and lifted each set of cotton pajamas in turn. "No," Susie screamed. "Not that one. No."

"Did you have a nap when you got home from school?" May asked.

"No," Susie screamed, kicking her heels on her pale butter-cream carpet.

May moved on to Delia's room, dutifully knocking on the door before pushing it open. "Can I come in?"

"Fine," Delia spat out. She sat in a corner of her cake-frosting-pink room, staring at the wall. "I won't bring in a diorama. I never bring in snacks for my class. Nobody wants a playdate at my house, and big deal Susie is wearing Pocahontas panties. What about my panties? They're digging into my legs so hard they're burning me. Look." She pulled down her underwear to show her mother the mark cutting into her leg.

"Oh, sweetie. They're too small. You're growing so fast. I'll get you new ones. I'm sorry." Delia relented, crawled onto her mother's lap, and let herself be hugged.

"Help." Susie hopped into Delia's room, the top of her pajamas half on, both arms poking through one sleeve, the neck hole partway over her head. "I'm stuck," she screamed. "Mommy, get me out."

"Mrs. Morrison, we've got a little problem," Pete said, appearing in the doorway holding a half-rusted pipe that looked worryingly similar to the one that used to be under her kitchen sink. From downstairs she heard the sound of gushing water.

Collapsing on the floor in a mock faint, she called out, "I give up."

Pete smiled.

"How can you smile?" she yelled.

With a final tug Susie rearranged her arms and pulled her shirt on. Beaming proudly, she lay down awkwardly next to her mother. "How can you mile?" she yelled, trying to exactly imitate the position of her mother's arms even though hers were inches too small to reach.

Delia couldn't help laughing as she quickly lay down alongside her sister. "Yeah. How can you mile?" she yelled

at Pete. As May laughed, a few tears seeped out of the
corners of her eyes. Her daughters began to chant. "How
can you mile? How can you mile? How can you mile?"
She joined them. "How can you mile? How can you mile?"

Pete rolled his eyes, whistled, then disappeared downstairs to attend to the pipes.

Delia rolled on top of Susie, smothering her with kisses.
Susie yelled go away but could barely be heard through
her giggles. Finally they collapsed in an exhausted heap.

"Hallow?"

May sat up to find Ovaa-Iita standing in the hallway
wiping her damp cheeks on her Harvard University
sweatshirt sleeve. "I'm having to go."

"Pardon?"

"I'm sick of home. I have to go back. In Finland."

May didn't correct her English. "I'll make the arrangements."

Delia, and then Susie, cheered.

9

IN THE MORNING MAY CALLED THE AU-
pair coordinator and adamantly refused her offer to
come right over and work things out.

"Ovaa-Iita needs to go home," May explained.

"Give me ten minutes with her," Carol pleaded. "I can
explain to her how normal it is to be homesick. I'm sure
we can get her to stay."

"Ovaa-Iita needs to go home," May repeated.

Carol quickly realized her best bet was to move on to a fresh candidate. "You won't believe the application that just landed on my desk. You are so lucky. She's a gem, and you've got first crack at her."

May took the phone number, but the gem wasn't home.

"She's gone to call at the animal hospital," Louise's mum said, "where she does her volunteer work. She loves animals, you know. Can you ring later?"

May agreed she would and then went on to her next call, arranging Ovaa-Iita's seat on Finnair's Friday night flight. That done, and two missed trains later, she left for work.

She assumed that was why Gil glared at her when she joined everyone in the conference room meeting— she was nearly an hour late.

Then she noticed he wasn't sitting in his usual spot at the head of the long table and that the look she'd first read as annoyance was closer to fear. She wondered if the man in Gil's usual seat might be the network comptroller affectionately known as Sir Hatchet, but when the unwelcome guest turned to look at her, she realized it was the detective who'd been up to see Gil the day before. His partner stood leaning against the window ledge, his narrow eyes unreadable.

Never mind that she'd sworn off romance forever. She couldn't help that she felt a jolt, like electricity, when the seated detective turned his eyes on her. Deep-set, slightly sad, a hard-to-pin-down color that first seemed green, then coffee—she had experience with eyes like his, had married a pair once, believing at the time she could save Todd from the darkness they couldn't completely conceal. It was a mistake she swore not to repeat. She braced herself and took in the rest of him, looking for his flaws.

For one thing there was just too much of him. He

was tall and broad—the brown tweed jacket that stretched across his back unable to contain him easily. His long legs shifted as he struggled to find a comfortable position for them under the table. Even his hair seemed ill at ease, sprouting up like leaves on a celery stalk before falling onto his high forehead. And then there was his nose, the slightly bent shape indicating it had probably been broken more than once. If she concentrated on his nose, she could convince herself he was a thug. A thug with poet's eyes.

Her attention was drawn back to his partner, whose leather jacket announced itself each time he shifted his position. With the body language of a seen-it-all drug dealer, he had the tough-guy look Paula preferred. If Iris's death didn't prove too upsetting to her, he could easily end up watching the sky turn from pink to ink out of one of Paula's large windows during an after-hours private consultation.

The young detective scratched the back of his head, and as his jacket lifted, May got a glimpse of his gun, which reminded her why they were there. She sat down next to Gil, whose jaw was now crunching at the speed of a jackhammer.

Detective O'Donnell watched May take her seat. She watched his hands, splayed out flat on the table, his long, slim piano player's fingers drumming slowly. Automatically she registered the absence of a wedding band, then fingered her own, which she wore like a talisman to ward off unwanted advances. When she saw the detective watching her twist the thin gold braid, her cheeks flushed and he marked it. His penetrating stare scanned from May to Margery as if he was taking inventory. But he was quick. Bunny, who'd been speaking the whole time, never even noticed his attention had strayed.

"After we tell people how to keep from getting car-jacked," she plugged away, "we can go to pickpocket prevention before wrapping up with a segment explaining stranger danger to kids. Do you like kids?"

"I like mine."

"Perfect. We'll put them in the front row. We can introduce them on air. How about your wife? Would she come in?"

He noticed May staring, slipped his hands off the table into his lap. "Only if the subject matter is how cops make bad husbands, in which case I'm sure she'd be delighted to attend." His smile was easily given, modest, and slightly self-conscious, the kind of smile the camera loved. It was a detail none of the assembled producers missed.

"So? Can we book you?"

"You can book me if I can book you."

May laughed at his joke, giving permission for everyone else to join in a second behind her, none of them wanting to admit they hadn't been sure he was kidding at all.

"Actually the department has someone trained to do the job you're describing," he said, his suddenly serious tone quieting them all. "And it isn't me."

"Sheila White," Margery interrupted. "Bunny knows her well. In fact, Bunny honey, it hasn't been six months since you dragged her on to do this very same show. Just because you didn't get much of an audience that time it's no reason to inflict it on us again so soon."

Margery stood up, walked over to the detective, stretched out her hand to shake his. "I do all the important cop shows here. Sheila is a close personal friend of mine. I spoke with her last night. She was going to come by this afternoon to give us a little pep talk. How'd we get so lucky to have you come down at this ungodly hour instead?"

"That's the difference between Detective White and myself. Community Relations can sleep late and come by in the afternoon. Homicide doesn't sleep at all."

May's eyes widened at the word. O'Donnell noted it.

Margery was unfazed. "I have the perfect show for you. 'Women Who Kill.' I've been developing it all week. And, sugar, a drop-dead handsome homicide detective to sit in as an expert panelist is just what my show needs."

Detective O'Donnell shifted uncomfortably.

"I've got three women," she explained. "Two first-degree murders and one manslaughter. I've got jailhouse camera hookup okays on all of them. I've got one victim's wife and the mother of another to sit in the studio with Paula. What I don't have yet is someone to explain how this is the wave of the future. It is, don't you think— women and crime?"

"Ladies, this isn't a booking meeting," Gil interrupted. "Detective O'Donnell has been kind enough to stop by to calm Paula's nerves. Let's not fight over his carcass. So to speak," he added quickly.

The detective took a small pad out of his suit breast pocket. "I'm not here to calm anyone's nerves but my own. Are you the hostess?" he asked May. Again her cheeks heated up, but before she could answer, Margery butt in.

"You're talking to May Morrison, our human-interest producer, whose current record time for getting eyes to well up is seven seconds, but, believe it or not, she's determined to bring it down to five. Our host, Paula Wind—and do yourself a favor, do not call her a hostess to her face—is taping her first show of the day across the street. She'll race over as soon as they're done. Which leaves us a little more time to chat." Her voice got softer, dreamy. "So what do you think of my idea?

You have a future in television—I can promise you that—if you want one."

The detective's courteous refusal was cut off by the unexpected ring of the slim red phone that sat on the table before him. Gil stretched over to grab it and screamed into the receiver, "What?"

May winced. Good news did not come over the studio phone during taping. Her eyes darted to the big clock on the wall. Paula and Colleen were ten minutes away from the end of their show.

"Tell her not to breathe. Tell her not to blink." Gil slammed down the phone, then tried to look collected. "You'll have to excuse me. Our guest lost one of her false eyelashes in her cup of coffee, and now she doesn't want to part with the other one." He backed out of the room slowly, but as soon as he closed the door behind him, they could hear his expensive loafers speeding down the hall.

Without pause Bunny and Margery resumed their maneuvering to win the detective. Cops were a catch. All the ratings-winning dark aspects of human nature were revealed under their watch. Good-looking cops were delivered by divine intervention. Even if O'Donnell couldn't be convinced to become a resident guest, he could still be a "friend of the show," leaking stories and introducing the producers to photogenic victims and perps.

"Maybe Detective O'Donnell has his own idea for a show," Margery suggested, correctly reading that her mark was not warming to her. "Maybe you have an unsolved case gnawing at you? One that's keeping you awake at night."

"This I have to see," Bunny growled. "Our new show, *Paula Wind's Most Wanted.*"

"All my open cases gnaw at me," the detective confessed. "Every single one keeps me awake at night. They keep me awake during the day, too. I think about them all the time. I'm thinking about them now."

Something in his voice made Margery quickly return to her seat.

"For example, right now Miss Ehrlick's death is gnawing at me. And to tell you the truth, one of the things that's bothering me is that no one here appears too disturbed by it. I guess she wasn't exactly anyone's friend."

Margery laughed out loud. "Sugar, I'm from Georgia. The only way I would know how to kill someone is with kindness, and if I thought it would have worked, I would have been fatally kind to Iris years ago."

He didn't laugh. "Why is that?"

She chuckled. "Where shall I begin? We could start with that she was a guest snatcher. She never even bothered to deny that charge. In fact, she was proud of it. Didn't she almost get that mute boy of yours?" she asked May. "The one who played the piano?"

"She tried," May said, remembering how hard she'd worked to gain that young boy's trust and how she'd almost lost him when Iris showed up at his house with a limo and a fat wallet to take him on a shopping spree at the Disney Store. May still remembered when the boy's mother called to report that they'd bought videos of every Disney movie, stuffed animals of every character, and nightshirts, sweatshirts, and backpacks for a clan of relatives. "By the way," the mother added, as if it was an afterthought, "we're still coming on your show."

"We play hard here," Margery told the detective. "Iris played dirty. Bribery, burglary—there was nothing she wouldn't do to scoop us on a show." She turned to May. "Am I right? Am I telling it the way it was?"

May nodded, but not without some discomfort at the direction the conversation had taken.

Whether O'Donnell was repelled or intrigued by news of Iris's unscrupulous behavior was impossible to tell. He turned his expressionless face to May.

"Okay. So you weren't friends with the deceased. Neither was I. But were you enemies? If you were, if people are going to be calling up the tip line with your name, you'll save me a hell of a lot of trouble if you tell me now."

May didn't like the question, but she answered anyway. "We had very little to do with each other," she started, but before she could finish the thought, the conference room door burst open. For a moment she imagined it was Iris's killer come to get her next. She envisioned him dressed all in black, a ski mask hiding his face, taking aim, about to fire, stopping, pulling off his mask to reveal Todd's tanned visage. Then Paula's high-pitched scream cut through her nightmarish daydream.

"That's ridiculous," came her voice from the hall. "One minute they're going to be watching her eyelash fall off; then boom they're going to see some clip from a flick she was in twenty years ago. The audience isn't that dumb."

Bunny got up, ready to face the ugly reality that her show, which would begin taping in less than half an hour, would be featuring a host in full-blown hysterics. "If you'll excuse me, I have to go," she explained to O'Donnell. "I've got a couple of compulsive cheaters in one greenroom and their wives in the other. If they meet up before the show, you'll have more than one murder to worry about."

"Paula," she called as she ducked out to the hall, allowing Colleen to sneak by her into the conference room. "I need you in makeup in five minutes."

It was the wrong thing to say. "Makeup? The only

reason I'd go near Betty now would be to kill her. Where's Colleen?"

Colleen sat down beside May, plunked down her Ro- lodex, and began flipping through it quickly. "Jayne is going to pay," she muttered, referring to the powerful publicist who sold her on the aging starlet as a guest.

"Where is she? Where the hell is Colleen?" Paula stormed in after her. "That's what you get me? An over- the-hill, no talent, dried-up has-been who can't even put on her own makeup?"

"Everybody booked her, Paula. If we didn't get her on, you'd be screaming about that."

"I hope her goddamn nose falls off on *Rolonda*." As she turned back to Gil, she suddenly noticed the detec- tive and his partner. "Hello there. I'm Paula Wind. Par- don the explosion." In an instant her fury vanished, her mood brightened, her on-air persona was reclaimed. It didn't matter that she didn't know who these men were. Later she'd beat up Gil for not prepping her. In the meantime, she turned her warmth on the stranger at the head of the table as if he were her long-lost brother. Moving with the ease of a dancer, she glided over, melted into the seat next to him, floated her hand atop his, and whispered, "Tell me what happened."

"Detective O'Donnell, this is Paula Wind," Gil jumped in before further damage occurred. "Paula, Detective O'Donnell is the man in charge of Iris's murder."

"Murder. I told you," she snapped at Gil. "Didn't I tell you?" She turned around. "Where's Frankie? What the hell good is a bodyguard who has to take a leak every ten minutes?" A hulk with a neck the size of an ele- phant's leg lumbered into the room. "Maybe you shouldn't drink so goddamn much water."

May watched the tendons in the mammoth neck flare. Paula focused back on O'Donnell, who stared back at her, impassive. She shot his partner an exploratory smile, which he instantly returned, starstruck. "What happened to dear Iris?" she asked him.

O'Donnell took over the questioning again and turned it back to her. "She a friend of yours?"

Paula could feel everyone staring, waiting to see the depth of her lie. "She was very"—she struggled for the right word—"ambitious. I have great respect for that in a person, don't you?" She seemed pleased with that. "You're positive it wasn't a stroke? Gil said he heard it was a stroke. She definitely was the type."

"It was murder."

Paula slumped back into her seat. "That's it, then. There's a serial killer out there. All right. I'm going to stay calm. So far they're only going after producers, so I'm safe. At least I think I am. Do you think I'm safe?" Before he could answer, she asked, "Do you do any private-duty work?" She looked toward his partner. "How about you?"

"Why do you say it's a serial killer?" O'Donnell interjected before Paradiso got a chance to make a fool of himself.

"What are you? On loan from the hostage negotiation team? Don't you own a television set?"

"I own two television sets, Miss Wind. I just don't get to watch them much, what with all the killers roaming the streets. However the particular killer I'm interested in today is the one who killed Miss Iris Ehrlick. To qualify as a serial killer, we'd have to have at least two more bodies. I'm curious. Are there some bodies I don't know about yet?"

"I don't know what you know about, but I know there's no way James Barnett committed suicide." She leaned towards him. "Do you even know who I'm talking about? Have you even heard about James Barnett and his supposedly suicidal leap?"

"I'm well aware of Mr. Barnett. Why do you say it wasn't suicide?"

"At one time I knew him quite well. Quite well," she repeated so that he'd be sure to get her drift. "Too bad you haven't been up to his apartment."

"Matter of fact we have," Paradiso said, happy to join in now that there was something worth talking about.

"Did you notice the paintings?" Paula asked. She stood up and walked to the window, gazing out as if the paintings were hung there, in the air.

"Detective Paradiso, did you notice any paintings at Mr. Barnett's domicile?" O'Donnell tried not to laugh as he thought about the dozen or so snapshots piled up on his partner's desk. Paradiso had gotten the crime-scene team to take Polaroids of the paintings, but he still hadn't figured out what to do with the damn things.

Paradiso nodded. "I remember the paintings. They were all over the walls."

"Do you remember the huge one above the fireplace? Very discreet. The woman had a throw—a deeply colored Flemish tapestry—draped over her so you don't see too much. If you were there, you couldn't have missed it." She moved so close to Paradiso that the hairs on her angora sweater came erect, stroking up against his leather jacket. "That one was me," she said quietly. "I modeled for it in James's class. Years ago. Years and years ago," she added, doing the math.

"I remember that one." Paradiso said. "It was beautiful."

"Thanks," Paula said, sitting down. Calmer now, she went on. "Trust me on this. James Barnett would just as soon have jumped as I would. I mean, I wouldn't jump because I'm afraid of heights. But Barnett—what was in it for him? He got a total of three lines in the *Daily News*. I counted. I'm telling you the only reason he would have jumped is if it got him *Time* magazine's Man of the Year cover. That's what he wanted. Glory. That's why he worked thirty-six hours a day getting Simon the best guests on the planet. That's why he painted beautiful women. The man was driven. He was a lunatic. But he wasn't crazy." She'd worked herself up to a panic again. "What am I supposed to do, Detective? Wait around to see if I'm going to be up next?"

May figured the detective must have had a lot of experience dealing with hysterical people because Paula's rising panic didn't suck him into its whirlpool. If anything, it made him calmer.

"What you should do is to remind yourself that as of this morning the New York City Police Department regards Mr. Barnett's death as an unrelated incident. As for Miss Ehrlick's murder, we're investigating with our full power as well as with the knowledge that the primary cause of premature death by murder is ill-chosen friends and lovers."

"That doesn't make me feel better. Do you know how many people consider themselves my friends? Thousands. Tens of thousands."

"Not to mention lovers," Margery muttered, unable to contain herself.

"I'm not happy, Detective."

"Neither am I, Miss Wind. Open cases make me very unhappy. And when I'm unhappy, I get jumpy. Usually the only person more jumpy than me is the perpetrator of the crime."

Gil's hyperkinetic jaws froze. He gulped, swallowed hard, stayed still.

"I bet it was a guest," Paula speculated.

Detective O'Donnell felt around his pockets for a pen,

then leaned over to Gil. "May I?" Smiling weakly, Gil offered up his Bic.

"Face it," Paula babbled, "most guests are wackos. I mean, would you come on the show?"

"We've been trying," Margery muttered.

"And he won't, right? You won't. Because you're a normal person. What normal person would come on this show? They're all nuts." She stood up.

Despite her better judgment May rose to the bait. "Come on, Paula. Plenty of normal people come on our show. They come to set things right, to help others learn from their mistakes. They come to purge themselves, to get a new start. Sometimes they just come to boast a little. They're good people, most of them."

"I don't believe she believes this crap," Paula said, heading toward the door.

"Are you going to your dressing room?" Gil asked her.

"I'm going on hiatus. How many shows do we have stockpiled?"

Gil stood up, popped another plug into his mouth. "Detective, I know you didn't come up here to hold our hands. But I'm sure your intention was not to make us feel we're in imminent danger."

"You're right. The only one in imminent danger right now is the killer, who, after I catch him, is looking at either a very long stretch in a very crowded and un- friendly prison system or a short stay, followed by death."

"Get me out of here, Gil. Get me on location. There must be some disaster area I can go visit."

"Paula." He was begging now. "Listen to me. The de- tective just told you somebody had it in for Iris. Not for talk-show producers. Not for talk-show hosts. Just for Iris."

"If it's someone she knew, it's someone I know." She

turned to Paradiso. "You never said if you do any private-
duty stuff. In case I ever feel well enough to work
again." She turned to Gil and coughed twice. "Now that
I have the flu."

"You look well taken care of to me," O'Donnell said.

Paula glanced over her shoulder to where Frankie sat,
arms folded, a sumo wrestler in a suit.

O'Donnell stood up. "You can all go back about your
business now. Detective Paradiso and I will be circulat-
ing through the offices to talk to each of you in turn.
Miss Wind, I have to ask you not to go home just yet."

"Believe me she's not going home," Gil said. "She's
taping a show in five and half minutes."

"What show?" she asked as Gil guided her out of the
room. He answered too quietly for anyone else to hear.
"Cheaters?" she shot out. "I'm supposed to go make
small talk to a bunch of goddamn cheaters?"

May was on her way out the door when O'Donnell
stopped her. "Mrs. Morrison, would you mind waiting
here a minute?"

Without looking back, Paradiso followed the rest of
the producers into the hall, closing the door behind him
as if this had been prearranged. All color drained from
May's face.

"You're like a human mood ring, aren't you?" he
asked once they were alone.

Instantly her color returned, then deepened, flaming
red. O'Donnell laughed, shaking his head. "Don't ever
play poker," he advised, then added, "or commit murder. Cop joke," he told her.

She returned the smile, felt her hot cheeks beginning
their cool down until he smiled and they heated up all
over again.

"It's a curse," she admitted. "Even my kids tease me
about it." She thought of Delia, wondered if her di-

orama got to school in one piece, figured it must have or she'd have gotten a tearful phone call. The school secretary seemed to enjoy it when children called their parents at work to share news of their pint-sized heartbreaking catastrophes.

"It keeps you honest," he observed.

She felt a twinge, vaguely familiar, a tiny spark. Then she thought of Todd, his broad naked back turned toward her as he told her about Chloe; the spark went out.

"This won't take long," the detective told her, lifting a large envelope from the floor. He emptied most of its contents on the table. "You have to bear with me. There are some things I just don't understand. Like this. Can you tell me about this?"

He slid over a stack of papers. May looked at the first page. There were names and phone numbers of public-relations heavy hitters, movie company sharks, magazine publishers, newspaper editors. There were names of a couple of hot TV stars, even two well-known politicians. Gil would have loved to have gotten his hands on this. "It's a call sheet," she explained. "A list of all the phone calls someone has to make in a day."

"A dead woman's call sheet."

She dropped it on the table, wiped her hands on her black wool skirt.

"I'm told it's Miss Ehrlick's morning call sheet from the day she was murdered. I'm told the afternoon call sheet is even longer. That sound right to you?"

She nodded.

He whistled as he shook his head. "I haven't gotten this many calls in my entire life."

May relaxed a bit. It was only a guide he needed, a translator. But when he leaned closer to look at the page over her shoulder, she wondered why this good-

looking cop with an ex and some kids had picked her.
He could have asked any one of them to stay. Margery,
for one, was dripping with desire to be helpful.

His closely shaved cheeks only inches away from her,
she could smell the thin, fading scent of his aftershave.
But she didn't want to smell it. She had sworn off romance. She leaned away.

"Talk-show hosts are the celebrities," she explained.
"But a good producer's job is to know everyone. Your
contacts are what gives you power."

"Would you mind turning to the third page?"

Complying, her eyes scanned the list. It had been well
prioritized—the first page composed of big-name jour-
nalists, publicists, a senator, the third page littered with
lesser mortals unknown to May until her eyes skipped
to the bottom of the page, drawn by a line of color, red
marker, that underlined her own name.

"I'm on this list," she observed unnecessarily.

"Did you get a phone call from Miss Ehrlick?"

"No."

"Well, your cheeks aren't turning into tomatoes, so
maybe you're telling the truth."

She laughed until she saw how serious he was.

"How frequently did you and Miss Ehrlick speak on
the phone?"

"We avoided each other at every opportunity."

"Any thoughts on why she might have intended to call
you? Or why she underlined your name?"

May had assumed it was Detective O'Donnell who'd
underlined her name in red. She noticed her hand
trembling slightly and leaned it against the table to
steady it.

"You're the only one underlined, if that's what you're
looking for," he said quietly.

She took another look and thought, *He's wrong.* "I

don't think I'm underlined. I think I'm crossed out.
What if whoever killed Iris crossed me out because
I'm next?"

"Sounds a bit far-fetched to me. I wouldn't worry
about it. Unless there's something I don't know that
you'd like to share."

May shook her head, quickly.

O'Donnell checked his notebook. "By the way, can
you tell me your whereabouts last Sunday night between the hours of nine PM and six AM?"

That was easy. It was the same place she was at that
time every night. "Asleep," she answered. "In bed at
home asleep."

He shifted but stared hard as he asked, "Alone?"

Skipping the blush of pink, her face went straight to
red. "I'm never alone. I have two young children and an
au pair living with me."

"And they all sleep with you in your bed?"

"No."

"Was anyone with you in your bedroom who can confirm your whereabouts?"

Her face was crimson now. She let out a breath willing the blood vessels to constrict, and they did, a bit. "I
sleep alone."

"Thank you very much," he said quietly, then handed
her his card and gently plucked the list from her hand.
"If you think of anything, give me a call." He opened
the door, signaling their meeting was over. She offered
a weak smile, then quickly left.

As soon as he closed the door, O'Donnell reached in
and pulled out the calendar from the envelope. The pho-
tocopy was folded into a small square. He opened it
carefully, laying it out flat on the conference table,
studying its large grid as he weighed the importance of
the fact that the murder victim had been clutching it so

tightly they had to break two fingers to pry it loose from her grip.

There were a few notations: a couple of lunch dates, a few dinners, two birthdays, an anniversary. But when his eyes reached the marking for Memorial Day, he looked back at the top of the page and wondered if it was possible he'd been wrong when he barked at hot-rod Paradiso not to be so quick in thinking it was anything more than a coincidental accident that Iris Ehrlick died in the middle of February clutching a page of a calendar bearing the name of the sunny spring month of May.

Paradiso rejoined him, staring over his shoulder at the calendar. He flicked his stubby finger at it as if he were flicking away a bug, and said, "You'll see. We'll dance with them all, but we'll come back to her." He grinned. "In fact, I have a feeling she got around more than we know. I'm going to take another look at the photos of those paintings. I'm thinking maybe one of them is going to look a hell of a lot like our frizzy-haired calendar girl."

"And what if it does? What's the motive, cowboy? She didn't like how her portrait came out?"

"Stranger things have happened."

"And how does it tie in with Ehrlick?"

"You heard them all go after Ehrlick. She was a woman waiting to get dead."

"Open your eyes, Paradiso. Didn't you get a look at Morrison's face? It's like she's got her own personal lie detector stuck inside her."

"Uh-huh. Right," Paradiso said, and left the room.

O'Donnell didn't need this crap, but no one was giving him a choice. He gathered up his evidence, popped a Zantac in his mouth, swallowed it with spit, and followed his punk-faced partner into the hall.

10

IT WAS AN INBRED BUSINESS. Sooner or later everyone would work everywhere at least once. But even though Iris Ehrlick's associate producer, Peggy Golding, had started out at *Paula Live*, their shared history wasn't helping May now.

"I can't talk about this," Peggy insisted. "I don't even know if I've still got a job."

May wouldn't be put off easily. "Iris never called me, not even to gloat. Why did she suddenly want to talk to me yesterday?"

"Lay off her, May. She's no worse than the rest of you. I mean she *was* no worse." She stopped for a moment, considering her words. "It was about that surprise dinner," she said finally. "Will you go away now?"

"What dinner?"

Instantly realizing her gaffe, Peggy quickly moved to cover it. "You're heartless. I'm facing unemployment, Iris is dead, and what do you do? What do the cops do? What do half the producers in town do? Spend all their time pumping me. You know I don't live on Avenue B anymore. I live one block from Gramercy Park. Eighteen hundred dollars a month for a one bedroom apartment, and I don't even get the bedroom. How much of that do you think unemployment will cover?"

"Did you talk to Detective O'Donnell?"

"Absolutely heartless, that's what you are. Iris was like

a mother to me—a mean mother, granted, but a mother. Yes, I talked to the detective. And I wish I'd told him that May Morrison was a cold self-serving witch who could care less if I end up sleeping on the street."

"Did you tell him why Iris was going to call me?"

"You want to make a federal case out of it? Yes, your name came up. I went through the call sheet with him." Suddenly she got quiet, a vulture who'd just picked up the scent of fresh kill. "Why?" Then, trying for casual, she added, "How did you know Iris was going to call you?"

It was a bad idea to make Peggy suspicious. May quickly backpedaled. "The detective told me. I don't mean to grill you. I'm just upset. You understand?" She didn't wait for an answer. "Is your job on the line? Do you want me to ask Gil if he knows anyone who's hiring?"

"That would be great," Peggy said, but May couldn't miss the arrival of discomfort in her voice as they quickly got off the phone.

When she emerged from her office, she found Henry waiting outside her door. He scrutinized her face, analyzing how much rosiness was in her cheeks, how much static in her hair.

"I hear there's a serial murderer stalking the talk shows," he admitted when it became clear May wasn't giving. "I hear he's the same guy who killed ten people in San Francisco and five in Los Angeles."

"How about a show on gossip?" May suggested, attempting to derail him. "People whose lives have been destroyed by it. Get together a list—a mix of ordinary people and a couple of big names. We can meet back here in an hour." Henry didn't move. "It's gossip you're hearing. Unfounded."

Gil, rounding the corner at a fast clip, grabbed May by the hand. "Come with me."

Henry wanted to be one of the guys too badly to do the smart thing and disappear. He followed them to the threshold of May's office. "It's awful about Iris," he tried.

Gil offered a stony stare, but Henry couldn't stop himself. "At least—" He had nothing in mind to say, but he desperately wanted to sound insightful. He started again, "At least it wasn't you."

Gil blinked so slowly even Henry couldn't ignore it. He retreated, having shrunk an inch, to his desk.

"I got Paula to stop hyperventilating," Gil said once they were in May's office, the door closed, "after I negotiated a deal." May knew it was going to be bad, a three-Advil headache at least. "No men."

"What does that mean? You're fired?"

He didn't crack a smile. "No male guests."

"Come on, Gil. The detective said we're not in any danger. And even if we were, why should we only be afraid of men? Haven't you talked to Margery lately? According to her, women are the crime wave of the future."

"Paula wants women only. End of discussion."

There was an edge to his voice she had never heard before that made her capitulate quickly. "Okay. No men." The parameters changed more often than the weather—no ugly people, no fat people, no acne, and now no men. In the end, what was the difference?

Except then she remembered the tipping show. Henry had worked quickly to come up with the preliminary guest list. He'd found a travel editor who appeared periodically on *Regis and Kathie Lee*, a restaurant critic currently doing short spots on the Food Network who'd been on *Paula* before, and a woman who'd written the definitive book on tipping around the world. May had followed up on all three.

"I'd love to gripe about this," the travel editor had purred. "Last week when I was in Dallas getting my hair cut, the woman who gives out the robes had a little dish at her counter with a dollar bill taped on top. Can you believe how tacky? I stiffed her."

It was just the right mix of folksy information and good humor. May told Henry to book her. Next she called the woman who wrote the *International Tipping Guide.* That call hadn't gone as well.

"Paula loves pet peeves," May had offered trying to help the woman get started. She'd seemed nervous—usually a bad sign.

"*Um.* I don't have any off the top of my head. Can I get back to you on that?"

May's eyes flitted down the page of Henry's notes. "I understand you decided to write the book after a business trip to England where you didn't know what to tip the hall porter. What did you end up giving him?"

"*Um.* I can't remember. That was ten years ago. Before my first was born. I haven't left Long Island for more than a day since. But what would you know about that? You probably have enough frequent-flier miles to go to the moon."

May had quickly extricated herself from the call and phoned Bob Swann to invite him on the show instead. The restaurant critic had a caustic sense of humor that played well against Paula's easy charm. The problem was there was no way to avoid the fact that six-foot-three-inch, legs-like-tree-trunks Bob Swann was a man.

"Bob's flying in from Atlanta tonight," May told Gil. "Paula won't mind. She knows him. He's been on the show before."

He shook his head and swallowed hard, sending a plastic pellet into his steely gut.

"Wouldn't gum be better for your teeth?" she asked.

"What exactly do you mean by that?" Gil snapped. A vein the shape of a lightning bolt rose up like a mountain range across his forehead.

"What's going on Gil?"

After checking behind him to be sure no one else had sneaked in to eavesdrop, he reached inside his jacket pocket and threw another *Paula Live* Bic across her desk. "This is going on. As if you didn't know."

"What? I don't know."

His eyes swept over her while he decided whether or not to believe her.

"I don't have any idea what you're talking about," she insisted.

Gil crossed his arms, as if to protect himself. He still wasn't convinced she didn't know, but he told her anyway. "They found another pen at Iris's apartment. First Barnett's. Now Iris's. And this one had the blue plug missing, which made guess who their number one suspect?"

"You?"

He nodded. "That is, I was number one. Then they asked for my alibi." He said the word with contempt.

"What was it?"

"It was impeccable, is what it was," he said, warming up to the story now that it got to the part where he was off the hook. "When we left here yesterday, Stephanie decided to take my mind off my miseries by making me stop off to visit her father. God bless her—at the time of the murder I was being attacked by Mike Wallace on the subject of tabloid television. Ask me how happy I am that a detective is going to call Mike Wallace to check out my alibi?"

"How happy are you?"

"Deliriously happy, ever since Stephie pointed out that being a segment on *Sixty Minutes* is a hell of a lot better than twenty to life at Riker's, where, she pointed out, if I ever go, I can forget about conjugal visits. It seems it's a package deal—I get arrested and for no extra charge she throws in the divorce for free." He dropped his voice. May leaned forward to hear. "It wasn't just the pen they found. They also found my scarf."

The *Paula Live* scarves had been last year's Christmas present. Their bonus checks came wrapped in them— royal blue cashmere with the *Paula Live* logo stitched on in gold thread. Stephanie had come up with the idea. Paula adored it. Everyone on the show had gotten one. It was a well-liked gift until word leaked out that only some of them—Gil's, Paula's, Joan Budney's—came monogrammed.

"How did your scarf get there?"

"Good question," Gil asked, staring her down. "Now I have one for you. Do you know where I keep my scarf?" Before she could answer, Gil raised his voice in an attempt to mimic hers. "Check your hat rack, Gil."

May's spine stiffened. "So what? Everyone knows you keep your scarf on your hat rack and your briefcase on your credenza. Face it, you're completely predictable."

"Actually, you underestimate your powers of observation, May. Not everyone knows. In fact, in my informal survey I've found very few people who noticed where I kept my scarf."

"What are you saying, Gil?"

"I'm not saying anything." He let his silence sink in. Then he asked, "Where were you last night? Where did you go after I left?" His eyes scanned her desk, finding her diary. He tried to read the entries upside down.

She slammed the cover shut and snapped, "You'll find out at the end of the month when you get my expense report." But what she was thinking was, *I went to Barnett's building. I talked to a stranger on the street. I can prove nothing.* "Get a grip, Gil. I know you're under pressure now. But if you don't hold it together, who's going to hold Paula together?"

"You're right," he said, settling in the chair, sweat gathering in beads above his ears as he thought of his host's volatility. "We have to keep a united front. I admit it. I panicked when they told me they found my scarf in Iris's apartment. That's the only reason I told them you knew exactly where I kept it."

"You told who?"

Gil slinked down further in his chair.

May stood up. "You told the detectives I'm the only one who knew where you kept your scarf?"

"No. I told them you knew, not that you were the only one." He spoke so quietly she could barely hear him. "Just one of the only ones."

"Thanks, Gil. Now they think I killed Iris."

"Maybe you did." He hunched his shoulders up to his ears, then let them fall down as he exhaled a deep breath. "Okay, okay. I don't think you killed anybody, May."

"Thank you."

"So let's forget it."

"Fine."

"Let's get back to work."

"Okay."

He stood up, ready to leave. "No men on the show. No exceptions. No discussions. When your restaurant critic gets here, send him back." He left before May could protest.

She sat for a moment, stunned. Was it really possible

that Gil had handed her over to the detectives? That now she was at the top of their suspect list? But Detective O'Donnell had given no such indication. She was overreacting. It was all going to be okay.

As usual her discomfort made her think of her children, made her want to check in to make sure they had gotten off to school without any problems. As she speed-dialed home and listened to the phone ring, she felt woozy, dizzy, as if she'd gotten more information than her brain could digest all at once. The day had turned dreamlike, unnatural. She was yanked back to reality when a deep voice came on the line.

"Morrison residence, Mr. Jackson speaking."

And why shouldn't he answer the phone, May thought. *He spends more time there than I do.* "Hi, Pete. How's everything?"

"Oh, fine. I'm just about ready to go pick up your new door. You're lucky it's a standard size. You'd have to wait two months if it was custom."

"I guess I'm just a lucky person. Is Ovaa-Iita there?"

"Lucky again. She left about ten minutes ago. Something about picking up a friend at the airport. She said she'd meet me at the bus. I told her I'm old enough to walk home from school by myself."

"She meant she'll meet Delia at the bus," May told him. "At least I hope that's what she meant."

"Mrs. Morrison. I'm just goofing with you. Ovaa said she'd get the girls. I think. She's hard to understand, you know? But I'm pretty positive she said she'd get them. You want me to stick around to be sure?"

Although that was exactly what she wanted, it seemed like overkill, paying her contractor to spy on her babysitter, especially since so far Ovaa-Iita had at least done that part of her job right, meeting the girls on time at the bus every day. "Go ahead and pick up my door," she told Pete.

"By the way," he said, "you did a great job on that Indian diorama. Only thing is, I hope you don't mind, I had to rebuild the tepee. It kind of collapsed while Delia was showing it to me. We put it back together, though. And now it looks authentic. I hope you don't mind."

"Not at all."

"Catch you later, then."

As May put down the phone, Margery scooted in and sat down. "What's the latest?" she wanted to know.

"According to Gil, they found a *Paula Live* pen and Gil's own *Paula Live* scarf at Iris's apartment."

"So that's why he asked me if I knew where his scarf was. I told him I don't even know where his brain is." She got serious. "So are they bringing him in for questioning? That's a lot of evidence to have lying around a murder scene."

"He says he didn't leave them there."

"What a surprise."

"He has a great alibi, too. He was up at his father-in-law's office arguing with Mike Wallace at the time of the murder."

Margery broke into a lusty laugh. "Mike Wallace is his alibi? My goodness, sugar, that's brilliant."

"Mike Wallace wouldn't lie."

"I'm sure he wouldn't," Margery said. "But do you really think a couple of detectives are going to hike up to *Sixty Minutes* to question the emperor? It's a beautiful alibi. I wish I had an alibi like that."

"Do you have one at all?"

"For last night? Sugar, I've got an alibi for every night this week and last. And can you believe it? Not one of them has called me back. So much for Colleen's magical 'Book of Rules.' "

"Gil says maybe I killed Iris. Maybe I left his scarf up at her apartment."

"Well, did anyone think to ask whether he'd been up there before? Maybe they had a thing." She thought about, and said, "Then again, maybe not. Anyway, it's not what Gil thinks that matters. It's what your boyfriend the detective thinks." She got quiet, then asked, "What did he interrogate you about anyway?"

"It wasn't an interrogation," May said, but now she wasn't sure. He never said a word about the scarf or anything, really. It was as if he was waiting to see what she had to say for herself, first. She sank, the full weight of the investigation settling in to rest on her shoulders.

This was crazy. She was a worrier—expert at squeezing in at least a few minutes of disaster visualization every hour. But she'd never entertained the thought of anything this bad happening, being a suspect in a murder case. Still, after years of scouting stories, she knew—better than most—bizarre things happened every day even to people like her.

"So what did Detective Gorgeous want you for, then?" Margery asked.

"He wanted to know why Iris was planning on calling me the day she was murdered."

"Iris was going to call you?" Margery whistled. "Why would she do that? Did you check it out with Peggy?"

"She's not giving. At least not to me." May was quiet for a long moment, before adding, "O'Donnell also wanted to know where I was last Sunday night."

"Uh-oh. That's the night Barnett went splat. Where were you and can you prove it?"

"In bed and no."

"Poor you. You didn't do it, did you? And don't pull out a letter opener and kill me for asking, either."

"Come on. Me? If I walk across the street against a light, I think I'm going to get arrested. I'm the most law-abiding citizen I know. It's practically pathological with me."

"So everybody's overreacting. That's all."

"I just don't want them overreacting me right into jail."

"They can't do that without evidence, sugar. You want me to call around and see what they've got?"

"Could you?"

Margery nodded.

"And I'll call around, too," May said, "to see what everyone else is thinking. There must be a hundred rumors, a thousand suspects. Maybe I can even find out whether Gil did a little embellishing on his alibi."

"Great idea. Cause it sounds like Gil might be the one thing standing between you and a pretty unpleasant date downtown." She left, leaving her words to slowly sink in.

11

SIXTY MINUTES AND *PAULA LIVE* didn't chase the same kind of stories, but through their mutual friends May had heard a lot about producer Holly Lovett. Word was that even beyond the obvious similarities—profession, marital status, number and ages of children—the two women had a serious potential to be soul mates, if only either of them could ever find a spare moment to call and arrange a dinner or drinks. Neither had, which May regretted now that she was finally calling with the singular mission of checking out Gil's alibi.

After the obligatory sharing of the names of all the friends who'd been trying to get them to meet over the years, May got to the point. "I'm doing some checking around, and I need some help. It's personal," she added quickly.

"I'm all yours. Just tell me what you need," Holly offered.

May decided the less explained the better. "Gil got into a shouting match with Mike Wallace yesterday. I want to know roughly what time it was and if anyone else was there to hear it." There was a pause, during which she imagined Holly trying to figure out the angle. May closed her eyes and crossed her fingers. Holly owed her nothing. She could easily beg off, hang up, and have a field day gossiping.

Instead she said, "No sweat. Mike's secretary likes me today. Don't go away." She put May on hold for several painful minutes.

"It was the old man's birthday," she explained when she got back on. "They ate chilled Brie in the penthouse dining room, which they booked from five to seven. Apparently there was quite an audience to their little squabble. Mike and Gil were going at it. Dan gave commentary. Dave scribbled notes, threatening to put it in his monologue."

"Anyone else there? What about Stephanie, Gil's wife?"

"I don't think so. Mike's secretary read me the log, and Stephanie wasn't on it. And I can tell you, no one gets on the elevator to the penthouse without signing in. I think the guard is former Secret Service. Does that help at all?"

It doesn't help me, May thought. "It helps a lot," she lied, and after extensive thank yous and promises to call back to set up a date, she got off the phone.

By the time she tracked down Henry at the Xerox machine, she had the distinct impression that people were looking at her strangely, as though she had a sign on her back saying Suspect Number One. Henry eyed her with mistrust, though with Henry it was hard to tell.

"Paula's banished all male guests, including Bob Swann," she told him, eager to focus back on her work, where she felt safe.

He checked his watch. "He's landing in an hour. What are we going to do?"

May relaxed a notch, relieved that her assistant's nerves weren't shattered because of her. "Not to worry. I'm going to take him to a fabulous dinner at Lespinasse. You call and see if they'll let us have a table in the kitchen. I'll wait until dessert to tell him the show got bumped, and by then he'll be too stuffed and happy to care."

"Brilliant," Henry said.

"And see if we can get him upgraded to a suite at the Ritz-Carlton," she told him, happy to be back dealing with things she knew how to control, shows fizzling, guests getting bumped. Then send over a phenomenally large and exotic flower arrangement."

"Doubly brilliant," Henry observed again.

"And expensive," May countered, taking a tiny bit of pleasure in making Gil pay, literally, for his panic. Then she noticed Henry hadn't made a move to go take care of things. In fact, he seemed to have stepped back, as far back as he could go, back up against the wall.

"Everything okay?" she asked him.

He nodded quickly, but didn't move.

May felt her stomach tighten. His fretting wasn't about Paula's newest edict after all. "Why don't we go out to lunch?" May suggested. Clearly he needed some maintenance work, some massaging and reassuring. She couldn't afford to have Henry fearing her, doubting her. It was worth a lunch to get him to calm down.

"I can't."

This couldn't be possible. She'd often kidded with Margery and Bunny about Henry, how he'd skip his mother's funeral to have lunch with a producer. How he'd give up his vacation to avoid missing a chance to suck up to a superior. This was bad. She turned and headed back to her office. If people were gossiping about her, it was Gil's fault. He was going to have to fix it.

Henry followed her, keeping his distance. "I was wondering about something," he said, letting his pace quicken slightly so he remained within earshot.

May stopped and turned to listen.

"Did you and Iris ever work together? I mean did Iris ever work for you?"

"Why do you ask?"

He stared at his feet, shuffled a bit. "I just heard some people talking, saying there was a grudge between you two, that's all. Is it true?"

"I don't know what your lunch plans are," May told him, "but cancel them. I need you to arrange the dinner with Bob Swann. I need you to call the tipping book lady and find a way to get her here in time for tomorrow's show. And I need you to do some preliminary research for a show on scapegoating, people falsely accused, convictions overturned based on insufficient evidence. Do you get my drift?"

He didn't answer, didn't know what to say.

"Go," May told him, stepping aside to let him pass. "Now."

He scurried to his desk but wouldn't look at her when she passed him on her way into her office.

May dialed home and let the receiver hug her shoulder as it rang while she slipped open her top drawer, pulled out a folder, and marked it "MURDER." She stuck the *Paula Live* staff phone list inside, relabeling it "Suspects." Henry buzzed. She disconnected her call. "What?"

"Your mother's on line two."

Since the move to Florida her mother called half a dozen times a day. The calls were brief, just long enough to cover all the vital subjects. May punched the button on line two.

"May, dolly," Shirley said. "What are you doing for dinner tonight?"

"I'm taking a guest to Lespinasse. A married guest," she added quickly.

"Don't you have any single guests on the show anymore?"

"No."

"What's the matter, dolly? You don't sound good."

"I'm not good. I'm having staff problems, people talking behind my back, that kind of thing."

"Oh. I'm not surprised. You always did have a temper."

"I have to go, Mom. I have people here waiting." She hung up the phone and dialed home again. Ovaa-Iita should have gotten the girls an hour ago. They should be there, Delia doing homework, Susie finishing her snack. She let the phone ring, eight, nine, ten times and gazed out her large window past the rooftops of Manhattan to the river and, half-hidden by heavy gray clouds, New Jersey. Squinting hard, as if maybe then she could see all the way to her house, she looked at the buildings spread out before her, wondering how all the other people working in all the offices below managed to balance their lives, whether anyone had figured out a way to do it that really worked, whether anyone else's life had gone so completely out of control.

At the sound of a sharp knock on her open door, she swung around. Paula walked in, slid her feet out of her suede slippers, and sat on her heels on the chair across from May, ready for girl talk. Still no answer—May hung up her phone.

"What's that?" Paula asked, pointing toward the open folder on May's desk.

May quickly closed it. "It's just notes. About Iris and Barnett."

"For what?"

"I don't know. A show, maybe."

"Great idea. You follow that nose of yours and catch the damn killer. I don't know what the cops are doing, but my ulcer's growing faster than a cold."

May relaxed a notch, relieved that Paula wasn't plugged into the peon gossip that seemed to have decided if May was a suspect, she must have committed the crime.

"Are you mad at me?" Paula asked, shifting gears quickly as she always did, never waiting for an answer. "You know what we'll do? When things calm down around here, we'll take some time off and Canyon Ranch it for a week. Do nothing but get massaged and wrapped." Even though she sat facing the smiling visages that made this trip an impossibility for May, it didn't connect. "In the meantime, we'll have fun with the chocolate show." She saw May's puzzled look.

"He didn't tell you, did he?" she asked. "What's wrong

with him? Okay, here's the deal. I can't do your shelter lovers for Valentine's Day because I've been advised that taping a show about shelter people would be dangerous right now."

"Who told you that?"

Paula jerked her head toward the doorway. May saw Frankie's thick shadow lurking a leap away. "Don't worry. I've figured out what we're going to do instead."

Gil strode into the room as if on cue, carrying a large tin box decorated with old-fashioned Valentines.

"You were supposed to tell her, Gil," Paula barked. "You didn't tell her."

"Pardon me, but I didn't plan on spending half the day being questioned by the police."

"Why are they questioning you?" Paula wanted to know.

Gil glanced at May, and for a moment she thought he was going to do it again, serve her up to save his hide. But he didn't. He said, "Routine stuff. Nothing to worry about. We were just shooting the breeze for such a long time I never made it over here to tell May. Sorry. I'm here now."

"Too late. I already told her. Chocolate," she repeated to May as if it meant something. "Open the box, Gil."

Gil lifted the lid to reveal dozens of chocolate hearts, stars, angels, and little mounds that May realized with a start were supposed to be breasts.

"We've got Lindt," Gil began the tour, pointing, "Godiva, Toblerone, Cadbury's, and Adult."

"My mountain-bike pro read me this article over the phone about a doctor who just discovered chocolate is good for you. Isn't it perfect?" Before May could answer, Paula went on. "The only problem is you have to make sure the doctor isn't a man. I can't have any men on right now. Did you at least tell her that?" she asked Gil, who nodded slowly like the worn-down man he was.

"And while we're at it, Gil, find some money in our budget for a metal detector. And a lie detector. Maybe we can give our guests a little Rorschach test before we book them. Do you think a Rorschach test would tell us anything? Maybe we should get a fortune teller up here. We did a show on a bunch of fortune tellers last year, didn't we? I could ask my psychic to come up. Can we at least get a lie detector?"

"Excellent idea," Gil said. "And why just use it on the guests? I'll be first on line to go through it. How about you, May? Would you go through it?"

"Of course she would," Paula said when May failed to pipe up fast enough. "You know," Paula went on, "I'd feel a lot better if we could get Detective Paradiso to work for us full-time. Can't we make him an offer? How much can a cop make?"

May picked up the phone. "Will you excuse me while I track down your chocolate doctor?"

Paula smiled and stood up. "Sure." Then she turned to Gil. "I want to talk to you about today's numbers. Did you see them? They're in the toilet." She led Gil out of May's office, venting. "Two of the best producers in New York are dead. You'd think at least our ratings would improve."

"There's a dozen more born every minute. There's Chuck Mills, Letty Altman, Bernie Goater."

"My vote goes to Chuck Mills," May called out.

"Hey, y'all," Margery shouted from her office next door. "Do me a favor and don't say my name out loud. Don't say my name at all."

"We were just kidding," May called back. No more kidding allowed, she told herself as she closed her door and dialed home again. This time when there was no answer, she fished around on her desk until she found the pile of call slips lost amidst the clutter. She remembered seeing one with Emily Cooper's number on it, and when she found it, she quickly returned her next-door neighbor's call.

"Thanks for calling back," Emily said. "I hate to bother you at work, but I hate to bother you at home more. We want to invite you over for dinner."

"I have a favor to ask you," May said, ducking the invite.

With this Emily perked up. "Anything."

May reminded Emily she had her spare key, then explained that she was worried because no one was answering her phone at home. Emily raced over and called back several minutes later.

"Susie and Delia are here, and they're fine. Your au pair is gone, though. She left you a note taped to the front door. It says, 'Flight to Helsinki called to put me on early and it was afraid of me to tell you so thanks for being great.' Does that make any sense to you?"

"Yes," May said weakly, wishing it didn't.

Emily continued. "Delia said they've been sitting watching cartoons and eating Mallomars all afternoon. I guess the TV was on so loud they didn't hear the phone ring." She whispered the next. "The little one must have peed in her pants. She's damp as a sponge, but thank goodness, she doesn't seem to care."

May gave Henry the job of taking Bob Swann to dinner and breaking the bad news. Carter Cooper surprised her on the early train.

"Emily told me what happened at your house today. You know, I can get your baby-sitter on this. You leave two children at home alone, that's reckless endangerment. It would be my pleasure, gratis, no thanks necessary, to handle this for you."

"I don't think so," May told him. "I don't have the energy to sue anyone right now."

"You don't have to have any energy. This is a dream case, so easy I could win it in my sleep. You know," he leaned closer, "I think it's a great idea for a show. You get a baby-sitter who left the kids at home alone, a couple of parents who've left the kids at home alone, a lawyer—doesn't have to be me—and the kid from that movie. What do you think?"

"Great idea, but Ricki Lake did it when the sequel came out."

"Damn—I know an idea when I see one. Okay. Forget the show. Let's sue her, then."

"I appreciate the offer, Carter, really, but I don't think so."

It took enormous control for her to feign exhaustion when she was wired, fueled, on rage. But she did it—closed her eyes, let her head drift to an uncomfortable angle, let the newspaper fall out of her hands, and increased the volume of her breathing ever-so-slightly, adding a tiny snort for extra effect.

This time when she sent Todd tumbling through a broken fence at the observation deck of the Empire State Building, she made sure he was tightly grasping Ovaa-Iita's hand for the ride, free fall, to the ground. As she watched them meet their fate, she heaved a deep sigh. She would make another call to Louise, the English au pair who Carol swore was bright, articulate, poised, and experienced. Then, at the next bookers' meeting, after her pitch on "People Falsely Accused," she would offer up a show on the "Baby-sitter Blues."

12

O'DONNELL HELD THE STIFF PO-
laroid in his hand. But looking at it longer wasn't making it any clearer why Paradiso had marched over to
his desk and presented it to him as if it were the Dead
Sea Scrolls. Since the picture wasn't talking, he raised
his eyes to his partner, who stood over his desk watching him. O'Donnell waited. Then he waited more.
"Yeah?" he said finally. "So? What is this?"

"You don't know?"

O'Donnell's gut turned into a fist. He slid out his top
drawer and sucked down another pill, then stared back
at the picture. "I know I don't like guessing games,"
he said.

"Hey," Paradiso said, holding up his hands as though
he were giving himself up, "I don't want to put any ideas
in your head. All I want to know is what you think
you're looking at."

"Okay. I'm looking at one of Barnett's masterpieces
you've been hoarding over there. Right?"

Paradiso nodded, his face a study in smugness.

O'Donnell looked at the picture again. In his own unschooled view it was pretty damn bad, a product of the
guy's I-wish-I-was-Picasso period. It was a nude, like all
the others, but the body parts were scrambled, as if the
whole thing were a puzzle someone had taken apart and
put back together wrong.

"I'm looking, but I'm not seeing. So talk to me. What am I looking for?"

"Who is it?"

"How the hell should I know?"

"I'll tell you who it is. It's her."

"Who?"

"Her. Morrison. It's her."

He couldn't believe this, didn't want to believe it. Maybe he'd call up his old partner, Bingo, and beg him to come out of retirement and back on the force. How much fun could it be having a stationery store, selling Lotto tickets and the *Daily News* and baseball cards to kids. Crap, it sounded too good to be true. And with Bingo's pension and his kids all grown, he certainly didn't have any money worries. But O'Donnell had three at home who all knew damn well they were going to college, so he was stuck here for a while. And for now he was stuck here with Anthony Paradiso and his pile of naked women.

"Give me a break. What do you mean 'it's her'?"

"Look," his partner said. "See that hair. That's her hair. All wild and messy. And look here." He pointed to a thick pink line at the top of the painting. "That's her mouth, right? She's got those lips, doesn't she? And this." He pointed to a splotch of red. "That's her cheeks. You told me yourself how they're always heating up."

"That's her cheeks? What are her cheeks doing down by her foot?"

"It's art. It's art. It's her."

"It's not her."

"You'll see. I'm going to ask her if she was ever painted by the victim, and she's going to heat up all over and say yes."

"Victim? Whoa, cowboy, I thought Barnett jumped. Didn't you tell me he jumped? Why do you have it in for this woman, anyway? Why do you want her so bad? You know something about her I don't?"

"Just that she did it."

"You don't know that." O'Donnell popped his third Zantac of the hour, but nothing helped. "You just *want* that." He had to be careful here. Something about this woman had struck him, too, but it wasn't that she was a killer, and it wasn't something he wanted Paradiso sniffing out. "Listen up, cowboy," he said. "You're not going to do anything here that's going to compromise my case. You hear me?"

Paradiso, seething, stared at the cracked linoleum tiles and nodded.

"You think it's her, we'll question her. You want to spend some time watching her, you watch her. But you keep your distance and you keep your hands off. You're not in Narcotics anymore. You don't take anyone out to any alleys to convince them you're in charge. You're not in charge here. I am. You got that?"

Paradiso snatched back his picture, said nothing.

"It's been a long day," O'Donnell said, a peace offering to let them both off the hook. "Let's go home." He patted his partner on the shoulder. Paradiso patted him back. They walked to their cars talking about traffic, the weather, how many guys had come to work sneezing their guts out all over the place. They talked about anything but the case that was making them both edgy, and mean.

13

MAY FINISHED READING THE last page of *Ramona the Pest* and closed the book. Delia smiled and snuggled closer, having loved the story. In a corner of the room Susie sat playing with a pile of Pound Puppies as if she were alone, playing that it was their first day at puppy school and none of them wanted to go because the puppy teacher didn't like them.

Preoccupied, May didn't stop to inquire about whether there was any real-life inspiration for Susie's game. Even Delia, used to her mother's demanding delving, noticed the sudden absence of all questions.

"Want to know what I did at the Cooper's house today?" she offered, hoping to get her mother's attention, nervous that May no longer cared what she or her sister thought or did.

The question was like a wake-up call. May's older daughter had perfected the art of the nonanswer, the "I don't remember," the "nothing and stop asking me." Now she'd begun teaching this skill to her willing pupil, Susie.

"What did you do at the Coopers'?" May asked, stepping up to the plate.

Delia snuggled closer, twirling her mother's hair as if it were an extension of her own. "I don't remember." Neither of them could help but break up laughing. Susie, who had no idea what had just happened, laughed along so as not to be left out.

Pete interrupted them, knocking on the molding he'd replaced just a few weeks before when a bout of door banging accidently caused the original wood to splinter off.

"I'm just going to wash up," he announced. "I'll change in the basement."

Delia giggled. "You're all gray."

He was, dusted all over with a mixture of sawdust, plaster, and grime.

"But the bottoms of my shoes are clean." He lifted one and then the other work boot to display his soles for inspection.

"I tracked mud all through the house yesterday," Delia explained to her mother who nodded, happy to have heard about it even a day late. "And I got a little crayon on the wall. Just a smudge."

"But we cleaned it up real good, didn't we?" Pete boasted. "A little bit of WD40 on a paper towel and . . ."

"Presto," Delia said, and they both laughed, remembering. "Good-night hug," she called out opening her arms wide.

"Didn't you tell her?" Pete asked.

May shook her head. Maybe she hadn't mentioned it because she still couldn't believe it had come to this, that she had asked her contractor to baby-sit so that she could take advantage of having gotten home early by running some errands—indulgent, exciting errands like going to the supermarket and the mall.

The mall was not her idea of a good time, but each of the six children's birthday party invitations stuck to the bulletin board in her kitchen meant a gift needed to be bought. Then there was Delia's underwear, which was cutting into her thigh, and her down jacket, which wouldn't zip anymore. While she was at it, she might as well take care of all the other things that had gone waiting: replacing the twin sheets that had begun to shred and Susie's lunch box, which had developed an unidentifiable odor that no amount of scrubbing cured. She could use a new phone, too, since the one on her night table had been accidentally dropped so many times it was now loosely held together with Scotch tape and was useless for calling anyone whose number included a six because the six button no longer worked.

There was also the condition of her kitchen cabinets to attend to, her pantry having recently morphed into an echo chamber. Even those canned items that were easily a few years old had been opened and consumed. The refrigerator was so bare Susie was now using it as part of her play kitchen, storing empty cereal boxes and coupons in the fruit bin. Happily, the mall was only a ten-minute drive from the twenty-four-hour Pathmark. This shopping trip could easily become an all-night affair.

May didn't expect the girls would mind Pete baby-sitting. In fact, she suspected they'd be delighted. So starved were they for a man around the house they'd all but adopted him anyway, a kind of temporary dad.

"All right, girls," she announced. "I hate to break it to you, but Pete is baby-sitting tonight."

Susie looked up from her game of make-believe. "For real?"

Pete and May nodded.

"*Yesss,*" Delia cheered.

"While I'm washing up, I want you to memorize my rules. No laughing, no joking, no talking. And if you listen real good, I'll teach you how to unclog a toilet."

She left them sitting mesmerized as Pete took apart the toaster, which Ovaa-Iita had managed to overheat and blow up in her last attempt at making Susie a breakfast of pale toast.

Since the children were sincerely happy to be left with Pete, May forced herself to take her time, to wander, not rush, through the stores. After a while she was able to stop thinking about them, and as she progressed up and down aisles and past mirrored columns and blank-faced mannequins, she even forgot about the mess that was her current life at work.

She set a new personal record for her longest mall trip ever—two hours—then continued at the same pace up and down the supermarket aisles. It was relaxing now—no one hounding her with a deadline, no one whining for a toy, no one accusing her of being a killer. Then exhaustion hit her. She had to pinch her ear to keep herself awake as she drove home. By the time she pulled into the driveway it was nearly eleven.

As she turned off her engine, she eyed the vehicle parked behind Pete's truck. Leaving the groceries and shopping bags in the back of her van, she rushed inside, hoping Pete hadn't invited one of his carpenter friends over to sit around and drink beer in her living room.

She found them, Pete and O'Donnell, sitting side by side on the pillow-less wicker couch in the sunroom, watching CNN.

"Hello, dear," Pete said when he saw her. "We have company."

O'Donnell stood, nodding hello. May, flustered, turned to Pete. "Thanks for watching the girls. What do I owe you?"

"Eleven thousand dollars," he said, deadpan. "I'm burying tonight's cost in gutter repair." He could see no one was in the mood to joke, so he put on his jacket and saluted the detective. "Pleasure to make your acquaintance. See you tomorrow, Mrs. Morrison."

The door slammed. May and O'Donnell studied each

other. He looked tired, she thought, and sadder than when she'd seen him last.

"I hope you don't mind that I stopped by," O'Donnell said as she turned off the TV. "I won't stay long. Is there somewhere we can talk?"

"Not here," she said eyeing the couches, whose pillows, she assumed, had been dragged into the basement, as usual, to make a fort. She led him to the living room, but it was bare except for the two authentic Mission straight-back chairs she'd fought Todd to keep, then realized were much too uncomfortable to sit on for more than a minute.

The kitchen was a disaster, the table covered with a week's worth of bills, catalogues, and flyers, the chairs a mess of crumbs, dried pasta, and streaks of old chocolate. There was no comfortable place to sit and talk, she realized, a fact that had been easy to ignore, since before tonight she hadn't tried to sit and talk with anyone in this house.

She watched him notice things as they walked, the blank spot on the wall where a picture of Todd and the girls used to hang until she couldn't stand looking at it anymore, two half-empty bowls of macaroni and cheese, that night's picnic dinner, on the hardwood dining room floor. She wondered what he was detecting from all this, other than that she wasn't much of a housekeeper, a fact she was perfectly willing to confess.

In the dining room O'Donnell stopped and pointed to a pair of Queen Anne chairs. "This okay with you?" He sat down before she had a chance to protest.

"My ex-husband got the table," she explained as they sat, both facing the empty center of the room.

He laughed easily. "Maybe he'll give it back to you someday."

"Right. And there really is a tooth fairy, and I really will win the lottery even though I never buy a ticket."

He reached into his pocket and pulled out a Lotto stub. "When I win, the dining room table's on me."

Her cheeks flushed. He looked away, embarrassed. When he turned back, his laugh lines were gone. "I have a few questions for you, Mrs. Morrison." His formality reminded them both this wasn't a social call. "By the way, where were you?"

"Running errands. Is that legal?"

"Last time I checked." He pulled out his notebook. "Bear with me a moment." She waited while he refreshed his memory, rereading his notes. "Within the past few weeks have you received an invitation to"—he read the rest off his pad—"a surprise dinner?"

Peggy Golding must have told him something. "Which one?"

"Does that mean yes?" He wasn't giving anything away.

"That means no."

"Did anyone mention such an event to you recently?"

"Yes. Why?"

"Who?"

"What when?" she tried, to see if his humor could be resurrected. His mouth curled into a half-smile, but his eyes saddened even more.

"Peggy Golding mentioned it to me," she told him.

He nodded and scribbled something. "Do you usually have appointments after work?"

She wondered if this qualified as questioning, if she should refuse to speak to him without a lawyer, if she should get a lawyer, if she should kick him out.

"I'm just trying to put things together," he said, as if he'd sensed her hesitation. "This is a friendly visit."

"Okay."

"Appointments after work?" he asked again, reminding her she hadn't answered him the first time.

"I try not to," she said, gesturing upstairs to where her children slept. He seemed as though he understood.

"Did you have an appointment yesterday after work?"

It was something she instinctively knew he wouldn't understand—that because she normally worked a whirlwind of meetings, lunch dates, and conference calls, she relied entirely on her pocket diary to jog her overloaded mind. She found her purse, took out her calendar, and opened it. The small boxes were chockablock with notations made by a multitude of pens. Yesterday evening was blank. Feeling more than a bit like Delia, she told him, "I don't remember."

Then it came to her. "I left early. I stopped in front of Barnett's place. I stayed too long and missed my regular train. I don't know exactly why I went," she added quickly, before the detective had a chance to ask.

"Did you talk to anyone there?"

She looked around the room, memorizing it. She loved this house, even if it was falling apart. She loved her life, her kids. She tried to protect them, support them, couldn't help but love them. How could this be happening to her?

When she answered him, her voice was low, soft, all its energy drained away. "There was a woman. I don't know who she is. A talk-show groupie. We said a few words, and I left. I walked to the train. I can't prove any of this. Do you believe me?"

He met her stare, clenched and unclenched his jaw, his eyes drilling into hers, looking for something. She felt that he wanted to, was trying to, believe her. Again she felt a spark and this time thought it was coming directly from him.

The temperature in the room seemed to have risen

ten degrees. Her palms felt sticky. O'Donnell's hand went to his shirt collar, an unconscious gesture, to loosen it.

"Is it too warm in here?" she asked, to cover her embarrassment.

"I'm here to investigate a murder," he said as if to remind himself.

"I know," she assured him. She had sworn off romance but hadn't bothered to think about the possibility of passion. Passion had been beyond her imagination. So why was she feeling so dizzy? Nothing was going to happen here. O'Donnell was a seasoned cop. She was sure thoughts of passion were forbidden to cops on the job, especially ones investigating murder, especially with suspects, which, she had to keep reminding herself despite her disbelief, she was.

He cleared his throat. "Are you familiar with Mr. Barnett's collection of paintings?"

"Yes," she said quietly. It was hard to keep up with him. She wondered if that was his technique, to keep her off guard.

"You knew Miss Wind was one of his subjects?"

May smiled. "Yes."

"What's funny about that?"

"He had a lot of subjects."

"How about you?"

"I have no subjects." She knew the question he was really asking, but she didn't answer it because she didn't like it.

"Did Mr. Barnett ever ask you to model for him?"

"Yes," she answered, wishing she could have said no, wishing she could lie.

"And did you model for him?"

"Why do you want to know?"

"I'm investigating a murder," he told her.

"But what does that have to do with me?"

"I hope nothing," he admitted, choosing his words carefully. "Mr. Barnett did ask you to model for him."

"He never met a woman he didn't ask to model for him. It was quite a line, and he used it a lot. I was married when he asked me, so it made it easy to turn him down. He really was a son of a bitch."

"Then he must still be one, because in my experience I've found people don't change much once they're dead."

She thought it was a joke, but she'd lost the urge to laugh. "Look, Detective. I don't get why you're here. I don't get why it seems no matter what happens, you keep coming back to me. I didn't do anything. I knew Iris, sure, but so did hundreds of other people. And what's the interest in Barnett? I thought he was a suicide."

"I'm just doing my job, Mrs. Morrison. I want to find Miss Ehrlick's killer. So does my partner."

She thought he was going to say something more, but he stopped, as if he'd censored himself.

"So why are you here?" she asked once it was clear he'd decided not to go on.

"Do you have a pen?"

She sighed deeply, then started fishing through her handbag.

"A ballpoint would be best."

She dug out a gold-flecked *Paula Live* Bic, which, as soon as she handed it over, made her think of the pen found at Iris's apartment, and the one at Barnett's.

As if reading her mind, the detective stopped scribbling in his notebook and asked her, "How many people have pens like these?"

She thought a moment. "Everyone I know. Our competitors collect them, for fun. I hear they especially like the ones Gil's chewed to bits."

He pocketed her pen. She wondered if it was an unconscious thing—plenty of people stole other people's
pens—or whether he had lifted it for prints.

"Is Gil still a suspect?" she asked.

He thought about whether to answer, measuring his
words to get them right. "I can't comment on that
right now."

"I hear he's got a great alibi."

"It's so good it's almost hard to believe."

"And me?" She spoke so quietly she wasn't sure he'd
heard her, but he had.

"You. You have an alibi I could blow away like a
feather." He blew into the air and studied her, watching
her color drain.

"Do you want to arrest me?"

"Want to?" O'Donnell shook his head, glancing at the
floor where several framed school photos of the girls
sat leaning against the wall, waiting for someone to
hang them. "No. I don't want to. Which is why I'm
working hard to find a crack in a golden alibi or a damn
clever someone who's doing an excellent job of blending
into the shadows." When his sad eyes rested on her,
refusing to look away, she colored.

"You believe me, then?"

"I do. But I can't say the same for everyone else."

"What's going to happen?" she asked as he got up and
picked his coat off the banister where he'd left it.

"I hope nothing tonight," he said, then added, "Lock
the door," before softly closing it behind him.

She watched as he walked down the path, watched
him stop to peer into the front seat of her van. She
waited until he was gone before carting in her shopping
bags, but she couldn't get his sad eyes out of her mind
as she slowly put her purchases away.

14

THE DOOR WAS OPEN, SO HE LET himself in. The place looked different from the last time he was up, but that didn't surprise him. He remembered what it was like working for Paula Wind. The best way to get her over her obsessions was distraction. Give her a bunch of leather swatches, ask her opinion on reupholstering the couch, and her fears of the pneumonic plague would get bumped for a morning's worth of meetings with designers. Tell her the receptionist was allergic to roses, and she'd make some already overworked producer call a dozen doctors for the latest stats on the side effects of nonsedating antihistamines.

He wondered if Linda was still the receptionist. He'd always liked Linda, at least her legs. Her face was hard, but her legs were great. He kicked himself for thinking about her. As of tonight his days of straying were over. The party wouldn't be the only surprise for Colleen. In his pocket was a velvet box holding a diamond ring that cost about three times what he'd paid for his first car.

It was going to feel good, springing it on her in front of everybody. He hadn't seen some of them since the day he left the show. Thinking about it now made him wonder again why he'd been invited at all. Gil wished him dead, he knew that, and the feeling was mutual. Paula simply wished he'd go away. Just last week when he and Paula had found themselves yet again at the same opening night party, they both spent as much time working on avoiding meeting each other's eyes as they did on working the room.

But someone knew enough to invite him to Colleen's surprise fortieth. Someone mighty swift, since his romance with her had been conducted solely behind closed doors, sometimes these very doors, in a supine position and with no audience participation.

He had no idea who the someone was, other than that the person was pretty damn sneaky, leaving no clue like a return address, no number to call to RSVP. This was going to be some surprise.

For a moment he wondered how the hell they were going to get her back to the office at—he checked his watch again—eight o'clock at night, but then he reminded himself, it wasn't his problem. Tonight he was the guest. His only problem was going to be making small talk with Paula and keeping far away from Gil until Colleen arrived.

He followed the dim sound of music, Edith Piaf, to the conference room. *Damn they planned this well.* Colleen was deep into her French period. Perfume, wine, food, poetry, music, everything was French. Piaf was perfect.

He worked up to a decent swagger only to find the conference room was empty. The party stuff wasn't even set up. He'd come on time as the invitation had requested—demanded—and wouldn't you know, he was the first one there. He peered into the one bowl of chips in the middle of the table. Whoever figured this thing out had been batting a thousand until they decided on those chips. Colleen's kitchen was stocked with carrot sticks, melatonin tablets, rice cakes, and a case of green tea. If their lives together had meant she'd be cooking him dinner, he'd have looked elsewhere for his companion. But they both ate out seven nights a week, so what did he care? She could eat rice cakes—hell, she could wear them—so long as he didn't have to join her. And he didn't. He was a meat-and-potatoes, salt-and-fat kind of guy. At least he'd be satisfied tonight at this party where there were no other guests and nothing to eat but a lone bowl of gourmet, oversalted chips that Colleen would never touch, but he could polish off in minutes. He did, devouring its contents just as—finally—another guest arrived, bearing drinks.

This was too good to be true. Macallan's, neat. He wondered if someone had made one of the production-assistant slaves do drink-and-snack bios on everyone they'd invited. Whatever—they might all hate him, but they knew what he liked.

He was just about to make small talk about how it felt to be back on his old stomping ground, but before he could get out a word, he was suddenly woozy, his knees buckling, as if he'd been shot with a stun gun.

He heard the question, "Are you all right?" but it sounded as if it had been said through a long, echoing tunnel. His head was throbbing, his brains felt as though they were being squeezed by a vise. The pain was strong, and it careened straight to his gut. He was reeling, might as well have been strapped into a lifeboat in the middle of the Atlantic during a storm.

He needed a bathroom, needed one fast. He ran, thought he knew where the closest one was, but—someone was calling him. He couldn't make out the words, didn't dare stop to listen. He stumbled on.

He made it into an office—Paula's, he thought—with relief. But as he headed toward her bathroom, he realized he was wrong, this wasn't hers, he was completely turned around. Another roar of pain rushed through his body, blasting out his equilibrium. He toppled over a chair, lost his scotch glass, nearly lost the contents of his stomach.

Then a hand clutched his elbow, led him out into the hall and around the corner until, *Yes, this is it,* he remembered; Paula's office, Paula's bathroom. He stuck his head in her toilet bowl just in time.

His stomach was a bottomless pit. It seemed to take forever to empty it. When he was done, he was so dizzy he thought he might pass out right there, with his head in the bowl. He might have except his head was suddenly yanked back with such force that his jaws clamped shut. He could taste his own blood, where he'd bitten off a piece of his tongue. His hand moved to feel what was around his neck, but by the time his fingers met the phone cord, stretched and wrapped around twice, there was no life left in them. His head rolled forward into the bowl, and the newly installed ever-flush mechanism engaged, washing his spit, blood, and bile away.

15

"LUCKY FOR YOU, HE'S NOT here," Stephanie told May after hearing it was to plead for several days off that she'd called. "To say he's in a bad mood is about as accurate as saying it's not sunny out right now."

May glanced through the kitchen window into the black of the new-moon night, wondering what made people feel so compelled to tell her she was lucky when facts so clearly indicated otherwise.

"This morning," Stephanie went on to confide, "he came out of the bathroom holding an empty toilet paper roll, wielded it around like a gun, and fired our house-keeper because she forgot to put a spare roll in the basket. She's been with us for twelve years. That's like dog years, for domestic help." She dropped her voice. "I hired her right back and told her the pathetic truth. If she changes her hairstyle and pretends she doesn't speak English, Gil will never figure out it's her. You could try the same thing if he fires you, but I don't think it would work."

"Let me ask you a question," May said, quickly moving in to take advantage of Stephanie's chatty mood. Gil's alibi was gnawing at her with the determination of a hungry squirrel picking through trash. She had no good reason to doubt it. And if she could prove it false, it wouldn't necessarily improve her own status in the case. Still, she wanted to know more. "Gil's been a wreck ever since that run-in with Mike Wallace. What exactly did Mike say to him?"

"Those two go at it all the time."

May noted the duck and tried again. "Were you there?"

"Neither of them takes it seriously, May. You shouldn't either. Listen, I have to run. I'll do you a favor. I won't tell Gil you called." Abruptly she hung up.

Was it her imagination that Stephanie had rushed to get off the phone? And why wasn't she on anyone's short list of suspects? May pulled her folder out of her bag and made a note to do some digging, put together a background check on Gil's wife. After all, her father was loaded. Didn't murder usually have to do with money?

She didn't have time to ponder this for long. She was already late for a phone appointment with the English au pair, her final interview.

"Of course the last time I lived abroad was with my auntie in Australia," Louise said in response to May's questions about homesickness. "I can't say I didn't miss my mum at all because that wouldn't quite be true. Around my birthday I was a bit down, and at Christmastime it's hard, isn't it? Actually, what I really love to do when I'm feeling a bit low is craft projects. All that cutting and pasting, it's relaxing, isn't it? Do your children like craft projects?"

As soon as she got off the phone, May called Carol, who promised to make the arrangements as quickly as possible. Still, the earliest Louise could arrive would be Saturday afternoon. So May turned her attention to the task of cutting and pasting coverage together for the girls until then.

It took two hours to set everything up. Eleven people were involved, including Pete, Emily, two old friends she barely spoke to anymore, and several serial playdates. Everything would work if no one got sick and it didn't snow. If snow canceled school, she was sunk.

Finally, she closed up the house, ignoring the creaks that seemed to have multiplied in number and volume ever since O'Donnell left. She turned on the TV, climbed into bed, and surfed the news stations, waiting for mention of Iris's death, but there was none.

She thought about the last time she'd seen Iris, about how rude she'd been at the Women in Broadcasting lunch, where she demanded to have her table changed because she'd decided her seatmates were B-list. It was exactly the kind of thing Barnett would have done. They had that in common, a guaranteed spot on anyone's Top-Ten-Most-Reprehensible-TV-Producers list. If Todd ever turned into a producer, he'd end up on that list, too. Her mind drifted, carried along by the pleasant thought of his demise. She went through the alphabet thinking of all the painful ways she could kill him. *Asphyxiation*, she began, and by the time she got to *smothering*, sleep came for her.

It seemed only moments later that the phone rang, but the light peeking through the thin planks of her white wooden shutters told her it was her morning wake-up call.

"Dolly, are you up? Don't go back to sleep now."

"I have an alarm clock, Mom. It works just fine."

"I'd feel better if you had a husband."

May carried Susie, limp, to her neighbors' house. Delia ran on ahead, her parka flapping open in the biting morning wind, revealing to the world that her thin cotton pajamas were suddenly two sizes too small. Delia couldn't wait to get next door, and May now knew why. In the dreamy voice she'd probably use one day to describe her first kiss to her friends, she'd told her mother when she'd woken up, "At the Coopers' house they don't have any rules."

"Look," she screamed out with delight when they walked into the Cooper kitchen, "Froot Loops."

Emily shrugged. "Sorry."

"A little sugar in the morning won't hurt her." May handed over Susie, who clung to May for a moment before giving in to the change of arms. Emily smiled blissfully. She hadn't held a child as small as Susie in a long time. Delia disappeared into the basement with Evan, who promised an even better breakfast of edible Creepy Crawlers in a bowl of chocolate milk.

May called down her good-bye, kissed Susie, and forced herself to leave. Saturday was only a few days away. Exposure to the Cooper kids wouldn't cause long-term damage that quickly. She stopped at a tall oak tree to quickly knock on wood, just to be sure.

As soon as she got settled on the train, she made a list of all the people she would call when she got into the office. She'd go after Peggy Golding first, this time more aggressively, about the surprise party O'Donnell had mentioned. She'd call Judy next to see if the buzz had changed on *Simon Says*. She'd give a shot at pumping Wendy to see what information she could gather on the status of Gil and Stephanie's marriage. Then she'd check in with Margery to find out what her cop buddies had told her.

She closed her notebook and opened the top newspaper on her pile. Work had to go on. New shows needed to be found. Paula had to be kept happy. May had to remain employed.

Newsday hooked her with a few paragraphs about a man who was awarded custody of half a dozen frozen embryos after a lengthy battle with his ex-wife. The story might be worth pursuing, but she wasn't feeling particularly generous toward men these days. She'd have to scope it out further first to see if she could legitimately build the story so that the court decision was revealed to be a bad one. She added it to her "To Do" list. The train pulled into her station.

By the time the elevator doors opened on the twenty-second floor, she had a full morning's work planned— and then realized she was taping the tipping show. She looked at her notebook, puzzling out how to juggle it all.

"Your name, please?"

She glanced up to find a uniformed policeman blocking the double doors leading to reception. He searched his list for her name but couldn't find it. "Do you have some kind of photo ID?"

She fumbled through her oversized leather bag, finally turning it upside down, letting the pieces of her life pour out. Frayed newspaper articles she'd ripped out, put aside, and forgotten; a half-finished lollipop stuck back in its own twisted paper; dusty lipstick; spit-out wads of gum peeking through clumps of tissues; ponytail holders knotty with strands of Delia's chestnut hair; three tiny Puppy In My Pockets, and a McDonald's "Little Dutch Barbie" toy still in its plastic wrapper.

As she struggled to scoop her belongings off the floor, another set of elevator doors opened behind her, letting out a tall, spindly woman whose name the officer quickly found on his list. May fumbled for her wallet. Twelve credit cards flew out in twelve directions on the muted blue carpet.

"Thank you, Mrs. Silver," the cop said, stepping aside to let her pass.

"Mrs. Silver," May called out. It was the tipping-book lady. "Lottie." But already the author was on the other side of the double doors, talking to Linda, the receptionist.

"I've got to get her across the street to the studio," May told the cop, but he blocked her way. "Ask Linda who I am. The receptionist. She'll tell you. I've got to get in. Ask her if May Morrison can go in."

"Let me tell you something, May Morrison," the cop explained, "even if you do locate some acceptable identification, which isn't looking too good, you're still not entering the premises because you're still not on my list. And no one's entering the premises who's not on my list." He seemed to be enjoying himself.

"Where the hell did you get that list?" she asked, trying to read it upside down. He covered the paper and ignored her question. Another set of elevator doors split open, spitting out Margery. A uniformed cop trailed after her.

"Problem?" the new cop asked his friend.

"Is this Paula's idea of security?" Margery asked, sidling up to May. "Don't you think it's kind of overkill?"

"Name, please?" the first cop asked Margery, not about to lose another customer. He put a small check next to Margery's name, which he found right away. At May's request, Margery got reinforcements.

"What's wrong now?" Wendy asked.

"I'm not on his list."

"Of course you are. I typed it up myself." She quickly scanned the names, then walked to the far end of the lobby to speak with the cop. After a long huddle she disengaged herself, returning to May with a brisk, "Let's go." The cop stepped aside but refused to meet May's eyes.

As they sped down the hallway, Wendy turned to her. "I'm sorry. It was my mistake. I had a few other things on my mind. I assume, considering what's happened, that you understand."

"What's happened?" May asked as they turned the corner. But before Wendy could reply, May saw a yellow plastic crime-scene tape blocking the hall that went to Paula and Gil's suite of offices. As she stood watching, a cluster of policemen walked into view, joined immediately by a man she recognized by the tweed of his jacket as O'Donnell. He barked orders at two men wearing blue overalls, plastic gloves, and booties. They all ducked back inside in a rush.

Wendy dashed into Paula's secretary's closet-sized cubicle, where Patty and several of her cronies were squashed together gossiping. May was about to join them when a cold hand grabbed hers. Margery pulled her along the hallway to the kitchen.

They joined Colleen and Bunny, huddled at the small round kitchen table. Under the glare of two long fluorescent lights Colleen's tear-and-mascara-streaked face looked pale, petrified, and twice her age.

Bunny pulled the Rolodex out of Colleen's tight grip and squeezed her hand. "Steady yourself now. You need to be strong. When Paula finds out, she's going to blast off."

"Finds out what?" May asked.

As Margery spoke, Colleen closed her lids tighter to shut out the words. "Last night when Rosa came to clean she found Chuck Mills in Paula's bathroom."

"Paula and Chuck Mills?" May rolled her eyes. "Who's she going to sleep with next, Godzilla?"

Colleen began to sob.

"She didn't know, sugar," Margery tried to comfort her, "about you and Chuck." She glared at May, who grimaced, realizing her mistake.

"I'm sorry, Colleen. I didn't know. I'm sure it was just a one-night thing with Paula. You know how she is with men."

Colleen stopped wailing long enough to get out, "Someone tell her before I kill her."

Bunny volunteered. "Chuck was in Paula's bathroom all right, but when Rosa found him, he was alone with his head in the toilet bowl."

"Was he sick?" May asked.

"He was dead," Bunny said because someone had to. "Stiff, stinking, dead."

"What time was he killed?" May shot out, daring to hope it was when O'Donnell was with her, that she was finally off the hook.

Colleen stared hard, her bloodshot eyes wide open. "Who said anything about him being killed?"

"Bunny did. Didn't you, Bunny?"

Bunny looked away.

"All Bunny said was that he was dead."

"It is an honest assumption, sugar," Margery said, defending her friend. "Given the circumstances."

"Was he killed?" May asked.

"Yes," Colleen hissed. "As if you didn't know."

The four women sat perfectly still, silent but for the mournful sound of Colleen's heaving sighs.

16

GIL POKED HIS HEAD IN THE doorway. "What is this? A prayer group? Come on people. We've got to hustle."

Wendy, standing beside him like an overgrown appendage, whispered in his ear, showing him her watch.

Gil nodded, then upped his volume. "Are you people deaf? What do I have to do to get you to move? Scream bloody murder?"

They all rushed up, talking at once.

"Stop," he called out, blocking the exit. His two-fingered whistle got their attention. "Everybody sit."

They scrambled back to their seats. Gil was at a new level of panic, bordering on shock. His face looked serene. His tics had vanished. His mouth was nibless. "We need calm," he instructed. "I want everyone calm."

No one moved. May sat so still she had to remind herself to breathe.

"Listen up. In a moment you will all stand and very

slowly, in total silence, walk to the elevator banks. When Paula gets off the elevator, you will explain to her that she can't go to her office right now. You will tell her we're installing a new security device. You will tell her we're painting with lead paint. You will tell her we're fumigating with toxic chemicals. I don't care what the hell you tell her." His serene demeanor slipped away in a hurry as he hissed, "Just get her across the street to the studio. Do you understand? I pulled rank up through a battalion of police officers and stopped just short of calling in a favor from the mayor. Today's shows will go on. But if Paula Wind gets wind that a corpse lay collapsed on her bathroom floor all night, those guests across the street so patiently waiting for a scintillating show on the rules of tipping will be waiting for a very long time."

He took a deep, cleansing breath. Then, in a careful, measured tone he went on. "I need Paula to make it through this show and the next. Once she finds out about Chuck Mills, she'll be useless. It could take days to get her up and running again. It could take months." His voice dropped lower. They all leaned in to hear him. "This is a crisis, people. I expect you to rise to it." The women stood and marched down the hall to the elevators as if to their own funerals.

"Cancel your lunches," he called after them. "Consider yourselves under house arrest."

"What's this? A surprise party?" Paula asked when greeted by the phalanx of producers. There was a moment of silence, none of them sure who should speak, or what to say.

Then May came forward, taking Paula by the arm. "I need you to come to the greenroom with me. Lottie Silver is afraid to meet you. Lottie is afraid to talk to you. I told Lottie"—she repeated the name again so it would be emblazoned and unforgettable in Paula's brain by the time she went on the air—"that you're really a pussycat."

"Meow meow. Did you tell her if she doesn't talk to me, I'll claw her eyes out?" She let herself be led inside a waiting elevator. Someone had passed on the word to the policeman, who stood aside, offering a subdued, "Good morning."

"New security?" Paula asked with interest.

"The first thing Lottie asked me this morning," May went on, ignoring the question, "is if you're as beautiful in person as you are on TV."

"Am I?"

"I told Lottie yes."

May soothed her host's nerves all the way across the street to the greenroom, where Lottie looked only mildly baffled when Paula reassured her she was a totally regular person, no different than anyone else.

But totally regular Paula's mood crashed quickly once the cameras rolled, revealing Lottie to have all the sparkle of a medium-sized potato. At the first break Paula stormed into the control room demanding May feed her guest some lines. "I'm dying out there. Save me."

May hustled Lottie back to the greenroom and served her a tumbler of brandy. When she returned her to the studio, she whispered to Paula to go for the story about the Chinese waiter.

"Tell me about the waiter who chased you down the street for a tip." Paula smiled warmly in anticipation of an amusing anecdote. Lottie smiled back, then yawned, the huge highly contagious yawn Paula had been fearing for years.

"We're not keeping you awake are we?" Paula kidded, struggling to stifle a yawn of her own. The audience tittered with what May knew was discomfort. Then, like dominoes crashing, they began yawning, too.

"Have a sip of water and relax," Paula said as contagious coughing started up next. "We're all friends here, right?"

Eager to be helpful, the audience applauded. Paula turned to the magazine editor, whose dangling chains bumped into her body mike with every breath, sending the sound guys into cardiac arrest. "Now that we're on the subject of salons," Paula confided as it they were friends for life, alone at last, "don't you hate it when everyone in the joint is practically sniffing around your purse looking for dollar bills?"

Before the editor could deliver her little salon story, Lottie Silver piped up. "It's a known fact that in Chinatown the busboys steal the waiters' tips all the time."

The techies sitting alongside May began muttering and cursing as the rattle of the travel editor's chains collided with the sound of Lottie's rambling voice. May thought of Chuck Mills, of her early days on *Paula Live* when he was the tyrannical executive producer. He would have fired her for what was happening in the studio now. Before the show was over, he'd have emptied out her desk and had her personal possessions searched through and boxed.

"All the busboys I've ever met in Chinatown have been honest," Paula was saying, "which I'll be sure to tell them when they call me to complain this afternoon." The audience laughed.

Paula would make her suffer for this, but Chuck would have made her sick over it. He made everyone sick. He single-handedly increased the billing of an entire group of Upper East Side physicians, making several gastroenterologists and psychiatrists downright rich, though doctors treating eczema, acne, migraines, and missed menses were also uncommonly busy during his tenure.

"Let's have some questions from the audience," Paula said to save herself. "What's on your mind? Other than a sudden craving for cold sesame noodles." More laughter.

May remembered the day Gil asked her to help him organize the producers to sign a petition threatening that if Paula didn't fire Chuck Mills, the rest of them would resign. Some of their colleagues had balked, afraid Paula would call their bluff. May had been instrumental in assuaging their fears, even though she was worried, too.

But Paula went for it. Six months earlier Chuck had inspired a rash of resignations that had crippled the show for weeks. She was still throbbing with the pain of getting used to those new hires. She didn't want to go through it again. In a never repeated demonstration of courage—or was it survival instinct?—she took the petition, went to the men upstairs, and demanded Chuck be dismissed.

Gil's ascension to executive producer was immediate. Chuck resurfaced soon after in a new and hotter job where the names of all *Paula Live* producers were banned from being spoken aloud. The bad blood between them was intense and well known. Chuck's death wasn't going to be good news for May.

Gil's voice broke through her consciousness. "Cut off that moron's goddamn mike. Cut off her goddamn head. What—are you asleep in here? Why can't we just hear Paula work the audience?"

"Because," one of the sound guys complained, "those chains are screwing us up. We're on the ceiling mikes now."

"Let's talk about hotels," they watched Paula try from

way at the back of the room, as far away as she could get from Lottie Silver. "They used to say you only tip a chambermaid if you're there for more than a day. Do we have anyone here who works in a hotel?"

"Chambermaids are the worst," Lottie interrupted, practically jumping out of her seat to share this news.

Joey, the cameraman, hesitated, then zoomed in on her face.

"They go through your drawers. I don't care how much you're paying. Last night at the St. Regis my earrings disappeared."

"When we come back, we'll solve the case of Lottie's missing earrings."

Paula stormed into the control room, her nostrils flaring like a taunted bull's. She stomped over to May. "Give me your earrings so I can show everyone Lottie had them all along and we can avoid a lawsuit from the St. Regis." May handed over her hoops. "This is not in my Folder. I want her off my set now."

"Lottie," May called, from the wings, keeping her distance from the grumbling audience. "Phone call. Hurry up."

May raced ahead to the greenroom to retrieve Lottie's coat and bag, which she gave to one of the stagehands with quick instructions to get their now-former guest a cab.

"Thanks for coming," May called as she began backing up to the control room.

"What about my phone call?"

"It was a wrong number."

"What about the show?"

"That was really a wrong number."

When the show was over, Paula stood at the exit shaking the hands of each member of the audience while Gil crouched just out of her sight, begging O'Donnell to leave her alone until she was done taping the second show, Bunny's "Wicked Stepmothers." Begrudgingly O'Donnell agreed, leaving behind several task-force cops to ensure that Paula and the producers were escorted directly back to the office as soon as it was over.

While Wendy and two production assistants assembled a fresh audience, Paula ducked behind a screen in her peach-painted dressing room to change into a new outfit. Betty, the recently forgiven makeup artist, popped in to do a touch-up and left immediately after finishing, sensing the resurgence of another threatening mood.

Looking fresh and revived, Paula turned to Gil, who sat slumped on a stool in a corner of the room. She smiled broadly, then cooed, "When I'm done making nice to those evil stepmothers, I want everyone back here for a postmortem on that pathetic excuse of a tipping show." She opened her door and extended a bright, charismatic smile to her next group of guests.

By the time the stepmothers were redefined as kind caregivers, Gil had gathered all the producers in the control room. The techies huddled in the hallway, happy to have been excluded. Paula whined about the idiocy of conducting the postmortem in the windowless control room, where no-smoking rules were completely ignored, instead of in the airy conference room across the street as they usually did. Then she turned to the task at hand.

"I know what I think. Let's hear what everybody else thinks."

Everyone else, thinking about Chuck's prone body, said nothing. Paula hated silence. "What? You're all suddenly shy? Bunny, you're about as shy as a stripper. What do you think?"

"It stinks. The whole thing stinks."

Paula smiled. Postmortems were akin to a gathering of a gang of ninth-grade troublemakers in the assistant principal's office. No one wanted to be expelled, but neither did they want to turn stoolie. "Margery?"

Margery eyed May, Paula, Gil. "I'm a bit shaken up myself. I'll have to pass."

The corners of Paula's mouth turned down. Postmortems usually meant all the producers, except Bunny, whose negativity was as dependable as nightfall, tried to act as if things weren't as bad as they seemed, particularly when the show was produced by someone as well liked as May. The failure of May's allies to rally round her meant the show must have been worse than Paula realized. She sank down in the uncomfortable swivel chair, bracing herself for her descent into depression.

There was a sharp knock. Gil jumped to his feet and slipped out before any of them could see who it was. From the muttering audible through the closed door May quickly deduced the cops were getting impatient. Gil had told them this would only take a minute. When he returned, he looked pasty and worn down. "We have to finish up here."

"What should I do?" Paula asked, meekly. "Fire May?"

Gil shook his head.

"Good. I don't want to fire you, May. I like you. But this can't go on. I want quality. I want integrity. I don't want to be another second-rate show where guests go home and shoot themselves or someone else. I'm tired of mediocrity, of being on at six AM in Phoenix."

"You're on at ten in Phoenix," Gil corrected her. "You're on at six in Tallahassee."

"Quality shows. Quality guests. Quality work. Do you people understand me? Am I speaking English?"

"Quality English," Bunny muttered.

Paula put her arm around Colleen's narrow shoulders

but didn't notice how they quivered. "You look like shit. Let's go get a facial and cheer ourselves up." It was another thing she did well, playing the producers off each other. While one was being crucified, another was getting a skin peel at Georgette Klinger.

"Paula." Gil forced himself to stop her. "I need a minute."

"Does it have to be right now? I'll feel much better after a facial."

"It has to be right now."

The producers rushed out of the control room, were hastily buttoning their overcoats and being hustled to the door by the task-force cops, when they all heard the shriek that told them Paula had just learned about the corpse they hoped no longer lay flat out on her cold bathroom tiles.

17

AS SHE WAS ESCORTED THROUGH the office, May saw that most of the staff, already interviewed by the police, were gone, sent home for the day. In the cubicles and offices normally occupied by the overworked production staff, cops now went about their business. But despite their busy presence, an unnatural silence had settled in, punctuated by the constant interruption of the trilling of unanswered phones.

When May got to her own office, her fellow producers right behind her, she found Detective O'Donnell standing just inside, waiting for them. Paradiso had made himself comfortable, sitting in the middle of her uphol-stered couch, filling it up, his arms spread-eagled across the back. Slowly he pushed himself up, his eyes never leaving hers, and took his usual position, leaning against the wall, his back to the window.

May strode past O'Donnell and said, "I have to check on my kids," as she took her seat behind her desk.

O'Donnell held himself back from commenting, but Paradiso let out a snort of a laugh.

"Why don't you ladies make yourselves at home," O'Donnell told the rest of the producers, who were clog-ging the doorway.

Colleen and Bunny took over Paradiso's spot on the small couch. Margery settled into the club chair, sliding her well-formed legs slightly to the side, the well-groomed talk-show guest's best leg position.

"Hi. It's May," she said into the receiver, keeping her voice low, conscious of the many ears listening in. "Ev-erything okay?"

O'Donnell shut the door, closing them in while May listened to Pete's update. Then she placed her next two calls, confirming her daughters' after-school pickups.

"Anyone else you want to call, sugar?" Margery asked when she was done. "The piano teacher? Your plumber?"

O'Donnell spoke before May could answer. "I have a few questions for you ladies. When we're done, Detec-tive Paradiso and I will be coming round to see you each individually."

"Maybe I should call my lawyer," Bunny grumbled.

"Be my guest," O'Donnell said, gesturing to the phone. "I am not dissuading anyone from bringing along legal counsel. I say 'bringing along' because those of you who choose to have a lawyer present should immediately in-form your attorneys that we'll meet you both down at the station house later tonight. We'll be happy to see the rest of you here, this afternoon. Lawyer anyone?" he asked, lifting up May's phone as though he were offering a drink.

May sniffed. She smelled something, a familiar odor that she couldn't place. She met O'Donnell's eyes, saw his nostrils flare, too. She looked at Paradiso, but he had his back to the strong winter sun, his face a silhouette, unreadable.

"I want to know more about after-hours security in this building." O'Donnell moved on, doing his job. "Anyone want to enlighten me?"

"There's a couple of guys," Bunny offered. "Jack and Bob. You ring the bell next to the door, and a year later, when they come back from wherever the hell they go to pick their noses, they answer it."

"The door is supposed to be locked every night at eight," Margery said. "Isn't that right?"

May nodded, but added, "It's a heavy door. It closes slowly. If you don't really slam it, which most people don't, it never really latches." She sniffed again and wondered, *What is that?*

"I see. But when it is locked, what do Jack or Bob do? Check for ID? Make you sign a book?"

"I don't know what happens if they don't know you, sugar," Margery told him. "If they do know you, they leer and let you by."

"If they don't know you," Colleen explained, "you have to produce a note on company letterhead saying you're allowed on the premises after hours. Then you have to produce some kind of ID. I know because Chuck came up a few times," she said quietly, then added, "after hours."

"Were you here last Tuesday?" Bunny asked. "I

thought I heard something last Tuesday. I decided it was the wind. Moaning."

"Sugar, were you actually moaning?" Margery joked, but Colleen's face remained impassive, so they all shut up.

"What about leaving the building after hours?" O'Donnell asked. "Do Bob and Jack have to let you out?"

"No," Bunny told him. "There's a button you push, a buzzer sounds, the door opens, and off you go."

"And is Jack or Bob there to see it?"

"No, they're in the closet picking their noses, remember?" Bunny reminded him. "Is this inquisition going to go on all day?"

May got another whiff. It seemed to be coming from under her desk. She leaned down. The smell was definitely stronger there, in the dark cave that was the underside of her fake antique banker's desk. She recognized the smell now. It was scotch. She wondered if Rosa, the cleaning woman, had been drinking under the desk, if maybe Colleen and Chuck had been partying there. Then she saw a plastic cup lying on the top of her garbage. She picked it up, sniffed it, coughed from the smell, old scotch, then sat upright in her chair. All eyes were on her. Her hand was still under the desk. O'Donnell's nostrils were flaring wide. Paradiso moved from his post and came toward her. She might as well have been hiding a gun the way he was staring at her.

"Bring your hands up slowly," he told her.

She did, then held both arms over her head, the empty cup clutched in her right hand. Through the bottom a quarter inch of amber liquid sloshed.

"What you got?" Paradiso asked.

"A cup," she said.

"What's in it?"

"Scotch," she said. "And it's not mine."

"Then how do you know what it is?" the young cop asked her.

"I can smell it."

"Why don't you sip it?" Paradiso taunted.

O'Donnell stepped forward quickly, a plastic bag that he'd whipped out of his pocket already in his hand. Like a magician, he took the cup away from her, placing it in the bag without touching it, and without spilling a drop.

He strode to the door, unlatched it, kicked it further open with surprising force, and called out, "Curtis."

A man in street clothes jogged over, listened to O'Donnell's hushed instructions, took the cup, and left, closing the door behind him.

"I think we're done here for now," O'Donnell said.

Everyone rose.

"No," Paradiso dissented. "Tell me you're not bringing her in."

"We'll be coming round to see each of you this afternoon, so stick around," O'Donnell instructed, ignoring his partner.

May couldn't. "Bring me in for what? For finding a cup of scotch in my garbage? What are you? The drink police?"

"We're not bringing you in," O'Donnell said, but he wouldn't look her in the eye.

"I'm kind of curious," Margery said, "as to why such a fuss is being made over that little cup. What's the deal, sugar?"

May turned to Paradiso. "Do you think it has the murderer's fingerprints on it? Do you think if I was the murderer, I would have left the thing with my prints on it in my own garbage can? Do you think I would have pulled it out of the trash while you were in the room if it was some kind of incriminating evidence?" Her face felt on fire.

"So smooth," Paradiso said, admiring her. "You've got this routine down so well it almost sounds real."

"Are you accusing her of lying?" Bunny asked, moving between Paradiso and May as if she were a human shield.

When the door burst open, May's eyes happened to be on O'Donnell, so she saw his hand quickly move toward his jacket, to his holster, then fall to his side when he saw it was Paula, with Gil right behind her. From the action of Gil's jaw she could guess that though he had tried to get their host to calm down, he'd failed.

Paula didn't stop to figure out the mood of the room. "What the hell are you people doing to protect us, other than nothing?"

"Let me explain what she's trying to say," Gil said, his voice tight with forced friendliness. "We know you're here to help us. We know you've got a job to do. But all of us are beginning to feel somewhat uncomfortable."

"I don't blame you," O'Donnell said, turning to Paula. "Someone was murdered in your bathroom last night. You'd be crazy not to feel scared. Unless, of course, you were the one who committed the crime."

"That's it. I'm out of here." Paula headed toward the door.

"I'm afraid not yet." The detective's words, cordial but firm, stopped her.

"Officer," Colleen interrupted. She wrung her hands, then rubbed her arms as if trying to warm herself up. Her eyes were teary, and her voice cracked. She was holding on, just barely. "I think we're all jumping the gun around here. I mean the wound is so fresh we can barely feel it. Maybe if we went around the room and shared what we felt in our hearts, we could open our ears and really hear what's being said."

If she hadn't been so mad, May would have smiled at Colleen's earnest plea. But her smile muscles had taken a sabbatical.

"I'd like to do that," O'Donnell said. "But with the unfortunate demise of Mr. Mills we now have two task forces and a major case unit helping us out. That's over twenty additional officers waiting for me downtown. So I don't really have time to explore anybody's feelings.

"I do, however, feel I need to make myself completely clear. We didn't come here to arrest anyone in this room. You are not currently suspects, just as you are not currently victims. Is that clear enough?" He directed the questions to May. There was no gentleness in his eyes now. She gave a tiny nod.

"What about the press?" Gil asked. "Paula's nervous about what happens when the press finds out we've had a murder here."

"The press has already found out. Despite our attempts to keep this quiet, a reporter from *Live at Five* picked something up on the scanner. She's en route here now, along with the rest of the world. We're going to lay some crime-scene tape in the elevator banks. That will keep the reporters off your floor. But when you leave here tonight, you should know they'll be waiting for you. They'll be calling out your names like you're all long-lost friends. I ask you to remember, they are not."

"Maybe not," Gil said, considering it, "but the show could get some major publicity out of this."

"The more publicity this creep gets," O'Donnell remarked, "the more reason he has to go out and do it again."

"Get me out of here Gil," Paula pleaded. "Cook up a

show that takes me on location, or it's going to be on your head if I'm next."

"Miss Wind, I'd like to remind you that you are not to leave town until we've had a chance to speak to you, either here or down at the station house, whichever is more convenient for you."

"Am I supposed to spend the day hanging around here like a sitting duck?"

"At this particular point in time there are over a dozen police officers here gathering evidence. These include some of the best on the force. I think at least for this afternoon you're safe."

"Really? How do you know the murderer isn't sitting right here in this room?"

"Actually I don't know that at all."

Half a dozen pairs of eyes darted to May, then looked away.

18

O'DONNELL AND PARADISO STARTED with Paula. Their closed-door discussion, punctuated by bursts of her shouting, lasted for more than an hour. When it was over, Paula bundled up in her floor-length black fur coat, put on her floppy hat and sunglasses, and headed to the basement, where building security had arranged to accompany her on a mazelike escape route to the service entrance. To prepare for the unlikely event that a small break-off faction of reporters lay in wait there, she practiced evading questions as she breezed down the hall by refusing to answer those shouted out by her staff.

"Will you be back tomorrow?" Gil cried out. "Will you be in on Friday? Will you be in on Monday?"

"Don't let me down," Colleen called after her. "I've got three herbal physicians coming in next week. Three beautiful female physicians. One of them was Chuck's." She began to whimper quietly, but Paula's face remained a mask. When the elevator doors opened, with a building guard waiting inside, Paula entered and remained statue-still as the whoosh of the doors closed her in.

May tracked down Patty at the Xerox machine. Paula's secretary was one of the few support people who, though interviewed, had been permitted to stay.

"What happened in there?" May asked.

In the instant before Patty answered, May could see her suspicion engage. Patty's easy rapport with her was discarded, replaced by, of all things, fear.

"They told her to put together a list of people she thought might be suspects." Patty liked May too much to close her out completely, but her voice was devoid of its usual warmth. She turned back to the papers groaning out from the copy machine.

"Does she have any? Suspects?"

Patty laid a hand atop a high pile of papers. "I've copied her Rolodex, my Rolodex, and her Christmas card list." She was working hard to avoid meeting May's eyes.

"What's wrong, Patty? Am I on her list?"

She nodded, but kept her eyes on her shoes. "Everyone she's ever known is on her list. Her father is on her list. The president is on her list."

"What about your list?"

Patty faced her, their eyes finally meeting. Now May could see the full weight of the rumors bearing down on her. "I don't know," Patty said quietly. "I just don't know." She turned back to her task, turned her back on May.

"Crap," May muttered as she walked down the hall to her office. If Patty was allowing even the possibility that rumors about her were true, May was in trouble. Patty liked her. She relied on May as a steadying force of nature when Paula started making turbulence in the atmosphere.

May slammed her door, mad at the world, then tried to put her fury aside as she called the homes where her children were safely ensconced, too busy with their friends to get on the phone and say hello. Ridiculously, she felt relieved when neither playdate mother insisted on sending her daughters home early, neither having heard news, rumors, or gossip that Delia and Susie were daughters of a maniacal serial killer. She was stuck ruminating about this when Bunny stopped by and began unpacking a grocery bag filled with a party-sized pack of potato chips, a large bag of Hershey's kisses, a small deli container stuffed with something white and creamy, and a liter of Dewar's.

"I called out for provisions. Name your comfort food. You want the chocolate kisses or the rice pudding?"

"How can you eat?"

Bunny spilled all the pens and pencils out of May's plastic Delia-decorated pencil cup and filled it with scotch. "If I don't eat, I won't have anything to wash down." She took a big gulp, then offered to fill up May's empty coffee mug, but May declined.

"You got to loosen up, kiddo," Bunny told her. "You're living your life like you're in a race without a finish line.

Stop and live for a minute." She took another hearty gulp.

"That's easy for you to say. No one's accused you of being a murderer."

"You're supposed to be the murderer? Don't make me laugh."

"Well, if you don't believe it, you're in the minority. Gil isn't convinced, but he's warming up to the idea. That detective, Paradiso, has already made up his mind. Henry's been looking at me cross-eyed."

"Since when does he count for anything?"

"Patty is afraid of me."

"Patty is? Our Patty? Not really."

"She is. I was just with her."

Bunny opened the container of rice pudding and scooped herself a large spoonful, then swallowed. "I've been doing my own noodling on this, trying to come up with some ideas. But you? May, kiddo, imagining you as a crazed killer is a lot like imagining Lassie turns into a werewolf when the moon gets full."

"That's how I feel," May said quietly.

Bunny finished the last of her pudding. "If Gil starts believing it, you know you're cooked. The man was born without a spine. At the first sign of trouble he'll drive you to jail himself. You got to keep him on the hook about this. You got to convince him you're not really a suspect, even if you are. Keep reminding him that he's a better choice. He is, anyway. He knows it, too." She opened up the bag of Hershey's kisses. "Have some of these. They'll make you feel better."

Again May declined.

Bunny shook her head. "I can't eat this here if you're just going to watch me. Look, kiddo, you know I think you're the best. You're the best producer—you deserved the promotion. You're patient as hell—I would have fired Henry six months ago. You're nearly perfect. In fact, I'd like you a hell of a lot better if you started smoking cigarettes or got a tattoo or a nose ring. But a killer? I'm telling you, I'm working on my own theories here, none of which make any sense yet, so don't ask me to share them. But none of them, not even my wildest ones, I repeat none, involve you." Shaking her head in disbelief, she left.

May considered finishing Bunny's drink, maybe finishing the entire bottle. Only she hated scotch—probably because it was Todd's favorite drink. Besides, she needed to stay sober so that she could pick up the girls after work, if she was still a free woman.

Time seemed to stop as May waited for O'Donnell to wind his way to her office. Even reading the trade papers required too much concentration. All she was good for was cleaning out her desk. She fished through a dozen nibs, a bottle of expired Advil, a package of melted Mentho-Lyptus cough drops, a handful of dried-out felt-tip pens. There were old "To Do" lists, the doing either done or by now completely undoable, a few no-longer sticky Post-Its saying "call home," and two crumpled lists of ways to kill Todd.

She was down to the unrecognizable bits of fluff and shavings in her top drawer, about to empty them onto the floor, when Stephanie walked by her office and, seeing May alone, stepped inside. Her face looked as desolate as was possible considering all the work she'd had done to make sure no new lines would be formed. May thought, *I can't let her become suspicious*, and forced a smile.

"Hey." May willed her smile to widen further. "It's great to see a friendly face around here."

"Thanks, May, but I'm not feeling very friendly right now. I'm so sorry to hear about Chuck. I mean, I know you and Gil loathed him." She stopped, looked around. "By the way, does anyone else know that?"

"Neither of us kept our feelings a secret," May admitted.

Stephanie shook her head, then checked her hair to make sure it had stayed vaguely in place. "Gil is in with the detectives now. Wendy asked if I could join them, and they had the nerve to say no. Why are they meeting with him, anyway?"

"They're meeting with everyone," May said; then, remembering Bunny's advice, she added, "It's scary. First Iris, then Chuck. It's as if everyone on Gil's personal hate list ends up dead."

"It doesn't make sense," Stephanie muttered.

"What?" May asked quickly. "What doesn't?"

"Come with me."

"Where are we going?" May asked as she raced after her, her face heating up at the thought that Stephanie was about to share something big

"To see Colleen. I heard about her and Chuck. I can't face her alone."

Deflated, May continued along. They got to Colleen's office just as Paradiso was leaving.

"Don't go away," he said to May as he slid by, too close to her, into the hall.

"Come on," Stephanie chided, dragging May into Colleen's office.

Colleen didn't acknowledge them. She sat, wet-eyed and still, listening to Charles Aznavour's voice pour out of a CD on the credenza behind her. Only when Stephanie reached up and jingled the crystal wind chime that hung from a hook wedged into an acoustical ceiling tile did she finally look at them. Then, pointedly, she stared down, as if meditating, at a photograph in a magazine that lay open on her desk.

May tried to make out the upside-down image. She could tell from the color of the page, powder blue, and the type at the bottom, it was a Tiffany's ad—a hand displaying a large pear-shaped diamond ring. Absent-mindedly Colleen ran her fingertips across the facets of the stone, then finally looked up. "I admit it. It was my fault. He's dead because of me. I'm supposed to feel better now that I've said it. Why don't I?"

"It's your fault? Did you kill him?" Stephanie sounded almost relieved. "Don't worry. We'll hire you the best lawyer in New York City."

"Of course I didn't kill him. I loved him." She collapsed, head down on her desk, but still managed to slide the magazine toward where May and Stephanie sat. "But he died because he loved me back. That's why he came up here. And look at what he brought with him."

"A magazine?" Stephanie asked.

Colleen sat up, met Stephanie's big blue eyes with eyes even wider. "A ring. A huge, gorgeous ring, which will probably end up locked in a Hefty bag at police headquarters as evidence for the rest of my life." She sniffled, struggling to compose herself. "All the lousy detective would tell me was that it was from Tiffany's. So I called the store and tracked down the woman who sold it to Chuck. She told me to look at page twenty-three in this week's *New Yorker*. She said Chuck walked in with the magazine and said, 'I want this one.' He's so romantic." She thought about that. "For a dead man."

She lay her head back on her desk and let the tears seep out until, after several moments, with great effort, she straightened up. The whites of her large doe-brown eyes had turned unnaturally red—like eyes caught by a flash in a bad photograph. "Who would do this?" she hissed, grabbing the magazine back. "Someone sick," she answered herself, then shot her bloodstained eyes at May. "Was it you?"

"Of course not," May said, lurching up as if she'd been kicked out of the chair.

"Poor thing," Stephanie said. "She doesn't mean it," she told May. "Did you mean that?" she asked Colleen.

"Not really." Colleen sniffed back her tears. "I'm just a wreck. They found an invitation in his pocket. He thought he was coming here for a surprise birthday party for me."

"Another one?" May asked, sitting down. She was thinking of the surprise engagement party that had lured Iris Ehrlick to her death, but Colleen misunderstood.

"I know. I told Chuck last week you all threw me a big party for my birthday, but I guess he wasn't listening. That's what our last fight was about. I gave him that book *Why Men Forget to Listen*. And he forgot to read it." She rested her head on her desk, then wrestled her resources back under control and sat up once more. The magazine stuck to her damp cheek. She peeled it off and asked, "Why would anyone want to kill Chuck? He was such a gentle soul." She saw May's and Stephanie's dumbstruck faces. "Get out," she yelled. "Get out." The walls shook as she threw her slim weight against her slamming door.

By the time O'Donnell and Paradiso stopped in to see May, she was down to dusting her bookshelves, a reassuringly mindless task she suddenly felt great guilt about when the young detective asked, "What the hell do you think you're doing?"

She sat down, hands folded on her desk, like a scolded child.

O'Donnell sat across from her, fumbling to get a stack of papers in order. Paradiso took up his post at the window. They said nothing, content to wait for her to speak her piece, to wait forever.

Her instinct directed her to take the offensive. "What's the connection between the surprise party Iris went to and the party Chuck Mills was invited to?"

"I see. Now you're passing yourself off as an armchair detective," Paradiso observed. "What's your style? *Murder, She Wrote? NYPD Blue?* I don't think she'll be able to get either of those programs at the Women's Correctional Center, do you, Detective?"

Her cheeks turned red. She cursed her genes under her breath and pushed on. "Who do you think did it?"

"That's direct." Paradiso turned to O'Donnell. "What do you think? Should I answer her?"

"We're working on finding the link between the victims," O'Donnell said, studying her. She gave him back what he gave her—nothing.

Paradiso broke up the stare contest. "I don't have all day here. What was the problem between you and Chuck Mills?"

"I didn't like him, and neither did anyone else on this floor. Except for Colleen. She has a weak spot for rotten men."

"Aren't there any good guys in your business?" O'Donnell asked her, then added, "Other than you."

May felt her skin turn red as a sunburn.

"Look at that," Paradiso let out. "It's impressive."

O'Donnell explained, "I told him I'm having trouble considering you a suspect because your face won't let you lie."

"My partner thinks that it's something that happens without your control," Paradiso explained. "I'm not as easy as him."

Their good-cop–bad-cop routine was certainly working. May found even looking at Paradiso made her arms sprout goose bumps.

As if sensing she was sufficiently unhinged, O'Donnell said, "Tony, why don't you start taking the statement next door? I'll finish up in here."

Paradiso seemed reluctant to leave. O'Donnell gestured toward the door with his head. Paradiso thought about it and left.

"Do you drink?" O'Donnell asked her.

"I'm not thirsty, thanks." He didn't laugh. Neither did she.

"I'm not offering you anything. I'm just asking, do you drink?"

"An occasional glass of wine, sure."

"Who drinks around the office?"

"Not me."

He waited. Then asked, "Then who?"

Bunny's bottle came into sharp focus on her desk. The smell was overpowering. She didn't know why she'd forgotten it.

"That's Bunny's. She stopped by for a drink. I didn't join her."

"I see. Do you all drink around here a lot?"

"I never do. Bunny always has a bottle in her desk."

"How about your boss? Does he drink?"

She had to stop to consider this. She couldn't remember ever seeing Gil drink, not even a soda, but then his mouth was always full of plastic. "I don't know."

He moved on. "Have you heard anyone make any threats around here?"

"What kind of threats?"

"Wishing someone would die. Saying someone deserved to die. That kind of a threat."

"Gil has," she said, then felt guilty for saying it. "But

talking about it is one thing. He's not the type to kill somebody. He's too much of a coward, really."

"You think it's brave to kill someone?"

She was talking herself into a corner. "No," she said quietly. "That's not what I meant."

Anybody else doing any threatening around here?"

"No."

"What about Todd?"

Her instant sunburn was back. "How do you know about him?"

He felt around in his jacket pockets. "I must have left it on my desk. It was a small piece of paper—a little list with just one item crossed out. I believe the exact wording was 'Kill Todd.' "

This time her cheeks hit the hot color of scarlet. If her face got any hotter, it would blister. "Did you go through my garbage?" She leaned under her desk to examine her overfilled wastebasket, hoping she wouldn't find another surprise there.

There was garbage, nothing more, and clumps of crumpled paper that had overflowed, scattered on the floor like snowballs.

"We don't do that kind of thing, Mrs. Morrison. We're very concerned that our cases hold up in court. But I did open my mail this morning. And a paper saying 'Kill Todd' was lying there waiting for me to read it."

"What makes you think it was mine?"

"It wasn't any great detective work. I didn't have to match up ink samples or dust for fingerprints or send it out for DNA testing. I just had to read your name on top. Purple ink. Bold type. 'From the desk of.' "

She knew the notepaper he described. Her mother had given her the personalized pads for her birthday after reading in a magazine that the color purple attracted men.

"Who's Todd? Another producer? A live one, I hope?"

Her face mutated to the colors of a half-ripe mango, a mix of bright red and pale green. "Todd Morrison is my ex-husband. The only place I kill him is in my dreams. Is that illegal? I think I need a lawyer." She grabbed a couple of chocolate kisses that Bunny had left behind and stuck them in her mouth.

"May, do you believe in listening to your gut?"

He had never called her by her first name before. It brought all her nerves to attention. She nodded, chewing quickly, then swallowed so that she could say, "It's how I do my job." She willed her blood vessels to constrict.

"Well, that's something we have in common, then. Sometimes my gut is the only thing I've got. Now, me and the guys, we're having a hard time here because someone keeps leaving us little presents. A lot of the presents lead directly to your boss, but he's got alibis like I've never seen before. The rest point to you. My gut is telling me, that's not right either. But the guys on the task force, they don't give a crap about my gut. All they give a crap about is not looking like an a-hole when your boss goes on the stand and gives the alibi that he was with Walter Cronkite when Chuck Mills got dead."

"He was?"

"We're checking it out, but I kind of doubt he'd make that up, don't you? Now, I know I asked you this before, but I'm going to ask you again. Where were you when I stopped by your house last night?"

"The mall. Kay-Bees. Macy's. Rite Aid. Pathmark. Where I bought nothing memorable. Where I saw not one person I know. So is this how it is? Are you saying I'm it?"

"I'm saying watch your back. I'm saying there's pressure to find this killer. I'm saying try not to be alone. Make sure if anything else happens, you got people who can testify they were with you. And think about why some individual with access to your trash would take the trouble to send me a love note you wrote yourself about your ex-husband. Who would want to do that? You have any enemies?"

"Just my ex-husband. Who lives in Los Angeles," she added. She wished it were as easy as blaming it on Todd. But Todd was too self-absorbed to spend his time setting her up for anything other than single parenthood.

"Maybe I should have a talk with him," O'Donnell said.

"Be my guest." She scribbled his number on a Post-It. "What exactly should I do?" she asked him.

"Go about your business," he said. "Live your life like nothing's wrong. But bring a lot of friends with you wherever you go. Go nowhere alone. And watch your back."

May hurried down the hall. The elevator was waiting. She ducked inside just as the door began to close.

"Quite a cold one today, isn't it?" she said to the man in the blue overcoat inside. He offered a begrudging nod.

"I'm May Morrison. I work here, at *Paula Live*," she babbled. "Where do you work?"

"Forty-four," he said pointing to the column of floor numbers. "Adelstein Group. Public relations."

"Oh," she said, impressed. "We happen to be looking for a new PR firm. Do you have a card?"

He plucked one from his wallet and gave it to her, waiting for her to say more. But she had nothing more to say. He looked at her hard, as if she were nuts.

She didn't care. So long as he remembered her.

19

"DO YOU WANT ME TO LAY IT OUT for you again?" Paradiso asked.

"Quiet the hell down," O'Donnell replied. "I can hear you just fine. You don't have to broadcast your news to the whole damn world."

"Everybody's gone," he said as quietly as he knew how. "You want me to lay it out for you?"

O'Donnell didn't answer, but that didn't stop him. "When Iris Ehrlick got dead, Miss Morrison was strolling to her train. Usually she's on the same train every night, but that night she missed it, took a later train. She can't explain why, can't produce one, not one person to place where she was before she got on the train."

"That's nothing. That's bullshit."

"Okay. How about this? Ehrlick left the killer's name at the scene as sure as if she'd written it on a mirror with her lipstick. May. The calendar said May."

"She grabbed her calendar and got the month of May. If she got April, would you be scouring the city for a woman named April? If it was December, what would you do then?"

"It wasn't December. It wasn't April. It was May."

"I want to be there when you bring this to the DA. Can I be there? I could use a good laugh."

Paradiso just smiled, then pulled out a pad from his coat pocket. He showed O'Donnell a list of names.

"Twenty-five people say they heard Morrison remind Gil Lee exactly where to look for his goddamn scarf, the one that turned up wrapped three times around Iris Ehrlick's throat. Twenty-five people."

"And eight million people didn't hear her. How about fingerprints? You ever hear of those?"

"Oh, and I guess you never heard of gloves. Fine. Let's move on to this. She was shopping, but no one remembers her, when Chuck Mills got dead. No one. What is she, the Phantom? She glides through crowds, but not one person sees her? You want to believe that, be my guest. I'm sticking with what I know, and what I know is she turns up on the phone-call list of victim number one even though she claims they never ever talk. Victim number two is someone she has publicly said she hates and wishes would vanish from the earth? Still not enough?"

O'Donnell was quiet now, seething. He didn't buy this crap, but Paradiso was like a ferret, digging up these half-baked snippets of nothing. But the nothing was piling up high enough that he might actually convince someone, someone desperate to have a live body to bring in for a change. The press was putting on the pressure. Paradiso was caving.

"I got my picture puzzle put together." Out of his inside pocket Paradiso pulled the Picasso Polaroid. Only he'd cut it up into pieces and pasted it back together in a closer approximation of a face. "You can't tell me that's not her."

"Now I know you're dreaming."

Paradiso ignored the comment. "You don't want to talk about the painting, let's talk about the cup of scotch she found in her trash."

"What was in that cup was not the cause of Chuck

Mills's death. Gil Lee's phone cord was the cause of Chuck Mills's death. Why don't you bring him in?"

"That's the one I want to see—when you march Gil Lee, Mike Wallace, and Walter Cronkite into the DA's office. Talk about a good laugh."

"You got a laundry list there. It adds up to nothing. Zero."

"I know. You're the big guy around here. I'm the runt from the streets uptown. So tell me, according to you, what do I need? You're not going to bring her in until she calls up and confesses? You're not going to get a search warrant until you see a videotape of the murder?"

"We're going to be working together for a long time," O'Donnell told his partner. "Even though it's obvious we're not each other's idea of a dream date. So let's concentrate on getting the job done right the first time. We're here to gather evidence, not wishful thinking. I know there's pressure, Paradiso. There's always going to be pressure. And, yeah, you got a few arrows there pointing over to Morrison. But there's nothing there that's good enough. You got to keep looking. And until you get something real, you got to keep your distance from her. Because let's say it is her. We got to do it so it sticks. We got to be sure."

"How many more bodies do you need to be sure?"

"I'm telling you, you're wrong here."

"But you're not telling me why." Before O'Donnell could answer, Paradiso went on. "I'm telling you you're not thinking clear about this babe. There's not one good reason not to bring her in. So let me bring her in. I'll question her. I'll crack her right open. It won't take any time at all. You can watch through the mirror if you want."

"Not yet."

"When? Tomorrow?"

"Not till you get something real."

"What I got is real. What you got is nothing." Paradiso studied his black shined shoes. "Twenty-four hours, that's all I'm waiting. Unless you come up with someone better in twenty-four hours, I'm bringing her in even if I have to climb over you to do it."

"Give me forty-eight," O'Donnell negotiated. He couldn't argue his way out of it any other way, not without looking as if he was protecting her.

"Two days?" Paradiso agreed, a happy man. "You got it."

They didn't bother shaking on the deal.

20

PETE WAS PACKING UP HIS TOOL-box when May walked in with her tired girls. Keeping up their end of the deal they had negotiated at McDonald's, Delia and Susie raced upstairs to prove they really could change into their pj's on their own, thereby earning doughnuts for dessert.

Pete led her down to the basement to show her the problem of the day.

"You ever notice the crack in the floor of your powder room?"

"Yes." It was hard to miss it, a scar that ran diagonally across the tiny black and white tiles from corner to corner.

"This post here"—he pointed to a column that ran from the floor to the ceiling—"it was never put in right. So the floor upstairs has sunk. And unless you shim it up, it's going to sink some more."

"What about this floor? Is the whole basement going to sink?"

"You're talking about the foundation of your house. I wouldn't worry about it. It's solid."

"What's it made of?"

Pete stared at her. It wasn't like her to get into these kinds of details. She was more a tell-me-what-I-need-to-do-it-right and how-much-will-it-cost-me? kind of homeowner. "It's concrete," he said, eyeing her.

"What's under the concrete?"

"Dirt. Look, I'd love to discuss your foundation with you, Mrs. Morrison, but can we do it tomorrow? I kind of got myself a girlfriend, and I kind of promised to take her to the movies tonight. Got any recommendations for a, what do you call it, woman's picture?"

For a moment May considered being honest with Pete, explaining that she was stalling because she really wanted him to stick around so she would have a witness who would testify she was home all night. But that was crazy. Bad enough she'd asked him to baby-sit her kids. She wasn't going to ask him to baby-sit her as well.

"They're having a Truffaut retrospective at the art museum," she suggested.

He rolled his eyes. "I better hurry in case there's a line. You going to be okay?"

"I'm fine," she said, as if willing it would make it so.

After doughnuts and milk the girls tried all their usual stalling tricks—"I'm still hungry," "I'm still thirsty," "Take my temperature," "One more story," and "I don't feel right." They never questioned why on this night their mother seemed just as willing as they were to stall, or why she kept announcing the time every half-hour. And what would she have said if they had? That it was because she wanted to be sure, if anyone asked them, they'd remember what time they'd come home, what time they'd had doughnuts, what time they'd had stories and gone to bed? Susie picked up on something, though. This night she took six stuffed animals in bed with her to make her feel safe.

As soon as their lights were turned off, May got on the phone. Her first call was to Margery, to check in.

"I'm glad you called, sugar. I've been meaning to call you all night."

"What's up?"

"Nothing good."

May braced herself. "Tell me anyway."

"I was up at the office, working late, when I passed by cop central. They thought no one was around, that we'd all gone for the day. I listened at the door. Let me tell you, May, that young fella, he wants your pretty little neck strung up for all the world to see. I don't know why. But he thinks you did it. All of it. He's sure of it."

After taking a moment to consider this, May confided to her friend, "The more I hear how sure people are that I did this the more I begin to wonder if it could be true. Think of that show Colleen did on multiple personalities. Maybe I'm a multiple. Maybe one of my other selves did it. Maybe I should get hypnotized to see for sure."

"Now, stop that. That's dangerous thinking. That's what they want. I called some of my friends downtown, and they told me Paradiso doesn't have enough, but he's on fire to get you, and sometimes that's worth more than a smoking gun. You can't waver, sugar. He smells doubt on you, he'll bring you in faster than a fly can get to honey. Problem is they have no one else. Nothing else. Just you."

"I have to find them a better choice."

"No shit."

"What about the scotch glass in my garbage that O'Donnell whisked out of my hand? What was that all about?"

"I'd say that was about a twenty-minute trip to the crime lab."

"Checking for what? Fingerprints? Blood? Poison? Was Chuck poisoned?"

"He was strangled. Least, that's what I heard. Course I don't know, for sure."

"I'll tell you who would know for sure."

"Who?"

May told her and then asked her friend if she could set up a meeting. Margery admitted it would be a tough one to pull off, but agreed to call in a few favors and give it a try.

May stayed on the phone for much of the night, calling old friends across three time zones, calls that would appear itemized on her next bill, with particulars like time of night and length of duration. By two her voice was hoarse and her store of old friends used up. She went up to bed and crashed to a sleep dense with chasing dreams. She woke out of breath several times in the night.

21

GIL'S WAKE-UP CALL SHOT HER out of bed. He was without apology as he explained that since Paula refused to go into the office for their morning meeting, they would hold it at her apartment instead.

"What's wrong with your face?" he asked her two hours later, when he opened the door to let May in.

She didn't want to tell him the truth, that she had woken up that way, her worry having taken a physical form: wide blotches of red on her cheeks, tiny bumps all up and down her neck.

"Windburn," she said quickly, remembering Bunny's admonition to keep Gil in the dark about her suspect status and her fear. "Pillow burn," she'd said when Delia had asked about it. "Allergic reaction to raspberry jam," she'd told Pete.

Wendy arrived and posted herself in the hallway as lookout against intruders and the press. Stephanie popped out of the kitchen to pass around a tray of drinks.

Bunny and Margery were the last to arrive. They entered breathlessly and marched over to Gil to report that when they stopped for coffee and a slice of marble pound cake at the Starbucks on the corner, they realized they'd been followed. The stalker was a man in a trench coat who began to sound, the more they described him, like Humphrey Bogart in *Casablanca*. They had every detail: the color of his shoes, of his scarf, of his hat.

"I knew it," Paula said, plopping down on her suede couch. "I just knew it." She turned to May. "At least I don't have to worry that it's you. Did you know half the office thinks you're the killer?"

"You've got to be kidding, sugar," Margery said, her voice a bit too cloying. "They said that about sweet thing, May?"

Colleen walked over to Margery. "Wait a minute. You're telling me that you two"—she walked over to Bunny—"went out for coffee together this morning?"

"What's the matter, sugar? You mad we didn't invite you along?"

"No. I'm just a little surprised. Not that I'd ever tell a soul the awful things you've each confided to me about the other."

May caught a flicker of guilt on Bunny's face and in an instant knew she and Margery had conspired to concoct this story to protect her.

"Didn't you hear that Bunny and Margery made up?" May asked Colleen. "You really are falling behind on the gossip."

Colleen wasn't buying it, but Paula, pacing across her antique rug, didn't give her a chance to get into it.

"Frankie, go check and see if he's hanging around outside my building."

The big lug—who'd been fired and rehired the night before and now sat like a Buddha, watching them from his perch on a tufted, tasseled hassock—got up and lumbered out of the apartment.

"Gil, if there's a stalker out there, that's it for me. Tape me here and edit in an audience later. That's my final offer. I am not stepping back in that studio until they catch this creep."

"Paula," Gil moved in quickly to calm her. "Colleen has raised a very good point. Since when do Margery and Bunny have coffee together?"

May could see it coming. To save his ass Gil was about to offer her up as sacrifice. But desperation made May a quick thinker. Acting on a hunch that Paula's bike pro, now boyfriend, Eddy, might go a long way toward bucking up her failing nerve, she quickly got Paula to agree to give her latest hunk of muscle a starring role on Friday's Valentine's Day chocolate show. With the promise that he would remain on the set for the whole hour, as a well-developed example of the benefits chocolate had on health, Paula begrudgingly gave the green light for the next morning's taping. To get Paula to allow chocolate doctor Richard Williams, whose name correctly indicated he was a member of the recently forbidden sex, to appear as the featured guest, Gil promised the entire front row of the audience would be filled with off-duty cops. As to whether or not Bunny and Margery had lied about their stalker. Gil no longer cared to pursue it now that Paula had agreed to come in.

At noon, ignoring Gil's protestations, May and Margery got up to leave. "Where are you two going? Why do you have to leave? We're ordering in lunch. You can have anything you want. Ben Benson's. Hatsuhana. Petrossian. Where the hell are you two going?" he shouted as they continued down the hall to the elevator.

"Don't give yourself a stroke, sugar. We're just going to get a bikini wax. We'll back in a couple of hours."

"Who's doing it?" Colleen called after them. "Is it Bella? Bella is the best in the city." But the elevator door shut her out.

They snagged a cab at the corner.

"Thanks for arranging this," May said, impressed that Margery had worked her magic so quickly.

"No problem. So you know, this favor is brought to you directly from Sergeant Sal DeMarco. Do you remember him?"

May couldn't forget the big, burly cop Margery had adopted for several months last year to hug and lug to theater openings and cocktail parties as though he were some prize she'd won.

"Want to make any last-minute confessions?" Margery asked as she paid the driver.

"Just that I'm scared out of my mind. And that I'm grateful for your help."

"Don't mention it. My mother trained me to be helpful to people in need. I couldn't stop now if I tried. Now, let's get going inside. We don't want to waste the doctor's valuable time. Not that his patients mind waiting," she added with a laugh.

They turned up their coat collars and stared at their feet as they brushed past cigarette-smoking cameramen and bored newspaper stringers lingering outside the New York City Medical Examiner's Office, just waiting for a break.

22

THE RECEPTIONIST IGNORED them as long as she could before finally sliding open her frosted-glass window. She waited with exaggerated patience for them to announce what the latest irritation in her day was going to be.

Margery handed over her card. "We have an appointment with Dr. Moss."

The receptionist slowly lifted the phone off its cradle. With a large fatty finger that was packed inside a size small plastic glove, she pressed a red button, then slid her window closed for privacy. She opened it seconds later with the instruction, "Straight back. The wooden door. Not the steel door." She narrowed her eyes. "The wooden door."

"How about a show on jobs we'd hate to have?" May suggested as they walked down the narrow hallway past metal doors on which they dared not knock.

When they got to the end of the hall, the wooden door seemed to open by itself. A squat rectangle of a man in a white lab coat hopped out from behind it, hand extended.

"Sorry I kept you," he sputtered.

May shook his hand, quickly looking away from the stains on his lab coat, especially the dark blotchy ones across his chest.

"I'm Margery Riegle. Pleasure to meet you." Margery

gave him a glorious smile behind which she struggled to suppress a gag.

He ushered them into his office, toward the two gray steel chairs opposite his gray steel desk. The smell was overpowering. Three Pine Scent Lysol cans stood at attention on his desk, caps off. Fir-shaped car deodorizers hung everywhere, dangling from bookcases, lampshades, even tied to the end of the venetian blind cords. The air stank of perfume.

"Do you think it smells in here?" he asked, noticing May's flaring nostrils. "My wife came in with me this morning, and her lividity went right to yellow. She is prone to that, though—a yellow, jaundiced look. Me, I don't smell a thing. How about you?"

May shook her head, politely, and felt all the color drain from her cheeks.

"Some people just have better smellers, that's for sure. I can understand it. Evolutionarily speaking that is. What I can't understand is rolling your tongue. What's the genetic advantage to rolling your tongue? Do you know?"

"I'm sure I don't," Margery admitted.

"Me either. My wife's theory is it's tied to sperm count. She's a biologist. She does cells. I do bodies. A couple of live wires, right?"

May forced a weak laugh.

"Pardon me a moment, would you?" He picked up the phone. "Gloria, can you go next door and pick up a few sandwiches? I'll have tongue." He looked at Margery. "And a roast beef on rye." He glanced at May. "And chopped liver. A double-decker." He put down the phone and told her, "You need some color in your face. You don't look healthy."

"Actually I'm not very hungry," May told him.

"So you'll take it home. Now, my wife," he said, finding his way back to his train of thought, "she can't roll her tongue for beans, but she has a nose like a bat. She also has an overdeveloped gag reflex. She won't ever eat here with me. I have to shlep to the deli. Should we have gone out?"

May heard a quick intake of breath as Margery got ready to break into the doctor's monologue, but she wasn't fast enough.

"She doesn't care that I'm allergic." He slid open his desk drawer. The sweet scent of potpourri wafted out like a cloud. He sneezed, then shut it. "She buys me this stuff by the bushel." He sighed, then seemed to notice he'd gone off track. "I forget. Who are we here to discuss?"

Margery jumped in. "Detective Sal DeMarco called you. May and I produce for *Paula Live,* the talk show. We're helping the detective out on his investigation of the recent talk-show murders."

He rubbed his forehead, thinking hard. "I don't know that show. I did watch one of them once, when Noguchi was on. It was *Oprah,* I think—something like that."

"It was *Oprah,*" May confirmed.

"She's the one married to Danny Thomas's son, isn't she? He was a fine man, Danny Thomas. Good strong bone structure."

"You're thinking of Phil Donahue."

"Right. She's married to Phil Donahue. I met him once at Gracie Mansion. He's got that white hair. Amazing thick hair but no color pigment whatsoever. You girls work for him?"

"We work on *Paula Live,*" May reminded him. "Do you know her?"

" 'Paula Live'? The name sounds familiar. Is she dead?" He rubbed his forehead. "We've had a couple of television personalities in here. The press has been swarming like maggots. We've locked them out. You didn't see any press out there did you?"

"Paula's alive," Margery explained, ignoring his question. She leaned forward in her chair as if getting ready to lunge. "She's our host. Her name is Paula Wind. The show is *Paula Live*. I'm a close friend of Detective De-Marco. He called and asked you to speak to me. He told you whatever you said would be held in deepest confidence." She waited, leaning toward him, willing him to understand.

"I think it was Gross who kept his TV going all day in the morgue. Face it, the patient is not going to be disturbed. Unless you have a family member present. Doesn't happen much, but every once in a while you get someone named after a building or a deli. Then you're stuck with them or their lawyers hanging around all day. You know what I do when that happens?"

"Well, actually," Margery tried to change the subject, but the doctor, on a roll now, couldn't stop.

"I don't mind telling you. It's no secret. I take out the buzz saw. Talk about a room emptier. I haven't met a person yet who stuck around once I got that thing crackling through the rib cage."

"Have you ever seen our show?" May interrupted.

"I never put on the TV or radio while I'm cutting. I don't want to hear anything that might make my hand slip. Not that it matters. After all, this isn't exactly brain surgery, is it?" He laughed at himself. "I have a cassette player. Vivaldi, Wagner—it depends on the body. I'm sorry. Did you want some coffee?" There was a light tap on the door. A slim technician walked in to deposit a brown grease-stained bag on Moss's desk.

"We just got the call, Doctor," the angular woman told him. "The Providence police found the head."

"Finally. Good. They got the head; it's their headache.

Ask them how they want the rest of the parts delivered." The woman let herself out. Moss opened the bag and unwrapped the wax paper packets. "You don't like chopped liver?" he asked when May left her sandwich untouched.

"I'm not hungry."

"You'll take it home, eat it later. So what can I do for you today? You're not reporters, are you?" He fumbled on his desk, looking for their cards.

Margery handed him another one of hers. "You do know Detective Sal DeMarco, don't you?" she asked, beginning to despair.

"Sal? Sure. Sure. He's a good friend. Spoke to him just this morning."

"Right. About me," Margery reminded him as she bit into her roast beef sandwich, pulling on and finally swallowing a long stringy piece in an effort to be a good sport.

"Sure. Sal called about you. I don't know where my brain is today. Left it in a jar downstairs," he said, laughing. "What did I say I would do?"

"You said you would tell us, off the record, the cause of death in the murders of Chuck Mills and Iris Ehrlick. We're helping Detective DeMarco investigate."

"I told him I would do that? I can't do that. I'm sorry. I can't discuss current cases. Anything else?"

Margery put her head in her hands. May fortified herself with a tiny bite of chopped liver and took the lead. "What about if we forget the particulars of those cases, Dr. Moss. What about if we just talk generally about your experience with serial killers. Did Detective De-Marco mention that we're planning on doing a show about serial killers? We'd love to know if you'd consider coming on as a guest expert."

The ME leaned back in his chair, mulling over the

offer. When he started patting down his hair and clearing his throat, May knew he'd been hooked.

"I'll tell you the first thing we do when we know it's a serial killer. We look for the pattern. Once we get the pattern, we're over halfway there. That's why my personal theory is these guys want to be caught. All a serial killer would have to do to throw us off the track is switch his weapon. So why don't they do that more often? Because they want to be caught. God forbid we ever get an ME serial killer." He thought about it for a moment. "I should take a look through my files."

"Dr. Moss." Margery, recovered, was back in form. "Can you at least say if the murderer was a man or a woman?"

"What murderer?"

"Any serial murderer," May jumped in to keep him from telling them of the press blackout yet again. "Serial murderers in general."

"Common sense." He stood up. He was just May's height. "Stand up," he told her, so she did. "I'm coming at you with a knife, I'm going to kill you. I'm bigger than you. I'm stronger than you. You know, you're not very tall at all," he observed.

"I know."

"So you're dead. Someone your size comes at me with a knife, I'm going to take it away from you. You're dead. Unless you're a black belt in karate. We have our exceptions."

"What about strangling?"

"Very straightforward. It's not like drownings. I hate drownings. Was it accidental? Who the hell knows? That's when you get families calling in the psychics. We had one last week. The woman wiggled her fingers and said, '*Oooh*, he's trying to tell me something.' A lot of mumbo jumbo. A corpse doesn't talk back. Period."

"If it's a strangulation," May tried, keeping him on track, "what's more likely, that it was a man or a woman?"

"Manual strangulation? Two hands around a neck?"

"Or with a scarf, a pair of panty hose," Margery offered, afraid he would veer off again.

"Depends. You're pretty tall; you look like you've got well-developed muscles. You probably work out at a gym three times a week."

"Personal trainer," Margery corrected him.

"Same thing, but okay. If someone like her"—he pointed to May—"wanted to strangle someone like you, how's she going to do it? She has a lot of choices, but they all amount to one thing, disable you first. Otherwise, you're going to fight back, and she's going get hurt. It's common sense. That's half the job, having common sense. What, are you writing a book on this or something?"

May forced a smile, but her impatience announced itself as her cheeks colored deeply once more.

"Will you look at that," the doctor exclaimed, leaning across his desk. "That is the most transparent skin I've ever seen." He got up and walked closer to better inspect her. "It's like the chopped liver went right to your cheeks."

May felt her whole body turn crimson.

"Holy toledo. Has it always been like this? Do you mind if I touch it?"

"Actually yes," May said, forcing another smile.

"Your skin is thin, but your teeth are nice and strong."

May pressed together her lips.

"So what about this talk-show killer," Margery tried, "man or woman?"

Dr. Moss wagged his finger at her. "Nice try, but we're on full press alert. Came from the mayor's office direct.

No details to be released. You girls work for a television show?"

"We're producers," Margery told him again. She sounded close to tears. "We're producers who are helping out Detective DeMarco."

"Right. The television ladies. Forgive me. I was in the decomposed room all morning. If you think it smells in here, you should stand around in there for a couple of hours. I tend to hold my breath for long periods of time when I'm in the decomposed room. Cuts off oxygen to the brain. Very dangerous. Makes me dizzy for hours. What can I do for you?"

"Detective DeMarco called. You told him you had news about the cause of death in the Ehrlick and Mills murders. You said it's not being divulged yet, but you'd let us know, off the record."

"Off the record? All right. All right. Ligature marks, eye hemorrhages—it's a no-brainer. We've got a couple of straightforward stranglings. We've also got a sadistic killer."

"How do you know that?" Margery asked.

"Because both victims had elevated blood-alcohol levels with large traces of Antabuse. Took a while to find the Antabuse, let me tell you. You don't see that too often, anymore. Used to be the drug of choice for curing drunks. Now, people prefer those spill your guts programs. I would, too, I guess. Because let me tell you, if you think drinking and driving don't mix, you should definitely not try an alcohol and Antabuse cocktail. It doesn't really burn up your insides, like drinking a quart of lye does, but that's how you feel. If I served you a drink like that right now, there'd be nothing you'd be able to do to stop the pain. You'd just have to roll around on the floor waiting until the goddamn stuff goes through you."

"Antabuse and scotch," May said, thinking of the glass in her garbage can. "Why would someone do that?"

"We're still off the record, right?"

May nodded.

"Because if you share any of this information, I will deny that you heard it from me. I'll deny that I ever met you. Is that understood?"

May and Margery nodded eagerly.

"It means that someone wanted to make their victims suffer like hell before they killed them."

The phone rang. He picked it up. "I know. I know," he said into the mouthpiece. Then he covered it with his hand. "Can you excuse me. If I don't get those arms and legs to Providence today, I'm going to have to bury them in my backyard."

"It's fine," Margery whispered. "We're done."

May let out a dim smile. The air fresheners were beginning to get to her now. If she stayed much longer, she'd have to avail herself of one of the airplane puke bags she'd noticed on top of the bookshelf behind the doctor's desk.

"Unusual skin," the doctor muttered as she left.

"Antabuse and scotch," May muttered in the hall.

23

MAY STUDIED THE MONITOR, watching the doctor explain it was his sweet tooth that drove him to study chocolate. Eddy, bonding with him immediately, jumped right in to share the anecdotal evidence that he biked faster after eating a Milky Way than he did after scarfing down two banana PowerBars. Paula, looking left out, admitted an affinity for hotel turndown pillow chocolates, then passed around a large basket filled with them for everyone in the audience to taste. The front row off-duty cops grabbed them by the fistful.

May struggled to concentrate. She stared at Gil, who couldn't stop twitching, rotating his neck, pacing, chomping on his nib. *Why couldn't it be him?* May asked herself. His alibis could have been carefully constructed to protect him while someone he hired did the dirty work. That happened. They'd done shows on that. It could be him.

Of course, the medical examiner believed the killer liked to see his victims suffer, which in itself made the probability of it being Gil unlikely. Around the office everyone knew better than to go to him with a physical complaint. His reaction, when those too green to know better sought comfort from him, was an unintelligible mumble followed by immediate flight.

The person to go to for comfort, the one who was

unflappable, unable to surprise or disgust, was May, who was also the one with no alibi at all. It wasn't fair— she'd never won a contest in her entire life, and now that she'd finally won first place, it was on the suspect roster of a murder case.

"The show looks great," Margery said, drawing her out of her misery. "You survived this one by a hair."

"Which one?" May snapped back, thinking, hoping maybe someone had gotten killed while she was stuck in the control room. At least then she'd have an air-tight alibi: four engineers who'd swear under oath she hadn't left the room for an hour. Then her children wouldn't have to be shipped off to Malibu and raised to be skinny, blonde, and tan. She wouldn't have to pass her time knitting them tennis skorts from her jail cell. It was bad form to wish someone else had died, but for now it seemed her only hope. "Was there another murder?" she asked, too quickly.

"I'm talking about your show, sugar. That bike pro seems to have cottoned to your doctor a little bit more than Paula appreciated." She walked over close to May so that only she would hear her whisper, "We need to talk."

"At least that's what it looked like to me, sugar," Margery went on, resuming her normal volume, winking at the techies, who laughed at her assessment. "In fact I wouldn't be surprised if the nice doctor ends up making a house call at Paula's tonight." She cozied up close again and whispered, "Smile and start walking."

As soon as they got to the hall, Margery dragged May to the greenroom, ignoring her pleas for explanations until they ducked inside. Remains of the morning's doughnuts sat, broken and hard; the air was heavy with the smell of stale coffee. Margery fell onto the old nubby couch and pulled May down with her.

"You've got one day to figure out who did it, or else they're bringing you in."

"What do you mean?"

"I've heard from two close personal friends that Detective Paradiso has been boasting to his buddies he's worked out a deal. In one more day if there's no one better, they're coming after you. Get yourself a lawyer, May. A good lawyer."

The door swung open. Paula entered smiling. "Here you are. So? What did you think of Doctor Chocolate?"

"Sweet," Margery said. "Very sweet."

"I think so, too," Paula agreed. "Thanks, May, for making me come in today. Listen, I'm going home. If you see Gil, tell him to let me know when my bathroom has been completely retiled. Until then I'm not stepping back inside my office. Got to go. Got a date." She winked and was gone.

There wasn't anything more to say. May and Margery left the studio in silence. Margery caught a taxi downtown for a meeting with another one of her sources. May went back up to her office, riding in the elevator alone, feeling nauseous, tasting bile in the back of her mouth, her shoulders and neck a relief map of ridges of tension.

The hallways were empty, nonessential support staff having been given the day off. The desolation was a perfect match for how May felt.

She walked quickly, spooked, past the open conference room door, the room still hazy from the smoke left behind by the cigarettes of half a dozen cops. She rushed past the area around the fax machine, deserted even by the machine itself, which the police had carted away as evidence of something. She walked into her office.

Paradiso was waiting for her, swiveling back and

forth in her desk chair. He stopped abruptly when she walked in. May froze, unsure of what to do.

"Have a seat," he said, studying her.

She sat on the wrong side of her desk, looking at the photographs of her children's gleeful faces staring at her from her credenza.

Paradiso followed her glance to Susie's and Delia's snapshots, then turned away, irritated. He put his hands behind his head, linking his fingers. She heard his foot tapping a beat. "You're a busy lady," he finally said, staring her down. "And I'm a busy man. So why don't we stop wasting each other's time."

"Okay."

"And don't bother holding your breath to get your cheeks to flame up. That doesn't do shit for me. I've seen guys make themselves sneeze, fart, puke, and fake a fever of a hundred and four. It means nothing to me. I am completely unimpressed. You got that?"

May felt as though she were far away, watching this happen to someone else, watching someone else nod their head and say, yes, I got that, sure.

He stood suddenly, sending the desk chair sliding back away from him. "Looky, lady. I'm dying to know. I want to learn something new. The only celebrities I've ever hung out with are famous junkies. So come on. Teach me something here. I want to learn. Why'd you do it?"

"Do what?"

He laughed as if she'd told him the funniest joke in the world. Then he stepped over to her. "Stand up."

She wanted to say no, knew there was no reason to comply, but she couldn't—she was so tired—so she simply rose.

He walked up so close to her that their noses were almost touching. "I'm going to get you."

"Am I breaking something up here?" Bunny barged in.

May jumped back, reclaiming her distance. Her body began trembling. Tears streamed down her face.

"What the hell is going on here?" Bunny barked.

"We're just having a friendly talk."

"Doesn't look too friendly to me."

"You should see it when it turns unfriendly."

"Don't say another word to this creep until you talk to your lawyer," Bunny told her friend.

Paradiso cracked his knuckles. "What are you a team? Bunny and Clyde? Hey, you want to do it this way, that's fine. I just figured you might prefer to cut the shit now rather than eat it later."

"Come on, kiddo," Bunny said to May. "We're closing early. I'll share a cab with you to the train."

In the elevator May began to shake all over, as if she'd suddenly come down with a case of the flu. Bunny made her stop in at the restaurant in the lobby of their building for a drink at the bar.

"He's trying to scare you, kiddo. That's all. Because he doesn't have anything better to do. You have to pull yourself together. You have to stay calm. It isn't enough to be innocent in this world. You have to act it, too."

All May wanted to do was to get home and be with her kids. She downed the rest of her wine and convinced Bunny she was better now, ready to go home. She just made it to the train. As soon as she sat down, she started making conversation with the woman next to her.

"I'm May Morrison. Do you ride the five-thirty-five every day?"

The woman, smelling the wine on May's breath, leaned away and closed her eyes. But May didn't care. All she needed was to be memorable. She couldn't keep up a conversation anyway. She was drained, exhausted, worn down.

This time she slept deeply, waking only moments before her stop. As she walked home, her sluggishness dissipated quickly in the brisk wind. She slid behind the wheel of her minivan. The car coughed, then started up. She drove too fast to Isabelle Donovan's house to pick up Susie, rehearsing her introductory speech to her unknown lawyer the whole way there.

The children first, she told herself as she got out of the car to retrieve her youngest. She plastered a smile on her face, walked to the door, and rang the bell.

24

SUSIE LOOKED AT HER MOTHER and burst into tears. May's other worries fled to the back of the line.

"They did great," Isabelle's mother reported. "She was happy all afternoon." Susie continued to wail, open-mouthed, her face like the one cartoonists drew to show despair. "I don't know what's wrong. She's probably just tired."

"I'm not tired," Susie screeched as May carried her all the way to the car.

When she rang the bell at Elisabeth's house, May watched through the broad parlor window as Delia's smile was replaced by a sullen mask. She saw her daughter grab her shoes, stick them behind the pillow of the plaid couch, then whisper urgently to her friend before diving behind the love seat.

Elisabeth opened the door. Rosy-cheeked with long, dark eyelashes that couldn't possibly be real but were, she smiled and said, "Delia's not here."

"I'm not going home," Delia insisted when she finally got into the car, then accidentally bit her lip. "Now look what you made me do," she wailed. Susie, too tired to find words, joined the fray with a purebred primal scream.

They're just as exhausted as I am, May reminded herself as the girls wailed in the back of the car all the way home until she couldn't stand it anymore.

"Go to your rooms," she barked as soon as they were inside, then instantly regretted it. She hadn't been with them for more than a few hours all week. Most of their time together had been spent like this, tears, screams, exasperation. Tomorrow, Saturday, their new au pair, Louise, was coming. That left only one more day for them to have the house, and each other, to themselves. Remembering Margery's warning she thought, *I only have one day left.*

"Let's start over again," she told her girls. "It's the weekend."

"How about a group hug?" Delia quietly suggested. They gathered in the hall, hugging tightly, the girls nestling into May as if they were trying to burrow their way to her heart. May's body shuddered. No one could tear her away from this. The world couldn't be that cruel. She'd done nothing wrong. A cry came out like a cough.

"What's wrong?" Delia asked.

"I coughed," May lied.

"Can we have a picnic for dinner, Mom?" Delia asked. "Please?" It was the end of the day, the time the girls always chose to test her resolve. Tonight the test was more challenging than usual.

May took a chance. "Sure."

"Mommy," Delia sang out, "I was only kidding. It's freezing outside."

Ignoring her daughters' wide-eyed stares, May fished out a red-checked tablecloth from the back of the linen closet, laid it out on the living room floor, changed into shorts, gave the girls their bathing suits, brought out sun hats and visors, turned up the heat so they would sweat, and lathered their cheeks and noses with sunblock. Then she banished all thoughts of Paradiso, Gil, Todd, Paula, Chuck, Iris, O'Donnell, Dr. Moss, and Ovaa-Iitas past and future so they could celebrate the unexpected arrival of a February summer's eve.

Taken off-guard by their mother's abrupt agreeableness, the girls returned the favor with complete compliance. In good humor, with no battles, they were bathed, storied, and in bed by eight-thirty. By nine May was on the phone with her cousin Ritchie. Ritchie was a good lawyer who'd helped her out on several closings, two versions of her will, and her divorce. This request was out of his league.

"You need a criminal lawyer," he told her after hearing her story. "I'm not a criminal lawyer."

"And I'm not a criminal."

"It's just words, May. Like 'civil' trial. They're never civil. It's just words. You understand?"

"I guess."

"I have a good friend from law school, Jack Forest. He's a brilliant guy. Pain in the ass but brilliant. I'll call him for you. Sit tight."

She did, just sat there, memorizing the details of her kitchen, her house, her life. She thought about how full her life was, how easily taken for granted, how easily taken away. Twice she picked up the receiver before it rang. Finally there was someone on the other end.

"Jack Forest, here," he boomed into her ear. "Ritchie

tells me you're in trouble. I owe that son-of-a-bitch something awful. Anyone else, I would have hung up the phone, calling me at nine o'clock on a Friday night. But Ritchie I owe my life."

May spilled out her story, giving details as requested.

"All right," Jack said when she was done. "I'm going to help you. I can't make any promises. I don't make any guarantees. But I'm going to help you. First thing—you don't like it, I apologize, but I have to ask—do you have anything, no matter how remote, to do with either of these crimes?"

"No."

"Good. Do you have any idea, no matter how remote, of who committed either of these crimes?"

"No," she said again.

"Can you spell the name of the detective who's gunning for you."

May did.

"There's two ways I can buy you some time here. Either way is fine with me. Let's start with the easy one. Has Detective Paradiso impugned your reputation in any way?—because if he has, that's good. That's actionable. That's defamation. I can stop him if he's made any statements in front of your coworkers accusing you of committing these crimes."

She thought about it, then said, "He did refer to my colleague Bunny and me as Bunny and Clyde."

"Is 'Clyde' a nickname? Anyone call you that at work?"

"No," she answered.

"Then forget it. That's one for Bunny's lawyer, not me. Who's Bunny's lawyer? These things are even better if we go in together."

"I'll find out."

"Good. Let's move on to battery and assault. Bottom line: has the son of a bitch touched you?"

"Does harassment count?"

"Harassment? That's just a cop doing his job."

"Intimidation?"

"Very hard to prove. If I'm a tough questioner and you're a delicate flower, you might feel intimidated, but that's not my fault. If you feel threatened by him, that's different. We can work with that. I'm talking physically threatened."

"He's never touched me, but he's come so close I could feel his breath on my cheek."

"Breath on your cheek? I can go with breath on your cheek if you don't have anything better. It's not much, but you're Ritchie's cousin. So here's the deal." Jack spoke so fast he made May breathless. "I'll track him down tomorrow."

"Tomorrow's Saturday."

"Not a problem. He won't like it no matter what day I tell him. For starters I'm going to threaten to bring action for assault. That should give you some more time. That's what you want, some more time, right?"

"Yes."

"Okay. I'll get you some, not much. But I'll tell you, if this guy wants to bring you in, he'll find a way. And if he finds a way, you call me. Day or night, whenever." He gave May his office number, his private line, his beeper, his secretary's home number. "It's going to be okay," he told her, but didn't sound too convinced. "If he lays a hand on you, it'd be even more okay. If he comes that close again, so close you can feel his breath, maybe you can help things along. He lays a hand on you, he's mine and you're rid of him. Do you know what I'm saying?"

May did and the thought of it kept her awake for half the night.

25

SHE WOKE TO THE SOUND OF THE doorbell, shot up in bed thinking of Paradiso, and checked the clock. Somehow night had passed. It was seven-fifteen in the morning. She threw on her robe, raced down the stairs, and then stopped just before opening the door. In the next moment her life might be forever changed. She unlatched the lock and threw the door open. A plump man with a thick, frozen mustache grinned widely as he handed her two long boxes.

"Got to get an early start today," he told her. "Valentine's Day," he reminded her, winking. "Doubleheader for you." He winked again, then ran back to his small white truck.

She threw the boxes on the kitchen table and ripped off the lid of the first, irrationally mad at the box, at the doorbell, at the delivery man. Mad that she'd been woken up and frightened. She lifted a small envelope out of the box and focused on wondering who had sent them. Maybe Gil, she thought, in apology for all the aggravation at work these past few days. But Gil wasn't a roses kind of guy. More likely it was Paula, suffering from a middle-of-the-night panic attack that she'd been too hard on her. Detective O'Donnell's face briefly passed through the lineup—an intriguing idea until she remembered she was just a suspect to him. Paradiso, she thought, but discarded that choice, since, after all, the roses weren't dead.

She pulled a cream-colored card out of the envelope. "To Delightful Delia," it said, "Happy Valentine's Day, with love, Daddy." She didn't bother opening the second box, the one for Susie. She left the long-stemmed beauties to wilt on the table and crept up to bed, imagining, with each step, the plunging of a thorn into another one of Todd's organs: a hole in his trachea, a puncture in his lung, a perforation in his liver. She crawled under the covers. The brand-new phone on her night table rang, too loud.

"Hi, Mom." She tried to sound cheerful. From Delia's room she could hear the sound of quiet singing.

Her mother sighed. "I won't tell you what day it is today, dolly."

"I already know."

"Let me know if you get any cards. Other than mine. Mine is in a purple envelope. You don't have to call me if you just get mine. Happy Valentine's Day, dolly."

After yelping with delight when they saw their flowers, the girls pleaded to call their dad and thank him. May briefly considered explaining what a time zone was, but then decided the concept was too advanced for them and agreed.

Delia dialed, gushed for several minutes and then passed her the phone. "Daddy wants to wish you a Happy Valentine's Day, too."

"Are you completely insane or merely demented? It's four-thirty in the morning here," Todd growled.

"Thanks, dear," she replied. "Same to you."

In the end it was the best Valentine's Day she'd had in years. As always Delia and Susie forced her to stay in the present, forcing even the awful fears haunting her—visions of being carted away and locked up forever—to be tabled for later. They had grander things to deal with, for example the pile of cards they'd made. It had become a contest, who could make more cards for Mommy, and the bounty was hers. There were a dozen pictures of tadpolelike figures—Susie's—surrounded by strange objects she took to be hearts. Delia, better able to manage a marker, had made more elaborate master-pieces, stick figure families with speech bubbles pro-claiming their love. Carried along by their own enthusiasm, they next insisted on bringing her breakfast in bed. She gave up trying to explain how that was more of a Mother's Day tradition and settled back on her pil-lows to enjoy the feast the girls had lovingly prepared: every kind of cereal they could find mixed together in a bowl swimming with milk, a large apple rubbed to a shine, and a mug filled to the rim and spilling over with orange juice.

Breakfast lasted so long it merged with lunch, and then it was time to go to Newark Airport to pick up Louise. Along with the rumpled other passengers disem-barking from their on-time flight, their new au pair ap-peared looking just like her photo, crisply dressed with a cheery smile.

"We're going to have quite a bit of fun," she told her charges. "I can see that. My two beautiful girls, brighter than the sun.

"Would you help me find my bags?" she asked them. "We're looking for one with Charlie Brown stickers all over it that might have some more stickers inside. And maybe some lollys as well. And some chocolate eggs. Probably Kinder Surprise. Have you not had them, chocolate eggs with little prizes hidden inside?"

"No." The girls, completely won over, each clutching one of their new best friend's hands, moaned at the thought of what they'd been missing all these years.

They wandered together to the baggage carousel. May watched, letting a small smile settle on her face.

"I'm glad to see you're picking up. I was worried you were taking off."

She swung around, and there he was, smug as ever, Paradiso.

"You wouldn't do that, would you, Mrs. Morrison? You wouldn't leave town now, with this case still open, would you? My partner did tell you not to leave town, didn't he? Or didn't he?"

He made it sound tempting. She could do it now, just hop on a plane, go somewhere far away with the kids, disappear. They'd had people on the show who did that. Except Paradiso's voice had made every one of her muscles constrict. She couldn't move a step forward, let alone across state lines.

Delia came running over. "We found the first bag." She noticed Paradiso. "Who are you?"

"A friend of your mom's."

"Oh," Delia said, then ran back to beat her sister out of pulling off the next piece of luggage.

May stood, watching over her children. Paradiso stood right behind her.

She swung around suddenly, facing him. "I'm not going anywhere. You can go home now."

"What a coincidence. I'm not going anywhere, either."

May waited. She waited until Louise had found all her bags, until Delia had taken two dollar bills from her and given them to a porter, until the porter had loaded the luggage onto the cart. She waited until she and her family were in a crush of people heading toward the exit. Then, with Paradiso so close behind her she could feel him pressing into her, she stopped, turned, and screamed, "Get your hands off me now."

Stunned, Paradiso stepped back, away from her.

"I said get your hands off me now."

It wasn't often you could hear a pin drop in the International Terminal at Newark Airport, but it was that quiet now. Paradiso knew better than to defend himself. He flashed his badge to an approaching security guard, and while he quickly explained himself, May and her family fled for home.

26

AWAKENED BY THE SMELL OF strong coffee, May lay still as a corpse for several seconds, trying to figure out if she was in jail. Afraid of what she'd find, she opened her eyes. She was in bed. Home. Safe. The weekend was over.

Sunday had passed uneventfully. Louise had busied herself unpacking, settling in, while the girls took turns recounting their life stories in excruciating detail. As it always did, Monday came too fast.

May got up and showered, was pulling her black chenille sweater on over her narrow black pants when her alarm clock went off. She was fifteen minutes ahead of schedule. This was a first. She inhaled the scent of the coffee and thought, *This is it; this is as lucky as it gets.* Now that she was about to be hauled off to jail, she'd finally struck gold in child care.

She found Louise in the kitchen wrapping a washcloth around Pete's left hand. "I was in the loo when poor Mr. Jackson turned on the faucet in the kitchen sink," the au pair explained. "When I flushed, he ended up positively scalded. He hasn't been here more than five minutes and already he's wounded."

"I'm fine," he told her, turning, embarrassed, back to May to focus on something concrete. "You probably need a new valve, but I'm not a hundred percent sure yet."

"Jolly good news to wake up to all around, then."

Pete waited, then asked May, "Don't you want to know how much it's going to cost you?"

"Oh. Right. How much is it going to cost me?"

"You okay, Mrs. Morrison?"

Louise studied her, waiting for her response. On Saturday when May had tried to explain away her encounter with Paradiso, she was delighted Louise was so easily satisfied by her story—that it was a big problem in America, getting felt up by strangers in airports, and the best way to handle it was to just walk away. But now she saw Louise hadn't been quite so appeased. Suspicion lingered.

"I'm fine," she told her contractor. "How much?"

"I don't know yet," Pete reported. He went down to the basement to figure it out.

May disappeared upstairs to wake the girls. They followed her down, still sweet with the residue of sleep.

"Good morning, princesses," Louise greeted them. "I've got a wonderful breakfast surprise for you. Have you ever eaten coddled eggs? They're the queen's favorite breakfast, you know."

"Susie has to bring a snack for her class today," May remembered, just in time, as she buttoned up her coat. "Graham crackers, top shelf of the pantry."

"Will do," Louise said.

"Mom, did you buy the cherries?" Delia called out from her perch atop the stool Louise had moved close to the stove top so she could watch the eggs coddle.

May froze. Delia didn't notice.

"I need them for Washington's birthday," Delia explained to her baby-sitter. "For the fruit tree we're making today. For the play." She turned back to her mother. "You got them, didn't you?" Her voice dropped. "You promised you would."

She had promised to do it. She'd meant to do it. She had planned to take a taxi downtown at lunchtime Friday. She'd planned to go to Balducci's and if they didn't have them, to Dean and Deluca. She was willing to go all the way up to the Fairway in Harlem if that's where she needed to go to find fresh cherries in February.

"Don't say it." When Delia looked down, her dark eyelashes spread out like a fan over her wide cheeks. "I know. You didn't have time."

"I had time, sweetie. I just forgot." She couldn't explain why she'd forgotten, that the detail had gotten upstaged by other concerns—life, liberty, the pursuit of a killer.

"I guess I'm easy to forget."

"Not to worry," Louise piped up. "We'll just pop round to the greengrocers on our way to school and see if they've got any frozen or canned. We do at home. I'm sure you must. It's America. You have everything."

Delia gave Louise a hug so tight May felt it, like a slap.

When May got to work, she was confronted with a new security system blocking her entrance onto her floor. The machine was set up to admit only those people whose voices had been programmed in. Somehow Wendy had forgotten to have the technician stop by to record May's voice.

May used her shoe instead, flung it against the double doors leading into reception, causing the ear-splitting wee-wong of another new alarm system. In a heroic gesture May would have to reward with a lunch somewhere good, Linda grabbed the sleeve of the new security guard's navy jacket just as he reached for his gun.

After registering her complaint with Wendy, May marched into her office to find O'Donnell standing there waiting for her. Paradiso was sitting on her love seat. She walked in slowly, took her seat behind her desk, trying to read the situation.

"Good morning," O'Donnell said.

That's good, May thought. *He's not reading me my rights.* "Good morning," she replied, then dared a glance at Paradiso, who glowered but said nothing. *Good again,* she told herself. *Jack Forest did his job.*

"Is this going to be another one of your friendly chats?" She had directed the question to Paradiso, who turned his head to look out the window. "Your partner wants me to confess to something I didn't do," she told O'Donnell.

"My partner is eager to find a killer, Mrs. Morrison. Maybe he's a little bit overeager. It sometimes happens when you get a lot of bodies piling up."

"Three," Paradiso called over. "You knew it all along, didn't you? That Barnett would end up on the list."

"It's official," O'Donnell explained. "We're looking for a serial killer."

"Does that mean you'll bring in the FBI?"

"The New York City Police Department doesn't need the FBI," Paradiso snapped.

O'Donnell ignored the outburst and slid a pile of papers across her desk. "You remember when I showed you Miss Ehrlick's phone list?"

"Yes."

"Would you mind taking a look at this?" When she hesitated, he added, "Don't worry. It isn't hers."

She lifted a corner of a page to peek.

"This one belonged to your good friend, Chuck Mills," Paradiso blurted out.

O'Donnell looked over his shoulder and glared at his partner, who glared right back.

May let the pages slip out of her hand. O'Donnell reclaimed them, flipping through until he got to the bottom of page three. He slid it over to her, his long index finger pointing to her name.

"Mr. Mills's secretary"—he checked his pad—"Dolores Maginn, said she told him she thought it was pretty strange that he got invited to a party here. According to Miss Maginn, Mr. Mills was calling you to check it out. Miss Maginn said it surprised her that he chose you to call. She said you couldn't stand each other."

"I've admitted that already. You'd have disliked him, too, if you ever met him."

"Lucky us," Paradiso said. "All the shit-heads we meet are already dead."

Her cheeks began to burn.

"Miss Maginn said not only did you dislike her boss, you disliked her, too."

"I don't even know her. I don't have any idea what the woman looks like."

"She looks a lot like you," O'Donnell reported. "Maybe younger. And not as pretty."

Suddenly her office felt tight, closed in.

"Mrs. Morrison"—Paradiso interrupted his partner's questioning—"why don't you explain to us how come you never mentioned Chuck Mills called you. And then, why don't you tell us why you never called him back? Was it maybe because you knew there was no point? No point in calling a guy you were going to meet later that night, going to meet for the purpose of getting him dead?"

"I'm calling my lawyer," she said, searching her desk for Jack Forest's number. "Chuck Mills never called me." She lifted memos, clippings, letters, shaking out stacks of paper. She knew she'd jotted Jack's number down somewhere.

She didn't bother hiding it when she found a message slip from a dead man at the bottom of the pile. Her cheeks turned into stop signs. "I guess he did call me."

"Nice," Paradiso observed.

"I never called him back. I didn't see the message until now." And she thought, *If I had, would he still be alive?*

"Do you mind if I hold on to that please?" O'Donnell asked. "You don't need it anymore, do you?"

May handed it over. "I never called him back."

"I know," O'Donnell said, then stood up. "Thanks for your time," he told her.

Paradiso followed him, backing out of the room so that he wouldn't lose sight of her. "By the way," he said real quietly so that no one else could hear, "I never laid a hand on you and you know it."

She tried to stare him down, but he wouldn't look away.

"Don't worry. I won't touch you. I don't need to touch you. I'm rehabilitated. You've taught me I need to be a patient man. So I'm going to wait. And I'm going to watch you." He stopped in her doorway. "You might want to go home now and pack. But don't take too much. You don't get to keep too many personal items in jail."

Home was exactly where she wanted to go, but Margery snagged her and dragged her into a meeting.

Paula's secretary was standing up. "She's gone."

"Paula is not gone," Gil protested. "She just hasn't arrived yet."

"Monday morning is her standing manicure, hair, and facial appointment," Patty explained. "She only has me cancel if she's going out of town, and she didn't call to have me cancel. You understand what that means?"

"She's going to be hairy and grumpy." Bunny offered.

"She's home," Colleen said. "Sleeping in."

No," Patty reported. "The doorman knocked, rang, and buzzed. She's not home."

"She's on her way in," Colleen said as if she knew. "She's in a taxi right now." She couldn't afford to entertain the idea that Paula might not show up. Tuesday was the female physicians. Thursday was Demi Moore.

At lunchtime Gil gathered the producers in his office. "Okay. Here's the deal. We've got ten shows in the can."

On cue Wendy held up a large calendar, red *X*'s marking the days.

"This puts us just out of sweeps. Now, I know Paula will be in tomorrow, but let's pretend, for argument's sake, she's gone out of town. We can still air for two weeks, no sweat."

May noticed a droplet trailing down the side of his head, following his hairline.

"She could be dead," Bunny pointed out.

"She's not dead," Gil screamed.

"We should call Detective O'Donnell," May said.

"I'm scared," Colleen admitted.

"Call no one," Gil yelled. "Paula is fine. She has gone off somewhere to be alone. Trust me. I will find her. In the meantime, anyone asks you where she is, you tell them she's in a meeting and can't be disturbed. If one of those detectives appears at your door, you plead ignorance and direct them to me." He was spitting now as he raged. "Everything is fine."

27

THE TRAINS WERE MESSED UP, and by the time she got home, it was just after eight.

"Both girls were rather tired. When they asked me if they could turn in a bit early tonight, I said all right. You don't mind that, do you?"

It wasn't hard to envision them exhausted, but it was impossible to imagine either girl would volunteer for an early bedtime. They were sleeping now, though, so May couldn't do any reliable fact-checking.

"Delia's homework is done. The laundry is done. I've tidied their rooms and the basement," Louise reported. "I'm up to my room to write letters. Night, night."

Her tone seemed cold, her manner distant, if May could trust her overtired perceptions. But she didn't bother to try to figure it out. She was so run-down she felt run over. Wearily, she checked window and door locks, then climbed upstairs to check on the girls. In their sleep they looked safe and serene.

As she undressed for bed, May thought of Paula, wondered if she had run away, tried to picture her in trouble. But despite Paula's endlessly mutating phobias, she just wasn't the victim type. She was too finely tuned to anyone who entered the range of her personal radar, too finely tuned to herself. May might be surprised to find a black-and-blue mark on her leg and have no idea of how she'd gotten it, but Paula would know the time to the second it had occurred. Paula memorized each beauty mark, each mole, even, it seemed, each hair follicle, in an effort to better conduct her vigilant search for everything from wrinkles and facial hair to faint blue spots that might, in a decade's time, turn out to be a varicose vein. Everyone she met was likewise studied for laugh lines, Band-Aids, knit brows, hair sheen, stutters, muscle tone, and phlegm. Paula would have no compunction crossing the street to avoid an oncoming walker who posed no more threat than appearing distracted. She memorized taxi drivers' names and license numbers. She wasn't the type to be easily surprised by an assailant. At least, not one she didn't know.

May tried to shake off the tension, to stretch the knots out of her neck, but she couldn't. The night lay ahead of her like a long road to nowhere. She didn't want to lie in bed tossing in the sheets, concocting poisonous cake recipes to bake for Todd as a belated Valentine's Day gift, or for Paradiso. She decided to try a hot shower to unwind.

The strong pressure supplied by the brand-new water heater Pete put in earlier that day beat down on her like little whips that made her breasts ache. She stood there, receiving the water's lashing; she couldn't have said for how long, didn't realize her eyes were closed until she opened them and found herself face to face with the thick white bath towel she'd draped between the slats of the grate atop her mirrored shower door, whose opaque white interior panel gave the stall the privacy of a tomb. She stood there perfectly still and watched as her towel slowly moved through the grill. Someone, she thought as goose bumps sprouted on her arms, was on the other side of the door pulling on it.

She looked around. It was pathetic. To fight back she had the choice of a pinkie-sized sliver of Ivory soap, a nearly empty plastic bottle of Dry Scalp Head and Shoulders shampoo, and her own clipped short fingernails. She was unarmed, soaking wet, and naked.

If she'd been alone in the house, she might have shrieked, prayed, and waited for the end. But all she could think of now were her two children sleeping unguarded down the hall and of their motherless, Chloe-filled future.

The white towel continued its steady withdrawal up and out until the tag in the corner got stuck in the grill. Then with an unmistakable tug, it was gone.

She took a deep breath and thought, *What would Paula do? What would Oprah do? What would Arnold Schwarzenegger do?* Enhanced with adrenaline-infused strength, she propelled herself forward, smashing open the door.

The crash of her upholstered bathroom stool mingled with a piercing wail. Susie lay on the tile floor, her nose spurting blood. May moaned as she bent down to wipe her daughter's nose with the white towel that lay puddled at her feet. As Susie howled, May quickly examined her to make sure nothing besides her nose had been bruised in the fall. Then May picked her up and carried her, murmuring, "It's all right, it's all right, Mommy's here," as if it hadn't been Mommy who'd caused her pain in the first place. May was standing there, naked, blood dripping between her breasts, when Louise appeared in the doorway.

"Is she all right?"

Susie looked up and stretched her arms out toward her baby-sitter, as if maybe Louise could do what her mother wasn't able to—make the hurt go away.

Softly, Louise began to sing, "Clap handies, Mommy comes. Bring little Susie sugary plums."

Desperate to escape her pain Susie's eyelids instantly

shut. She lay her soft, damp cheek on Louise's shoulder. May gently dabbed the blood off her daughter's tiny lip with a corner of the towel. When Susie winced, Louise pulled back, ever so slightly.

May suddenly felt cold and very exposed, standing there naked and wet. She watched as Louise carried Susie away, back to bed. Then she quickly slipped into her bathrobe, and turned off the shower. By the time she got to her daughter's room, Louise was gently laying Susie down.

"I thought someone had broken in," May explained, but she knew it sounded ridiculous, improbable, hysterical.

"It's not my business," Louise said, but her words didn't hide the judgment in her voice as she turned and marched up to bed.

Cold water on her face couldn't cool down the heat in May's cheeks. For the second time that night she checked every door, every window, moved the phone into her bed, forced her fists to unclench. She got up at fifteen-minute intervals to wake Susie, checking to be sure she hadn't suffered a concussion. In between that she struggled, unsuccessfully to make her eyes stay shut.

There were moments in the night when she drifted off to sleep—a minute here, a few more there. But it wasn't until the first chirp of the earliest dawn-loving birds that she finally allowed herself to plunge into a light sleep, still ready, at a moment's notice, to spring out of bed and fight back.

28

IN THE MORNING SUSIE SAID HER nose felt funny, but since the sight of the purple bruise would surely make it feel even worse, May worked interference to keep her from checking it out in the mirror. Pete, who'd been tinkering under the sink to find out why, now that he'd made several repairs including installing the new water heater, the pressure in the kitchen had dwindled to a trickle, didn't help things when he congratulated Susie for making it through the school of hard knocks.

May watched Delia's eyes narrow with jealousy, watched as she abandoned her bowl of cereal and began walking into walls saying, "Ouch, ouch, ouch." Unschooled in the art of subtlety, she pulled at Pete's legs until he slid out from under the sink.

"Is my nose purple yet?" she asked.

"Why don't you tell your mum about the hat we made yesterday," Louise suggested to change the subject.

To May's surprise, Delia obediently returned to her seat and, between mouthfuls of Rice Krispies, explained that she and Louise had worked all afternoon to make her hat for the Crazy Hat Day parade, which her first grade class was to lead. Constructed out of toilet paper tubes and old batteries, hers was to be the crown of the Queen of Recycling.

With Susie's multicolored nose now integrated into

the scenery of her life, Delia went on, in minute detail, to explain exactly how they'd finally managed to get the tubes to stick to the paper frame. Weary with lack of sleep, May drifted in and out of the conversation. She replayed the accident in the shower, saw the blank face of a killer stalking her, saw Paradiso stalking her, imagined Todd bursting into the room like some superhero to rescue his girls.

Suddenly she felt Delia pause, knew she was waiting for a response. To be safe she let out a soft sympathetic laugh. Susie continued to chew on her bagel, oblivious, but Delia, Louise, and Pete all stared at her as if she'd told them to swallow a rat. "What's wrong? What did I say?"

Delia stomped up to her room.

Louise was eager to explain. "If you'd been listening, you'd have heard her tell you that last year, when she wore your spangled beret for Crazy Hat Day, she was the only child in the entire school who hadn't created a homemade hat. She said all her classmates laughed at her. Even her teacher laughed at her."

"And then I laughed at her."

"I must admit you're fair about it; you don't actually favor one girl over the other, do you?"

"Don't feel you have to be charming all the time," May said. "Make yourself at home."

"I'm going to check out the heater in the cellar," Pete put in, eager to get out of the way.

When May bent down to give Susie her good-bye hug, she accidentally pressed too hard against her nose, causing Susie to howl in pain. Delia refused to come down and acknowledge her mother's departure at all.

On the train May tried to disappear into the daily papers, her eyes passing over columns of newsprint, but not a word sunk in. When she got to her building, she breezed past the reporters without hearing their calls, wasn't even aware that her elevator was so full it approached the legal limit of occupants. When its doors opened, she walked into a mob.

Margery spotted her and pulled her to a corner where her laptop and cellular phone lay on the dark brown fur of her coat. "Don't step on my desk, sugar," she said as she guided May to a spot just beyond her splayed out possessions.

"Gil's gone completely out of his mind," she went on to explain. "First he announced that everyone has to go through a metal detector, which, if you've had even one tooth filled, I suggest you refuse to do. You'll set it off by smiling at it."

May glanced around the lobby, saw Henry scanning the out-of-town papers, the receptionist, frantic, on a cell phone. She continued searching the crowd, checking to make sure Paradiso wasn't lurking, watching her.

Margery continued. "He's got an old coot with a lie detector waiting for us in the conference room, which is bad enough. But when I heard he hired a supposedly female guard to frisk us, I organized this little strike."

Gil came out through the double doors. An alarm sounded, then died.

"People." He clapped his hands three times quickly, like an irritated grammar school principal. The grumbling crowd quieted. "I am not doing this for me. I am doing this for you. There's a madman on the loose. I'm trying to make this place safe for us all."

"There's more than one madman out there," a gravelly voice muttered.

"Who was that?" Gil snapped. "If the person who said that does not come forth right now, I'll fire you all."

May spoke up before Bunny could turn herself in. "We're all on the same side here, Gil. If you need me to prove it to you, I'll take a lie detector test. I'll gladly go through your metal detector. But why are you concerned about a gun? No one's been shot. Why don't you start checking desk drawers and briefcases for Antabuse if you want to do something productive."

The room became still.

"What are you talking about?" Gil asked, his voice low, his panic temporarily contained.

"Yeah. What are you talking about?"

May swung around, and there he was, Paradiso, materializing out of a shadow.

Margery sidled up next to her. "Ignore her. She's just babbling."

Paradiso came closer. He wanted this to be a private conversation. "I know how I know about the Antabuse," he quietly told May. "Now I want to know how you know."

"We both know," Margery said.

"Fantastic. And how exactly do you ladies come by this information, which as of this moment is something known by a handful of people, by which I mean two kinds of people. Police people and murderer people. You're not police are you?"

"We were told by. . . ."

"Confidential source," Margery cut May off. "We were told by a confidential source."

Paradiso's eyes went from May to Margery to May again. "Who?"

The elevator bell rang. May jumped. The doors opened, letting out no one.

"Nervous," Paradiso observed. "I don't blame you. I'd be plenty nervous, too, if I were you."

"What's the problem?" Gil asked, joining them. "What's this about Antabuse?"

"Ask her," Paradiso said, looking at May.

"Confidential source," Margery repeated, louder.

"All right. That's just fine." Paradiso pressed the elevator button. "But if I were you, I'd put a call in to my confidential source and ask—and beg him to come along downtown and make a statement on your behalf. I've got some paperwork to do. You don't have too much time."

The elevator appeared and Paradiso withdrew inside.

"All right, people," Gil said, clapping his hands again. "The show is over. Let's make a line. Miss Meddleson is waiting."

"This is demeaning, Gil," Margery yelled.

"Demeaning? I can't argue with that. But here's your choice: Do you want to be demeaned or do you want to be dead? Demeaned or dead? Demeaned or dead? Take your pick." Sweat was dripping down his face, detouring around his eyebrows, hugging his ears. "I've hired an entire platoon of the best security force available in New York City because I'm concerned about your safety. And hers. And hers." He began pointing through the crowd—Maria in the final scene of *West Side Story.*

"Do you want to take a vote?" he asked. "Would that be more fair? I'll take a vote. How many of you would rather be dead than frisked? Clap your hands. See? No one."

Try again, sugar," Margery shouted out. "How many of you would like to have some stranger rubbing her hands all over your body?"

The techies hooted and applauded.

"All right, now. Y'all know what I mean. Who wants to be frisked by Attila the Nun?"

Gil clapped his hands once more, asserting control. "That's it. No more choices. If you want to live, line up to the right of the double doors and be prepared to be admitted one at a time. If you'd rather face unemployment or death, you're creating a fire hazard. I have to ask you to leave."

Begrudgingly a line was formed. May got on the end of it—unemployment and death both being unacceptable to her. Anyway, she needed to get into her office. She needed to call and ask, and beg, Dr. Moss to admit to what he'd told her.

Her thoughts were interrupted when Gil marched past her over to Margery, who remained planted in front of her ad hoc desk.

"Fire hazard," Gil said.

Margery stretched herself to her full five feet nine inches—five eleven in heels—putting her just high enough to look down at the top of Gil's head. "I'm doing it, sugar. I'm going to walk through your metal detector. I'm going to let myself get all hooked up to your truth machine. But if that woman lays one of her latex-gloved hands on my body, I'll bite her head off."

A bell announced another elevator's arrival. Colleen stepped out, her expression instantly turning perplexed.

"Then I believe this car is for you," Gil told Margery, graciously extending his arm.

Margery strode to the end of the line, cursing, muttering, awaiting clearance.

It was May's turn to be felt up by the prison matron when Wendy burst into the room.

"Gil. She's alive," she quickly sputtered, adding the news that Paula had called from Sun Valley, where she was vacationing with Doctor Chocolate. "She told me she'll book her return," Wendy reported, "the minute the murderer is caught."

"I'll kill her," Gil snarled, then saw the wide-eyed

stares around him, the prison matron's eyes widest of all. "But first I'll kill you."

The drably dressed guard touched one latex-gloved hand to her mouth, then grabbed her purse from the table behind her and ran screaming to the elevators, giving the reporters in the lobby downstairs a lively treat for their evening news.

29

THROUGHOUT THE DAY GIL further fortified the office with motion detectors, anti-bugging devices, and a full-time fingerprint technician. With each upgrade in protection he called Sun Valley to report in, but Paula languorously reiterated the position that she would return only after the killer was caught.

May asked Linda to buzz her if Paradiso arrived back on the floor and told Henry to hold all calls except those from her kids. Then she closed herself in her office and tried Dr. Moss once again. Once again he refused to take her call.

She took out the folder she now thought of as her murder file and reread her notes. She could no longer wait for someone else to make sense of it all. Despite Jack Forest's efforts, Paradiso was still after her. She didn't know how long she'd be able to keep him at bay, how long before the pressure became so intense she confessed just to put an end to it. And wasn't that exactly what he wanted?

She couldn't, she wouldn't give up without a fight. She would do whatever she needed to track down this bastard killer. With the razor sharp focus she used to build her most challenging shows, she grooved herself up by imagining the killer was her greatest "get," a hot, wily guest whom every producer in town was hunting down. *Colleen is tracking him, too,* she told herself. *Bunny and Margery are close on his trail. Inside Edition, Montel, Oprah, Tonya,* even *Regis and Kathie Lee are a breath away from discovering his identity. But this guest would be a May Morrison win.*

First step, as always, in outthinking the competition was to enter the head of the get. She did it well, her empathetic nature making it less of a struggle for her than for some.

I hate Barnett, she said to herself, getting started. *I hate Iris Ehrlick. I hate Chuck Mills. Who am I?* She sighed because the answer was anyone working in daytime talk. She tried again.

I carry around a stash of Paula Live *pens that have bitten-off nibs. I drop the pens at the murder site. Am I clumsy,* she asked, *or am I wily? Am I Gil, or am I someone who wants you to think I'm Gil?*

She thought of Gil's scarf, of Iris's and Chuck's call sheets, of the cup of scotch in her trash can. *Is it a coincidence that I keep climbing to the top of the suspect list?* she asked herself. *Or is it something that someone has meticulously planned?*

"Who?" she asked the empty room. "Who has it in for me?"

Her first thought was of Todd, but he was happy in his new life. He didn't need to get rid of her anymore. Chloe popped into her head, but she vanished immediately, having already easily disposed of May with minimal fuss. There was Ovaa-Iita, but she was out of the country. Besides, Ovaa-Iita wasn't bright enough to commit a series of carefully planned murders. Who was?

Her intercom buzzed. Henry's voice announced, "Your mother on two."

She picked up the phone. "I'm in a meeting, Mom. I'll call you later."

She hung up and underlined Henry's name on her list. He was bright enough. He was ambitious. He knew all the victims, at least by reputation. But what would he have to gain? It wasn't as if he'd get her job if she went off to jail. The only thing he'd get was unemployed.

Again she thought of Gil, and then immediately of Stephanie. Something had been bothering her about Stephanie. She couldn't put her finger on it, but she felt it in her gut. Stephanie knew something. Fumbling through her Rolodex, she found Gil's home number. His wife answered quickly, as if she'd been waiting for the phone to ring.

"Gil's so close to the edge," May told her. "I'm really worried. I hear they're worried upstairs, too. We need to talk. Can you come in for lunch?"

After rearranging her afternoon obligations, Stephanie met May in the Trustees' Dining Room on the second floor of the Metropolitan Museum of Art. From the museum staff's fawning attention May gathered Stephanie's year-end contribution must have been just short of the size that got museum wings renamed.

They managed to make small talk until the waitress took their order. Then, after checking in her compact mirror to see who was sitting behind her, Stephanie asked, "Is he having an affair?"

"No."

"Thank God. The whole way in I was thinking that must be it. Why else would May sound so desperate?

She's going to tell me he's having an affair with one of those pretty young associate producers."

"Gil doesn't mess around. You know that. It's the murders I'm worried about. You do know that most of the evidence points to Gil? He has told you, hasn't he?" It was just like Gil to protect Stephanie from the details of the investigation, to protect himself from her disapproval.

"Come on, now. You've known Gil a long time. Can you imagine him killing someone? Doesn't that usually involve blood?" She took a long drink of merlot from her goblet. "Let me ask you something. Do you know where Gil was on the day his children were born?"

May didn't.

"For Amanda he was in London, but for Bingham he went all the way to Hong Kong. That's how much he wanted to see the miracle of birth. At first he pretended the trips were for business, but he finally admitted it was because he didn't want to see their little gooey heads pop out. Did you ever see him get a paper cut? It's not a pretty sight."

"I don't think fear of blood would be considered an airtight alibi for murder."

"Gil, a murderer? I admit, the man knows how to kill a show. He can even kill a joke. But something alive, that bleeds and has squishy parts?" Her laugh was close cousin to a groan. "How about we let the detectives talk to my father about that one. He's told the story to practically everyone in the world already, how when we go to his cottage in Easthampton and sit out by the pond, if a mosquito lands on Gil's thigh, he'll call over one of the gardeners to swat it."

Very quietly May said, "If you strangle someone, there is no blood."

"When did you become an expert on strangling?"

May felt the charge of Stephanie's suspicion shoot through her. Maybe she'd been wrong about Gil keeping things from his wife. Maybe Stephanie knew more than she'd let on.

She leaned in closer and said, "May, did you really think I'd just meet you here without protecting myself?"

"What do you mean?"

Stephanie smiled, the picture of calm, as the busboy brought more bread. When he walked away, she said, "Between the time you called and the time I got here, Daddy hired eight former Secret Service agents to dine with us in this room. I bet you my diamond ring you can't figure out who they are."

May took in Stephanie's multifaceted diamond, which on any other hand she'd have assumed was overdone costume jewelry. Then she scanned the room. It was a white hair and gray suit crowd, no one distinguishing themselves from anyone else.

"I'm not the killer, Stephanie," May said quietly, so as not to be overheard. "Don't waste your money protecting yourself from me."

"One can't be too sure."

"I know what you mean," May admitted. "I've been toying with the idea that maybe it's you."

Stephanie's hearty laugh rang out so loud it surprised them both. "That's a good one, May." She leaned in close. "What on earth would I have to kill for? I have everything in the world I want."

May wondered what it was like to feel like that. She had to admit it, Stephanie didn't look like a desperate woman, even if that was only because she had a good plastic surgeon. Still, it didn't surprise her to hear Stephanie's claim to a satisfied life. Her marriage to Gil was strong and steadfast. Her children were athletic and academically gifted, as well as blessed with their moth-

er's sunny nature. Her father kept her entertained with
celebrities and power brokers. And someday she'd in-
herit an actual family fortune that included the cottage
in Easthampton, a sprawling Park Avenue apartment,
and a small stone hideaway in the French countryside.
Now that May thought about it, if Gil was going to kill
anyone, it ought to be the old man, who everyone knew
couldn't stand him.

"You're just like Gil—paranoid that Paula isn't coming back. But she'll be back. Things will work out,"
Stephanie said, taking tiny bites of her perfectly
poached salmon. "They always do."

May didn't remind her that they hadn't worked out
for Iris, Chuck, or Barnett. "I want to know who killed
them," she said as much to herself as to Stephanie.

"We all do," Stephanie assured her. "Believe me we
all do."

As soon as May got back to work, she checked with
Linda, who told her that no detectives had stopped by.
Barreling on to her office, she was intercepted by
Margery.

A snarl of producers and assistants were clogging the
hallway ahead of them. Margery kept her voice low.

"Do not waste your time trying to call Dr. Moss. I got
through to him an hour ago, and he adamantly refuses
to help us out here. Forget him. The damage is done."

"Damn," May said, leaning against the wall, feeling
trapped.

"Now, don't despair yet, sugar. There's more. I hear
that Detective O'Donnell was unimpressed with his partner's latest revelation about you. Apparently he's surprised it took so long for the Antabuse news to leak
out."

The producers at the end of the hall broke up their

huddle. Colleen made a beeline for May. "Where were you?" she asked, her voice sharp.

"That's what I was wondering, sugar," Margery quickly joined in the change of subject. "Believe it or not, we all had lunch together—experimenting with collaboration. I'm not optimistic that it will work."

"Where were you?" Colleen asked again.

"Having lunch with a friend," May said, unwilling to share that her own suspicion had drawn her to pump Gil's wife.

"Well, while you've been out lunching with a friend, we've been figuring out what to do next," Colleen told her. "Hypnosis."

"Pardon me?"

"You heard me. Hypnosis. It's perfect."

"She thinks one of us did it and then repressed all memory of it," Bunny offered, and May couldn't quite tell by her tone if it was a joke.

"She's in love with your multiple personality theory," Margery reported. "Several angry demented selves hiding behind a charming facade."

May's cheeks colored. Every time she considered this scenario, it was with herself cast in all of the roles.

"Why so red, May?" Colleen asked. "Have I hit a nerve?"

"Lord, a person can't even joke around here without causing a pogrom," Margery said, turning her back on her colleagues. "I'm going to my office."

"What about my hypnotist? I told him to come up at three."

"Sorry." "See you later." "Not me." One after another the producers scattered, leaving Colleen, pouting, alone.

As soon as May closed her office door, Henry buzzed her. "There's someone coming back to see you to discuss your Dreyfus account."

She buzzed him back. "I don't have a Dreyfus account." It boggled her mind. She could barely bully her way through the layers of security in the outer reaches of their offices, but not one messenger, not one bearer of greasy Chinese food was deterred. Now sales reps were slithering in.

"Sorry," he reported over the intercom. "I couldn't stop her."

"Mrs. Morrison?" This rep looked nothing like the woman Todd had taken her to meet after her father died. That saleswoman, determined to convince May to invest her small nest egg in a highly speculative precious metals fund, had been a study in classic dress—tapered navy suit, cream-colored silk blouse, short dark hair, mild-mannered makeup. "You're young enough that you can take risks," she'd told May, then added urgently, "You're young enough that you must take risks." They did and lost every penny of May's investment.

The saleswoman standing in her doorway now was of a different breed. Thin as an exclamation mark, her cheeks hollow, her wispy hair held back with a dozen metal bobby pins, she wore a caramel-colored narrow skirt, a loose brown jacket, and thick taupe-colored vinyl orthopedic shoes. May figured she was aiming for a look of shabby rich, to resonate of annuities, safety, comfort. She figured they knew she was older now.

"I'm Mrs. Dowling." She presented a small brown wallet displaying her identification.

May quickly explained, "I don't have an account at Dreyfus. I don't want an account at Dreyfus. Dreyfus doesn't want an account with me. I'm broke. But thank you. I'll call you if I get rich." She stood up, but Miss Dowling didn't move. She just stared, blankly, blinking.

"Dreyfus? I'm not from Dreyfus."

"Oh." It was May's turn to stare like a dummy. This was it for Henry.

"It rhymes with Dreyfus. But it's DYFS. D-Y-F-S." She spoke slowly, enunciating crisply, "The Department of Youth and Family Services."

May had done enough shows on teachers who used corporal punishment, on mothers who locked their kids in the car while they shopped to know that DYFS was the State of New Jersey department charged with protecting children from abuse. "Did we have an appointment?" A mole inside DYFS was almost as good as a cop for a friend. "Would you like coffee? Tea? A bagel? Croissant?"

"We don't make appointments. People tend to go out of town without letting us know when we make appointments." The spindly woman shook her head, but as if she wore a helmet, no hairs budged. "I'm afraid you don't appreciate how serious these kinds of charges are."

May knew exactly how serious DYFS charges were. She just didn't know what particular charges they were discussing. "Why are you here?"

"Because of Susie."

"My Susie? What happened to her?"

"Mrs. Morrison, let's not play games with each other. I saw her, I saw her nose. You don't have to pretend."

"She fell in the bathroom. It was an accident. She was standing in front of the shower door when I opened it." She stopped defending herself to ask, "How did you find out, anyway?"

"That's neither here nor there. I'm your caseworker. An investigator will contact you to take your statement later. She'll make a recommendation on how we should proceed."

"I already know how to proceed. It was a freak accident. In the future I'll take baths. I want to know how you found out, and I want a lawyer."

"I see you're not ready to own up to this." She stood and said, "Taking responsibility is the first step on the ladder to good parenting." She walked to the door, then turned around. "Think about it. That's the second step. Before you act, think. The investigator will be contacting you shortly." She left, a trail of rose perfume lingering behind.

May pressed the speed dial for home. "How did everyone get off to school today?" She struggled to sound casual.

Louise's answer was a cold, curt, "Fine."

She called Jack Forest, but he told her he handled only criminal matters, which, he pointed out, this was not. She tried Ritchie next, but he was in court. Her neighbor, Carter Cooper, the last lawyer on her list, quickly agreed to meet her on the 6:07 train. He was seated, craning his neck looking for her, when she arrived. She quickly spilled out the story about the DYFS visit. When she was done, he dropped his voice and confided, "It's my fault. Damn. I was an idiot." Then he admitted that Louise had called Emily first thing in the morning to say her friend had witnessed an incident of child abuse. She wanted to know how these things were handled in America.

"I gave Em the number for DYFS," he confessed, hanging his head. "In a million years neither of us would have suspected she was talking about you." He sat quietly, turning the problem over in his mind until it crystallized into an opportunity. "Here's how we'll handle it. I'll represent you with DYFS, make sure things work out right. You can organize a show on the proliferation of unsubstantiated abuse charges. I'll let it drop with DYFS that the show is in the works. I guarantee you it will make them expedite your case. These things can go on for a while," he confided.

May agreed to let him represent her, sending him home a happy man.

She walked into the house calling for a "group hug." Her girls ran toward her. She held them tight.

"Mrs. Morrison?" Pete stood in the doorway to the downstairs bathroom, drill in his hand. "Can I talk to you for a minute?"

"Girls. We're going out. Go find something to play with in the car."

"Where are we going?" Susie called out as she raced her sister upstairs. "The circus?"

"It's dinnertime," Delia explained, exasperated. "Probably McDonald's again."

May met Pete at the bathroom door. "What's left? Haven't you replaced everything already?"

Pete shook his head. He looked embarrassed. "It's not that." He studied the tips of his workboots. Then he looked up at her. "It's your baby-sitter. There's something about her I don't like. It's none of my business, but I think you should can her."

"Thanks, Pete," May said quietly. "Consider her canned." She might as well let him think it was because of his advice, not something she'd decided hours ago. She called upstairs. "Louise? Come on down. We're going out. Bring your purse."

"Thanks, but I'll stay here. I want to ring up a few friends," the au pair explained.

May saw Pete disappear into the kitchen. He came back carrying the phone. "Sorry," he said. "Phone's out. I cut the line by mistake. I'll have it spliced by the time you're back."

"I need you to come along," May said.

"Do you?" Louise asked, but she grabbed her purse and followed May, Delia, and Susie out the front door.

When they pulled up in front of the brick house where the au-pair coordinator lived, May asked Louise to come with her to the door. Carol didn't hide her displeasure at having her dinner interrupted.

"I'm sorry to bother you," May apologized, "but it turns out that Louise and I are like chalk and cheese. Ever since she called DYFS on me today accusing me of child abuse—I don't know, I just can't seem to breathe so long as she's alive. It's best for everyone if I leave her here." She turned and started down the flagstone path back to her car. Louise remained frozen in place. Carol ran after her.

"May, wait. We can work this out. You have to be willing to talk these things through. The key to a good relationship with your au pair is open, honest communication."

"Good idea." May swung around and marched back to Louise.

"You're dangerous," she told her, "because even now you think you did the right thing. I'll drop off your suitcases in the morning. I'd advise you to get out of town before my lawyer has a chance to get you hauled off to jail." It was true, May thought as she got back in the car: the key to good relationships was honest communication.

The Happy Meals did the trick. By the time the girls finished their McNuggets, twirled their plastic transformer tops off the table, and rolled in the colorful balls in the indoor playground, they were tired but cheerful. Like three drunks, they marched up the front path to the house singing songs from the *Magical Mystery Tour* that the girls had memorized from the CD, thinking they were new.

May stopped in her tracks. Her front door was ajar. She covered Susie's mouth so that she wouldn't scream, then hustled the girls across the lawn to the Coopers, where she rang the bell and waited, clutching her children to her.

30

CARTER PLACED THE CALL TO the police. May paced through his house, the girls pacing behind her, Susie thinking it was a game, Delia less sure. To keep busy Emily put up coffee and set about filling platters with shortbread and butter cookies, cheese and crackers, as if it were a party. When Carter got off the phone, he bundled up in his coat and stood peering through the sheer curtains of his living room window, watching for the arrival of the police.

May stopped in their dining room and looked out of the tall casements that faced her house. The roman shades were only half drawn, so if she ducked, she could see right into her sunroom. Something caught her eye. She strained, looking harder. Someone was walking around in her sunroom, keeping in the shadows. A light flicked on. The taut muscles in her face tightened more. She marched back to the front hall and grabbed her coat.

Emily, following her, grabbed it back. "Where do you think you're going? Stay here."

May reclaimed her coat and opened the front door.

"Get my gun," Carter shouted out to Emily.

Delia began to cry, which made Susie cry, too.

May stopped dead. "You don't need a gun. Call the police and tell them not to come. It's not a burglar."

By the time she reached her sunroom, Todd was sitting on the cushionless sofa watching Nick at Nite. He saw her but didn't budge. She moved in front of the television to block his view. He continued to watch *Gilligan's Island* through her legs. "Where are the girls?" he said finally, without looking up.

"I want your key. That key is supposed to be used when you have the girls, not to let yourself in whenever you want."

"Nice walls," he said, pointing to the naked studs, a product of Pete's busywork. "Where are the girls?"

"You cannot let yourself in as if you live here. My next-door neighbor called the police. We thought you were a burglar. You could have gotten yourself killed."

His large weary eyes looked up at her.

May looked away from him and said, "You're right. I wouldn't care, but your daughters would be devastated."

As Todd stood up, she wished, and not for the first time, that he weren't so damn good-looking. His thick wavy hair had lightened in the California sun, making his shocking blue eyes seem even bluer. Only his toothpaste-commercial smile was gone, turned off, set aside to charm someone else.

"I didn't have to come here," he said quietly. "I flew in on the red-eye. I've moved into the Wyndham." In answer to May's surprised look, he quickly added, "The studio is paying."

She wondered if this meant that his endowment with

Chloe had run out, but then she heard a noise, and when she swung around, there was Chloe, hovering nervously in the entryway. "Sorry," Chloe mumbled. "I didn't know you were here."

"I live here," May reminded her.

"Could you please wait in the car?" Todd asked.

Chloe, unsure of how she fit into this group, grabbed her fur-lined suede coat and left, her clicking heels echoing on the hardwood floor.

Todd resumed. "My lawyer told me not to come. He wants to handle this lawyer to lawyer. But I thought maybe some sane part of you would agree that this makes sense, that it would be better for both of us if the lawyers stayed out of it." He waited for her questions, but she didn't know what was on his mind, and she didn't want to give anything away, so she just waited, saying nothing.

He went on. "Bottom line, I think the girls would be safer staying with us in Los Angeles right now."

The "us" stung like a wasp, but if he knew, he didn't let on.

"The wife of a guy I'm working with at the studio is a teacher at an all-girls private school—one of the best in Beverly Hills. He told me his wife can get both girls in. We just have to send over their records."

"Which of Susie's records would they want? Her finger-painting skills or her block-building IQ? Oh—I forgot—it's LA. You probably need birth certificates from all of her previous lives."

"Let it go, May. Los Angeles is more of a family town than New York. It's all anyone talks about these days—their kids, their kids' schools."

"Not having your kids living with you could be a real disadvantage then, couldn't it?"

He seemed to consider agreeing, but instead sighed

noisily, staring at the floor. His eyelashes were just too long for a man. She hated them, wanted to pluck each one out. She hated that he looked so good, even now as he threatened to dismember her life. When he looked back at her, she could feel the anger percolating just below the surface.

"I saw on the news that Paula was missing," he said, "and you know what my first thought was? 'Good.' Here's a woman whose job is communicating and did she ever get my name right, even once? She called me Ted. She called me Rod. She called me 'May's situation.' Give me a break."

"What does that have to do with us?" May asked.

"Then I hear she's fine; she was just on vacation. But in the dead of the night"—he glared as he went on— "the day after you had your daughters wake me before dawn, I get a call from some detective. I hear about a serial killer. I hear about a long list of suspects. I am asked whether I've been in New York during the past two weeks. Apparently I am a suspect. I quickly figure out that you, too, are a suspect. How did he put it? 'We're looking at everyone.' I ask him, 'Are you looking at May?' He gets all tongue-tied. Are you involved with a cop now?"

He said it as if it were something to be ashamed of, which made her want to answer yes, I'm a cop groupie, sleeping with entire precincts at a time. Instead she let out a laugh, and said, "If I was, it would be none of your business."

"My kids' safety is my business. What's going on, May? Are you in trouble?"

She struggled before answering. He was absolutely the wrong person to confide in, but the impulse to unload on him, to let down her guard and take off her armor for a moment, was compelling. For all the failings of their marriage, she had never held back anything from Todd. Suddenly she was aching to tell him how horrible Louise had been, how frightened she was by Paradiso's suspicions, how confused by O'Donnell's hot and cold attention.

That was what she missed most of all, confidences shared in the dark.

"Things are not going all that well right now," was what she allowed herself.

"Then you understand," Todd offered, relieved.

"I know. You love the girls. You're just concerned. That's normal," she said, to confirm his feelings. She had to admit it felt good that he was concerned.

He nodded, somber, lay a hand on her shoulder, raised it to her face, stroked her cheek. For a moment they were silent, remembering. Then Todd went on with business. "We only have two bedrooms, but they're huge, and they'll have their own bathroom with a Jacuzzi. The girls will love it. And the house is right on the beach."

He waited for May to be impressed, but she said nothing.

"Chloe's already signed Delia up for an art class at the museum and found a movement class for Susie after school. They'll miss you," he added softly.

"No they won't."

"Don't sell yourself short. Even when you were never home, when it seemed like you lived at the office, they only cared about you. I'd help Delia with her homework, brush her hair, feed her, get her dressed, and she would rush in after school and say, 'Wait till I tell Mommy this.' Susie would get a scrape and scream at me that I could put the Band-Aid on but only you could take it off when it was healed. I was an afterthought for everyone. It's the best thing for them now, though. We both know it. No matter how much they'll miss you."

"They won't miss me. They're not going anywhere. They're totally safe. Get out of my house."

"Do you want the lawyers to handle this? I'm warning you, May. My New York lawyer is a shark. He was recommended to me by Robert Shapiro. That's Robert Shapiro of the Dream Team. You really want someone Robert Shapiro recommended calling Cousin Ritchie?"

Her eyes were caught by the flashing red lights of a police cruiser pulling up in front of her house. She walked to the window, saw Carter motioning, trying to explain why they didn't have to come in. She opened the front door. Todd didn't budge.

"I'll tell the police you broke in," she said. "In ten seconds I'll start screaming rape."

Again he heaved a sigh. "You're so self-absorbed you can't even see."

"Get out, Todd, before your ice princess freezes to death in your car."

He grabbed his coat. "Tell your lawyer to expect a call from Bill Giasullo. As long as this killer is out there, the girls are not safe in this house. And I'm not going back to California without them."

He was almost out of the door when May remembered to ask for the key.

"You'll get your key," he promised, "when I get the girls. Don't look so glum, May. It's a good life they'll have in California. And you'll finally be able to devote all your goddamn precious time to your goddamn precious show, free and clear."

May took a breath, was about to scream, when Todd turned and walked away. He stopped to speak briefly to the policeman before disappearing up the driveway, where his rental Thunderbird idled, the tailpipe spewing a steady cloud of smoke.

May wiped her fresh tears on her sleeve, then marched outside, her eyes stinging, to retrieve her daughters. She'd check the yellow pages for a twenty-four-hour locksmith, and if she couldn't get one to come before morning, she'd pile the girls in the car and spend the night in the nearest hotel. She'd do everything necessary to keep them safe, but they were going to be safe with her.

31

IT WASN'T THE SOUND OF CARS on Route 21 or the teenagers celebrating someone's birthday in the room next door that kept her awake through the night. It was the question drumming through her mind like a mantra: *Are they safe, are they safe, are they safe?*

At five she carried them, one and then the other, to the mini-van. There was no traffic as she zoomed into the city. She eased her car down the curved ramp, glanced at the skyline of Manhattan across the river, and entered the dim light of the Lincoln Tunnel just as the dawn broke.

The city was awakening, its traffic a quiet conglomeration of newspaper trucks, empty busses, and bedraggled troops of the night shift dragging off while the early morning shift drowsily came on. When she pulled up to the parking lot across from her building, the steel gate was being rolled up.

"Come on." She softly prodded the girls. "You can go back to sleep in my office."

Half-awake, their pajamas soft and crumpled under their coats, the girls wearily followed their mother. The building's night guards were already off duty, the revolving doors now open to all. May squeezed into a section with Delia and Susie and pushed them through.

"Is it Take You Daughter to Work Day again?" Delia asked, coming awake as the elevator door closed.

"Where are we?" Susie mumbled.

"I have a few things to do in the office, and I thought it would be a special treat if you could come with me before you went to school."

"We're going to work on a school day?" Susie asked, suddenly wide awake with incredulity. The doors opened on twenty-two.

The private security guards' shift had just changed. The guard who'd nearly shot her for hitting the door with her shoe now adjusted his belt and cap, ready for action. He knew who she was—she was sure of it—but he insisted on pretending he didn't, on making her go through the process again.

"Name."

"Give me a break. You know my name."

"Name?" he insisted.

"She's May Morrison," Delia said, glaring at her mother's disrespect for authority.

The guard started at the top of his list and slowly, very slowly ran his finger down one name at a time. May stole a glance, saw the list was alphabetized. "*M* comes after *L*," she offered, but he gave no indication that he'd heard. His stubby fingers continued its descent, unwavering and slower now.

"All right," he said, finally finding her. "You can go in. Who are they?"

"Who do you think they are? Midget murderers?"

"Mom, stop," Delia hissed, embarrassed at her mother's rude behavior.

The guard, sensing he and Delia shared a common enemy, softened. To bond further he offered his new pal a look at his gun. When Susie asked if she could try it, May barked, "Come with me now," and her children followed, struggling to keep up with her quick pace. She knew—they didn't—there wasn't much time before the early-bird workaholic shift arrived.

Delia was easy to entertain, happily stationed at Henry's computer playing the latest version of Carmen Sandiego. Susie got a stack of magazines, a pair of scissors, a large piece of poster board, and instructions from her mother to cover all the white spots with the prettiest pictures she could find. For insurance May promised if they let her do her work, she'd stop off at Carvel for a mid-morning snack on their way to school. This was a first. Cooperation was complete.

By the time she tore down the hallway, it was six-thirty and she hadn't gotten any further in her plan than that she would start out by searching Gil's office. After that she'd methodically move down the corridors searching the rest. She'd search them all until she found something, something that would exonerate her, send Todd back to Malibu and Paradiso back to the creeps he was used to intimidating. She was driven now, energized by a force stronger than fear of wrongful capture. If Todd was going to try to prove her girls were in danger, to try to take them from her, then she had to make sure that danger was removed. If the cops were missing something, or didn't even have sufficient evidence to look, then it was up to her to find it for them.

The hallway was quiet, deserted—the guard on his rounds on the other side of the floor, too far away to hear her. She put her hand on Gil's brass doorknob, then stopped for a moment. A ripple of fear coursed through her body, irrational fear, as if she might find something awful, a body sprawled across the desk, a corpse dangling from the ceiling.

She flung open the door before the fear had a chance to take on a life of its own. An ear-splitting scream shot out, the sound so loud it froze her feet and brain. She fought to think and, with some struggle, realized the sound was an alarm. Newly installed lights flashed on and off, further disorienting her, the bright rays causing her to blink quickly. With new understanding for the plight of a deer caught in the glare of headlights, she tried to move but couldn't. Not even when she felt someone rushing up behind her, running into her with a force that made her fall to the floor.

"Freeze," the guard shot out, and she did. He twisted her arms, pulling them behind her back, cuffing her tightly. Within moments Susie and Delia were at her side, wailing with terror, their tears dripping onto her like rain. Despite their pleas the guard refused to remove the cuffs until O'Donnell arrived, fifteen long minutes later.

32

THEY RODE TO SCHOOL IN SI-lence. Susie clutched the card on which Detective O'Donnell had scribbled his home phone number, as if it were a magic shield. Delia, using a pencil, had bored a hole in hers. Then, using a piece of string O'Donnell had pulled out of his pocket, she'd made herself a charm bracelet.

As May negotiated the counter-rush-hour traffic out of the city, she silently tried out explanations not only for why the girls were late for school but for why they needed to be allowed to keep the card of a New York City homicide detective with them all day long.

It's her new security blanket, she imagined telling Mrs. Ditrolio, Susie's teacher. *It's her special bookmark,* she tried out as an alternative. *How do you like her jewelry?* she imagined kidding to Mrs. Fine when she brought Delia into her class.

But the girls were such sticklers for the truth she knew they'd chime in with their own dramatic versions of what it was like when Mommy was handcuffed by a mean security guard and then rescued by a nice policeman who told her she ought to go to the police school if she wanted to grow up to be a detective. Her best bet was to say nothing, and hope the girls would say nothing, too.

This morning rated right up there with the night of Todd's good-bye speech as one of the worst moments of her life. Forget that she never got to search anyone's office, that the fact that Gil installed an alarm system made her even more sure he had something to hide. Forget that she was completely humiliated by the sadistic guard and that her children were so terrified they both wet their pants. Forget how humiliating it was to hear Paradiso and O'Donnell argue over her as if she were invisible.

"Breaking and entering. Stalking. Tampering with evidence. Take your pick," Paradiso shouted, "and then bring her the hell in."

That's when O'Donnell had handed each of the girls his card and asked them to wait in Mommy's office. As soon as they'd left the room, he turned to May, said, "Excuse me," then faced his partner.

"You talk like that in front of those kids again—in front of anyone again—I'm going to bust your ass so bad you'll be standing up at desk duty for the rest of the century. You can't prove this woman was doing anything other than working. Me, I think she was investigating. You ever hear of that word? That's when you look for evidence, like Antabuse, that will actually hold up in court."

Paradiso muttered something that May couldn't quite hear. Then he glared at her as if she were less than human, a bug he was hot to crush and get out of the way.

As O'Donnell led her to her office to reclaim her kids, he warned her, "Your lawyer really stirred him up. He's not going to touch you, but he's not going to make it easy on you, either."

All that was bad. What was worse was this: If Todd found out his daughters went to school clutching Detective O'Donnell's cards, she might as well go ahead and purchase their one-way tickets to Los Angeles herself.

She knew he had only been trying to be a good guy, that O'Donnell had offered his cards as a distraction to take the girls' minds off Paradiso's vicious accusations, off their own damp bottoms and their mother's wet eyes. His sympathetic wink had told her he didn't really believe they were in danger. It was a trick—a benevolent policeman's trick—to make a pair of frightened children feel secure. How could he know he was planting evidence in their hands that would only serve to strengthen their father's case against her?

Luckily, Susie fell asleep several minutes before they got to school, and the card drifted out of her open hand to the floor. By the time May roused her to gently lead her to her classroom, the morning's drama had faded like a dream.

Delia, on the other hand, marched into her class waving her right arm wildly, waiting for her classmates to notice and ask about her unusual bracelet. She quickly joined in the singing already underway—"from sea to shining sea"—waving her arm back and forth like a flag caught in the wind. As soon as the anthem was over, the children noisily scurried to their chairs. May knew she should leave, that she shouldn't just stand in the doorway like a dummy watching, but she so rarely got a glimpse inside her children's classrooms that she wanted to extend the moment, drink in the details.

Delia's right arm shot up, then started waving with the frantic motion of a child desperate to be called on. When her teacher asked, "Delia, is this really something that can't wait?" May quickly slipped out of the room lest she be asked to give amplification to the unbelievable story her daughter was about to tell.

She stopped back home to meet Joe from Lots of Locks and left him there, putting bars on the basement windows, locks on the casements on the first, second, and top floors, and a new Medeco on the front door. As for the door's fifty-year-old chain, despite Joe's professional opinion that it offered about as much protection as a piece of string, May decided to leave it on anyway, if only because it made her feel safe. For the back and side doors, they chose gleaming new locks that were the latest in nonelectronic security. Joe promised to have an estimate for the electronic system written up by the end of the day. The quickest he could install it was next week, but he had a pair of motion detectors she could plug in downstairs if she wanted to in the meantime.

By the time she got to the office, news of her early morning capture had circulated all the way around the floor and back to reception. A new guard greeted her, a slim, attractive Hispanic woman who knew who she was without introduction.

Linda got out a quick, "Are you all right?" but May didn't stop to answer. She was several feet away from Gil's office when Wendy caught up to her.

"I want you to know I fired that awful guard," she explained. "He was totally out of line." She dropped her voice. "I told Gil you set off the alarm because you were dropping a folder on his desk. I didn't tell him which folder it was. You'll have to figure that one out yourself."

This was the other Wendy, the kind, solicitous one who always eased the way for Gil. She was soothing, confident, competent, assuring May everything would turn out all right. May couldn't help but wonder what she'd done to earn the respectful attention.

"It was my fault," Wendy explained as if sensing the question. "That guard had it in for you from his first day on the job. But to handcuff you in front of your children—that's unforgivable."

Now May understood. Wendy wouldn't have cared at all that the guard had been abusive except that it happened in front of the children. They were her soft spot, and May knew it just as she knew that all the birthday cards and Easter baskets signed with Paula's and Gil's names came only at her initiative.

"Go on," Wendy urged her into Gil's office. "It'll be fine."

As soon as Gil saw her, he hung up the phone, folded his arms, and waited for her to say something. Until that moment it hadn't occurred to May that he might be mad at her, might view her walking into his office as a break-in. After all, they ran in and out of each other's offices all day long. Again she thought, *He's hiding something—what?* Her eyes roamed the room for clues. She saw awards on shelves, newspaper clippings under brass paperweights, pens scattered like pickup sticks, posed family portraits—Stephanie and the children in the backyard, at a pool, at a lake, on horseback, on bicycles, in a canoe.

"Are you planning on explaining yourself, or am I supposed to read your mind?" His voice was high, as if he was holding something back, holding his breath, holding it in.

"I'll be happy to explain myself. I came in early with the girls to try to get some work done around here. I heard someone and thought it was you. I ran down to your office to talk to you and walked inside. Next thing I know I'm spread-eagled with the fascist guard handcuffing me. My children are hysterical, thinking either I'm dead or I'm about to be hauled off to jail." She'd worked herself up. Her anger sounded real because it was. "I think you're the one who owes me the explanation."

Gil's quick blinks told her he'd taken it in and knew he was in trouble now. She let her anger blossom fully.

"How could you forget to warn me about the alarm? What are you protecting—your priceless art?" She gestured toward the vintage posters that Stephanie had picked out on his behalf when after a year he still hadn't gotten around to putting anything up on his walls. "I haven't spoken to my lawyer yet, but I fully intend to file charges against both the guard and the security company." She let her anger fly out, raw. It wasn't hard to do. Her heart was racing, her skin bright red, her voice beginning to quake. "If the New York City Police Department isn't bringing me in for questioning, what the hell was that guard doing cuffing me like I'm some drug dealer on the street corner?"

Gil sank a few inches in his seat. "I'm sorry," he said quietly. "I should have sent a memo about the alarm. It was a mistake not to tell you."

"He handcuffed me in front of my children," she re- peated, enjoying how her rage made him squirm.

"He's been fired. Did you know that? Wendy fired him. I didn't even have to ask her. She did it on her own. I have a call in to the head of the security company. I'm going to demand he apologize to you himself. By letter, phone, fax—all three if you want. You want to sue them, go right ahead. I'll help you. Just tell me what you want."

"Time off," she said. "My kids need me."

"They can have you. Just not now." Gil looked som- ber. "I need you here when Paula gets back. You have to wait till then. Once she's back, I'll send you and your family anywhere you want to go. Where do you want to go? Disney World? Switzerland? Hawaii? You name it."

"I don't need a vacation," she insisted. "I need a leave of absence."

"The only leaves I'm giving now are permanent. You work here or you don't work here, May. What's your choice?"

"Lotto," she muttered as she left, but he didn't hear her.

As soon as she got to her office, she called her mother.

"I'm sending the kids to you for a visit. I'm pulling them out of school for a week. I'll fly them down and come right back."

"That's crazy. Don't do that. Wait for vacation."

"I need to send them now."

"You're always in a rush. Dolly, I wish I could help you out, but now's not a great time."

Bunny popped her head in the doorway. May mo- tioned for her to come in and sit down.

"What do you mean now's not a great time? Is every- thing okay?"

"Of course, dolly. I'm fine. Don't worry about me. Just go back to work. And remember: You have to put your-

self out there if you want to meet someone. I love you."
Her mother signed off.

"You okay?" Bunny asked, studying May's face. "I
heard you had a little incident with security."

May switched her attention back to the crisis at work,
hoping there wasn't another crisis building in Florida.
"I came in early." She hesitated, considering how much
to share. But she couldn't lie to Bunny. "I was going to
search Gil's office. I accidentally set off his new alarm."

"Better you than me. I was going to go through it
after work."

"Who's done this to us?" May asked.

"I don't exactly know yet," Bunny mumbled, and got
up.

"What are you going to do?"

"I'm looking at a bunch of old shows, looking for
ideas. You want to help?"

May followed her to the small closet that was their
cassette library.

"What kind of ideas?" she asked after Bunny loaded
up May's arms up with as many boxes as she could
carry. "Disastrous shows? Disgruntled guests?"

"No," Bunny said, balancing her own tower of cassettes. "This isn't about a guest, that much I know."
She walked off, deep in her own thoughts, leaving May,
bewildered, watching her.

Henry came up behind her, out of breath. "I've been
looking for you everywhere. Your cousin's on the
phone."

She raced to her desk to take Ritchie's call, dumping
the cassettes in an empty shopping bag she found stuck
underneath her credenza.

"Toddy's lawyer is threatening to file on an expedited
basis," he explained. "They're claiming there's imminent
danger to the kids. I don't think they'll move as fast as

they say. I think right now they're posturing. I think Toddy's probably trying to round up witnesses who'll testify that the kids are in danger living with you. It might be fairly convincing."

"Could they win?"

"Normally I'd say no. Judges hate to overturn custody decisions. But the minute the word murder, or murder suspect, comes out of Todd's lawyer's mouth, you're in trouble."

"What do I do?"

"May, maybe it wouldn't be the worst thing if the girls went to California for a few weeks."

She didn't want to hear it. "If they go, I'll never get them back," she told him.

"We can be very specific in our terms. We can describe exactly how many weeks, days, even hours that his custody lasts."

"No."

"Okay. So how many impeccable witnesses can you give me who will swear under oath the girls are in no danger whatsoever?"

May thought of O'Donnell, and of the cards he gave them for protection. "I can't think of anyone off the top of my head."

"Then think harder," Ritchie advised. "Hang up the phone, close your door, and come up with names for me."

She hung up the phone and closed the door. But all she came up with was the wish that she hadn't followed Todd's stupid advice and emptied her bank account to invest in precious metals, that she still had a nest egg she could empty. If she did, it would be easy. She'd just scoop up her kids, pack them in the minivan, and drive somewhere faraway. Someplace where the decisions of the day were never more complicated than should I use waxed or unwaxed floss, super or special gasoline, Sprint or MCI? There were a hundred choices she was happy to make in a day, a thousand problems she was willing to face straight on. But this one was too big. This one kept changing shape, and every time she got a handle on it, it slipped right out of her grasp.

33

PETE TOLD HER THE GOOD NEWS, nothing new had broken, and the bad news, Delia was told to sit on the bench at recess. Then he left, as the girls hunkered down for another gourmet meal of swirly pasta, chicken nuggets, and baby carrots in stage-one limpness. They ate, subdued, in silence. O'Donnell called as May was doling out the SnackWell's brownies.

"Are the girls okay?"

When Susie figured out who was on the phone, she grabbed it. "Know what? My teacher told me policemen are heroes." She listened, laughed, and told her mother that this policeman said he was a grilled cheese on rye with tomato. Delia grabbed the phone out of her hand.

"Mrs. Fine thinks I made you up," she explained; this was news to May. "She said you were probably a guest on Mom's show once. She said anyone could get a card from a policeman if they wanted one and it was nothing to boast about." Delia listened closely to what the detective had to say. "You can? You will?" She hung up the phone before May had a chance to speak, happily reporting that the detective promised to come to her class to corroborate her story.

When the phone rang seconds later, it was the au-pair coordinator making her final pitch for the best au pair in the world, who happened to be available to arrive by Sunday afternoon.

"Your girls couldn't be in better hands unless they were your own," Carol assured her. "I'm telling you, I'm jealous. I've checked Sabrieke out better than I've ever checked out anyone."

May thought, *That's not saying much.*

"I have to admit," Carol went on. "I considered keeping her for myself. But my kids are too old. They don't need an au pair anymore. They need a driver with a lot of cash."

May got off the phone and began the tedious task of telling the girls all about their new baby-sitter, trying to make her sound great.

"She's a nurse," she told Susie while bathing her.

"Does she give shots?"

"No. But she loves kids."

"Will she love me?"

"How could she not?"

Susie's head was lathered with shampoo when the doorbell rang. May feared Paradiso, wished for O'Donnell, found instead a woman who blended in so well with the dark outside it took a moment for May to make her out—black jacket, dark chocolate skin, dark skirt, brown shoes. The woman took off her black leather gloves to lift out her identification from a slim brown wallet. May stepped out under the light of the lantern overhanging her front door to read it. Her sudden fear, that the woman was a cop sent to bring her in, was proved wrong when she saw that the bold letters on the bottom of her card spelled out DYFS.

"I'm Ms. Thomas," the woman explained, offering a cold, fleshy hand. "Did Mrs. Dowling tell you to expect me?" As May shook her head she realized the question wasn't meant to be answered. Neither was the next one. "May I come in?"

"Mommy?" Susie called. "There's soap in my eye."

"I have to get my daughter out of the tub," May explained, hoping that leaving Susie unattended in the bath wasn't a chargeable offense.

"Take your time," Ms. Thomas said as she stepped inside, quickly removing her coat. "Do you mind if I look around?" she asked as if May had a choice.

"Ow," Susie called out as May struggled to quickly comb her knotty hair.

"I'm not hurting you," May told her harshly, mindful of the woman roaming the house.

"Do you mind if I come up?" Ms. Thomas called out.

"Not at all," she called back.

"I don't want to brush my teeth," Susie insisted, pushing May's arm away just as Ms. Thomas, in her soft-soled shoes, appeared in the bathroom doorway.

"You want to have big strong teeth, don't you?" Ms. Thomas asked, revealing her own oversized pegs.

Susie burst into tears and drew close to her mother, hiding her head between May's legs. "She's shy," May explained, thankful.

"Mom," Delia called out from her room. "Where's my card?"

Ms. Thomas, sympathetic, smiled. "May I say hello to your other daughter?"

"Delia, there's someone here I want you to meet."

"I don't know where my card bracelet is," Delia hissed. May needed to change the subject quickly.

"Delia, this is Ms. Thomas."

"Is she our new baby-sitter?" Delia muttered, looking wary and resigned at once.

"No, dear. I work for the Department of Youth and Family Services," the woman explained. "I visit children in their homes and make sure everyone's all right."

"What if everyone's not all right?" Delia asked.

"Then we do everything we can to make it all right. Would you like to show me your room?"

Delia shrugged and looked at May, who nodded, struggling to appear good-natured about it all even though her cheeks had turned fire-engine red.

"Can I go, too?" Susie asked.

Ms. Thomas's smile broadened. "I'd love that."

When May started after them, Ms. Thomas turned and said, "I'll meet you downstairs in a few moments," leaving no room for discussion.

For the ten long minutes that her children conferred with Ms. Thomas, May managed to go through the motions of reading through the pile of mail that had accumulated on her kitchen counter. She separated out bills, sorted flyers, and skimmed catalogues. When she heard the faint sound of Ms. Thomas's light footsteps tapping down the stairs, she gathered the papers back into a big pile, undoing all her work.

"May we sit for a moment?" Ms. Thomas asked. May complied, falling into the nearest seat at the kitchen table. Ms. Thomas lifted Delia's backpack off the seat next to her and slid into it.

"I've read all the papers in your file. I've spoken to Mr. Cooper, your attorney. I've had a lovely informative talk with your children. Is there anything you'd like to add?"

She didn't want to speak, shook her head no, but in spite of herself she blurted out, "What happened to Susie was an accident." Her eyes welled up.

"I know that."

She regained control, blinking back tears. "Then why are you here?"

"We have to check everything out, don't we? These days it's better safe than sorry."

May sighed so deeply it came out like a groan. Ms. Thomas's expression softened. She slid an open folder across the kitchen table. A form letter sat atop a stack of pages. "There's a course given up at Community Hospital on managing stress. You're to go to it. Bring this form and have the teacher sign it before the class begins and again when the class is over. Then send it back to me in this envelope. Once I receive it, your case will be closed."

"If I had time to go to a stress-reduction class, I wouldn't be under so much stress. If you really want to help reduce my stress, just close my file and go home."

Ms. Thomas, used to worse, was unruffled. "The course is meeting tonight, and then again in a month. If you want to close your file quickly, you should get over there tonight. That's up to you."

"And while I'm reducing my stress, who's watching my kids?"

"I've taken the course myself and gotten a lot out of it. We're not adversaries, you and I," Ms. Thomas explained. "I'm a single mother, too."

"But you don't have to justify to anyone that you're a good mother, do you?" May asked.

Ms. Thomas looked distressed. She gazed off in the distance, considering something. When she finally spoke, her voice carried less authority. "From what your older daughter told me, I gather you're having something of a custody battle with your ex-husband. The children made it clear to me they don't want to leave you. Now, understand, our policy on custody is clear.

We don't disclose ongoing investigations to a noncustodial parent unless and until the time comes that we've found the custodial parent to be unfit, but that's another matter.

"What I'm trying to say is, I don't know if your ex-husband knows of our investigation yet, but if he finds out, however he finds out, I can be subpoenaed to come to court and testify about your case. It's happened to me before. Once I'm in court, it doesn't matter what I say. The fact that I'm here seems to be bad enough. It's in your best interest," she said, drilling her eyes into May's, "and in the best interest of your children," she added meaningfully, "to close this case quickly. The course tonight begins at eight."

The layers of pressure were making May feel as squashed as a train-flattened penny. She watched Ms. Thomas's Hyundai chug up the street. Then she called Emily, who, feeling culpable in May's DYFS affair, immediately offered to send over her oldest child, eleven-year-old Timmy, to baby-sit.

May poked her head in Delia's room, where Susie lay alongside her sister, sleeping curled up like a giant stuffed animal. May carried her to her own bed, then came back and sat down next to Delia.

"I'm going out for a while," she explained. Delia, reading *The Twits*, didn't even look up to let May know she'd heard. "Timmy is coming over to stay with you until I get back." Delia shrugged, as if to say okay, who cares, whatever. She was already world-weary, a seven-year-old used to being left.

When Timmy arrived, he went straight to the TV and turned on *Beavis and Butthead*. May hoped Delia would fall asleep reading in bed without ever making it downstairs, but she knew that wasn't likely. The sounds of the grunting cartoon characters were already winding their way up to Delia, as irresistible as the smell of freshly baked cookies.

May sped to the hospital, quickly finding her way to the community outreach classroom. It was as inviting as a morgue: underheated, with beige speckled squares of linoleum flooring and Band-Aid–colored folding chairs; even the walls repelled her with their sallow yellow paint.

Surprisingly, most seats were filled. Half of the crowd was dressed in hospital greens, their name tags identifying them as doctors, nurses, technicians, and they chatted amiably among themselves, as if they'd just wandered in on a break looking for a place to sit down and put up their feet. As for the others, they were a mixed crew, some dressed in suits, looking as though they'd come straight from the train, some who'd rushed out of the house with their babies' dried spit-up still decorating their shoulders.

At a podium in the front of the room a speaker arranged a stack of notes. May left her coat on her chair and approached him.

"I'm supposed to sign in," she said, hoping he'd wave her off, tell her that wasn't necessary, that she didn't really belong here anyway, that he understood, even if no one else did, it was all a terrible mistake.

He took the slip of paper from her and signed it, without looking up. Then he reminded her to bring it back at the end of class so he could sign it again.

She sat down, glum, annoyed, defiant. She knew exactly how to reduce the stress in her own life, and it wasn't, as the instructor now began claiming, going to be a matter of seizing the moment, just saying no, buying a pair of rollerblades, or making lists. She made her own stress-reduction list as she listened: call Newt Gingrich and lobby him to cut off funding for DYFS,

poison Todd in a painful way, catch the talk-show killer,
win the lottery, and quit her job. That was all she had
to do. She couldn't wait to get started.

The class tittered. The person next to her poked her.
The teacher was looking at her. The whole class was
looking at her.

"Sorry?"

"Daydreaming is an excellent way to reduce stress,"
the teacher pointed out. "Unless you're driving, in which
case it can be an exceptionally poor choice. Anyone else
care to share the ways in which they unwind?"

The arm of the man next to May shot up. "I watch
the idiot box all day," the senior citizen explained. "I'm
addicted to those damn talk shows. I hate 'em, but I
can't stop watching 'em."

May didn't mean to groan out loud, but when she did,
the teacher's eyes jumped right to hers. "The woman
next to you doesn't think that's a very good way to
relax."

"It's not that," she said in a loud whisper. "Never
mind."

"Don't be shy. If you think watching TV doesn't reduce stress, offer our friend another suggestion."

She shook her head, then said quickly, "It's just that
I'm a TV producer, that's all. Ignore me. I produce for
a talk show. Go on. Skip ahead to someone else. I'm
relaxed. I'm so relaxed I could faint." Her face, bright
red, belied her words.

"Which talk show?" the woman behind her asked.

May's shoulder's sank, *"Paula Live."*

"Ooh. I love that show," another woman called out.

"Is she the one who's dead?" a nurse asked from
across the aisle.

The teacher broke in. "My favorite way to reduce
stress is to allow spontaneity into our lives. So why

doesn't our relaxed producer come up to the podium to take a few questions. Maybe we can break the ice."

"No thanks," May tried.

The teacher frowned. "It's called learning to go with the flow. It's in my lesson plan," he added with a stern look that lifted her out of her seat.

She knew how to do this. She plastered a smile on her face and marched up to the podium becoming more The Producer with each step.

She didn't keep track exactly, but her guess was that by the time the teacher reclaimed his spot at the front of the room, she'd answered over a dozen questions, charming the group with her candor and amusing them with several hardy anecdotes. Afterward, as he signed her out, the teacher thanked her for making his lecture fun.

She sped home, her head throbbing, her stomach as tight as a clenched fist, her stress level holding at high. It rose even higher when she saw the patrol car parked in front of her house. Racing up the path, she slipped on a slick patch of ice. Eyes stinging, she limped inside.

34

THE YOUNG POLICEMAN, HIS face a celebration of freckles, came quickly toward her, but his respectful soft-spoken voice was overwhelmed by children's chatter.

"A car, a man, watching us," Timmy and Delia

shouted, their voices colliding. Susie, covering her ears, ran to hide between May's legs.

"It was after we watched TV," Delia bellowed, winning the audience. She lowered her voice and continued. "Susie woke up and couldn't fall back asleep, so she came down, too. I told Timmy we had a bottle of Coke in the refrigerator in the basement. Sorry," she said because the soda was for special occasions.

"I showed him where the popcorn was, and he knew how to make it, but then we dropped the bowl. It didn't break, but the popcorn went everywhere. We were chasing it, cleaning it up. Susie ate some off the floor."

"I did not," Susie said.

May looked at the white puffs littering the floor. They'd had fun. Then something had happened.

"We were getting the pieces that rolled into the dining room when Timmy saw the car across the street."

May walked to the dining room window, looked out, saw houses, trees, nothing.

"Timmy got the idea to get Susie's binoculars. He told me to turn off the lights so we could see better. You tell it," she instructed Timmy, shrinking away from the scary part.

"When I looked through the binoculars, I saw a man. He was sitting in his car looking through binoculars at us."

May didn't want to scare her children any more than they already were, so she tried to contain the shiver that sparked down her spine in a rush.

Carter explained the next part. "While Timmy was in the kitchen calling me, the car drove off. I called the police. I hope you don't mind."

How could she mind? She had no time to mind. She had to get the children organized for their move to California. Their summer clothes were still in the storage boxes in the basement. She'd need suntan lotion, tennis rackets, a Ouija board.

"The boy gave us a good description of the car," the policeman told her.

"He reads racing magazines," Carter boasted. "We just finished our first MG kit last weekend."

"The car was a dark-colored Thunderbird," Timmy reported. "An early eighties model, I'd guess."

Carter motioned for him to simmer down. Susie, lying down on the couch, was wrapping herself up in a crocheted blanket, readying to fall back asleep.

Timmy shrugged and backed off, sullen. Delia, who recognized the mood, knew what to do.

"Can we go out in the backyard if we put on our boots? Please. Just for a few minutes? Just while you're talking? We'll stay in the back. Please?"

"It's okay with me," Carter said.

May agreed. There was no danger now. She watched the two children race out to stomp over the thin layer of fresh snow that blanketed the grass.

"We've got two squad cars touring the neighborhood," the cop explained. Then his eyes went to the window, to the cars pulling up in front of the house. "And here comes one of them now."

They turned as one to see a dark car park in front of the house, a police cruiser behind it. When a policeman escorted Todd up her walk, May seemed to be the only one who wasn't surprised. It summed up just about everything she knew about cars—that her ex-husband had a crush on Thunderbirds, used to scour rental agencies whenever they went on vacation to find one that could provide the beloved wheels of his youth.

Todd burst in on the offensive. "Where were you May? How old is Delia's boyfriend. Nine? Ten?"

"He's not her boyfriend. He's her babysitter. And it's

none of your business. What were you doing spying on them?"

"None of my business? You left your kids with a nine-year-old baby-sitter and that's none of my business? Thanks, May. You're making this easy for me."

"I'll have you know my son is eleven years old," Carter interrupted, "and he has far better manners than you."

"Who is this?" Todd asked, his voice dripping with sarcasm. "Your detective boyfriend?"

The freckle-faced cop walked between them. "Let's stay calm, here. Everybody take a deep breath and take a step back. Ma'am," he said to May, making her feel older than matronly. "Do you want to press charges?"

"Why are you asking her if she wants to press charges?" Todd yelled. "What kind of charges is she going to press? I'm the one who's going to press charges."

Their voices collided, May shouting that peering at the children through binoculars was harassment, Carter jumping in with a dissertation about restraining orders and right of way, Todd chanting, "We'll see about that at the custody hearing."

When the kitchen door slid open with a whack, they all shut up. Delia raced in breathless, laughing. Timmy followed, his hair wet down, his eyelashes dotted with drops of melted snow as he yelled for help while Delia giggled, delighting in the joke. But what took May's breath away was the coiled phone cord wrapped around Timmy's wrists, one end of which Delia held on to as if it were a leash.

"Where did you get that thing?" May asked, trying to force herself to lighten the question with a laugh, hoping Todd, who knew her too well, didn't hear the panic in her voice.

"In the backyard," Delia answered.

May turned back to Todd. "I'm not going to press charges. Let's just forget it."

Todd eyed her suspiciously. It wasn't like her to give up without a fight.

"I don't want the kids to grow up with us hating each other," she went on. "I'll call Ritchie in the morning. Wherever you want to meet is fine with me. Let's just get this over with."

"That's smart, May," Todd said, relaxing now that she'd all but admitted defeat. "If nothing else, I always knew you were smart."

It was ten-fifteen by the time she got rid of Todd, the cops, Timmy, and Carter. She half-dragged Delia, wired enough to win a marathon, to bed, but once she got her there, Delia fell instantly, deeply to sleep.

May crept around her room, trying not to wake her while she searched for the bracelet that held as its charm the card with O'Donnell's home number. She found it. He was home, and promised to be there within the hour.

35

"THEY'RE FINE IN THE CAR," O'Donnell said, gesturing back to where he'd parked at an odd angle, the way cops do when they arrive in a rush.

May peered through the darkness to make out three huddled shapes, one in the front, two in the backseats.

"My sister watches them for me," he felt he had to explain. "But she has the flu. First time in her life. My other sister would have taken them, but she's working the graveyard shift at St. Vincent's tonight."

"Don't leave them in the car," May told him. "Bring them in. My girls are asleep. They won't bother anyone."

O'Donnell, clearly uncomfortable with the situation, brought his sons in. May stuck a video—*E.T.*—in the machine and the three boys filed into the sunroom to watch it. None of them, not even the big one, who looked to be about ten, complained. They were well trained in disappearing into the woodwork.

"Where does your ex-wife live?" May asked. She liked it that gun-toting, corpse expert O'Donnell had the same baby-sitter problems she did. What surprised her was that no sweet-talking woman who swore she loved his kids as if they were her own had snagged him yet.

"My Mommy's in heaven," the youngest boy, five-year-old John, answered for him, appearing in the doorway to politely explain that the video wasn't tracking right.

After May fixed the tracking O'Donnell said, "Cancer. Last year. It's easier to say she left me." Then he changed the subject back to police business, where he was safe. "Where's the phone cord?"

Respecting his obvious need to keep his sorrow private, May asked no questions, just handed over the cord.

He studied it. "How many people have handled this?"

She quickly calculated: in addition to O'Donnell and herself there was Delia, Timmy, and the cop, who'd warned the kids—this was the kind of police work he was used to and did well—that wrapping a cord around any part of their body was dangerous.

"Five," she told him. Too many, she thought.

He put the cord in a plastic bag, but May guessed by

the way he handled it that it was unlikely it would answer any questions, including the one that was dogging her—how did it get there?

"We all know Chuck was strangled with Gil's phone cord," she told him. "It could be a coincidence that this turned up in my yard, right? A squirrel could have picked it out of some neighbor's garbage can, right?"

"It's possible," O'Donnell said, sounding unconvinced, as he went outside. May watched his flashlight mark his trail through the backyard. When he came in, he dusted off the snow that had fallen in clumps from the trees onto his shoulders. Then he told her what she could already see for herself: the kids had stomped everywhere, obliterating any chance that he might find a useful print.

"I don't like it," he told her. "I don't like this cord turning up here. It makes me think someone's watching you, trying to scare you. But the bigger problem for you is that it's going to make my partner think it's proof that you're a demented killer doing a good impersonation of a human being."

"What should I do?"

"I'm going to hand this over to a criminalist first thing in the morning. Tomorrow afternoon you're going to walk in, on your own, to the station house for questioning. Believe me, I say this to no one, but I'm saying it to you: It's better if you come in on your own terms. And bring a lawyer. A good one. The best you can afford."

His pager beeped. He excused himself to use her phone, leaving her feeling dizzy, stunned. When he came back, he looked grim. May thought, *He's going to take me in now. Who'll watch my kids?*

Instead he said, "I've got myself another body."

"Who?"

"Don't know yet." He walked into the sunroom studying his boys, trying to figure out what to do with them.

"What's up, Pop?" Sean, his middle son asked.

"I got to go to work."

"Don't worry. Just drop us off at home. We can stay
there. Aunt Beth lets us stay alone sometimes."

"I'm going with you, Dad," Brad, the ten-year-old,
announced.

"Then who's going to watch me?" John asked quietly.
"Why can't Aunt Beth watch me?"

"She's sick," O'Donnell told him. "And no one's coming with me." His head dropped as he stared at his
shoes, trying to figure out what his options were.

"Leave them here," May offered suddenly. "I can use
the company."

"Thanks," he said. "But I'll take them along. They can
stay in the car."

John burst into tears. "I don't like to stay in the car.
It's scary in the car."

"Let him stay here," May said quietly. "Unless you
think it's not safe."

O'Donnell took a long listen to his powerful gut, then
went with her on a tour of the house, collecting spare
blankets, pillows, and sleeping bags, checking with John
in closets and under the beds to make sure there were
no monsters.

"Brad, Sean, John, you're in charge of taking care of
Mrs. Morrison. You have my number. You beep me anytime you need me." Then he left.

May got everyone settled into some semblance of a
bed, bid them all good night, and dragged herself, exhausted, to her room. She pulled off her clothes,
dropped them in a puddle on the floor, and climbed
into a pair of respectable flannel pajamas and robe.
She'd call Jack Forest first thing in the morning and go

with him to the station house. She'd get Ritchie to come, too. Maybe Carter could pitch in. For a while she studied the ceiling, wondering exactly how she'd ended up with so many lawyers. But before she finished reconstructing how she'd gotten to this point, she crashed to asleep.

When she woke, she had no idea of the time, thought it was morning, then realized the light streaking across her walls came not from the sun but from the headlights of a car that had pulled up in front of her house. She got out of bed, crept into the darkened bathroom, moved a slat of the wooden blinds, and peeked out, careful not to make any sudden movements that might catch the driver's attention.

She was at the threshold of rage, figuring it was Todd come back to spy on her, but even with her limited knowledge of cars, she could tell the one now parked in front of her house was not the Thunderbird he'd been driving. It was too small and light-colored, maybe pale gold or silver.

She crept downstairs and found Brad sitting up, staring out the window. He was like Delia, his family's designated worrier, the one who sat up until his father came home every night. For a moment she wondered if his self-appointed vigilance was building his character or stealing his childhood. Then he looked over, saw her staring, looked back outside, and she saw he was afraid.

She stepped around his sound-sleeping siblings and joined him at the window.

"That's not Dad's car," he reported, in case May didn't know.

Don't overreact, May thought. Cars were allowed to park on the street. She kept her voice calm as she told him, "It's probably someone visiting a neighbor." She hoped he was easily convinced because she was afraid if she had to talk for too long, he'd hear the tremor in her voice. "I'm sure that's all it is. Let's both try and get some sleep." But as she left him to go back upstairs, she could see he didn't buy it, didn't move from his new post, guarding at the window, as vigilant as his father would have been.

"Go to sleep," she called out in a whisper from half-way up the stairs. He motioned to her the way she imagined his father would, his hands saying what would have been too rude to articulate: *Don't worry, don't worry about me, just go on.*

Though she'd been lying in bed for a while, she hadn't yet fallen back asleep when she heard light footsteps coming up the stairs. She forced her eyes to stay open even though they wanted to clench shut. Brad emerged out of the shadows and whispered, "Someone's trying to get into your house."

Together they quickly padded downstairs. At the bottom step they stopped and watched the knob slowly, unsuccessfully, turn.

The Medeco was fully engaged, but she lunged to put the chain on, too. Then they both heard the sound of footsteps racing down the path and the quick cough of a car starting up.

It was gone before either of them had a chance to make out the licence plate in the dark, but Brad insisted he'd seen a hat on the driver, one that, as he described it, made May picture the brown fedora Gil had worn to work just the day before.

36

THEY WAITED, PLAYING WAR ON the floor in the front hall until sunup, but still O'Donnell didn't call her back.

"When Dad is deep into a murder case, he forgets everything. Sometimes he even forgets to eat," Brad told her as if his father needed defending. "It drives Aunt Beth nuts when he doesn't answer his pager. She says it used to drive my mom nuts, too, but I don't remember that."

Appreciating the weight of the shared memory, May quickly reassured him, "We're fine. He's fine. I just don't want him to worry about you, that's all."

When Susie got up at six-thirty, May left her with Brad, attentively listening to the rules of war. May quickly showered and changed and repeatedly reminded herself that the important thing was to keep calm, to keep the kids from getting scared.

Amazingly, even after his brothers and Delia joined him to help build an enormous card castle on the floor, Brad still didn't boast of the scare in the night. But as the morning progressed, he began to eye his brothers and May saw the story straining to come out. The look was a familiar one, one she'd seen often on the faces of her guests at *Paula Live*. The need to share a story would grow urgent, as if only in the telling would the fear, guilt, or desire be brought back to a manageable level.

While Susie and Delia were arguing over whether to watch *Rugrats* or *Muppet Babies,* and Sean and John were wrestling over a Lego Maniac set John had brought along, Brad started biting his lip, getting ready to tell his tale.

"Come on, everybody," May called out. "We're going to the diner for breakfast. By the time we're back your dad will be here."

Pete, spackling on the second floor, agreed to keep a lookout for O'Donnell and to tell him where they were when he showed up.

"Are we in Orlando?" John asked once they'd arranged themselves in one of the Florida Diner's pink six-seater booths.

"We're in New Jersey," Susie explained.

"Looks like Florida," John insisted.

Sean, just back from trying out the video games in the front lobby said, "Yeah? What does Florida look like, John? Tell one thing." He looked at Delia and rolled his eyes. "He's never even been to Florida."

"They just call it Florida because it's pink and green," Delia explained as if that made sense to her. "That's what Daddy said," she informed her mother.

"It's because the ceiling makes you feel like you're at the beach," Susie piped up, and May glanced over her head to notice for the first time that the ceiling in the Florida Diner was sky blue, with painted clouds.

She rushed the children through their assorted cereals, sausages, pancakes, and French toasts. She changed dollar after dollar into quarters, letting them each take turns picking out songs from the tabletop jukebox. After a while Brad seemed to forget he had a story to tell, concentrating instead on eating anyone's leftover bacon and home fries.

When they finally pulled into her driveway, May saw

O'Donnell and Pete waiting for her on her front steps. Pete disappeared inside right away, as if he'd been prompted, to drill in some wallboards. The kids ran in after him, to watch.

O'Donnell escorted May into the kitchen. "Can you prove where you were last night between eight and nine o'clock?" He wasn't bothering with small talk.

On top of the pile of papers on her kitchen table was the yellow card certifying that during the hours O'Donnell specified May had been suffering through her mandatory stress-reduction course. She handed it over to him.

"Congratulations. You have just reduced your stress considerably. You're not a suspect in last night's murder. You've just fallen to the bottom of the list."

Without thinking, she grabbed him. He hugged her back hard. The children, as if smelling something going on, came downstairs and stood, watching.

"Is she trying to warm up?" Susie asked. "Is she cold?"

Delia rolled her eyes.

"We're leaving in a couple of minutes, boys," O'Donnell told his kids, stepping away from her. "You're going to be late but you're going to school." The boys raced to the sunroom to grab a few last moments of TV.

"You'd better sit back down," O'Donnell said.

"Why?" She felt unburdened, nearly airborne with her new-proved innocence. She didn't want to sit; she wanted to fly, to laugh, to dance.

"Bunny's dead," he told her straight out.

May plopped into the nearest chair, the wind blown out of her.

"She was murdered in her office last night."

"This can't be true," she told him as if that would change things.

O'Donnell knew in these situations there was nothing

to do but state the facts. "We found several people who spoke to her on the phone between seven and eight o'clock last night. At nine she was found with a phone cord wrapped around her neck. An exact duplicate of the one your daughter found in your backyard."

May raced to the bathroom and retched into the toilet bowl. When she was done, she washed her face with cold water, as if that would wash away the cries lurching out of her.

"Mommy?" she heard Susie call. "Mommy, are you okay?"

"I'm fine," she answered, struggling to compose herself. "Just fine." She rejoined O'Donnell, who waited, his face blank. Then he laid a hand on her shoulder. "You okay?"

"No," she said. "Who is doing this?" she whispered when she'd composed herself enough to speak.

Before O'Donnell could reply, Brad walked into the room and asked, "Did you tell him yet?"

But May had forgotten about their night visitor; it had been eclipsed by this, the loss of her friend. Brad didn't know.

"At two-thirty-six this morning we had an intruder attempt to enter the premises," he said in perfect policeman pitch. "Mrs. Morrison scared him off when she double-locked the door."

Weary, his father took out his notepad. It showed on his face. This wasn't just any house, not just any witness telling him about an attempted break-in. This was his son, describing danger he'd claimed as his own.

As soon as Brad finished his report, O'Donnell tousled his hair, said a brusque, "Good work," then pushed him off toward the other children.

"This isn't good," he told her, in case she hadn't figured it out for herself. "Whoever tried to get in here last night is liable to try harder next time. If they can't get in your house, they might try at work or at school. You've got to get your kids out of here."

Goose bumps popped out on her arm as the phone rang.

"How are you, dolly?" her mother asked, not expecting much of an answer.

"I'm bringing the kids to you for a week."

"What?"

"'I'm bringing them today, as soon as I can get a flight."

"You can't."

"Our new au pair is coming Sunday, I'll have to fly back here to get her. Then I'll bring her out to you. She'll baby-sit whenever you need a break. She's a nurse. Won't it be nice to have a nurse around?"

"What do I need a nurse for? You can't bring them right now, dolly. That's all."

"Why not?"

"Why not? Do I have to explain myself to you suddenly? Am I a child suddenly?"

May quickly explained the reason for her urgent request. She made the murders sound as grisly as she could, which wasn't hard.

"All right. All right. I understand. I'll come to you," her mother said. "Is that all right? I'll come over the week-end. I'll take the children away somewhere. It doesn't have to be Florida, does it?"

May tried pleading and then bullying, but she couldn't convince her mother to stay in Boca and receive the kids there.

"I'm not arguing about this, dolly," Shirley said. "I'm going now to call my travel agent to see what kind of deal she can get me last minute."

Though it meant confessing he'd been listening in from the hallway, Pete, power screwdriver in hand, came into the kitchen to offer his own solution. He had a cabin upstate—Ulster County, New York—two hours away. It had three bedrooms—one with a water bed—a wood-burning stove, and a deck overlooking a pond. "I'll bring you the key tomorrow," he said. "You should listen to the detective. You should take your kids and your mother and your new Mary Poppins and go."

O'Donnell simply nodded his accord.

37

LATER IN THE MORNING WHEN May called in to work, she got a policeman on the phone instead of Linda.

"We've closed you down today," the cop told her after she explained who she was. "Maybe you'll be allowed back in here by Monday."

She kept the girls home from school. They hit the video store, taking out the entire collection of both Abbott and Costello and Jerry Lewis classics. Next stop was the supermarket where they stocked up on popcorn, pretzels, donuts, chips, and ice cream.

They passed the rest of the day and the next in front of the TV in a hypnotic stupor. Saturday was pretty much the same. If the girls noticed their mother's unusual compliance to all requests, they didn't say. But by Sunday morning the miraculous happened—they were sick of cartoons, thrilled to hear they'd been invited next door for breakfast.

Like prisoners released, the girls raced across the lawn to the Coopers' house. Emily's spread made Martha Stewart's presentation skills seem lazy. Susie dug in first, eagerly. Delia held back, nervous about destroying the pretty look of it all.

Then Susie overheard her mother talk about where she was going. She put down her plate. "Please. Please, can't I come with you to look at Bunny in the box?"

But Emily had learned nothing from raising five boys if not the power of distraction. "Guess what my boys did last night?" she asked, kneeling down next to Susie. Then she whispered, drawing Susie in closer. "Timmy pasted glow-in-the dark planets on the bathroom ceiling upstairs." She winked at May, motioning for her to get ready to leave. Carter, conspiring, ran up and called down, "I can't find Venus. Does anyone know where Venus is?" He held his hand over Timmy's mouth so he couldn't answer.

"I can," Susie and Delia both called out, racing up the stairs to be first.

"Thanks," May said, and gave Emily a heartfelt hug. "I should be back by noon."

"They'll be fine," Emily told her. "Carter and I won't let them out of our sight."

May arrived at the funeral home only a few minutes late. When the director escorted her into a cavernous auditorium filled to capacity with mourners, she whispered, "I said I'm looking for the Bunny Hoffman funeral," convinced he had led her to another one by mistake. After all, wasn't Bunny a loner, a curmudgeon who'd befriended May against her better judgment, a woman who knew no life outside of work? May had assumed that other than the office staff, there would be just a smattering of mourners, six or seven old ladies who came because that's what they did, because they had nowhere else to go.

"This is the Bunny Hoffman funeral," the director insisted.

Chastened, May quickly displaced a dozen mourners as she slipped past them into one of the few empty seats left. They barely noticed, their attention held by the running eulogies coming from the steady stream of people going to speak at a small wooden podium.

There had been no clues at all that Bunny was part of such a large and loving family. May had never suspected that the kindness displayed toward her was typical. Because Bunny never mentioned her personal life to anyone, they'd all assumed, May included, that she just didn't have one. Unlike May, Gil, Wendy, Colleen, and Margery, Bunny kept no pictures on her windowsill advertising her humanity. Yet here was a clan, huge and adoring, all mourning the loss of a woman whose life May had mistakenly believed consisted of a monastic devotion to work.

Now, by her count of the eulogies—and she'd missed at least one—she learned Bunny had four brothers, three sisters, and dozens of nieces and nephews, husbands and wives and children of nieces and nephews, and cousins, who sat in the front rows like ducklings, in size order. One after another they took their place at the podium to talk about their dear aunt, sister, cousin, friend, Bunny.

And no wonder she lived simply in a sparsely furnished studio apartment in a prewar building in Murray Hill. It wasn't, as gossip went, that she was miserly. On the contrary, with all the theater tickets, circus tickets, late dinners before *Letterman* and *Saturday Night Live*, shopping trips to Bergdorf's and F.A.O. Schwarz that

May now heard about, all the charity events she spon-
sored in her nearly nonexistent spare time, the benefi-
cent aunt, sister, cousin must have come close to
contemplating eating cat food for dinner some nights.

There was an eerie sense of her in the large room.
One of her brother's had the same raspy voice, another
her wet, smoker's cough. A woman May took to be a
sister wore her hair up in an old-fashioned twist that
made her look, from the back, like Bunny, as if she
were watching it all.

Halfway through the long service May picked out the
cluster of her colleagues, who'd arrived early enough to
sit together in a bunch toward the front of the room.
There was Gil, looking gray; Stephanie, dressed in black
Chanel, leaning in toward him, whispering urgently in
his ear; Margery beside them, a proper southern
mourner in a broad-brimmed black hat and sunglasses.
There was Colleen, weeping into a fine linen hankie,
grieving, May assumed, for Chuck while at the same
time keeping one dainty hand stuck inside her leather
carryall, nervously fingering her Rolodex.

Wendy sat right behind Gil, in a row of perfectly
poised support staff, hands all folded in laps, heads
cocked attentively. Henry was there, too, though probably only because he feared he'd be fired if he missed it.

Sitting next to Paula's secretary, Patty, was a man in
a navy suit, and then May noticed there were three
more just like him positioned in the shape of a cross,
in front of, behind, and next to, on either side, a woman
in a black-hooded cape. Though May couldn't make out
the woman's face—the hood was too large, the cape en-
veloped her—she could tell by her carriage it was Paula.

May listened, saddened, to the eulogies, but as the
hour wore on, her eyes were drawn back to her colleagues, to studying each one in turn, looking for a tell-

tale sign, a twitch, trickling sweat, crinkling brow, that might reveal a killer. At first as her eyes scanned them, she thought, *No way, not her; not him; she could but wouldn't; he would but couldn't; they might but no, not them; not him.* But then she remembered the cord in her backyard, the knob slowly turning on her new front door, and she thought again. *Maybe she might. Maybe together they did.*

Her formerly trusting self might have thought it impossible to believe any them could do such a thing. But a newer side of her, a side born the night Todd told her about Chloe and strengthened with each successive murder, thought anyone—Gil, Stephanie, Todd, Margery—anyone might turn out to be capable of killing.

It was only once the service was over, as she waited to walk down the aisle toward the anteroom where Bunny's brothers and sisters lingered to accept condolences, that she picked the somber faces of O'Donnell and Paradiso out of the crowd. They sat perfectly still in their seats at the back of the room, following everyone with their eyes, watching just as she had done, for a clue that might point to the darkness marking one of their souls.

Paradiso saw her first, didn't smile, muttered something that made O'Donnell's head swivel toward her. When their eyes met, he acknowledged her with a slight nod. She smiled and nodded back.

In the parking lot she joined the group of producers huddled around Gil's gold Mercedes sports car.

"They say we'll be able to get into the office tomorrow," he was telling them. "God only knows what they've done to the place." May saw a mass of blue walk by, then realized it was the clump of men surrounding Paula. Gil saw it, too.

"Paula," he yelled. "Wait up." He jogged across the lot, was nearly run over by the stream of cars maneuvering to follow the hearse to the cemetery. He got to his elusive host just as she slipped inside a black Lincoln town car. She listened, then slammed the door without reply.

Head hanging, Gil returned to where his workers were waiting. He struggled to snap out of his funk. "Tomorrow morning I want everyone back to work, back to normal. No sick days." He looked meaningfully at May. "No vacation days," he went on. "Eight o'clock in the conference room, no excuses no exceptions."

"Do you want some of us to stay home?" Henry asked. "Like we did after Chuck was killed? Or when you say you want everyone in by eight, are you including the associate producers, the production assistants, and the secretaries?" He really wanted to know.

"You don't have to come," Gil said, then raised his voice so everyone else could hear. "Eight o'clock tomorrow morning in the conference room or I'll take it as notice of your resignation."

"I don't know how much longer I can take this," Stephanie let out as Gil made his way back to Paula's town car, standing in front of the slowly moving vehicle to get it to stop. "My father's offered to finance a platoon of private detectives," she went on, "but Gil called him up and told him not to do it. He said the police are very close to an arrest and don't want interference. Have you heard that, too?" Her perfectly highlighted hair blew around her perfectly made-up face. Even in the glare of direct sunlight no hint of the expensive foundation she used to blend her skin tone was visible. Her face remained as placid as a pond, but her eyes looked out like little boats of misery.

"I'll tell you, this, sugar. I was on the phone with my number one assistant-district-attorney source this morning. And he told me that everyone on the show, from the mail-room clerk to your husband, is a class-one suspect now. Those of us who don't have, or cannot procure, a documented alibi are going to be invited downtown for questioning tomorrow. So if I were you, I'd call my daddy right now and tell him to hire that platoon of detectives. In fact, if you want, I'll call him myself."

"Gil must have his reasons," Wendy said, defending her boss, but she sounded unconvinced. "He wouldn't tell your father not to do it if he didn't have a very good reason."

As they stood together watching Gil jump up and down in front of the car, calling out, "Paula, Paula, Paula," they all silently tried to figure out exactly what that reason might be.

38

MAY ARRIVED JUST AS EMILY was setting out hot chocolate and cookies. The girls were in the backyard making a snow fort with all five Cooper boys under Carter's watchful eyes. Emily placed a ceramic bowl filled with freshly made whipped cream in the middle of the table.

"Are you as perfect as you seem?" May asked her.

"Are you nuts?" Emily answered. "I'd give anything to switch lives with you."

Both women laughed at the shared reality that neither of their lives was the fantasy the other pictured it to be.

Emily put an end to their sisterly spirit. "A car's been driving by your house every hour on the hour," she explained.

At the muffled sound of tires sloshing through slush, they both went to the window in time to see a bright red Volvo turn on to their street.

"Not that one." She turned back to May. "Carter wouldn't let me call the police. He said I should ignore it. He said it was your husband's car."

May's hot cheeks cooled instantly. Todd's surveillance was irritating, enraging, but it wasn't frightening. "I should let Todd know that if he's trying to drive me crazy, it's done. He can stop. I'm insane."

Emily laughed. "We should all be as crazy as you. Why don't you leave the girls here for the afternoon? They're having a great time."

May thanked her but declined. They had an au pair to pick up at JFK and her mother to get at Newark Airport after that. And even if they didn't have anywhere to go, right now she needed to be with them.

By the time she dragged the children out of their new favorite kitchen and battled the traffic to the airport in Queens, Sabrieke's plane was landing. May felt the residue of the day sticking to her; she felt heavy with sadness and edgy with fear. But her children brought her out of it.

"I can pick out all the au pairs," Delia boasted, and went on to explain that they were the ones with the smiles that weren't exactly happy and never lasted. "I hope she's not the last one off the plane," she grumbled. "The ones who are the last ones off the plane never work out."

May was still trying to figure out which au pair Delia was thinking of when her daughter called out. "Look. That's her. See the smile?"

May saw the smile, but it didn't look stiff or pasted on at all. She also saw the long wavy hair, the lanky limbs, the open face. The young woman moved with an easy self-confidence, as though she took it for granted that people noticed and liked her. As she headed for them, Delia extended her hand, the family member with the best manners and most practiced "Nice to meet you."

Sabrieke was charmed. "Nice to meet you, too," she said, her English heavily draped by a thick French accent.

"My mommy visited a dead person this morning," Susie announced by way of introduction. "She was dead, right Mommy?" She turned back to Sabrieke. "The woman was named after our rabbit, Mr. Bunny. She was dead in a box, right, Mommy?"

"We don't have a rabbit," Delia explained, offering Sabrieke her first eye roll. "There's just a wild rabbit who sometimes lives in our backyard."

Sabrieke's smile didn't fade, but it was joined by puzzled eyes.

On the way to the car Delia explained her version of the story of Bunny's demise. Susie giggled, thinking it was just another made-up tale, less scary than the ones she was used to, in which it was usually the child's mother or father who died.

They were nearly home when Sabrieke, seated in the front passenger seat with her lithe body twisted toward the children in the back, asked, "Is it a bad robber who did this thing?" Then May realized Sabrieke thought it was a made-up story, too.

As soon as they were in the house, she took her aside. May didn't have much time—in fifteen minutes she had to leave again to pick up her mother. Quickly she recounted the details of the past few weeks, leaving out nothing—not the murders in her office, the phone cord in the backyard, not Susie's bashed-in nose or Todd's unwelcome visits. She didn't want to frighten her, but neither did she want to pretend that at the moment theirs was an average household engaged in an ordinary routine. She didn't want to put the girls through another painful getting-to-know-you period only to have the young woman run home scared as soon as she figured things out.

It was a gamble. But although her trust in her instincts had wavered over the past few weeks, she still insisted on listening to them. And right now her instincts told her that Sabrieke was not the type to be easily scared away.

"It seems I have walked into an adventure," was her reply as she dragged her heavy bags into the kitchen. Her only question was, "The children, are they safe here?" providing May with the perfect segue to explain why in the morning Sabrieke, the girls, and Grandma Shirley would all be going to a place called Upstate New York to spend a few days in her carpenter's cabin.

"My grandparents have a cabin in the Ardennes," she said. "I like it very much going there. We can catch grouse and pull up carrots, in your upstate?"

May imagined this was unlikely, but since she didn't know for sure, she said, "You'll have to see."

"Of course. Soon enough I shall see for myself, no?"

The girls begged to be left home with their new babysitter. So after repeating careful instructions not to open the door for anyone until she got back, May left for the airport to pick up her mother.

"You don't have to worry about us getting murdered," she heard Delia explain as she closed and locked the door. "Because it's only people who work in my mother's office who get murdered. And it usually doesn't happen twice in a day."

39

WHEN SHE FIRST MOVED TO Florida, May's mother, Shirley, had made friends with a woman whose newfound hobby was taking snapshots with the disposable cameras she bought at the checkout counter of the drugstore. She gave the pictures to her subjects, handing them out like Life Savers, little rewards for being her friend. Shirley sent hers directly to May with an implicit understanding that May would send back photos of the girls in return. But May didn't have a friend with a camera, and the huge leather bag filled with filters and zoom lenses that used to take up half the floor of their downstairs coat closet was now Chloe's problem, not hers.

In fact, photographs of the girls had become rarities of late, regular documentation of their happy childhood ending with the departure of their father. Snapshots were now limited to school photos, awkward poses against backdrops that were meant to, but never did, look like nature.

The large assortment of photographs of her mother though—some of which were stuck with magnets on the refrigerator door, others of which had found their way up to Delia's and Susie's rooms—had given May the illusion that she was keeping up with how her mother looked, even though it was now over a year since she'd last seen her. It was a shock, then, when she picked her out of the airport crowd. For one thing, the pictures couldn't capture her gait, which was undeniably shaky. Nor did they accurately reflect how gaunt she had become.

Shirley did her best to appear put together, with an arsenal of promotional makeup giveaways in her purse at all times and her hair coiffed and dyed at the start of every month. But despite her efforts she looked unsteady, as if her spine had slipped slightly, as if she was settling down and to one side.

May got ready to bolster her with a torrent of compliments, but before she could begin, her mother blurted out, "I couldn't believe it when I remembered you're closer to forty than thirty. But now that I see you, I realize it's true."

May tried to find the right comeback, but her mother wasn't done yet. "Anyway, what did I think? I was getting older and you were staying twenty? When did you stop highlighting your hair?"

It was unlike her mother to chatter. Aware of it, Shirley forced herself to stop and took a breath. "I have some news," she said. "Important news."

May thought, *What kind of cancer?*

They found an unoccupied row of turquoise plastic molded chairs near an abandoned car-rental counter and sat down. Shirley took May's hand.

May thought, *Parkinson's, Alzheimer's, heart disease.*

Shirley took another breath, was having difficulty getting started.

May thought, *MS*, then gently urged her, "Go ahead. Just say it fast."

She squeezed May's hand tightly, then closed her eyes. "I'm engaged."

May shot up out of her chair.

Shirley said, "Arrest me. I tried to wait for you to find

someone first. But I can't keep waiting forever. They're lining up where I live, the single women. They join the computer club, the fishing club. You think they're really interested in computers? They're interested in men. I couldn't wait anymore."

May sat down. Her mother asked if she'd forgive her in time to give her away at the wedding.

"What do I have to forgive you for?"

Her mother clutched her chest. "Oy, this is hard."

May smiled. It was funny, her mother thinking this was bad news. It was surprising news, yes; she'd have to get used to it, sure, but it wasn't bad. It was good; in fact, it was great news. It meant maybe her mother would stop calling her six times a day. Maybe she'd stop harping at her to find a man. It meant maybe she'd be happy now. May grinned widely, the first time in days.

Her mother scowled. "It's Mr. Morrison."

May struggled to comprehend the problem. She knew Todd's father lived nearby Shirley's retirement community in Boca. She knew they occasionally bumped into each other in the supermarket, at the Shrimp House Restaurant, or the bank. Shirley used to dutifully report their meetings, including the fact that Mr. Morrison— they were always strangely formal with each other— never asked about either May or the children. But when Shirley saw that May became agitated by the news that her former father-in-law expressed zero interest in the well-being of his only grandchildren, she stopped mentioning it all together.

That her mother cared what Mr. Morrison thought of her engagement made May question the frailty of what she considered to be her mother's strongest asset—her fine mind. "What's the difference what Mr. Morrison thinks. He's a moron like his son."

"Oy vey," Shirley moaned. "He may be a moron, but he's the moron I'm going to marry."

By the time May pulled into her driveway, she wondered if maybe, like Alice, she'd gone through the looking glass and would soon wake up to find it all a dream. Things were so mixed up that hearing shocking news was starting to seem normal. Both her ex-husband and a murderer were stalking her house, her mother was planning to marry her ex-father-in-law, her carpenter greeted her at the front door with a list of the amenities at his homemade cabin hideaway, and her new au pair, dressed in a neon orange skirt not much longer than her belt was wide, announced that May's detective friend was on his way over.

"Is he your boyfriend? She should change before he comes over if he's your boyfriend," Shirley said as if Sabrieke weren't there.

"You like me to change? I can change. Is no problem if you think I look too good."

May quickly explained that O'Donnell was not her boyfriend and that even if he was, Sabrieke should wear whatever she liked. Her mother look on disapprovingly, as if this explained why May hadn't yet remarried.

O'Donnell arrived around eight, looking as though he hadn't slept. While Sabrieke got Delia and Susie ready for bed, the detective, May, Shirley, and Pete sat drinking coffee in the kitchen, planning the trip upstate. Pete drew a careful map of the back-roads route to his cabin, and then filled them in on details. If the ropes holding up the garbage can were gnawed through by raccoons, there was a spare coil in the loft in the garage. All toilets must be jiggled after flushing. The chimney flue needed to be opened. There was wood behind the shed. The water turn-off valve was in the cellar. They should tell the girls not to scream when they saw spiders, because it might bring out the mice.

O'Donnell followed up with his own set of questions. Where was the nearest neighbor? (half a mile); did the cabin have a phone? (not hooked up); did the neighbors have a phone? (sure thing); would Pete be sure to give the neighbor's number to O'Donnell? (no sweat).

Though the detective made it clear he was not delighted with the cabin's lack of a phone and remote location, he conceded it was a better choice for the children than staying home. When Shirley discovered May was not planning to join them, she tried to talk herself out of going along, too.

"Your nursemaid is a little wood nymph. She can gather kindling, feed the birds, take Susie's temperature, and teach Delia how to speak French all at the same time. If you're not going, I'm staying home with you."

But May held fast, negotiating back from two weeks in the cabin to one, and then settling (as she'd planned to from the start) on five days away—enough time, she hoped, for the police to have a suspect under arrest.

After Pete left and Shirley went up to bed, May and O'Donnell sat at the kitchen table, both lost in thought, not speaking. After a while May got up to make some tea. O'Donnell's cup had turned cold by the time he broke the silence with the advice, "You really should go away, too."

"I thought I'm not supposed to leave town."

"You're off Paradiso's suspect list. I'm telling you, leave town."

"I can't." She didn't explain why, didn't know if she could. It wasn't that to go meant being fired from her job, though that was part of it. It was more a feeling she had that leaving meant giving up control of her life, giving in to fear.

"Then I should stay here with you," O'Donnell offered.

"You can't do that," she reminded him. There were too many reasons; none he didn't know.

"I don't want anything to happen to you," he admitted.

May smiled; his admission, just words, was like a gift. "Then it won't," she said as if believing it would make it true.

40

SHE COULDN'T SLEEP, AND IT wasn't because her mother snored, either. What kept her awake were the images racing through her mind—phone cords wrapped around her neck, Todd winking at a black-robed judge, maggots crawling out of Bunny's nose.

She got out of bed and straightened the never-ending clutter of magazines and toys that surely was as alive as any bacteria, invading every crevice of available space in the house. She repacked the children's suitcases for the third time. She drank warm milk and then weak tea. Finally, exhausted and wired at the same time, afraid to even attempt to sleep now, she decided to turn off the pictures in her brain by plugging in one of the videos that Bunny had given her to look at.

Wendy's voice spat out, "It's Father's Day, but Father's

gone," her disgust giving a full editorial position without any comment. May pressed the fast-forward button and watched the silent speed-talking heads, Paula's bobbing up and down with what May knew in real time was deeply heartfelt empathy.

"Governor's book tour," Wendy announced, leading, bored, into the next show. This time the fast-forwarding looked no different than the slo-mo as the governor sat across from Paula at their small, round "important persons" table, answering her questions with minimal movement of his lips.

During " 'Hand Models, Can You Raise Kids with Gloves On?' " a show Bunny herself put together, May drifted off, then woke to the gray snow of a played-out tape. She reached over, hit Stop, then fell back onto the cushionless loveseat to steal one more hour of dreamless sleep. She woke abruptly several times thinking, *Bunny found something*, but fell back asleep before the thought was fully processed.

Pete was her alarm clock, arriving, as promised, at seven. "They should stop at the little market near the house to get a couple of lightbulbs," he advised. "And batteries for the flashlight. There's a flashlight in the garage on the shelf near the door. It takes two of the big ones—the D's." He waved a piece of paper covered with his compressed handwriting. "It's all here. So long as they can read, they'll be fine."

"Thanks," May said, taking the paper from him. "This is all very kind of you."

"It's nothing. You know, Mrs. Morrison, your kids, they get to me. They remind me of my own kids when they were little—way back in the days when they'd still be seen with their old man in public without getting embarrassed. That's what your kids need, you know? They need an old man. I'm not proposing," he added quickly.

NANCY STAR

"I know," she said, and they both laughed at the thought. "Don't worry, Pete," she told him. "They're doing okay. We're making the best of things."

Half an hour later Sabrieke, Shirley, and the kids piled into the van. Shirley volunteered to drive, the easier job, while Sabrieke played the part of stewardess, dutifully doling out chocolate milk and snack packs of Goldfish pretzels, working the cassettes, mediating between Susie's request for loud music so she could sing and Delia's request for no music so she could read.

As the car pulled away, Pete and May walked back to the house, looking to anyone who was watching like an old married couple saying good-bye to visiting relatives. Then they went in the house and back to their business of being alone. That's when May felt the hole the size of a crater in her stomach. She hated having her kids away, couldn't understand how people lived through sleep-away camp, college, life with them grown and gone. There was no way she'd let Todd take them from her.

Later May thought maybe it had been the sense of losses piling up that had left her turned so far inward she hadn't noticed the envelope lying on the foyer floor when she first came in the house. By the time she discovered it, she had accidentally dragged it into the dining room and could no longer judge whether it had been shoved through the mail slot or someone, somehow, had come into the house and dropped it.

O'Donnell answered her beep right away. She read him the invitation over the phone, describing it in her best imitation of police detail.

"It's a store-bought card with fill in the blanks. The person used a felt-tipped blue marker and wrote with a scratchy scrawl. It looks intentionally scribbly, maybe written by a righty with their left hand."

"Could be," O'Donnell replied.

268

"The party is at two-thirty next Saturday," she told him. "In the space where you're supposed to write who it's for, the person scrawled: 'Bring a naughty nighty.' Do you think he could be getting kinky?" she asked.

O'Donnell asked, "Is there a number to RSVP?"

There was, she told him, with a 718 area code, which meant Staten Island, Queens, Brooklyn, or the Bronx—"Nice and vague" she commented before telling him, no, she hadn't called yet.

O'Donnell went through all the reasons why he didn't think the invite was sent by the killer, the most important being that it didn't fit his MO. As for her offer to be wired before attending the party, he suggested a more prudent approach would be to RSVP that she was coming and let the police handle investigating it. When she didn't back down, his voice rose. "No wires," he insisted, and hung up the phone.

41

WHEN SHE GOT TO WORK, MAY felt as if she'd arrived at Sleeping Beauty's castle the day Sleeping Beauty woke up. Paula was back with a large staff of protectors: three off-duty cops, two private eyes, a bunch of bouncers, and Frankie at her side. All of them had a hard time keeping up with her as she raced around the office drumming up support for her latest crusade.

Bunny's funeral had stunned her and moved her, she

announced, more than anything else in her life ever had. She'd spent years pitying Bunny, she told everyone several times, only to find she should have been pitying herself instead. After seeing how many lives Bunny had touched, she decided the wrong person had been killed.

"It should have been me," she said.

Everyone knew enough to disagree with her quickly and with great passion.

To work through her feelings of grief and guilt, she and her therapists, including the on-call *Paula Live* psychologist whom they brought in to handle all post-show traumatic-syndrome problems, decided her cure would begin with creating a show dedicated to Bunny Hoffman. The producers were summoned. The protectors stood back against her wall of windows, hands over their crotches, at ease.

"Will anyone want to watch a show about an overweight, coarse, hoarse television producer? In the shadow of bombings, massacres, droughts, global warming, will the loss of one unassuming woman mean anything to our viewers?"

Gil seemed to brighten at Paula's question, but before he could answer, she answered for him.

"I don't care. Bunny's family is going to watch this show, and that's enough for me. So don't try to scare me out of it. For once I'm not the least bit scared. This organization is going to come together to create an entire show devoted to Bunny. By the time the show is over, the audience here and at home is going to feel like they knew her, or at least like they wish they did. May, you're in charge. I want you to bring on the tears. I mean torrents, rivers, oceans."

The producers sat stunned. It would have been in bad taste to point out the cavernous flaw in this bad idea, that though Bunny's life was absolutely worth celebrating, it was completely undramatic and, other than the captive studio audience, no one was going to watch.

"Go," Paula urged. "Delve. Compose. Create."

Glumly they marched across the hall. Gil held his door open, ushering the producers directly inside his office. He slammed the door. "What she doesn't know is how close she is to losing her markets in Santa Fe, East Lansing, and West Palm."

"My mother's in West Palm," Colleen reported. "She'll go into a major depression if we go off the air there."

"After this Bunny show, we'll be lucky to be on the air on the live feed. This is it. The moment of truth. For those of us lucky enough not to be killed or arrested, it looks like the only other choice is going to be unemployment."

Gil went on. "You people have to be either geniuses or magicians to make this one work." He sounded completely defeated. "I have a meeting upstairs in two minutes where I'm going to try to convince the bean counters that this show, that all our shows, are ideas still worth having. I'm counting on you to make it the truth."

"If you want a big idea," Margery offered, "here it is. We'll do a tribute to Bunny in the first segment of the show, scrape around like catfish to find something. Then, in the second segment we'll segue into a 'Who's the killer?' bit. Every one of us wants to catch him. The bastard." Never one of Bunny's fans, Margery was clearly shaken up by her loss.

"Forget it," Gil said. "Face the facts. We're a bunch of mediocre TV producers who can just barely sniff out a trend. That's a far cry from being able to track down a killer. That idea is DOA. Like Bunny. Like us, if this show sinks." He heaved a sigh. May studied him closely. He should have jumped at the catch-the-killer idea. It was in bad taste, sure, but it was the only way they were going to get an audience. And since when did Gil ever care about taste?

"I'm going upstairs," he announced. "May, you're in charge. You and your illustrious staff are going to figure out a way to save this slug of a show. And don't even think about leaving the room till you do it."

He opened the door and let himself out. May couldn't speak for the others, but until the moment he took out his key, she never believed he was serious about locking them in.

42 "IF BUNNY WERE ALIVE, SHE'D go out on the window ledge right now, sneak a smoke, and scream for help."

"If Bunny were alive, we wouldn't be locked in here in the first place," Colleen countered. "How can you kid around about this?"

"What do you want me to do, sugar? Change places with her?"

"Let's stay friends and get this show of Paula's over with," May counseled. "We're stuck here. There's a killer on the loose. Any one of us could be next. Our jobs are on the line. My kids are on the line," she added quietly. "Let's get Paula off our backs."

Her colleagues muttered, shifted in their seats, grumbled, then got up to grab pen and paper off Gil's desk.

"We'll shape the show like you suggested," May told Margery. "We'll do the first half about Bunny's life, focus the second half on the killer."

"Why bother?" Colleen slumped in her seat. "Gil already nixed the idea."

"He won't have a choice," May said. "It's all we'll give him. He can either sell Paula a show about Bunny and her killer, or he can tell Paula there'll be no show at all. What do you think his options are? You think Gil's going to get down in the trenches and produce a show himself? You think he even remembers how? If we're together on this, he'll agree. Are we?"

"You willing to do that, sugar? You ready to risk Gil's nervous breakdown? Pinkie swear?"

May extended her pinkie. "I'm willing if you're willing."

Margery linked pinkies with her and offered her other pinkie to Colleen. They made a circle, pinkies linked, then suddenly aware what a tiny circle it was, all quickly let go.

"Let's get to work," May said, "and figure out the beats of the show."

Without too much negotiation they worked it out so that Colleen got Bunny's work life, May took her family life, and Margery had the job of putting together the story of how Bunny Hoffman's life had ended. When they finished mapping out the shape of the first half, Colleen groaned.

"This part's going to be so boring our audience won't hear us over their own snoring. We might as well just put up a sign now saying *Paula Live* Going-out-of-Business Time-Slot Sale."

"It won't be boring. It will be moving," May told her. "And the second half will be gripping, frightening, real. Anyway, when was the last time we worked together on a show? And I don't mean one of those hysterical last-minute jobs, like the time that Washington hostess had her secretary cancel because she forgot she was giving a lunch."

"I like those last-minute read-the-mail-on-the-air shows," Colleen said.

Margery added, "At least people watch those. At least they're entertaining. At least the letters I pick to read are funny."

"There's a lot of talent in this room," May said to get the group to focus. "And a lot at stake. Come on. This barely qualifies as a challenge. Between the three of us, we should be able to make dog walking entertaining."

"Is that supposed to be a compliment?" Colleen asked. "Because I don't feel like it's a compliment." She took a few breaths before adding, "Do either of you have a Xanax? If I don't get out of this room in one minute, I'm going to have a panic attack."

The first time May buzzed Wendy and said they were stuck, Gil's assistant thought it was a bad joke. Only after they began banging on the wall of her small cubicle did Wendy realize Gil had really locked them in.

"Something's wrong," she muttered as the producers filed out. "It's not like him to do something like this. Something is definitely wrong."

May followed her into her cubicle. "What do you think it is?" she asked.

Wendy looked surprised, as if she hadn't realized she'd been speaking out loud. "Nothing. Everything's fine." She closed down, locked up, went back to her ordinary mode—no help—and resumed straightening up the top of her perfectly neat desk.

As soon as May got back to her office, she phoned her friend Judy at *Simon Says* to find out if there was any new scuttlebutt on Barnett.

"Not really," Judy said. "The police took Simon up to the apartment yesterday, though. He told me it looked pretty much the way it always did—like no one really lived there. At least they've finally admitted it wasn't a suicide," she confided, thinking this was news. "It wasn't a robbery, either. Everything was in perfect order. Simon says there wasn't even a fingerprint. And I hear they found Barnett's black book. Which means every unmarried woman in the business—who am I kidding?—every woman in the business is now a suspect."

May called Peggy Golding next. "I hear they're looking for a producer over at *Rosie O'Donnell*," she told her. "Do you want me to call there for you?"

"Actually, I'm going to stick it out here," Peggy said. "At least whoever got Iris is now finished with the *Tell Tonya* show. I heard about Bunny, so I guess you're safe, too. I'd be scared as hell to work on a show this guy hadn't hit yet. I've been trying to figure out the pattern, but I can't. It's not alphabetical. It's not musical notes. Did you ever see the movie where it was musical notes?"

"How is Tonya taking it?" May asked, ignoring the question.

"She's fine. She's convinced it's a spiritual thing. That the victims all got killed because they had bad karma. You know, what goes around comes around. You have to admit it's not like any of the dead people were particularly beloved when they were alive."

May decided not to enlighten her about Bunny's adoring clan.

"We've got every theory on earth going here in our office pool," Peggy went on. "Numerology, revenge, crazy guest, spurned lover, drugs, voodoo, Mafia—Chinese, Russian, and Italian—and knew-something. Poor Bunny. She was so convinced someone had found out something they shouldn't have. She was hounding all of us, calling over to trace Iris's steps the day she was killed, as if the police hadn't bothered to do it themselves. And look where it got her. Kind of makes you want to forget the whole thing, doesn't it?"

"Yes," she lied, and got off the phone. Extra supplies of adrenaline were racing through her system as she thought, *Bunny was on to something.* She tried to envision what it was, what stories Bunny could have been chasing that Iris, Chuck, and Barnett might have been hot on as well. Possible villains raced through her mind—cults, drug cartels, mobsters. But none of those were Bunny's style. Besides, O'Donnell had confiscated all the victims' work files. If they'd been chasing the same story, he'd have found out by now. So it was something else, something personal. She phoned O'Donnell to share her theory, to see if she could get him to agree that she was right.

When he finally answered his beeper, he said, "What you've got isn't evidence. It's speculation, grasping at the wind."

She let out a small "Oh."

"I'm not saying you can't find anything out that might help us," he went on. "I'm saying I don't want you to try. It's not safe, May. Leave it to the professionals. I wouldn't begin to try to figure out how to do your job. I don't want you to get hurt trying to do mine."

She didn't argue the point. She didn't remind him that he wasn't the only one with a powerful gut and that hers was insisting she push on. So what if no one wanted her to do it. She'd spent her life accommodating other people. This time she'd accommodate herself.

"I've got to run," O'Donnell said. "Will you promise me you'll leave it alone? I don't want to have to worry about you."

"You don't have to worry about me," she replied, then hung up and hustled to Colleen's office.

"I was just zapping through a bunch of shows Bunny gave me," Colleen said as she pressed the pause button, freezing the frame on the video. "I'm looking for some winning moments we can use as part of a testimonial. It is not an easy task." She realized May's thoughts were elsewhere. "You want something?"

"Question: What if Chuck was killed because he found something out? What if that's what happened to Iris? What if that's what happened to Bunny?"

Colleen closed her door and lowered her voice. "Did Bunny talk to you? She came to me with a conspiracy theory, too, and I will tell you the same thing I told her. I was the only secret Chuck Mills ever had. If he'd had any others, I would have known them. We shared everything. Everything," she repeated, her eyes flashing.

"I didn't know Bunny was pumping you about Chuck."

"How could you know? She was an expert at discretion, wasn't she? Chuck and I had a tough job keeping our little romance a secret. Bunny kept her whole life a secret. I think I'll do a show about that when all this settles down, if I'm still employed. 'The Secrets People Keep.' But first I have to finish watching this corker," she said, and unfroze the guests of "Miss America, Where Are They Now?" "Her shows weren't all this dull, were they?" The question was left in the air as May hurried back to her office, where Henry awaited her.

"Here's the list of Bunny's immediate relatives," he said. "I suggest you start with her sister Elaine. Elaine will be the most forthcoming of all of them." He handed her the bio of Elaine Hoffman he'd put together after interviewing Bunny's production assistant. "She's home waiting for your call. She told me if you want you can drive over to see her right now. I wrote out the directions. I don't think it's too far from where you live."

Finally, after a year, Henry had figured out how to do his job. But his timing stunk. She didn't want to leave now to interview Elaine. She wanted to interview Bunny's production assistant and her associate producer. If Bunny had been sniffing around about the murders and finally figured something out, they would be the ones who would know it.

"Can I come along?" Henry asked, looking for a reward for good behavior.

"It's better to do these things one on one," she said, rather than admitting the truth, which was that if she went alone, she could get in and out quickly and back to the office in time to snag Bunny's staff for a talk before they went home for the day. Then she had to hurry home, too. Her mother had promised to go to the country store at seven to call her. And May had promised to be home to get the call.

Moping, now that he'd been told to remain at his desk, Henry begrudgingly muttered that he'd rented her a car, a red Plymouth Reliant, already parked in the garage across the street. Normally she would have taken a moment to cajole him out of his mood, but it struck her now that his mood wasn't her problem, so she ignored it and rushed out to get the job done.

43

ELAINE HOFFMAN LIVED IN ONE of four twenty-story apartment buildings plunked in the middle of a grassy square that was fenced in by a figure eight of roadways. May concluded the residents of the red-brick buildings must be more interested in ease of egress—their location marking the spot where three highways intersected—than in physical beauty, of which there was none to be seen.

As soon as Elaine opened the door, May realized she was the family member who'd given the ghostly impression that Bunny had been at her own funeral. Though she was much younger, Elaine had groomed herself in her older sister's image, except that Elaine was a prettier, thinner version.

Bunny's presence was everywhere. The mantel above the fireplace was devoted to her, a record of her achievements displayed for all of Elaine's visitors to see— framed copies of *Variety* announcing her promotions, a lovingly polished Emmy, several awards from various women's groups, blown-up copies of advertisements announcing her appearance on seminar panels.

"We're very proud of her," Elaine explained.

"So were we," May told her. She then gently went on to explain the show Paula wanted to do now, a celebration of Bunny as an icon of their times, a good woman who asked nothing, gave everything, and had her life stolen in an awful act of violence. "We think this might help flush out the killer," May told her.

Elaine wavered at first. She wasn't sure Bunny would have liked the idea. She'd have to check with her brothers and sisters to see what they thought. But despite her gentle hospitality, despite the soft voice, the tea served in fine English china cups, the French bakery cookies spread out on antique platters, May sensed hostility simmering. Finally, Elaine exploded.

Bunny spent her life serving others, she told May suddenly. She expected and received little thanks. But the way the police were treating her now, like a body, nothing more, incensed Elaine to her core. The rude detective who'd come round to interview her hadn't even pretended to be interested in what she had to say.

"What did you have to say?" May probed.

Elaine was eager to get this off her chest. "I told him Bunny and I had plans to go to the Ninety-second Street Y the night she was murdered. He didn't even write it down. We were going to hear Maya Angelou read. Bunny wasn't a fan, but since I am, she said she'd come. That's how she is. She insisted we go to dinner first, but I didn't want to go. It's always the same thing: we go to some expensive restaurant; she insists on paying. I'm a bookkeeper," Elaine added. "I'm on a tight budget, and she knows that."

May squashed the urge to point out she was still referring to Bunny in the present tense.

"She called me that night," Elaine went on, "caught me just as I was going out the door to get the bus. Something came up, she told me. She was running late. She wasn't going to be able to get out of the office in time for dinner. She'd meet me at the Y instead. That's fine, I told her. Don't worry about it. I was actually relieved. I wasn't in the mood for a fancy dinner. I should have gone up to her office." She stared off into the distance.

"If you went to the office, you might be dead, too," May said quietly.

"Maybe." She didn't sound convinced. "I told all this to that young detective. He acted like I was talking too slowly, giving too many details, wasting his time. He didn't even write anything down," she said again. "So I hurried up with the story. I didn't even think about the rest until this morning. I guess I was in shock. But this morning I woke up with it on my mind as if I'd been dreaming about it. I know I dreamt about her all night. I was going to call the detective, but then I thought, what if he doesn't listen? What if he still doesn't write anything down?"

"What is it you remembered?" May asked in the gentle tone she'd seen Paula employ hundreds of times.

Elaine hesitated, then said, "She wasn't herself when she called. She was rushing to hang up, making light of what it was she had to do. But I didn't buy it. I said, 'Bunny, what's wrong?' She laughed this nervous laugh and said it was too long a story to go into over the phone. She said we could go for coffee after the reading and she'd tell me then. I don't like to wait, though, so I didn't let up. 'What is it?' I asked her.

" 'It's nothing at all,' she told me. 'I'm just sitting here studying a pair of photographs, trying to decide if two people who shouldn't even know each other might actually be related.' I said, 'I see,' but I didn't, really. I just figured it was research for a show. Now I'm wondering whether maybe it wasn't. Do you think it was why she was killed?"

May shrugged, admitting, "I don't know."

"I couldn't understand why she had to do it right then. It certainly didn't sound very urgent. Then she said, 'Gotta go, kiddo.' " Elaine's eyes filled with tears. "That was the last thing she said to me. 'Gotta go, kiddo.' "

She caved in to herself, trying to regain control, not wanting to break down in front of a stranger. "I'm sorry," she muttered into her chest. "I'm sorry. Excuse me. I'm sorry."

"It's fine. Go ahead," May said, then waited several moments before asking, "Was there anything else?"

Elaine looked up. "No. I sat through the entire reading, turning around every other minute to look for her. When it came time for questions, I went to the side of the auditorium and checked up and down each row. It's funny, how I can always pick her out of a crowd. But she wasn't there. I called her office from the phone in the lobby of the Y. When there was no answer, I took a taxi straight to the police station. I told them something happened to my sister. First I think they thought I was a nut. Then I think they thought I did something to her myself.

"I rode to the office in the back of a police car. When we got there, they wouldn't let me see her. They made me sit on a sofa in the reception room while they called the detectives handling the case. I didn't know she was in trouble. She never told me."

They sat in silence for several minutes. Elaine had crumpled up again, not wanting to show May her tear-stained face. Very quietly she got out, "Can we talk another time?"

"Of course. I understand. I'm so sorry. You must miss her terribly." When May was all bundled up in her coat, she said, "I hope you don't mind my asking, but who has Bunny's personal effects? From her office," she quickly added.

Elaine shrugged. "The police, I guess." She stood up, walked to the front door, opened it. "Call me tomorrow. I'll feel more myself tomorrow." She closed the door and returned to her seat by the fireplace to consider whether or not she ought to call back the police and give them one more chance to do right by Bunny.

44

MAY GAVE UP ON HER IDEA OF returning to the office when she saw the bumper-to-bumper traffic surrounding Elaine's building complex. After inching her way home in her rented car, she walked into her house to the sound of the ringing phone.

"It's dirty and dustic," Susie reported as soon as her mother picked up.

"Rustic," May heard Delia correct her. Then Delia got on the line.

"Grandma Shirley says it might be the only time we ever get to sleep in a house where we can see the sky between the cracks in the ceiling."

Shirley elaborated next. "The cracks aren't in the ceiling. They're in the roof. When you look up between the logs you can see stars."

"Sounds romantic," May tried.

"Oh, it's very romantic, dolly. If it rains or snows, it will be so romantic we'll be soaking wet with delight. Wait," her mother said suddenly, "the wood nymph would like a word with you."

"Allo?" came Sabrieke's voice. "I want just to thank you because this place it is just the same like my grandmother's. I never thought in America I would find such a place as this. You have a beautiful country."

Before May could respond, Delia was back on, reporting on the bug situation. "There are a million spiders in the house."

"And naps," Susie added when her grandma insisted she get a turn.

"Gnats," Delia shouted out to correct her.

Shirley took back the phone, and said "They mean bats," and she wasn't kidding.

Finally they ran out of change and said their speedy good-byes. May depressed the receiver and called O'Donnell's pager. She'd spent the car ride back from Elaine's figuring out her strategy for getting more information out of him without admitting what she knew. But when he returned her call and she heard his confident voice, her plotting was forgotten.

"I'm safe and sound at home," she told him, groping for a way to pump him. "I just wanted to let you know that. I'm home safe."

"I'm glad," he said, distracted. In the background she heard shouting, a siren, voices calling out orders. He was calling on a cell phone, she realized, from a crime scene.

"I just spoke to the girls. They're fine. Buggy but fine."

"That's the country for you."

"Sure is." It wasn't going to work; she was completely transparent. His voice had that quality Todd's sometimes got when he was half-listening while he waited for her to ramble around to the point. "They want to come home," she said, "if it's safe. Is it safe?"

"We haven't made any arrests, if that's what you're asking."

"Are you close?"

"We're working on some possibilities."

She went for the kill. "I was just thinking—I know I'm not supposed to be thinking about this, but you can't get hurt thinking, can you?" He didn't answer. She didn't wait. "I was wondering if you found anything in Bunny's office. Anything at all."

"Like what?"

"I don't know." She had to be careful here. "There are things that I might have in my office that someone like Bunny would never have in hers. Things that weren't 'Bunny.'"

"Like what?"

"I don't know. A hairbrush with someone else's hair on it. A bus ticket somewhere she'd never go. A chit with someone else's signature on it. A couple of photographs. You know. Something like that."

She couldn't see that he reached into his pocket, pulled out his notepad, and wrote down "hairbrush, bus ticket, photographs." He stared at his list, replaying the words as she'd said them to him. He had to admit, she'd given a good go at giving equal weight to each. But she wasn't quite able to keep from telling him what he needed to know. He crossed out "hairbrush" and "bus ticket," then circled "photographs."

"No," he said. "We didn't find any of those things. We found a telephone, which we examined but didn't remove. And folders full of papers, magazines, videos. Why do you ask, May?"

"I just thought maybe you might have missed a clue—only because you really didn't know her."

"It's possible," he said.

He did know something. May felt it. Suddenly she wanted to get off the phone. She wanted to go to the office, to Bunny's office, to search for what the police had missed. Bunny had been looking at two photographs when she called Elaine. The photographs were why she said she had to miss dinner. But no photographs were found on her desk—she didn't believe O'Donnell would have lied about that. And Bunny never kept any pictures in her office, at least not the last time May looked.

So she had to look again. She would go tonight, when no one was there, while the campers were safely away counting spiders and bats. She didn't look forward to sleeping alone in the house anyway.

"I'm worried about you alone in that house," O'Donnell admitted.

"If my mother and Sabrieke and the girls were with me, do you think I'd be any safer?"

"No. Then I'd just be worried about them, too."

"Well, don't worry," May reassured him. "I won't open the door for strangers. Anyway I'm going out with a couple of friends in a while. If you call back and I'm not here, it doesn't mean I'm dead."

"Maybe you should stay in tonight," he said.

"Why?"

"I'd just feel better if I knew you were locked in tight."

"Don't call back," she advised, "and then you can imagine I'm locked in as tight as you like."

He didn't respond to her dim attempt at humor, nor could he see that the silence made her cheeks turn red.

In her car, with the doors locked and the radio turned up high to Hits of the Seventies, May felt energized, invulnerable. She may have coasted into marriage with Todd, stumbled into a successful career by happenstance, procreated out of a desire imprinted in her consciousness before she was born, but this, this chase was her choice. This was May moving her life in a direction no one had planned for her. She wasn't a vulture, picking at the remains of someone else's life to see if it would make a good story. It was her life, her story. And the thrill of it, the fear itself, emboldened her.

Then a small voice in her head said, "Don't forget us." It was Susie's voice, and with it her brain made a connection to her foot and instantly her pressure on the gas pedal eased. She hadn't even realized she was doing eighty. Now, down to sixty-five, she began falling behind traffic.

She would have her adventure, but she'd have it smart. She was no teenage superhero on a suicide mission. She was a grown-up mother of two who couldn't afford to take chances that could orphan her kids.

Being safe meant having help. Who was she kidding, trying to do this on her own? Being a dead hero was not an honor she craved. If she told O'Donnell what she knew, he'd meet her in a minute. She plugged the car phone into the lighter, then realized she'd left the detective's beeper number at home. She got the number for his precinct and tried him there.

The cop who answered the phone laughed when she asked for O'Donnell's pager number. "I wouldn't give you his number if you told me you were his dying mother," the man said, in case she hadn't gotten his drift the first time he said no. "How about you give me your number and I'll get him to call you?"

"Do I sound like his mother?" she snapped.

"You sound like a goddamn pain in the ass."

She pulled the plug on the call as if she were pulling the plug on his life, then parked her car at the curb in front of her office. She plugged her phone back in and tried Margery next but got the machine. She left a message at the sound of the tone.

"It's May. I'm going up to the office. I wanted you to know in case something happens to me. If something does happen, promise you'll look out for the girls. Make sure their father takes good care." She disconnected, shaking off the words that had sent a chill darting up her back.

She turned away from her fear, locked the car, and rang the night bell. But Jack or Bob must have been in a closet picking his nose, so after waiting for a while, May just pushed in the heavy door, which hadn't latched, and rode up alone in the elevator to the twenty-second floor.

45

IT HAD TAKEN SO LONG TO GET used to having security guards around the office she was surprised that now that they were gone, she missed them. It made no sense. The protection they provided had turned out to be purely pretend. On the night of Bunny's murder, for example, the guard had been on duty, walking her rounds, patrolling the halls, opening and closing rest-room doors, checking empty offices. But it had been easy—fatally easy—to figure out her rhythm and avoid her.

So no one complained when Gil announced that the item had been axed from the budget. Nor did anyone pipe up when he told them if they wanted to, they could dig into their own pockets and chip in to pay for a guard themselves.

Yet now, without a guard on duty, the quiet halls

seemed darker, less safe. May groped her way to the latest security measure. Gil had replaced his office alarm system with a new one, put in to protect the entire strip of executive offices. Although no one had challenged Gil to his face, May knew she wasn't alone in wondering why he'd bothered to install the system only to share the code with everyone he knew.

She pushed the not-so-secret numbers, disarmed the system, and entered the cool reception area, switching on the overhead lights as she went along. For a moment she imagined how the building must look from the outside, from the vantage point of some sleepless New Yorker's apartment window: lights on the twenty-second floor going on, one, then another, then more. She imagined herself a resident in one of those apartments, a high-rise so tall it was easy to think you didn't need curtains or blinds, although anyone who watched her show on Peeping Toms knew better. Would she, she wondered, peering out at the darkness, watching lights go on—one and then another—think this was a normal night in the city? Would she, a sleepless executive staring out her window to pass the time, assume she was watching another sleepless executive return to work to get a jump on the day? Would she ever imagine it was someone like herself, a harried, overworked working mother seeking clues to, of all things, a murder?

For someone who made her living documenting oddball behavior, May realized, she had retained a surprisingly provincial view of life. Although she knew that strange people doing strange things lived in pockets of every town, she had somehow assumed her life would never intersect with theirs off the air. It was, she realized now, as if she'd felt her work producing shows about bad things happening to good people somehow protected her family from bad things happening to them.

She flicked on the light in Bunny's office. The crime-scene tape was gone now, but shreds of yellow plastic were still stuck to the molding along with scraps of the masking tape the police had left behind in their haste. The dust they'd used to raise fingerprints still coated much of the room, the floor a mess of tracks and lines made by furniture that had been dragged around, removed, replaced, as detectives looked under and around each surface—for what?

Bunny's glass desk, that she had so often cursed for showing every fingerprint, smudge, and particle of dust had, by now, been rubbed and smeared so many times it had the impenetrable look of frosted glass. All her papers, both public and private, had been removed and relegated to several cardboard boxes, heaved away and poked through by stubby fingers, glanced at by dispassionate eyes—for what?

May scanned the room, taking it all in, the clues to the woman she knew and to the one who'd been hidden from her. But there was nothing to explain why Bunny's life had been stolen, nor was there a hint as to why, while alive, she'd been so content to let her colleagues misread her. Not that any of them truly revealed themselves. While at work May made sure to keep her kids way in the background of her life. Colleen had worked hard to hide her romance with Chuck. And someone—who?—was engaged in the ultimate deception, masquerading as a human while making a hobby of murder.

There was nothing more to see. She turned off the light, closed the door, and continued down the hall.

She walked through Paula's office next, stroking objects as she passed them, glass paperweights, awards, books, pictures. May stood before the credenza, Paula's favorite spot for displaying the photo collection Patty tended to, taking care to remove the outgoing Romeo's visage when a newer beau came to replace him.

The men took turns, leaning against trees, sitting on deck chairs, sipping white wine at publishing parties, smiling at opening nights at Orso's, then one day vanishing, replaced by the next version of wide smile and eager eyes. Today it was Doctor Chocolate on skis in Sun Valley, but from experience May knew his time was running out. Neither he nor any of the mementos collecting dust on Paula's bookshelves looked out of place. May moved on.

In Gil's office she studied the papers on his neatly arranged desk, trying not to move them too much, peered down his phone list, flipped through his calendar. There were plenty of names she didn't know, but no one that seemed any more threatening than another.

She slid out his top desk drawer, half-expecting to find a stash of coiled phone cords. She dug down deep, beneath neatly arranged office supplies, notepads, boxes of Post-Its, until she found a stack of notebooks piled one atop another.

She took out the first one, found its pages filled with lists of all kinds. Lists of sweep ideas, of sweep numbers, of award-winning shows, of award-winning producers. She pulled out the notebook beneath it. More lists. Story ideas from this year, last year, the year before. Notes scribbled in margins, phone numbers, names, scribbles, doodles. It was toward the end of the last notebook, the one crammed in the back at the bottom of the drawer under a folder of yellowed clippings, that she found the list of addresses of AA meetings, the list of names of buddies to call, the list of inspirational thoughts to take Gil's mind off of drink.

That was Gil's secret, she thought, the reason why she'd never seen him drink anything stronger than Coke. And she thought of the Antabuse.

She quickly replaced the contents of his drawers, except for the last notebook. She held it, hugging it to her chest as she turned to his picture gallery, tended to lovingly by Stephanie, pictures added with precise regularity, one shot of each child a year and a group shot, always posed in the same spot under a giant tulip tree by the pond in their wooded backyard. The children grew taller each year, but Gil seemed to shrink—from what? she wondered. Drink? Disappointment? Despair?

It struck her again how she—all of them—posted photographs in public spots as unimpeachable but silent testimony that they had lives outside of the show. Everyone but Bunny, who had held one in each hand the night she was killed.

Still clutching Gil's notebook, she slipped into the cubicle next door, so clean she could smell the Lysol that Wendy used each night to disinfect her phone and computer keyboard. At the window ledge she picked up a small oval-framed photograph of Wendy's son, Charlie, his expression vacant, the eyes blank as those of a baby who couldn't focus yet. When the phone rang, she nearly dropped him, then steadied herself. She checked her watch, saw it was after midnight. Only Margery knew she was there. She reached for the phone just as the ringing stopped, her hand outstretched in midair. The silence seemed to deepen.

Quickly she turned her eyes back to the photograph in her hand. Looking at Charlie's sad face, she finally felt the luck people kept telling her she had. The luck to have daughters strong enough to occasionally defy her and an ex-husband with the audacity to want to protect them. She felt the weight of the picture, the weight of the boy's existence, felt suddenly like a voyeur, standing in Wendy's narrow space, invading her sad life. She looked to find the exact spot where the picture had sat so that she could return it there. It was easy to do, since Rosa and Emil were such bad cleaners. They dutifully emptied wastebaskets and skimmed dusters gently over cluttered office desks but left the rest alone, as if they'd once been told the hierarchy of office life dictated it was only what happened on the desks that mattered.

She carefully returned the frame to its place on the ledge, marked as it was by a perfectly shaped rectangle cut out of the dust where it had sat for over a year, where nothing had ever disturbed it. It was easy to fit it in, just right, like a puzzle piece.

Then she noticed the small picture next to it. It was the last in line and sat at an awkward angle, perpendicular to its dust-free outline, as if it had been recently removed and hastily replaced. On closer inspection May saw that while the other pictures were muted by a thin coating of dust, this one had been wiped clean in a circle around Charlie's face, as if someone had been trying to get a closer look. Quickly, like a thief, she pocketed it.

She scanned the room once more—the ledge, the desk, the floor. Then, with the photograph in her pocket and Gil's notebook in her hand, she returned to her office. Wearily, she sat at her desk to sort things out, but first she lay her head down, just for a moment, to rest.

"Sugar, are you out of your mind?"

May jumped up, startled, to find Margery staring at her with eyes so intense May felt her body go numb with fear.

"What the hell are you doing? It's five in the morning.

People are getting murdered right and left, and you're sleeping with your head on your desk."

May squinted at the gray dawn out her window. "I didn't mean to sleep," she admitted as she scanned Margery, looking, she suddenly realized, for a sign of a weapon.

"You are absolutely pale as a ghost," Margery said. She sat in one of the guest chairs, and as she crossed her arms, May let out a tiny sigh. She'd been wondering what was in Margery's left hand, saw now it was nothing.

Margery noticed the fear wash off her face. For a moment she looked puzzled, then laughed. "Good lord, you're frightened of me. Well, that's a healthy sign. You should be frightened of me. I'm frightened of you. I tracked down your boyfriend and told him either you're the murderer or you're going to end up getting killed. He's damned mad that you came up here in the middle of the night, I can tell you that. He didn't want me to come up either, but he's not my boyfriend, so I don't give a hoot."

"Where is he now?"

"Down at the corner of Seventh Avenue. He stumbled upon a robbery at that little card store next to the deli, so he got delayed."

A voice bellowed down the hall, "Police. Freeze." Neither May nor Margery moved as O'Donnell swept into her office, gun drawn, two Uniforms borrowed from the burglary crime scene on the corner covering his rear. He dismissed his backup as soon as he saw May was okay.

"Get it through our head. This is not a game. This is not a television program. This is real. Even the dead people are real." He shook his head, as if he was giving up, giving up on her. "What did you find out?"

May lifted the notebook off her desk and handed it over.

"It's a notebook." He opened it, started reading through.

She took it from him, opened it to the page containing the lists of AA meetings, and handed it back.

"Where did you find this?"

"In Gil's desk." She didn't offer more, didn't tell him about the photograph, heavy as a brick, in her pocket, didn't tell him what Elaine Hoffman had said, either. She was mad. She didn't like being bullied, especially by him.

He read some more, then closed the book. "Why didn't you tell me you were coming here?"

"You're not my father or my husband or my boyfriend. You told me I'm no longer a suspect in your murder case. I don't owe you anything."

He nodded slowly, then said, "That's true."

"Anyway I did try to call you," she said quietly. "But some cop with a stick up his ass wouldn't put me through."

O'Donnell smiled, and nodded again. Then his hand went to the beeper that hung off his belt. He read its message, then turned back to May. "What else do you want to tell me?"

She shrugged and shook her head. She wasn't ready to tell him anything else. She didn't want to be laughed at, sloughed off, reprimanded like a child.

When O'Donnell left, Margery said, "He didn't push you very hard, sugar. Which makes me think he's close. He's close or he's there."

"So why didn't he tell us?"

"If he can't prove it, he can't say it. But I'd bet money he's got someone in mind. And I hope to tell it isn't you or me."

Fear made them hungry. They left for breakfast at the Brasserie, where they ate heartily but didn't speak, each left to her own uncomfortable musings. When they got back to work, it was clear from their colleagues bland greetings that they'd left behind no evidence of their early morning wanderings.

46

SKIPPING THE USUAL SMALL TALK at the coffee machine, May shut herself in her office with thoughts of her kids. She knew sending them away had been the right thing to do. They were safe with her mother. Sabrieke was sweet. But she hated that she'd let them go somewhere with no working phone. She beeped Pete. He called back right away.

"You miss me already?" he asked her. He'd taken the day off from her house to repair a leaking skylight in a kitchen remodeling job he'd bid for and lost last year. It was something he had a weakness for, repairing other contractors' bad work, pointing out to the homeowner all the money-pinching mistakes and poor judgment calls the other guy had made.

"I don't like that I can't get in touch with the girls. Why don't you have a phone in your cabin?"

His voice stiffened. "Because I don't like getting calls. Because most of the time when people call me, it's not good news. Like right now."

"It's ridiculous for them to be up there with no phone."

"Did they call you from the store last night like you planned?"

"Yes."

"Was everything okay?"

"Yes. Except for a few complaints about holes in the roof."

"There are no holes in that roof." This was more than he could bear. "I put every one of those planks there myself, and there are no holes."

She decided not to mention the bats. "What if I need to reach them in an emergency?"

"Mrs. Morrison, if you need to reach them in an emergency, I'll drive you up there myself. Are you having an emergency right now?"

"What about the neighbors? Can you call them and ask them to check to see if everything is okay?"

There was a long silence. "If I have to," he said finally.

"You have to," May told him.

"Good-bye," Pete said.

He called back ten minutes later. "Old Albert drove his pickup over to my place, but the only one there was a big grizzly bear. Just goofing," he quickly added, in case she was dense enough to believe him. "They're fine. They're eating pancakes. They're still in their pajamas. Your mother said she'll call you tonight and not to worry. Can I get back to work now?"

"Thanks, Pete."

"No problem," he said, softening. "I'll be back at your house first thing tomorrow morning. Okay?"

"Okay." She hung up the phone. She still wasn't happy. She wanted her kids home. She needed the killer caught.

She fingered the picture in her pocket, took it out, laid it in the middle of her desk, studied it. She wouldn't have been able to argue with O'Donnell if he had been there now telling her that she was working on nothing more than a hunch, that it was all speculation that this picture—that this boy—held any answers. Probably he didn't. Probably Wendy had moved the picture herself, had picked it up to stare into the troubled eyes of her child, rubbed the glass that hid his lips so she could kiss them quickly, then hurried to put the picture back before she was caught with it in her hands.

But the image that was stuck in May's mind, the one pasted on the inside of her eyelids so that every time she blinked she saw it, was of Bunny holding a picture in her thick, fleshy hands, rubbing the glass with her thumb to get a better look at the face, thinking to herself, this is it, this is why.

"What did she know? May asked the empty room. "What does he know?"

She couldn't pump Wendy, not with the limp excuse that her gut had suggested Charlie, of all people, was involved in Bunny's death. Especially since she knew she would probably soon find out she was totally wrong. From years of following leads on story ideas, she knew these searches were like traveling blind through a maze. Dead ends popped up where you were sure the path ran clear. Detours you never noticed suddenly appeared before you.

She would have to find a way to check out the boy without Wendy knowing it. That way if there was nothing worth finding out, there'd be no one to apologize to, nothing to explain. Her plotting was interrupted by a hard knock on her closed door. She quickly stuffed Charlie's picture back in her pocket, shuffled around the papers on her desk unnecessarily, and told her visitor to come in.

A long-faced Henry walked in, sat down, and said, "I

went over my bank statement last night to see how long I can last on unemployment, and it's not very long."

"Why do you think you're going to be unemployed?"

"Because after this tribute to Bunny, we've got nothing grooved up. Nothing good. And the tribute to Bunny sounds"—he paused, considering precisely how honest it was safe to be—"doubtful. Plus Paula's been ranting to Patty that from now on she only wants uplifting, noble shows. With huge ratings," he added, his voice emphasizing the incompatibility of those two concepts.

"Great," May said, an idea suddenly gelling. "I've got a perfect show."

"You do?"

"I do. It will be enlightening, uplifting, and have a strong social conscience, too."

"I love having a conscience," Henry told her.

"I'm working with the title: 'When Our Kids Are Too Troubled to Live at Home: Do Institutions Work?' "

Henry bit his lip. "That might be too earnest. Or dull."

It was the final stage of his apprenticeship. Henry had learned how to challenge her. As always, his timing stunk.

"It's never dull if it makes you cry. If we can find two success stories, we can go directly from sobs to cheers. Paula will love it. Gil will love it."

"Then let's do it. If Gil will love it, let's do it."

"Okay. This afternoon we'll go and look at some residential homes. Do some research fast. I want a list of homes with great reputations. We'll pick the top two and go out and build a story."

With Henry surfing the Net for information, May, moving on pure instinct, went to see Wendy. At the threshold of her office she stopped, suddenly worried that, like a cat, Wendy had found her trail, sniffed a scent that told her an intruder had violated her space the night before. But when she spied Wendy seated at her desk being her usual briskly efficient self, she knew she'd left no trace.

"I have a favor to ask you," she began.

Wendy looked up, her eyes as vacant as her son's.

"My cousin's daughter's just came home from the hospital. She's got a list of problems three pages long. My cousin feels she just can't take care of her anymore. They're looking for a good residential facility. One like Charlie's. Would you mind if she called you about his place?"

Wendy's eyes flashed to the window ledge. For a moment May thought, *This is it, she's noticing the picture that's missing,* but when Wendy turned back, it was only to ask, "What's wrong with her?"—her interest as mild as if May were inquiring about the weather.

"I don't know the exact problem. They don't like talking about it. I just know they can't handle her at home anymore. They live in Connecticut. That's where your son is, right?"

"Yes."

"That's what I thought. They want a place not far from where they live, which is just outside of Hartford. Is your son's place anywhere near Hartford?"

"About half an hour," she said as she opened a file in her computer.

"What town?" May persisted.

Wendy looked up at her. "If you don't mind, I have a ten-page document to type." She looked back at the monitor. "Tell your cousin to call me." Her fingers flew across her keyboard. May had been dismissed.

She stopped by Henry's desk and told him she got a tip on a great place half an hour from Hartford. She left him pulling open files of maps and cross-checking against the lists he'd already compiled on children's residential facilities in the tri-state area.

Colleen called out from her doorway. "May. Got a sec?"

May joined her in her office.

"Believe it or not, I've found a few segments Bunny did that are actually amusing. And I got Paula to do about ten minutes of reminiscing for me on tape. What have you got so far?"

Henry knocked on the door. "Sorry to interrupt, but I wanted to let you know there are two places in the Hartford area."

"What kind of places?" Colleen wanted to know. "What are you two cooking up?"

"I made us appointments at both," Henry reported.

"Colleen," May said, "excuse us. We've got to run."

"Where are you off to?" Gil called after them when he saw May heading to the elevator.

"Where are you two going?" Colleen demanded, following right behind.

The elevator doors opened. May quickly ushered Henry inside. "Chasing a story," she said.

"About what?" Gil asked, holding the door.

Henry, for once, said nothing. The door began to ding. Gil struggled to hold it open. Finally, it heaved closed, his puzzled face shut out.

"Good work," May told Henry, whose smile threatened to take over his entire face.

They traveled the rest of the way down in silence and continued that way to the car Henry rented. He navigated the route to their first appointment. It was early afternoon by the time May pulled up the curving gravel driveway leading to the large white clapboard building marked "The Hubble Home."

47

"WE'RE DOING A SHOW ABOUT what caring can accomplish," May explained to the director, a tall, imposing woman with hard-set mannish features.

"I'll be honest with you," Mrs. Hubble explained in a disarmingly soft voice. "I have only one interest in allowing you to interview us, and that is financial. Public funding is drying up fast. I look more and more to private donations. We have many families who struggle to afford us and others who just can't pay at all. If you convince me that doing a show on us will help our bottom line, you can film here, simple and plain."

May admitted that though she couldn't make any guarantees, she could supply Mrs. Hubble with lists of names and numbers of people whose lives had changed in wonderful ways after appearing on *Paula Live*. She saw Mrs. Hubble's interest brighten.

The first stop on their tour was the sunny, bright school building, its walls painted in glossy primary colors. Everything looked clean, new, top-of-the-line. They wandered in and out of half a dozen classrooms where children struggled to learn. A little boy Delia's age stroked a piece of wood, then a cotton ball, as his teacher patiently chanted, "Is it soft? Is it hard? Is it soft?"

"Are there any other kids?" May asked when they came to the end of the building tour.

"The older children are in another building right now," Mrs. Hubble explained. "There are fewer of the older ones. That's our success, really. We work very hard to get the children enough medical attention, education, and training so they can return to their families and to independent lives. Of course, some can't because they're too ill. Others can, but have parents who aren't ready. We can't keep them forever, though. We're strictly a children's home. We have six or seven adult homes we feed into, but placement is difficult."

They had reached another, smaller building. As soon as they walked into the first room, May saw ten-year-old Charlie sitting by himself playing with a stuffed pig. Quickly she looked to see if Henry had identified him from the pictures on Wendy's windowsill, but there was no flicker of recognition in his gaze.

"Nice pig," May said. Charlie looked up at her, made a noise like a snort, then quickly looked away. *What could this boy have done?* May thought. *What could he possibly know?*

As they continued on their tour, Mrs. Hubble confided that when Charlie had first come, he couldn't speak at all. He had many mental, emotional, and physical limitations. He needed several operations before he could learn to walk. He didn't recognize sounds, was unmoved by music. "He's our little success story," she boasted. "I think as soon as his family gets ready to accept him, he's ready to go home. We're working on that now."

"I'd like to make Charlie the centerpiece of the show," May announced suddenly. More powerful than her discomfort at her deception was the need to find out how this fragile boy was connected with Bunny's murder. She had to find out whether or not there was anything to know, whether she'd arrived at another dead end.

"How wonderful," Mrs. Hubble said. "I'll discuss it with his parents as soon as possible."

May swallowed a groan. She wasn't thinking things through. She'd been riding so fast on instinct she hadn't stopped to consider that of course Mrs. Hubble would call the boy's mother. That would be the end of her investigation and the beginning of her new career—trying to explain this all to Wendy.

"I wouldn't dream of telling you how to do your job," May said quickly, "because you clearly do it so well." The woman beamed. May went on. "We gave you no notice. You didn't have time to pretty anything up, to put on a show. You've got a beautiful home here, and your children are lucky to have you." She meant it, and hoped that made up for the deceit that would follow.

"Thank you," Mrs. Hubble said, appreciative.

"However, my business is to know how to get people to agree to share their lives on national television. It's not difficult to scare people away if you don't know exactly how to approach them. And I'd hate to lose this opportunity because the boy's parents got scared off." She hated what she was doing, so she kept going back to the image of Bunny holding Charlie's photograph, comparing it to something—what?

Henry jumped in. "I'll be honest with you, Mrs. Hubble. At first I didn't see how this story was going to pan out. But once we met Charlie, I knew May was right on target again. This won't merely be a good show. This will be an important show." He lowered his voice. "You'll probably need to hire someone just to handle your mail once the checks start pouring in."

"I'll get you his parents' numbers," Mrs. Hubble said, quickly capitulating. She returned moments later with an armful of promotional material and a small envelope. "I've written down the mother's number. I only have an emergency contact for his father, but I put that in, too. They don't live together," she added. "Is that all right?"

"Maybe better," May told her, trying to sound pragmatic, trying to keep her breathing steady and calm so her face wouldn't heat up and reveal her excitement at the idea of getting Charlie's father's phone number in her hands.

"Definitely better," Henry added, because he didn't know.

On the trip back to the office Henry rambled on with ideas about how to build the show. Finally, May turned up the radio to drown him out.

His voice broke through, ". . . after I call Charlie's mother."

May reached over and took the small envelope that contained the phone numbers off of Henry's lap.

"I'll call," she said, good-naturedly, as if she was doing him a favor.

Henry glowered the rest of the way back.

48

BY THE TIME THEY GOT BACK TO the office, Gil and Wendy were already gone. Paula and her security force were next to leave, trailed by a troupe of tiny women dressed in white robes who'd stopped by to chant with Paula for peace of mind. Patty was just finishing up, standing at the Xerox machine, her coat already on and buttoned, copying letters she'd proof-read and seal on the bus ride home. No one wanted to linger after dark. No one but May.

Henry offered to wait while she contacted Charlie's parents, but she put him off, telling him she had some personal business to take care of first. Reluctantly, he followed the last of his coworkers out.

May tried to keep calm about the call, but it was tough to do. She didn't know exactly what she was going to say to Charlie's father, didn't have anything particular in mind she expected to find out, but it was an avenue untried, an opportunity for discovery. Later she'd deal with the consequence of Wendy's ire at her meddling.

She dialed the number Mrs. Hubble had given her. No one answered. She waited ten minutes and tried again. No answer. It was a city number, the same exchange as hers. For all she knew Charlie's father might live in one of the residential apartment buildings across the street or down the block. He could be on his way there now. He could already be home but in the shower. He could be out of town, away on a business trip, on vacation. He could be dead. She tried again.

It was just before seven, she was on her way back from the bathroom, when the service elevator opened, startling her. She squatted behind the giant blue recycling bin against the wall and hid, like a child, until she heard the familiar squeak of Rosa's cleaning cart. When she popped out from behind the bin, it was Rosa's turn to shriek and jump. When she saw it was May, she crossed herself and laughed. *Rosa knows about the murders too*, May thought, then asked, "Where's Emil?"

"Emil no work no more," Rosa explained. "He scared."

"Aren't you scared?" May asked.

Rosa shrugged, then rubbed her fingers together. "I need the money," she explained. "For children. Emil no need the money so bad. His children working, grown up big." She shrugged again, then pushed her cart along.

As soon as she was back at her desk, May studied Mrs. Hubble's careful royal blue script, the tiny arrow pointing to Wendy's name with the notation "Call first." Ignoring that, May tried the father again, this time putting the call on the speaker phone. She let it ring.

At first the sound of the amplified ringing kept startling her out of her thoughts, but after a while it disappeared into the background, like the noise of an air conditioner, traffic, ocean waves. She attacked her desk, busywork, reading through the piles of mail and memos she'd been ignoring for a week. The ringing went on.

By the time a voice answered hello, she had forgotten she'd been calling someone, forgotten whom she'd expected to answer the phone. It certainly wasn't the tentative female voice broadcasting over the speaker phone in stilted English. "Hello? He no here. Hello?"

May grabbed the phone from it's cradle. "Hello?"

"Mister not here."

The voice was familiar. She struggled to place it. "Who is this?"

"The cleaner."

"Who?" She hadn't meant for her voice to be so stern and accusing.

"Rosa. Rosa Marie Fernandez. I'm sorry I pick up. I can get someone here. Please forget I pick up. I can get someone here. Please forget I pick up. I'm sorry." The phone went dead.

When May found Rosa, she was in Gil's office running

the duster over his desk. Rosa looked up quickly, then glanced away, hoping May wouldn't notice the sweat on her brow. She didn't have enough English to explain why she'd picked up the phone, how the incessant ringing had gotten under her skin until she'd become convinced it was someone calling for help.

May said nothing, just sat in Gil's chair, picked up his desk phone, and dialed the number written in royal blue ink on the paper she clutched in her hand. As the phone on the credenza behind her began to ring, she conjured a vague recollection of the day Gil had it installed, a phone with an unlisted number he'd wanted so that Stephanie could reach him directly. They'd teased him about it for a day or so and then forgotten it. It was easy to forget. She'd never heard it ring until now.

Rosa refused to look at her, to acknowledge the peculiarity of the situation—May sitting at Gil's desk, receiver to her ear, ignoring the ringing phone only an arm's length away. Instead, she quickly piled her dust rags on top of her cart and, muttering, pushed her way out of the office.

After several more moments May hung up. The room was still. Her mind felt blocked, as if she couldn't think, didn't want to think, didn't want to know. She got up, went to her office, put on her coat. She glanced at her watch and saw she was late; she might not make it home in time to get her mother's phone-call from the grocery store. She had to hurry, hurry home to sort this out. She could think better there.

On the train she stared out the window at her own reflection instead of at the puzzle stuck in her mind. In a daze she walked up her front walk, put her key in her lock. When she heard the phone ringing, at first she thought she was imagining it, replaying the insistent ring of the phone in Gil's office in her brain. But as soon as she opened her front door, she realized it was the shrill sound of her kitchen phone she'd been hearing. By the time she reached it, the phone had stopped ringing. The house was silent.

49

JANE HUBBLE WASN'T THE KIND to brag. She didn't even like to be lauded within her small circle of friends. Occasionally, when one of their bridge buddies was over, her husband, Stewart, might recount a story Jane had told him about a child who'd had a small success or one who'd just returned to a family that had been afraid of him before. But even those small testimonials made her uncomfortable. She'd become quite adept at changing the subject, pretty quick at refocusing the spotlight away from herself onto someone else.

She imagined, as she heard Stewart's key in the lock, that when she told him her news tonight, he'd quickly point out that if she wanted to change the subject this time, she'd have to change the channel to do it. She listened to him hanging up his coat, lumbering to the bathroom, and wondered what had made her agree to the outrageous suggestion in the first place. Was it because of their increasingly shaky financial ground? Was it because the TV producer had convinced her the publicity might serve to encourage the private donation of money, now that public money had dried up? Had she gotten that easy to distract and flatter?

Things weren't good; that was for sure. They'd hit a new low earlier in the week when one of the board members proposed they close down the barn and lower the age limit to twelve. There were several good facilities, the woman pointed out, that specialized in the teenage years. The barn was underutilized anyway, she reminded her unnecessarily, as if that were a failure and not a sign of how many children they'd managed to help enough that they could leave.

Plus the neighbors were getting organized again. She had heard from one of the sympathetic ones, the man who ran the nursery that abutted the nose of the property at the north end: the current sentiment was that the new town planning board, sworn in that January, would be amenable to taking another look at the variances that enabled the school to exist in the first place. Wouldn't the show help fend off that inevitable attack? Still her decision nagged at her.

She'd told this all to her niece, Ellen, who'd called right after the woman left. Ellen, who lived in New York City, didn't believe her at first. She loved her aunt Jane, but thought her an oddball and decidedly unglamorous, spending her life doing the hard work others found too distasteful. How unlikely, then, to hear that she was slated for a guest spot on a talk show. "Did you say *Paula Live?*" Ellen had asked in disbelief. "The real one, that's on Channel Two?"

How could Jane admit she had no idea what channel the show was on, had never watched it? Once, years ago, when she was recovering from bronchitis, Stewart had turned on the television set and she'd watched Phil Donahue dressed up in a skirt. Then she'd fallen asleep, and when she woke up hours later, *Wheel of Fortune* was on, her fever had broken, and she felt strong enough to get up and turn the darn thing off.

"Of course it's the real one," she told her niece, because what else would it be? Within the hour relatives she hadn't spoken to in years were checking in, wanting to know the airdate. How could she know the airdate? she protested. They hadn't even made the show yet.

It didn't take long for her to realize this was a very big deal, not just for her, but for all her friends and relatives, who seemed to feel their status had suddenly improved through the mere fact that they knew someone who was going to be on TV. That's what finally made her face the impact the show would have on the boy. His was a success story—there was no doubt about it—possibly one that would be inspirational to others. No question the show would help the home. But what about the boy? He was still troubled, with little self-confidence, fragile self-esteem, and a limited support network. It would be so easy for his progress to be undone.

Then there was the mother. She came every week, was punctual and polite, but there was a skittishness about her, too, as if she might dissolve easily, bolt, run away, never to be seen again. Each weekend she sat beside her son, watching him as he played, accompanying him on walks through the grounds, but they didn't engage in conversation. There was no physical contact.

The problem of Charlie's placement had been weighing on Jane for some time, but his mother continually put off any discussion of the subject. Jane was sure he could make the transition, but she hadn't yet found the right route to getting the family to agree. The absentee father sent checks all right, but he made no attempt at contact; there were no phone calls, care packages, notes tucked in with the checks, no birthday cards, no gifts. She should have been more honest about that when she spoke to the producers.

That was the problem. She shouldn't have given them the names at all. No good would come of this for Charlie or his family. That was what had been gnawing at her all afternoon. It was wrong.

By the time Stewart kissed her, sat down at the kitchen table, and placed his napkin on his lap, she knew what she had to do. She presented him with her dilemma anyway. He listened without interrupting as she described the meeting with the television people. He seemed neither surprised nor upset when she told him she'd given out the parents' numbers. Likewise, when she told him she thought she should call them herself to admit her mistake, he made no effort to dissuade her.

She found all the numbers, including another one for the father that she'd unintentionally neglected to give to the producer. Then she retreated to the study at the back of the house. From her chair by the window she could look out at the building where the older children lived. She hated calling it a barn because she thought that made it sound as though the children who lived there were animals. When she admitted that once to Stewart, he'd merely said, "We're all animals," in that way of his that made her worry vanish. They both knew how much she loved the children, especially the older ones, whose departures she mourned even as she celebrated.

She put on her reading glasses, which she needed all the time these days, and checked her watch. She could usually get Mrs. Porter at home by now. She had never had the occasion to call Mr. Porter before. She tried all three numbers but got no answer. At first this worried her, but then she realized it meant the TV people wouldn't have been able to reach them either. It was only when she decided to try one last time that she finally got through.

"It's Jane Hubble from the Hubble Home," she announced herself, quickly adding, "Charlie's fine." She knew some people assumed when she called that it was with bad news, and occasionally when she told them everything was all right, she'd hear a sigh that seemed to admit disappointment. "I called to tell you I've made a mistake. I gave your name to a young woman who works for a television program." When she finished her story, there was silence, and then a quiet but unmistakable intake of breath.

Jane waited what she thought was a decent interval, and then said, "Are you all right?"

She couldn't see the person on the other end, couldn't see the head shaking, the teeth grinding, the lips pursing, the eyes closing, didn't know the horrible plan being formulated. All she knew was that the phone went dead, and when she called back again, there was no answer.

Stewart told her not to worry, that there was no figuring some people out. She decided to agree—the whole thing was giving her a headache anyway—and went to bed, promising herself that first thing in the morning she'd call back that television producer to explain that though she regretted it, she'd have to decline the offer to cooperate in a show about Charlie, since it wouldn't be in the best interest of the boy. That decided, she tried to sleep but gave up after an hour, taking to the chair in the study, where she sat staring out the window, noticing for the first time that the crater-carved face of the full moon was a sad one.

50

WHEN THE DOORBELL RANG, MAY was halfway undressed, getting ready for a shower she hoped would wash away the muddled feeling in her head. By the time she got back into her clothes, ran down the stairs, and looked through the peephole, no one was there. But a car idled in front of the house, white smoke chugging out of the tailpipe as if it were a fat cigar.

She opened the door. A figure hopped out of the car, ran toward her, breathless. "Where the hell are the girls?" Todd asked.

She forced a wide smile across her face. "Well, hello there. Can't seem to keep away, can you?"

"Where are the girls?"

She wasn't sure how much it was safe to tell him, so she stalled, ushering him to the uncomfortable living room chairs, suggesting he relax while she went to put up water for tea. When she got to the kitchen, she closed the door and phoned Ritchie. He was completely dependable—home by five-thirty, finished with dinner and in front of the TV by seven every night, the phone a reach away.

"The only way you're going to get rid of him is to confront him," he advised. "You go out there and tell him the girls are with your mother for the week. Then before he can ask any questions, you ask him why his lawyers haven't called me yet. Tell him I cleared my calendar so that anytime he wants to meet tomorrow is fine with us. Maybe he'll surprise you and be reasonable."

"Your side of the family always suffered from inappropriate optimism," she told him before hanging up and returning to the living room. Todd, already tiring of waiting, sat with his face scrunched into a suspicious pose.

"I just checked with Ritchie," she explained quickly. "He said we can meet anytime tomorrow. All you have to do is have your lawyer call him in the morning and tell him when and where to go." She opened the front door, making her intentions clear. He got up, followed her, slammed it shut.

"You don't get it. I'm not here to schedule an appointment with your lawyer. I want to know where the hell the girls are. If you even know."

"They're with your future stepmother at a friend's house," she told him. She knew better than to use the word cabin to a man who'd only lasted three days at sleep-away camp.

"What do you mean 'future stepmother'?" he asked, tipping her off that he hadn't yet heard the news.

She felt a surge of sympathy as she explained about their parents' engagement. It was just like his father, just like Todd, to have failed to mention it. He shouldn't have to hear it from her. "I'm sure Dad was just waiting for the right moment to tell you," she said, taking repossession of the word *dad* as if she had never lost it.

Todd looked stunned. "You know I think he did try to tell me," he admitted slowly, "but I didn't let him. Last week when I called him, he said, 'How about a double wedding?' I thought he was kidding around. I said, 'Sure, Dad, just let me know her name so I can add it to the invitations.' "

In an instant May's empathy vanished. "You're marrying Chloe?"

He nodded, sheepish.

"I thought you were 'fatally allergic' to marriage. Those were the exact words you used. 'Fatally allergic.' Like to a bee sting."

"She's young," he explained, as if that needed to be said. "She's never been married."

"Oh, well, then, by all means. Now I understand. That's an excellent reason. I'll have to point that out to the girls when they ask."

"She won't try to be their mother," he explained as if it was something that worried her. "She's not the type." He sat back down in the living room chair, legs stretched out in front of him, making himself completely at home. Too much at home, she thought. It wasn't his house; these weren't his things. She didn't want him sitting there looking like he belonged. His forehead uncreased; he jiggled his shoulders the way he always did to let her know he was beginning to unwind.

She wanted him out. The phone rang. Todd moved to answer it, then smiling, stopped himself. She smiled back, then regretted it. She didn't want to soothe him, to make nice anymore. She got to the phone, said hello, heard a click.

"Maybe it's Chloe checking up on you," she suggested. That seemed to remind him he should be on his way.

He put on his coat. "Are you okay?" he asked, softening now. "I didn't mean to spring that on you like that."

"I'm fine." She would be fine, she thought, if Todd would leave. Then she'd take her shower, clear her head, and call O'Donnell. It was time for full disclosure to O'Donnell. The phone rang again, but she opened the door first so that Todd would leave before she answered it. By the time she got back, the machine had engaged and the caller hung up. She played back the days' messages.

"It's your mother calling. At the time I said I would. Where are you? Never mind. Your children want to come home. They hate it here, and you can't blame them. What's to like? There's barely any heat. The spiders are bigger than my head. Delia thinks she saw a bear out the window. Whenever I need anything, I have to come to this godforsaken convenience store, which if it doesn't get robbed while I'm here is only because I'm not coming at the right time. And where are you? I'll try you in an hour."

"Hello?" The next message was Delia's voice. "Hello? She's not home, Grandma." The phone went dead.

"Hey. This is Pete. The heat isn't working right up at the cabin, so I'm going to go drive up tonight to see if I can fix it. Wanted to know if you care to join me, but I see you're still out on the town, so, later."

"Hello?" Delia again. "She's not home."

May took the phone off the hook so that if her mother called while she was in the shower, she would get a busy signal and keep trying. Then, finally, May stepped into the stall and let the water pound her back, her neck, her shoulders, her face, hoping it would wash away the fog that was keeping her from seeing the answer to the dizzying questions racing through her mind.

It was just as she turned off the water that she heard the phone ring, and she thought, *How could it ring when I've left it off the hook?*

Confused, she slowly opened the shower door. The room went dark so suddenly that for a moment she wasn't sure the light had ever been on. She felt her way to the switch and flicked it. Nothing happened. The lights had blown.

She toweled herself off, found the clothes she'd been wearing before, put them back on, then listened hard to the familiar house sounds. The radiators whooshed softly; the rain the forecasters promised would arrive then turn to snow began to hit the roof. She made her way to the window, lifted the blinds, and peered out to see if other houses had gone dark as well. Lights—yellow incandescents, white fluorescents, blue television glow—beamed out of houses across the street and from next door.

She found her way to the top of the stairs. Below her the house disappeared into a yawning darkness. Groping the wall, she went down slowly, counting the steps the way Susie always did, reminding her every time there were exactly twelve. But Susie was wrong. May realized as she stumbled down the last. There were thirteen steps. *Unlucky thirteen,* she thought, and laughed out loud, a nervous cough of a laugh that didn't conceal the tight sound of her own fear.

She cruised from room to room flicking on the light switches as she went, but no lights came on. When she opened the refrigerator door, she saw that light was off, too. She looked for a flashlight in the junk drawer but then remembered that after taking the girls to see *Harriet the Spy,* all flashlights, binoculars, magnifying glasses, and notepads had mysteriously disappeared, borrowed, then lost. She knew she had candles somewhere, but the only ones she could find in the dark were tiny pink birthday candles. She opened the refrigerator, felt around for something she could stick the candles in, located a stale loaf of Arnold's white sandwich bread. She stacked a few slices, one atop the other, and stuck in a bunch of candles. She reached around the top shelf

of the pantry and got the box of wooden matches she
kept there. She lit the candles, the soft light flickering
as she made her way to the phone.

She pushed 911, put the receiver to her ear, heard
nothing, tried again. There was no ring, no busy signal,
no static. Her phone was dead. Her phone had been off
the hook, then it rang, and now it was dead. She forced
out a nervous laugh, its hollow sound echoing off the
walls. *This means nothing*, she told herself, trying to
stay calm. There was a short circuit, a power outage,
maybe damage from the rain. She tried to, but didn't
believe it.

She would go next door; that was all. She'd go to the
Coopers' and call for help. *Help from what?* she asked
herself as she swung open her front door. Wendy stood
there about to knock.

"Is your bell broken?" she asked, her voice loud and
untainted by fear. "I've been standing here for ten minutes ringing and knocking."

Even in the pitch black dark Wendy could make out
the fear on May's face. "Are you all right?" Wendy was
sure now something was wrong. She walked into the
house, gently shutting the door behind her. Together
they walked through the dark rooms, May leading the
way, to the candle-lit kitchen. "I tried calling you to let
you know I was coming, but your phone is out of order.
I reported it to the phone company." Wendy added.

"Thanks," May managed to get out.

"Why is it so dark? Are your lights out, too?"

May nodded.

Wendy whispered the next. "Is something wrong?"
She reached out and touched May's arm.

May grabbed her hand and held it tight. She struggled
to regain her equilibrium. Then she whispered so softly

Wendy had to lean close to hear her say, "Someone is in the house."

Wendy whispered, "Right now?"

A rage of chills raced up May's spine while she quickly went over the facts in her head: the electricity was out, the phones dead. Someone was in the house. "Yes," she whispered back.

Wendy took her by the hand, her normally cool fingers made icy with fear, and slowly pulled May along with her like a recalcitrant child, cruising the first-floor rooms, locking doors as they passed them, front, side, back. When she saw the basement door stretched open, she quietly closed and locked it, too. May strained to listen for creaks, rumbles, footsteps, but they had stopped. He had stopped. He was listening, too.

Wendy interrupted the silence. "It's Gil, isn't it? I was hoping it wouldn't be Gil."

May nodded.

Wendy began to tremble. She rubbed her arms, then clenched herself tightly, struggling to regain control. After several deep breaths she was calmer. "I can't believe this has happened to him."

May needed to know. "Wendy, is Charlie Gil's son?"

In the flickering light she could make out Wendy nodding. "I had a feeling you'd figured that out. I knew eventually someone would. I didn't care of course. I'd have been happier for everyone to know. But Gil insisted that no one find out."

May smelled burning toast, blew out the candles. It was easier to ask this in the dark. "Is Stephanie Charlie's mother?" It suddenly made sense. There would be no room in Stephanie's life for a limited child. Having Wendy pretend to be his mother was just the kind of solution she'd come up with.

When Wendy laughed, May realized she had never

heard that sound from her before. There was something frightening in her laugh, as if all the things she'd bottled up for her entire life might fly out at once, a hurricane of emotion, and devour them both.

"Charlie is mine. Mine and Gil's," she explained.

"You had an affair?"

Wendy laughed again. "No. Stephanie had the affair. Gil and I were married. It was a hundred years ago. We met in college. You never knew that?"

May shook her head.

"I met him my very first week at school. I was pregnant by Christmas break. I loved being pregnant. Gil loved it, too. We were married just after Easter. Charlie was born the following summer. Then everything went bad."

"Is Gil the husband who abandoned you?"

Wendy nodded. "You can't imagine how much he'd been looking forward to that baby. He was like a kid himself; we both were really. The week before I went into labor, he went out and bought a dozen balls, all kinds of balls—rubber balls, beach balls, a tiny football, a little basketball. He said he didn't care if it was a boy or a girl, he was going to be the kind of dad who came home early every day to play catch in the backyard. We were living in a one-room apartment at the time, but we had big plans. We didn't know exactly where we were going, but it was going to be somewhere great.

"When Charlie was born, he was there, right by my side. But before I even had a chance to see my son, I saw my husband run out of the room and heard him puke in the hall."

"Why?" May asked.

Wendy shrugged. "He wasn't prepared for what Charlie looked like. It made him sick. So he split." Wendy sighed, took a deep breath, put it behind her again.

"Hey, it's not the worst thing in the world is it? I wasn't the first woman whose husband left her. I wasn't the last. You've done it. You've survived it."

They sat silently for several minutes. May struggled to listen, but there were no sounds at all in the house now. It was perfectly still.

"He's listening to us," Wendy said, and then went on, her voice gaining power. "Gil had already met Stephanie when Charlie was born, but I didn't know." She seemed to be speaking to a larger audience, performing, May thought, for Gil.

"I didn't know he was a climber. I didn't know Charlie and I had turned into gigantic blocks he needed to kick over in order to get somewhere better."

"How could you work for him? Why did he hire you?" May kept her voice low. She didn't want to be over-heard, but she did want to know.

"After a couple of years passed, Gil came back. I was easy to find. I hadn't gone anywhere. He asked about Charlie, pretended he suddenly cared. Then he dropped the brick on my head. Said he and Stephanie wanted to get married, but Stephanie's dad would forbid it if he knew about his past—which I quickly realized was Charlie and me. Then he made his pitch. He told me if he married her, I'd be able to get Charlie the very best care available. He promised me all the money I needed—no limitations, no caps. Apparently Stephanie was loaded.

"I didn't have much of a life myself at the time. Caring for Charlie was a round-the-clock job. I borrowed money from relatives who were starting to resent it. So, was I weak? Did I make a pact with the devil?" She looked at the basement door as if she knew that's where the devil was, down there. "I did that, and more. I took a job with the devil, is what I did. And I got lots of money for Charlie so long as I kept quiet. Remember when we went out to lunch after Todd left you?"

May nodded.

"That was almost it for me. Gil was livid. He said if he ever found me socializing again, he'd fire me and cut off the funds in a flash. I dared him to do it. I told him I'd expose him to Stephanie a blink later. He said, 'Go ahead. You and Charlie will live out your life in some slum, and when you drop dead, he'll wither and die.' "

"He said that? How could you even bear to look at him after that?"

"I forgave him," she said.

And, May thought, *you still love him.*

"I understood that all that time it had been eating him up inside, making him strange. Lies do that," she explained, in case May didn't know. "I kept hoping he'd come to his senses. But he won't because it's made him crazy. It's made him into a killer. I've known for a while but kept praying it wasn't so. I can't afford to keep Charlie in that home without Gil's help," Wendy whispered. "I can't afford for Gil to be a killer."

May could hear the desperation in her voice. But that's all she heard. Even the hissing of the radiators had ceased. "It's so quiet," May said out loud, and wondered if maybe she'd been wrong. Maybe there wasn't anyone else in the house.

She got up and unlocked the basement door, threw it open. There was no one at the top of the stairs.

"What are you doing?" Wendy asked, startled.

"Maybe there's no one here. Maybe it's just a problem in the circuit box. I'm going to go down and see."

"What if Gil's down there?"

"I don't think he is, but if I scream," she whispered, "or if I'm gone for too long, you run next door." She pointed in the direction of the Coopers'. "You tell them to call the police."

"I'll go there now."

"No. Wait here." She positioned Wendy at the top of the stairs. "I'll be okay," she told Wendy, believing it. "I don't think he's down there. And if he is, I know all the hiding places. Delia and Susie have shown them to me. If he's there, I'll hide and you'll go next door to get help."

Wendy nodded, clearly frightened, and took her position at the top of the stairs.

May crept down. She was used to creeping, did it every morning so as not to wake her children. She knew how to stoop slightly, keep close to the wall, where there were far fewer creaks, how to step lightly, feeling for the ones she hadn't yet discovered.

The basement was even darker than upstairs. As if she were blind, she used her hands, running them down the banister, then finding the wall, keeping them there. The basement was unfinished, the walls concrete, cold and damp. She stopped to wipe off a web that had gotten stuck to her. She listened, heard nothing. Her eyes strained to see in the dark, made out a large shape, the washing machine, and another, the dryer. Her foot stepped on something soft. She recoiled, then realized it was just a pile of dirty clothes she'd left there herself. Staying close to the wall, she found her way to the small, hot room where the furnace was churning up heat, where the circuit box was.

It was brand-new now, of course, one of the first things Pete's electrician told her she had to replace. *There shouldn't be a problem with it,* she thought as she inched closer to the wall.

It was slower going now. She had to avoid hot pipes, the water heater, old tools leaning against the wall, the tools Todd hadn't bothered to take with him but which May had packed and moved with anyway, just in case she ever figured out what they were for.

Finally her eyes made out the rectangular shape of the circuit box. Her hand found the door and after she'd opened it, the switches. They were all lined up on one side. She felt for the top one, flicked it over. She was pretty sure the top one was for the second-floor bedrooms. She called, the way the electrician had called to Pete.

"Wendy? Did anything go on? Go see if the light is on in my bedroom. Wendy?" There was no reply. And she thought, *Oh, my god, he's gotten her*, and went racing out of the room, banging into things, the ironing board, a broom, a net bag filled with beach toys, making her way up the stairs.

Wendy was not at her post.

"Wendy?" The light had gone on somewhere upstairs, giving the first floor a dusky glow. "Wendy?" She hurried through the kitchen, the dining room, the foyer, the living room, the sunroom, cursing herself for not taking Wendy's advice and going for help, hoping it wasn't too late.

She swung open the hall closet, saw only coats, shoes, nothing. She climbed the stairs. "Wendy?" All she wanted was a startled cry, a muffled yes, anything that would tell her at least Wendy was alive.

May was checking in Susie's room when the lights went out again.

She froze. This time she couldn't convince herself it was a problem with the wiring. This time she knew the wiring was just fine. Someone was in the house. Someone was in the basement all along.

She burst out of Susie's room, heading toward the stairs, when she heard a call. She stopped, waited, listened to be sure that she'd heard it. It came again, very quietly from far away.

"May?"

It was Wendy calling her. She struggled to listen, to place where the voice was coming from.

"May?"

No, it was farther. It was from the basement.

The phone rang. The phone that had gone dead. *How can this be?* she wanted to know. It rang again, but sounded wrong, too far away. Then, on the third ring, she realized it was the phone at the top of the house in Sabrieke's attic bedroom. She raced to her own bedroom phone, felt for the wire in the back, found that it had been unplugged, fumbled to connect it.

"Mrs. Morrison?"

She didn't know who it was, struggled to catch her breath so she could speak, considered hanging up instead so that she could call the police.

"It's Jane Hubble here. From the Hubble Home. I'm so sorry to call you so late, but you did say I could call you anytime. I didn't wake you up, did I?"

"No." She needed to catch her breath so she could speak, so she could explain that she couldn't talk right now.

"This will only take a second. It's just that I felt I should tell you that I called Wendy Porter, the boy's mother. I told her about our conversation and that I'd made a terrible mistake. I told her I thought the whole idea of a show about Charlie was a mistake. I'm afraid we can't go forward with it."

"Oh," May got out.

"The thing is she was quite agitated when I told her, extremely upset. I expect you'll be hearing from her. I hope I haven't caused you too much trouble. I hope you're not angry."

"No," May said. "That's fine." But what she was thinking was, *Wendy knew, but she didn't say.*

"May?" Wendy's voice was closer now. She was at the
bottom of the stairs. "Are you all right?"

May hung up the phone and stood at the top of the
second-floor landing. She could make out a slender silhouette waiting below. "Where were you?" May wanted
to know.

"Who was on the phone?" Wendy asked.

"Wrong number."

"Well, now that the phone's working, we should call
the police. I'll do it from the kitchen." May heard her
walk to the kitchen, heard her pick up the phone, heard
her tell the police the address, and she thought, *That
phone is still disconnected.*

By the time May got to the front door, Wendy was
back in the hall grabbing her wrist.

"Don't you dare leave me alone here," she said, and
her voice sounded more threatening than scared. "Let's
go sit down and wait."

May made out the shape of two glasses on the
kitchen table.

"I hope you don't mind," Wendy said. "But I poured
us some drinks. If I don't steady myself, I'll just faint."

"I'm not thirsty," May said.

"Suit yourself," Wendy replied, and downed hers.
"You really will feel better if you drink that," she said.

"No thanks."

They sat, waiting for the police, who May knew would
never come. May's eyes had adjusted well to the light
now. She could see Wendy playing with the scarf
around her neck. May got up.

"Where are you going?"

"I can't sit anymore."

"Come on," Wendy urged her. "Sit down. Drink up."

May sat down on the stool at the kitchen desk where the telephone was. With the dark as her shield she quietly moved her hand to the back of the phone. Her fingertip found the small empty hole where the phone line was supposed to plug in. The coiled cord connecting the receiver to the cradle was missing as well. She felt she might, but couldn't afford to, faint. Again she stood.

"I have to go to the bathroom," she said.

"Me, too," Wendy told her and stood up.

"I'll go upstairs," May offered quickly, heading to the hall.

Wendy followed right behind, stopping at the front door.

"You can use the powder room straight ahead," May told her as she ran upstairs.

"That's all right. I'll just wait here till you're done. I'll be the watchout," Wendy told her. "Don't take too long."

Moving with the stealth of a giant cat on the hunt, May made her way to her bathroom, shut the door without locking it, and, quietly, very quietly, pulled open the shower door, closing herself inside. It was dark in the stall with the lights out, dark and damp, like a coffin. After a minute had passed, she heard Wendy call upstairs.

"May? Are you all right? Is everything okay?"

She heard footsteps running up the stairs. She heard Wendy call out, "May?" then, "Shit," as she began her search. She heard Wendy opening doors, the hall bathroom, the girls' rooms, then May's room. "May?" she called, opening the closets. "May?" as she headed to the bathroom.

As the bathroom door opened, May took a deep breath and held it. She felt her adrenaline surge. Strengthened by the thought that if she didn't move fast and strong, her children might be orphaned, she flung open the shower door so hard the frame bent and the mirror cracked in half. Wendy was flung to the wall. Her eyelids flickered once, then closed.

51

SHE DARTED DOWNSTAIRS, MISS-
ing the last step again, falling hard on her face, but she
didn't stop to check for bruises. She found the portable
phone in the living room, disconnected like the others,
but forcing her hand to steady, she replugged it. Then
she raced to get O'Donnell's card from where it now
hung, tacked to the bulletin board in the kitchen. She
struggled to read the number in the dark, dialed his
beeper, hung up, and waited. The phone rang instantly.

"Mommy?" Susie's voice crackled over the phone line.
"We're coming home, Mommy. Do you want us to?"

At the sound of Susie's voice, May felt her body shud-
der, at the precipice of collapse. "Of course I do."

"I've been trying to call you for an hour," her mother
said after reclaiming the receiver. "I was beginning to
think you were dead. We're on the parkway. Delia ate a
spider tonight. She wants to come home and go to the
doctor so he can remove it. I told her it's nothing to worry
about, but she doesn't believe me. She wants you."

She'd been listening to her mother, had momentarily
forgotten Wendy on the floor upstairs, but suddenly the
hairs on the back of her neck rose as if her body had
sensed something her ears and brain had missed—a tiny
sound, a subtle smell, a barely detectable change in the
atmosphere. "Don't come here now. Stay away," she
hissed into the phone and hung up.

She left the phone on the desk, and when it began to ring again, she didn't answer it. She walked into the hallway, stood in the shadows listening, hearing nothing. She closed her eyes to concentrate, listening harder.

She gagged as something came around her neck, tight. When her hands went to feel what it was, the spiraling cord was pulled even tighter. She felt the blood pounding in her temples.

"Come with me," Wendy said, as if May had a choice, being pulled by the cord like a dog on a leash. Again her hands went to her neck. Again Wendy yanked at the cord, so tight now May's head felt as though it would burst.

"Sit down," Wendy told her, pushing her onto the stool next to the kitchen desk, but even after May did, Wendy didn't ease up the pressure. "I never did this to anyone who was fully alert," she explained. "But you know what? This time I can."

May tried to think of where the scissors were. Somewhere on the desk behind her were two pairs of safety scissors the girl had used to cut out valentines. But even Susie had complained the rounded safety scissors weren't sharp enough to cut paper. They made poor candidates for a weapon. Her mind raced. There might be a letter opener in the desk drawer, but with Wendy standing over her holding the phone cord tight, she wasn't sure she could manage to slide it open and look. She turned slightly, sitting sideways on the stool, then started to pull out the drawer very slowly, a centimeter at a time.

"What are you doing," Wendy snapped, snapping the cord tighter.

A noise came out of May, a stifled gag. She felt like she might get sick. Wendy let up her grip a little. She wanted to talk.

"You hadn't figured it out, had you?"

May shook her head. She could breathe now. In a moment she'd be able to talk. But Wendy had her on a tight leash. In a second, she could cut off all her air.

"This time I've written it all out in a note," she explained. "I never thought I'd need to be so goddamn specific. I mean, I started out with someone Gil wished dead, out loud, in public. Everyone knew he loathed Barnett. Blew that one, moved on to Iris. Everyone knew he hated Iris. He'd actually told Chuck Mills to drop dead. Then goddamn Stephanie dragged him to those parties with Walter Cronkite of all people. Little bitch."

"But Bunny?" May managed to get out, her voice cracking. "Why Bunny?"

Wendy sighed. May slipped her hand onto the kitchen desk, feeling around. She wasn't going to get more than one chance. She found a pencil. It had no point.

"Bunny figured it out. I didn't plan on Bunny. Or you." She waved her hand, dismissing Bunny's and May's demise from the conversation. "I stuck a letter on your refrigerator," she said, pointing. "It's from Gil. He admits he killed you. He says he wants to get caught. He doesn't want to hurt anyone anymore. I'm tired," Wendy admitted. "I never figured on a spree."

"What happens after they arrest Gil?" May managed to ask. She found a paper clip, a marker, a crayon, a roll of tape. The tape stuck to her arm. She carefully jiggled it until it came loose. It started to roll off the desk. May moved her arm and stopped it just in time.

"I've never done this to someone who was watching me," Wendy said. Her eyes burned into May's. "But I can't undo what's already been done. This is it. You're the last. Then I'm through."

May struggled to keep from unraveling. A tear leaked

out and traveled down her cheek. She had to stay strong and focus. "What's going to happen?" she asked, her hand still quietly busy, exploring the objects strewn about the desk.

"After they find you, after Gil's arrested, Stephanie will divorce him. Her father will insist. I have a lawyer all picked out for her. It will be done before the trial.

"I've got a lawyer picked out for Gil, too. Gil will plead temporary insanity. I'll testify. He'll go to jail, but my testimony will keep him from being sentenced to death."

"You'll save him."

Wendy nodded. "And when he's in jail, I'll visit him every day. It's what I do best, anyway, visit." She started pulling the phone cord tighter. "Gil will be a model prisoner. He'll be too scared to make trouble. When he finally gets out of prison, he'll come home to me and Charlie and we'll be a family. Finally."

May's hand rested on a tall, thin jar of rubber cement. She began peeling off the hardened glue that was stuck around the cap. "Why didn't you just turn him in to Stephanie?" May said, her voice barely a whisper. There was a piece of rubber cement stuck hard. Her fingers picked at it silently.

"That wouldn't have worked," Wendy said quickly, having already considered and discarded the notion. "He said from the start if I ever told, he'd deny it was true. We had all the documents altered. That was the price for the money. I needed his money. I've been saving, though. For years I've been squirreling away some of the money he sent me, a little bit every day. Waiting is a cheap way to pass the time.

"This is the only way," she went on wearily. "Believe me, I've considered the alternatives. After Stephanie and her father abandon Gil, I'll be all that's left." She pulled the cord tighter still.

May mumbled something.

"What?" Wendy asked.

"My kids," May got out. She turned the bottle of rubber cement upside down, letting the viscous fluid drain to the top. Then, holding it sideways, she began to unscrew the cap. "What about my kids?"

That one gave Wendy pause. May felt the cord loosen. Wendy looked at her sadly, and said, "I'm sorry. I'm sorry for them."

In the moment it took for Wendy to feel bad for May's young children, May brought her arm around and jerked the bottle of rubber cement at Wendy's face, taking careful aim so that at least some of the glue would find its way into her eyes.

Her aim was better than she thought. Wendy howled in surprise and pain. May grabbed the phone cord out of her hand, raced to the front door and across the lawn, to the Coopers'. As Wendy writhed at the burning in her eyes, the Coopers delighted at the chance to aid in May's rescue.

52

THE PARTY WAS IN A PRIVATE room at Tavern on the Green, the ceiling obscured by clouds of balloons imprinted with the names of the betrothed. Shrieks of delight, mostly female but with a few hearty baritones mixed in, collided with the whoosh of tissue paper as naughty nighties were triumphantly lifted out of overwrapped boxes, as if they were hard-won trophies. Black and red dominated, along with yards of lace and structural enhancements so firm some items looked as if they could stand up on their own, exhibits in the costume hall at the Museum of Metropolitan Art. Others had suffered so many cutouts it was hard to know which body parts were meant to go where.

The bride-to-be laughed like a teenager, egged on by her friends, while May watched, marveling that her mother, on the brink of turning seventy, could do a better girlish giggle than she.

In a nod to the times, Esther, the longtime friend who'd organized the party, had called the night before to say that male escorts were allowed. Most declined to come, to the delight of their wives, who were happy to have an afternoon out as long as lifts or car service was provided.

The prospective groom, however, came as directed, secreting himself for most of the evening in a small

room where cigar smoking was permitted. Todd chose
to hover alongside Chloe, a protective hand resting on
her back, which was exposed through a hole in her
dress quite similar to the styles of several of the nighties
Shirley had pulled out of her boxes. In fact, May
guessed Chloe was the most likely donor of the nightie
that Delia had remarked look like someone had attacked
it with a knife.

Sabrieke had been given instructions to take the girls
home by taxi if they acted up in any way, but that
seemed unlikely now. For one thing the girls, happy
and obliging ever since their return from their forest
adventure, were enjoying the attention of doting relatives and old family friends. For another, one of the
waiters, recently arrived from Belgium, was transfixed
by Sabrieke, their uninhibited flirtation causing several
of Shirley's friends to be disappointed by soup that was
served cold and a tray of warm rolls that had been offered once and never circulated again.

May felt something on her shoulder and turned to see
it was Paul O'Donnell's hand resting there.

"You okay?" he asked.

She smiled at his concern, happy she'd invited him,
happier still that he'd accepted. It had been two days
since Wendy's arraignment, time enough for May to
have learned that the police had been gathering evidence all the while. More plodding and methodical than
she, they'd worked hard to ensure that the pieces of the
puzzle O'Donnell had put together would actually stick
in court.

There was a witness O'Donnell found who had seen
Wendy hanging around Barnett's apartment building.
The doorman of Iris's building reported having seen Iris
enter the day of the murder accompanied by a woman
of Wendy's height. Chuck Mills's secretary remembered

once mentioning to Wendy, a casual acquaintance, that Chuck was practically addicted to single-malt scotch. Wendy was one of the few people to know that Gil's first attempt at giving up drinking was through the use of Antabuse, and she also knew that mixed with alcohol it could disable her victims long enough for her to overcome them.

Then, right after May's tip-off about the photographs, Bunny's sister Elaine had called. O'Donnell listened to her complaints about Paradiso and then started getting search warrants, gathering the final pieces of evidence that would allow him to wrap it all up tight.

He had to reassure May several times that there would be no bail, that all the pieces fit together perfectly. Wendy was charged with the murders of Barnett, Iris, Chuck, and Bunny, and, he was confident, she would be convicted. Even if the trial was unpleasant, the danger to May's life had passed.

It was still freshly felt though. When O'Donnell teased her that if she lost her job, she could always put up a shingle as a private eye, she could barely let out a laugh.

"I guess I'll relax again someday," she admitted, and when he squeezed her shoulders in reply, she felt it everywhere.

She wasn't sure this would work, this romance with a detective, but she was determined to give it a try. Leading a chaste life had offered some advantages. For one thing, she never had to explain to her children why a man who had insinuated himself into their family as if he belonged was suddenly gone. But with O'Donnell, she really believed that if it didn't work out, they'd end it like grown-ups. Besides, no matter what happened between them, he'd promised her kids they could carry his card forever, call him anytime they ever got into trouble. Even, as Susie asked, if it was in the "minnle" of the night.

"Speech," her mother's friend Gloria called out after taking too many sucks off her Bloody Mary straw. "May, darling—over here."

Reluctantly May obliged, smiling at the faces of her mother's friends, some of whom had known her since she was Susie's age, some since she was born, all who seemed unchanged, except they'd gotten older.

"Say something," Gloria whispered in her ear, her blood-red nails digging into May's arm.

Rita, who'd disowned both her children for reasons no one could remember, tugged at her sleeve. "Make it nice."

Champagne had been poured into small toasting glasses. May raised hers. "When I told Susie her grandma and grandpa were getting married, she looked at me and said, 'Grandmas and grandpas are always married,' I didn't argue. Here's to grandmas and grand-pas who are not just married, but happily married."

The crowd oohed. Todd clenched his jaw, then downed the contents of his glass. Chloe nibbled on his ear to cheer him up. Susie climbed into her grandma's lap. Delia explained the details of the murders to Aunt Josie, who was doing a good job of listening, for some-one trying to get her teeth to shift back into place. Cousin Sarah showed pictures of her grandchildren to Blanche, who wasn't looking. O'Donnell got an earful from Todd's father, who, having just finished his fat cigar, could now concentrate on what he did best, set-ting people straight.

"Let me set you straight on what the problem was between those two," he began. Quickly May walked to the other side of the room. She watched it all, the peo-ple she'd known all her life and the man she'd just met, and wondered if she looked as changed to them as she felt. Death had worked its spell on her. In a flash everything looked different. It was if she could actually hear time ticking, wasting away.

It was with this in mind that she had called Gil to tell him she was going to work three days in the office and two days at home from now on. She didn't wait for the perfect moment or ask his permission. It was not something up for discussion or negotiation. If Gil doubted she could make the job work this way, he could fire her. She'd find another job. If she couldn't get hired as a producer, she'd work as an associate producer, an assistant, an office temp, she'd answer phones. If she couldn't afford the taxes on her house, she'd sell it and rent an apartment. If she couldn't afford a big one, she'd rent a smaller one. She wouldn't starve.

As it turned out, Gil didn't object, though she didn't know if it was because of the new tone of authority in her voice or because he was too distracted trying to figure out which part of town his own apartment should be in, now that Stephanie had kicked him out.

Likewise, she'd laid down the law with Todd. She wanted the girls to have a relationship with him. If Chloe was his newly chosen life partner, then they should get to know her, too. Delia and Susie would spend one school vacation a year in Los Angeles and part of every summer, if it didn't interfere with camp. She wanted them to feel at home in his house, to feel that they belonged. With nothing left to argue, Todd booked the next flight out after the party. When May teased him that he was rushing back to Los Angeles to try to get a deal on a TV movie about Wendy's life, he didn't even bother to deny it.

As for her, she was going to take some time off. First stop was Orlando. Her mother's travel agent had gotten them a deal. She'd take the girls, and O'Donnell would bring his boys. It wouldn't be deluxe, but it would be away. And Fantasyland was exactly what they all needed right now.

"Mommy." Susie was tugging on her skirt. "Grandma is crying. She needs a tissue." May looked over at her mother, who was beaming and crying, all at once. May reached into her purse, handed over a small Kleenex packet, then noticed a piece of paper folded up and sticking out of her wallet. It was a typed sheet Carter had given her the night that Wendy was arrested.

He'd answered the door that night, ordered Emily to call the police, then gone out in the street to intercept Shirley, Sabrieke, and the girls when they pulled into the driveway so that they wouldn't go into the house. Pete had showed up, too, taking his post, guarding the door, making sure Wendy didn't escape.

Then O'Donnell and Paradiso had come, the photographers and reporters had come, the crime-scene team came, and Wendy was led away, head hanging down, hands cuffed behind her back.

The girls had finished eating all of Emily's homemade chocolate chip cookies and finished drinking their tall glasses of dark chocolate milk. Pete had cleaned up and carted away the broken shower door. May, Shirley, Sabrieke, Delia, and Susie had headed back home to see for themselves if things really did look just as they had left them. That's when Carter handed her the paper and suggested that she read it once everything calmed down. She'd been polite enough to take it, to stick it in her purse, but then promptly forgot about it. There were the girls and their grandma to comfort and hardened rubber cement to pick up off the kitchen tile floor.

She unfolded it now and read "Carter Cooper's Top-Ten List of Winning Talk-Show Ideas: 1) 'Marriage:

How Long Can the Flame Last?'; 2) 'Teenage Drinking: What Happens When the Parents Provide the Booze'; 3) 'Neighbors You Want to Send Packing.' "

That's it, May thought. That would be her next show. "Neighbors No One Wants: Can the People Next Door Be Too Nice?" She'd line up a bunch of neighbor horror stories, then have Carter and Emily come on as examples of people who lived to help you, whether their help was wanted or not. *Not bad,* she thought. It needed some noodling, but it might turn out to be fun. Those were the only kinds of shows she wanted to work on for now—fun ones. She looked up to find the whole room staring at her.

"There she goes again," Shirley said. "Concocting some cockamamie story. My dolly."

The room filled with the laughter of lifelong affection. Delia charged over to grab her leg possessively. Susie ran to seize the other one. From across the room O'Donnell raised his glass to her and smiled. With the warmth of her children snaking round her, she smiled back.